Tender Is LeVine

ALSO BY
ANDREW BERGMAN

FICTION

Sleepless Nights

Hollywood and LeVine

The Big Kiss-Off of 1944

NONFICTION

We're in the Money

Tender Is LeVine

A Jack LeVine Mystery

ANDREW BERGMAN

THOMAS DUNNE BOOKS NEW YORK
ST. MARTIN'S MINOTAUR

THOMAS DUNNE BOOKS.
An imprint of St. Martin's Press.

www.minotaurbooks.com

Designed by Lorelle Graffeo

ISBN 0-312-26205-1

First Edition: February 2001

10 9 8 7 6 5 4 3 2 1

For

Lulu,

Jake,

and Teddy

ACKNOWLEDGMENTS

There were a number of books about Arturo Toscanini that I consulted before writing this novel. Among them were Joseph Horowitz, *Understanding Toscanini* (New York: Alfred A. Knopf, 1987), Samuel Chotzinoff, *Toscanini: An Intimate Portrait* (New York: Alfred A. Knopf, 1956), and Samuel Antek, *This Was Toscanini* (Zurich: Müller, 1963).

For a general background into the lives of Meyer Lansky and Lucky Luciano, I used Dennis Eisenberg, Uri Dan, and Eli Landau, *Meyer Lansky, Mogul of the Mob* (New York: Paddington Press, 1979), and Sid Feder and Joachim Joesten, *The Luciano Story* (New York: McKay Publishing, 1954).

Invaluable for its descriptions of Las Vegas at the dawn of the 1950s was A. J. Liebling's article, "Our Footloose Correspondents: Action in the Desert," published in the May 18, 1950, issue of *The New Yorker*.

I would also like to thank the bassist David Walter, once a member of the NBC Symphony, for sharing his memories of Toscanini and of the orchestra's 1950 cross-country tour.

—A.B.

Tender Is LeVine

PROLOGUE

In the summer of 1950 I had my office redecorated. That may not seem like much to you, but it was a very big deal to me. Call it a sense of permanence or an acceptance of my limits; I had realized, finally, that a private detective was all I would ever be. The colossal and magical fantasies of my youth had extinguished themselves: I would never wear the uniform of the New York Yankees, my name would never be illuminated above the Morosco Theater, Rita Hayworth would never thrust her silken hand down my gabardine slacks. I was forty-four years old and this was it, this office on 51st Street and Broadway. This was my destiny. This was my lot.

I had come through a very rough period: long, ragged months of self-doubt and shallow, anxious sleep. This malaise had been building for years, but I had always managed to jolly or work it away. Then in March of 1948—the nineteenth, to be exact—my old man died, nice and easy, listening to Jack Benny on the radio. The last human voice he heard on this earth belonged to Dennis Day. I took it pretty hard, for all the reasons. No longer a father's son, I started sizing up my adulthood: divorced, childless, drifting through middle age with a PI's license and an expanding waistline. In eight years, I'd be fifty; in sixteen years . . . The math was not reassuring. I couldn't get a comfortable fix on mortality and began a period of retreat, turning down cases, choosing instead to stare out my office window or just stay home in Sunnyside, listening to ball games and eating western omelets. Ringing phones and doorbells went unanswered, dishes went unwashed. Poised over the bathroom sink one morning, I put down my razor and began to cry for no reason I could identify. I left a perfectly good toaster in the incinerator and ran down the hall back to my apartment, panicky and short of breath.

I dreaded the mornings and tried to avoid them by listening to the radio far into the night. I would stare out my bedroom window at the stars twinkling over Queens, listening to strangers talk about nightclub acts or the atomic bomb or all the commies running our government. The discussions would grow garbled and I would fall asleep, often waking up to static from the airwaves, the sky growing light. I would turn the radio off, suddenly wide awake and raging.

It was depression, pure and simple. The case of the depressed dick. My income, always marginal, sank to the janitorial level, but I couldn't have cared less. Money for what? Friends talked to me earnestly, gripping my arm, but I simply nodded, scarcely hearing them. I started drinking a little—Jewish drinking, nothing scary—and began to play the horses. I would take the train out to Jamaica, certainly the ugliest racetrack in America, and stand for hours by the rail, drinking foul black coffee and losing my money. I bought all the guidebooks, bet exactly four dollars on each race, and drew immense satisfaction from the inevitability of defeat.

I can't locate a precise moment or occasion, but after about three months I simply grew tired of my crisis. It ceased to engage my pity or my interest. Like a virus, perhaps, it simply played itself out. I stopped going to the track, cut the drinking cold—except for my nightly Blatz—and began shaving every morning at seven-thirty sharp. I started working more, and found that I was working better. Pedestrian cases took on profound interest, the dullest of clients immediately engaged my attention. I purchased an alpaca overcoat and attended all five games of the '49 World Series, and when Tommy Henrich stepped to the plate in the ninth inning of the first game, swinging his bat very slowly, back and forth, staring out at poor boozy

Don Newcombe, I began to put on the coat. Not out of hubris, not at all, but more out of a sense of order restored; the Yankees versus the Dodgers and the Yankees win. That was simply the way the world was supposed to operate.

From that point on, I emerged fully from my shell. Friends marveled at my rejuvenation and took me to dinner in celebration. They toasted the LeVine of old: nimble, sprightly Jack. My poker partners hailed the return of their favorite sucker, Jack of Eternal Hope. My vital fluids coursed; I got random, indiscriminate hard-ons and found myself once again the roué of the coffee shop, charming the tired, bleached-out waitresses, sliding that extra dime beneath the chipped saucer, spinning off my counter stool and onto the sunny streets. I breathed deeply, enjoying the Broadway bus fumes. Birds flapped overhead, flying north or south it mattered not to me; I knew they had their reasons, as I had mine. Each in its way, each in its place. The way the Good Lord meant it. I was, simply, a contented soul.

So I decided to redecorate my office, to reaffirm my career and my bald-headed place on this earth. I engaged three brothers named DiNapoli, who ripped the place apart in between mouthfuls of fried-egg sandwiches in the morning and meatball heroes in the afternoon. They never stopped eating or working. The War Bonds poster came down in the outer office, wood paneling went up. New lamps and a coffee table were purchased, as well as a generous supply of postwar magazines. The inner office was repainted (beige) and recarpeted (green), but otherwise untouched. I would not part with my ancient desk and chair, my lamp, my wooden files, my coat stand, my moosehead. These things were sacred. "This shit is really old-fashioned, strictly Sam Spade," said Tommy DiNapoli, showing me multicolored brochures in praise of metal and vinyl. "This is the trend now. It's a cleaner, more modern look." I simply shook my head. For the walls, the brothers strongly urged oil paintings depicting the Finger Lakes region, as rendered by their Uncle Augie; I resisted, despite considerable pressure, and put up some George Bellows fight scenes.

The hammering and sawing and sanding lasted about ten days, and I reveled in it. “Can’t hear you,” I’d shout into the dusty telephone. “Having the office done over.” I felt prosperous, burgherlike; I watched the progress of the work, hands in pockets, hat slung back on my head, smiling from ear to ear. Then Frankie DiNapoli repainted my name on the frosted glass door in bold blue letters and the brothers were gone, after hearty handshakes all around. They pulled the drop cloths, vacuumed, and stole off like Italian genies, leaving me alone and missing their perpetual motion.

I sat behind my desk and surveyed the newness and splendor of my office. In the center of my desk was an invoice for four hundred and fifty dollars. I was reviewing various options for raising this sum when my newly painted door opened and Fritz Stern walked in.

ONE

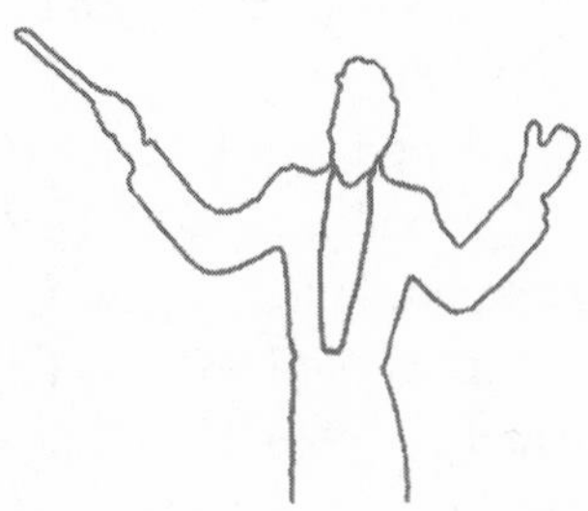

Fritz Stern was a small man with gray eyes, gray hair, and the nervous attentiveness of a refugee who had never stopped escaping. His sharp features were coated with a Florida tan that seemed as inappropriate on him as a zoot suit.

"I have been traveling," he told me somewhat apologetically. He held an elegant gray fedora in his lap and blinked several times. He was wearing a blue three-piece suit that looked to be ten years old and would probably last another fifty.

"Florida?"

Stern shook his head. "No, no vacation," he said. "I in fact acquired this suntan while on tour some months ago. And then with the summer months—"

"Tour?" I pulled open the top drawer of my desk and extracted a toothpick, then began working on a strand of bacon that was dangling precariously from a back molar.

"Yes," Stern said brightly. "We were in the southern states and Texas, the Northwest, the Midwest, all over." Stern had overcome most of his accent, but a phrase like "the southern states" defeated him entirely: the *t*'s came out in *s*'s and the *s*'s gave way to *z*'s.

"You from Germany originally?" I asked him.

He blushed delicately—God knows why, it wasn't his fault—and then nodded.

"The accent," he said. "I know is terrible."

"Not at all," said Ambassador LeVine. "You come over in the thirties?" The piece of bacon fell from my molar.

"I was born in Frankfurt in 1907 and came to this country in the year '38."

"Good year to come over."

"Good and bad," he said with some force. "Many were not so fortunate. I lost family, friends of a lifetime. We all did."

All I could do was nod. There isn't a lot of room for snappy patter when you start discussing mass murder. You nod a lot, you shake your head a lot, maybe you don't feel as guilty as you think you should, so you feel guilty about that. Nothing you can say will make a rat's ass worth of sense or difference. The best thing to do is just listen.

"But that is the past. I consider myself completely an American." Stern looked at his fedora, then smiled. "I even dream in English now."

"Me, too," I told him. "You have a family, Mr. Stern?"

"A wife and two daughters, one almost twenty-two, the other is thirteen. We live on Fort Washington Avenue in Washington Heights. It's a good neighborhood, well kept up. There are a great many other German refugees there, a beautiful park to walk in, good stores." He nodded, convincing himself. "I would say we are quite happy there."

Stern blinked a few more times and again studied his hat. He sighed loudly, as if to relieve a great pressure.

"Everything okay at home?"

He looked up quickly, as if startled.

"Oh yes, at home is fine. Fine." He nodded as he repeated himself. "Fine. Sure."

"Mr. Stern, not to be a busybody, but may I assume that something is less than fine or you would not be sitting in the office of a licensed private detective?"

Stern recoiled slightly, as if I had uttered the words "New Orleans whorehouse." He pulled on his earlobe, worried his bottom lip, rubbed his neck. He said nothing.

The circumcised Sherlock Holmes swung into action.

"You said you were on tour, Mr. Stern. You an actor, something like that?" It didn't seem possible; this guy was about as theatrical as a steamed carrot.

"A musician," Stern said after a moment.

"I see."

"With the NBC Symphony."

"I'm impressed. Jesus Christ, to play under Toscanini, that must be something."

"The experience of a lifetime, Mr. Levine."

"LeVine, capital *V*."

"LeVine, I apologize. The experience of a lifetime, I can assure you. I have been with the orchestra since 1940, since the South American tour. Before that I played in Buffalo for a couple of years. But those winters were terrible."

"I'm sure. What instrument do you play?"

"Second violin," he said a little ruefully. "A soldier in the ranks, one might say."

"Listen, just to play with that crowd . . ."

"Again I say, the experience of a lifetime. You listen to the broadcasts?"

"Sometimes," I told him truthfully, "if it doesn't conflict with the ball games. I'm no expert, but I like my Beethoven as much as the next guy. And you were on tour a while ago. Yes, I remember reading about it, quite a rousing success. Got a tremendous play in the press."

Stern stared at the floor through my blathering, preoccupied.

"One could call it a great success, yes." He wet his lips as if to say more, then sighed once again and shook his head.

"How come you're shaking your head, Mr. Stern?"

Stern looked at me evenly. His right eyelid began to pulse. He rubbed it.

"Do many . . . odd people come here, Mr. LeVine?"

" 'Many'? Well, I would say that all depends on your definition of 'odd.' More than enough, I'd say."

"And these people"—Stern leaned forward, gripping his fedora—

"what makes them odd, in your opinion? Would it be their requests or their behavior? I would like to know this."

"Hard to say, Mr. Stern. Sometimes the most peculiar-looking people will make the most conventional requests. Then an ordinary Joe—nicely dressed, fresh haircut—he'll ask you to do something absolutely grotesque. You get a fair number of delusional types in this business."

Stern drew a blank. "And this means what?"

"Guys who think their wives are sleeping with Eddie Cantor or the vegetable man, people certain they're being followed by dead relatives; I've had more than one ex-GI tell me he was afraid to walk his dog at dinnertime because he was certain that his lieutenant was hiding in the shrubbery, poised with a gun or a knife."

"And you do what?"

"I do what. I humor them, sometimes I try to guide them to professional help; I know a couple of sympathetic headshrinkers. If I'm seriously broke, I might take their cases. I once had a client named Thaler, a furrier who was convinced that his wife was having a torrid affair with Cab Calloway. I followed Frau Thaler for three weeks and, not surprisingly, came up empty. I told the furrier he was wasting his dough, but he was adamant and paid me to keep working the case. Two days later, I see the wife and Calloway checking into the Hotel Taft, where they spent most of the afternoon. I sat in the lobby until she left, alone; she was smiling and her hat was on backwards. One never do know, is the moral."

Stern had listened intently. Now he leaned forward.

"All right, so now I ask you, Mr. LeVine: Do I appear to be of these crazy ones? I would like an honest answer."

"How honest?"

"This is not a joke, I assure you. Do I appear to you to be a person given to delusions?" Stern's forehead had turned slick with sweat.

"You've said nothing to indicate that you are, Mr. Stern. That's an honest answer. My first impression of you, if you care . . ."

"Very much." He leaned even farther forward now, his hands knitted together.

"My first impression of you is that you are an intelligent, somewhat highly strung—no pun intended—individual of obvious breeding. How's that for openers?"

Stern seemed pleased with the description.

"Highly strung but not crazy, is what you are saying."

"That's what I'm saying." I put my Florsheims up on the desk. "So now you're going to tell me you saw Hitler driving a Yellow Cab on Park Avenue."

Stern did not respond to this at all. What he did was reach into his jacket and pull out a newspaper clipping. He placed it on the desk before me.

"I would appreciate it very much if you would read this news clipping," he said. "Then we can talk."

I took the clipping and studied it. It was from the *New York Times*, datelined Washington, D.C., May 25, 1950, and it was written by a music critic named Howard Taubman. Two paragraphs had been bordered with red pencil marks.

"You want me to read the part in red?

"Exactly." Stern put on a pair of half glasses, as if I needed help reading. "Read the whole, of course, if you wish, but the section in red I consider of the utmost importance."

I read the section in red.

> Mr. Truman, Mrs. Truman, and their party arrived at the hall at 8:28 and were greeted at the entrance by General David Sarnoff. They were led into a reception room backstairs. Then Walter Toscanini called his father.
>
> The Maestro was nervous. It was said that he had been worrying about this meeting with the President for a week. In the course of the conversation with

Mr. Truman, he showed his nervousness. When the President asked him what the program was, Mr. Toscanini could hardly remember.

I looked up.

"This is it?"

Stern removed his glasses. "It does not strike you as in any way remarkable?"

"Frankly no, Mr. Stern, unless I'm missing something. Toscanini meets the President of the United States and he's nervous. So what?"

Stern arose from his seat and walked around the office, his hands clasped behind his back. He gazed at the moosehead.

"You are a hunter, Mr. LeVine?"

"I don't know a moose from a goose. My ex-brother-in-law bought that for me shortly after I opened for business. He thought it added what he called a 'raffish charm.' He's that kind of guy, the kind who still says 'raffish.' "

Stern looked from the moose to me.

"You are no longer married?"

"That's correct. Divorced for nine years, to be precise. I'm currently living with Betty Grable."

Stern returned to the chair and sat down.

"Enjoy the walk?" I asked.

Stern merely blinked.

"May I have the clipping back, please?"

I slid the clipping back across the desk. Stern took it, folded it neatly, returned it to his jacket. He looked at me. I looked at him.

"So?" I said.

He cocked his head, as if overhearing a conversation in another room. I was getting aggravated.

"Mr. Stern, you hand me a clipping about Toscanini having the shakes when he meets the President. I read it and find it thoroughly unremarkable, but you find it compelling and obviously you have a reason for thinking it so. Now, I don't claim to be the busiest shamus on the block, but I'll be goddamned if I'm going to spend the rest of the morning trying to read your mind. You want a detective, I'm a detective. The question before the house, however, remains *why* do you want a detective. Shall we proceed?

Stern smiled. You wouldn't have confused him with Louis Armstrong, but it was a smile nonetheless.

"Very well put. So I will now open my mind to you." He cleared his throat. "The article by Taubman is not, as you say, Mr. LeVine, remarkable. Except for one detail which strikes me as unique because I have worked with this man—this genius, I should say—for the past ten years. What I am getting to is that it is absolutely inconceivable to me that Toscanini should be unable to remember the evening's program." He shook his head for emphasis. "Absolutely inconceivable."

"It could happen. He's excited, he's an old man—"

The violinist held up his long, slender hand.

"Let me continue this, Mr. LeVine, and then we can talk."

"Fine with me." I picked a pack of Luckies up off my desk.

"And I would appreciate it if you did not smoke. My lungs are not the best."

"Then you better get to the point. I won't last much longer without a butt."

Stern smiled. "That is unfortunate. I will reach my point quite soon."

I regretfully put the Luckies down and the fiddler continued his story.

"The Maestro, as you say, is an old man. Eighty-three, in point of fact. But his memory is absolutely unbelievable. He does not merely know by heart every note of every piece we play. There are other conductors quite capable of that. But he knows every note of works he has not conducted for a half century; he knows every note of pieces he has never conducted and in fact detests! It is a memory that cannot be fathomed by ordinary human beings. By which I include myself as well as you."

"Speak for yourself," I told Stern. "Ask me who's leading the American League in runs scored. Go ahead."

But Stern was on a roll now. There was no time to accommodate my lowbrow banter. "Thus I find Maestro's forgetting the program not comprehensible," he continued, "unless one realizes something. And that realization, Mr. LeVine, is one which has caused many weeks of sleepless nights not only for me, but for other members of the orchestra who feel as I do." Stern's eyes were bright.

"Who feel what?"

"Mr. LeVine, I believe that the man in the room with President Truman was not Toscanini. I believe that Maestro has been missing since sometime in May." Stern sat back in the chair. He took out a handkerchief and mopped his brow.

I took my feet off my desk and sat up. "And you say that other members of the orchestra feel as you do?"

"That is correct."

"That's over three months ago."

"Yes. Last week we are to begin rehearsals again and they are canceled. We hear that Maestro is ailing. Some of us just look at each other."

I ran my hand over my cool clean scalp.

"But you obviously don't feel that he's missing just on the basis of this clipping."

"Obviously, Mr. LeVine. I feel it because the relationship between orchestral players and a conductor, though formal, is quite intimate. We know each other's quirks and mannerisms so very, very well. About halfway through the tour, I began to feel that Maestro was not himself. It was hard to explain. His step was lively, like always, he looked the same . . . but he did not conduct the same way. Something was different. Rehearsals became shorter and shorter; Maestro hardly spoke a word. I assumed at first that because the programs were pretty much the same from city to city, Maestro did not feel the need to rehearse. That is not unusual. On a tour of this length, in fact, it is common. We gather in the morning, test the sound of the hall, then leave. Live a tourist's life, one could say. But something began to bother me, something told me this was not Toscanini. Something in the beat, in the way he moved, in the way he turned his head. . . ." He threw up his hands. "This was not Toscanini. I have no doubt."

"Physically . . ."

"Physically, no difference. Not on the surface—the white hair, the beautiful skin. But other things. I will give for you an example: The Maestro's eyes are very weak. Terrible."

"He doesn't wear glasses, does he?"

"Never in public, because he has great vanity. But one day this . . . this other Toscanini, he makes a joke about the first clarinet's necktie. We all thought this was strange because Maestro normally could not even see the clarinetist, much less his tie." He shook his head. "It sounds like ravings, I am sure, but believe me, Mr. LeVine, I am not one who imagines things.

"I'm sure you're not."

"One other thing, perhaps a pedantic one, but it is not minor. On the tour we played the Beethoven Seventh. You know it?"

"Hum me a few bars."

"There is a second movement, very famous, but always played very slow. *Da* da-da, *da*-da . . ."

"I'll be goddamned. I do know it."

"For years that movement was played so slowly, as would befit a funeral movement, like in the Beethoven Third. But is not a funeral movement. Maestro looked at the score and saw that it was marked *allegretto.*"

"Which ain't slow."

"Which isn't slow at all. Maestro conducted the movement as Beethoven had intended, in a kind of, let's say, 'flowing' manner."

"And on the tour?"

"On the tour, the alleged Toscanini just dragged it out. Da . . . da . . . da . . . *dahhh* . . . da. We all just looked at each other."

"It could be his age."

Stern shook his head very definitely.

"Impossible. The whole manner of conducting was different. The gestures were totally like Maestro, but the spirit was completely different."

"So you think it was some guy who rehearsed in front of a mirror?"

"I do not know what he did. All I know is that Maestro is missing and we were conducted by an impostor. I am as sure of that as I am of my wife's fidelity."

I didn't say a word. Stern allowed himself a small smile.

"Maybe surer."

"And the other men in the orchestra, Mr. Stern? They feel this also?"

Stern looked at the ceiling, at me, at his hat.

"Some do," he said to the hat.

"How many?"

"Enough. At least a dozen." Stern looked up. "This is not the sort of thing one discusses so openly, Mr. LeVine. Only to one's closest associates in the orchestra."

"You mean only the second fiddles believe this story?"

"No, it is a representative grouping from all sections of the orchestra: brass, woodwinds, strings. . . . Several have stated, in a very confused and concerned fashion, 'This can't be Maestro. This is a fraud.' "

Stern stared at me, waiting for a reply. I didn't have any.

"You think I am crazy," he said finally.

I turned and took a peek out my window, across the air shaft to the insurance company on the other side of the building. The agents and their assistants were marching back and forth to their file cabinets, busy as can be. The wall clock in their office said that it was half past eleven. When I turned back to the violinist he was staring at me intently.

"Say it. You think I am mad."

"I don't believe anything of the sort," I said, lying only the tiniest little bit. "What I don't really get, Mr. Stern, is what you expect me to do."

Stern nodded curtly. "This is my next point. I would like for you to determine whether Maestro is in fact missing, and if he is, I wish you to find him and return him to the orchestra and to the world."

He was dead serious.

"Is that all? Why didn't you say so? When do you want him?" I checked my watch. "How about four-thirty?"

Stern raised his eyebrows.

"You are joking at my expense?"

"At *your* expense?" I paused for dramatic effect. "Mr. Stern, do you have any idea of what you're asking me to do? I'm not an agency, for crissakes; I'm just one lonely Yid with a license to follow people around. I don't have the resources for this kind of thing. I mean, to level with you, I seriously doubt that Toscanini got himself snatched. That's not a reflection on the sanity of you or the other fiddle players; it's just real long odds against it. If he seemed different, maybe it's something medical. People do go into decline past a certain point, even geniuses."

"Mr. LeVine," Stern began, "if it was something medical—"

"Let me finish my point. I was going to say that if in fact you *are* correct and the old man is missing, I think that NBC has more than enough resources to track him down. I suggest you talk to someone over at Rockefeller Plaza."

Stern shook his head, saddened and a little embarrassed.

"It is impossible for ordinary musicians to speak with the top people at NBC. Just as a matter of protocol. And then, of course, we think of our jobs. To go in and say that Maestro is missing and the man conducting is a double . . ." Stern just waved his hand to complete the sentence.

"You think you'd get canned?"

"Very possibly. It's just not something one would do. And then if Maestro is in fact missing, as I believe, then perhaps NBC knows of this and has supplied the double."

"While searching for the genuine article?"

Stern shrugged and mopped the back of his neck with his handkerchief; he seemed to have aged five years since he had walked in the door.

"*Ich weiss nicht.* It is all doubts. There are so many things. . . . Maybe we are all crazy, but I tell you, in my heart, in my guts as they say, I know that Maestro is missing."

I could feel a familiar stirring of the blood, a sense of engines turning over. Despite all my best efforts to resist, this was beginning to intrigue me.

"So you'd like me to talk to the NBC brass, is that what you're saying?"

"That is correct," Stern said. He was now sitting at the very edge of his seat. "Without, of course, mentioning the source of your information."

"And you'll pay? You can afford me?"

"It is not just me, Mr. LeVine." Stern smiled modestly. "Approximately ten of us have agreed to pay, up to a point. May I ask the nature of your fee?"

"The nature is twenty-five a day plus expenses. I charge everyone the same, with certain exceptions, but you're no exception." I pulled out a Lucky. "And if I don't have a smoke right now, I'll start shaking uncontrollably, which is not a sight you're going to enjoy."

"Go ahead, Mr. LeVine. I'll be leaving soon."

I lit up. "One more question: Why me?"

Stern put his handkerchief away and looked at the floor. When he looked back up, his expression was somewhat sheepish. "I used the phone book, I have to say. You were close to Radio City and you had a Jewish name. Most of the detectives had *goyische* names."

"You think the names are *goyische,* you should see the faces."

Stern laughed like a man not used to laughing.

"I supposed it's ridiculous, Mr. LeVine, but I still have a refugee mentality. I look first for a Jew." He sighed. "Was not the nicest experience."

"I'm sure it wasn't."

And with that he arose, swiftly, like a man with errands to run.

"Should I leave some money now? I brought some just in case." He smiled again. "In the movies . . ."

"It's just like the movies, Mr. Stern. You can leave me fifty bucks."

Stern took out an aging brown wallet and started counting out fifty dollars. He counted the bills very carefully.

"Who should I see at NBC?"

"Thirty-five, forty . . ." He looked up from the money. "I think you should attempt to see Mr. Sidney Aaron, who is the vice-president for what they call 'special programming.' "

"Which includes the concerts?"

He nodded and finished his counting, then handed me the bills. I pocketed them without a glance; this guy would no sooner short change me than go over Niagara Falls in a barrel.

"He is not a nice man, Mr. LeVine," Stern said solemnly. "Nor do I think he is a truthful one."

"That's par for the course in my line of work, Mr. Stern. Let me worry about that."

Stern bowed politely and walked to the door.

"I hope I am wrong, Mr. LeVine. I hope none of this is true."

"I hope it is true. Just for the hell of it."

Stern began to say something, then thought better of it and left the office, shutting the door behind him about as quietly as it can be shut. I stared at the door and ran my hand across my brow. My brow was wet, which meant I'd been concentrating. That happens to me a couple of times a year. The phone started to ring, but I ignored it. Instead, I arose, grabbed my hat, and left the office for the three-block walk over to NBC.

TWO

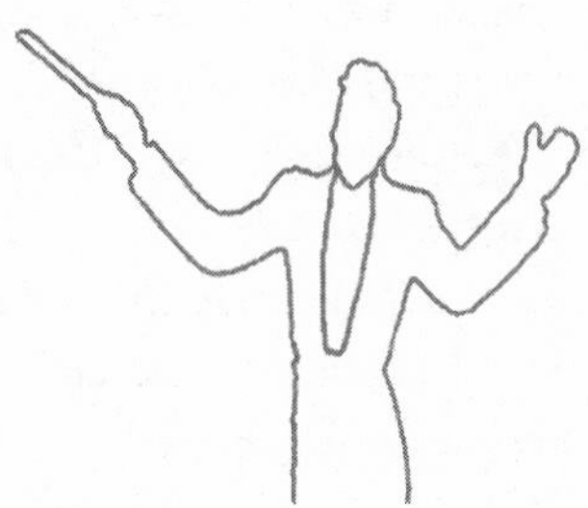

Sidney Aaron's office was located on the twenty-eighth floor of the NBC Building at 30 Rockefeller Plaza, more popularly known as Radio City. Thirty Rock was a building that had figured prominently in my storied professional history: In 1944 I had enjoyed the privilege of racing down its halls with a Philadelphia banker named Eli Savage, a pack of Democratic Party thugs in fevered pursuit of us. That's when I was big news. Today I sauntered unimpeded into the building, past the wide-eyed tourists in their bright suits and pastel dresses, past the sweating messengers, past all the men and women who entered Thirty Rock with something to sell over NBC's licensed airwaves—good health, fresh breath, clean teeth.

But Sidney Aaron on the twenty-eighth floor was beyond any such mercantile concerns. I knew that because he had an English secretary working his desk. When someone named Sidney hires a girl from London to answer his phones and keep people waiting, it tells you something. It certainly tells me something: It tells me I'm about to meet someone I'm not going to like.

"You have an appointment with Mr. Aaron?" she asked. Her name was Elizabeth Hamilton and she looked every bit of it: the faint blush in the cheeks, the lustrous straw-colored hair, the touch of lantern in the jaw.

"I'm afraid I don't," I told her with as much fawning respect as possible. "But it's quite important and I really only need about five minutes of his time. Maybe less, if I talk fast."

She smiled politely. "Well, Mr. Aaron is actually in a meeting right now, and then he has a luncheon engagement. Might I tell him what this is in reference to?"

"You might, yes. It's about the orchestra. Something's up in the string section."

She delicately bit her bottom lip. "Are you a union rep?"

"Technically, no. Let's say I'm a bearer of information your boss should know about."

"I see," she said, but her eyes told me that all she saw was a problem.

"It's important, trust me. If I take more than five minutes, you can throw me the hell out." I chuckled, a swell guy.

"I'm sure that won't be necessary, Mr. . . .

"LeVine. Capital *V*."

"Mr. LeVine. Let me just ask Mr. Aaron if there's a chance he could squeeze you in. . . . Excuse me."

Elizabeth Hamilton arose from her chair and headed for Aaron's inner sanctum. Beneath her tailored suit, it was evident that she had the goods—that firm, white, wind-buffeted English flesh in ample and elegant proportion. We were quite suddenly naked before a fire in a Welsh cottage, on a fierce winter night, cups of steaming tea on the floor, the wind howling outside the window. "Oh, Jack," she whispered, beads of sweat around her mouth. "Oh, Jack LeVine, you marvelous Hebrew."

"Mr. LeVine?"

Fully dressed again, she slipped out of Sidney Aaron's office and closed the door.

"Mr. LeVine, I'm afraid that today will just be totally out of the question and the rest of the week looks quite horrid as well." She returned to her desk and started scanning her appointment book in an unconvincing but oddly touching fashion.

"That's a real pity, Miss Hamilton." I removed my hat; people sometimes take pity on a bald guy.

"Meetings all next week as well . . . My God, how does this happen?" She lifted her head from the book. "Is it something that perhaps Mr. Peterman could help you on?"

"Peterman?" I said.

"David Peterman is Mr. Aaron's executive assistant."

"I'm afraid not." I walked to the door. "I'll call you the middle of next week; maybe we can work something out."

Elizabeth Hamilton gently chewed the tip of her pencil. I had wicked thoughts.

"I'm terribly sorry," she said.

"No problem." I smiled and left the office, then crossed the hall and waited. It was twelve-fifteen. If Aaron was indeed going out for lunch, he'd be departing his office within the hour. I'm a patient guy, so I waited.

At twelve-forty, the door to Aaron's office opened and a tall man of about fifty stepped into the corridor. He had curly salt-and-pepper hair, a Hank Greenberg nose, and eyebrows like graying caterpillars. His charcoal-gray suit was made to measure, as were his shoes and shirt and probably his socks and underwear. He looked like a man who had made it on his own, leaving numerous casualties along the way. If this wasn't Sidney Aaron, then I was Hopalong Cassidy.

The graying man called back into his office.

"Elizabeth, I'll be back at two-thirty. Push the Ben Grauer meeting to four." He closed the door behind him, inspected his shoes for high gloss, then made the right turn out into the corridor.

"Mr. Aaron?"

The man turned around. I stepped forward, a friendly hand extended.

"Jack LeVine, Mr. Aaron. Thank God I had a chance to catch up with you."

Aaron warily shook my hand. He had brown eyes, but not nice brown eyes.

"Do I know you?"

"You don't," I said oh-so-agreeably. "But I'll overlook that for now."

"I have a lunch date, Mr. LeVine," he said, and began to walk away, "and I'm late already."

I followed him down the hall.

"Busy day, huh?"

"They're all busy."

"I'll bet they are."

He hurried to the elevators. It wasn't that Aaron was anxious to shake me; as far as he was concerned, I wasn't even there.

"You handle the cultural end here at NBC?" I asked, curious as an Eagle Scout. Aaron pushed the elevator button. "Kind of the conscience of the company, you'd say?"

"This company doesn't need a conscience," he said to the elevator door.

"Maybe not. I need you for maybe three minutes tops, Mr. Aaron. Your secretary, Mrs. Miniver, told me you were booked up."

"That's right."

"She suggested I see Mr. Peterman," I yammered on. "But I told her I had to speak to the head dachshund, the numero uno." This guy brought out the absolute worst in me; I just couldn't help myself.

The elevator doors opened. Aaron walked into the elevator without giving me a glance.

"Afternoon, Mr. Aaron," said the elevator jockey, a light-skinned Negro in a blue uniform. I got in with Aaron. It was just the three of us in the cab.

"It's kind of a special matter," I continued.

"Beautiful day outside, Mr. Aaron," the jockey said.

"Certainly is, Sam."

"A very special matter, I'd say."

Aaron stared at me with a carefully calibrated blend of indifference and contempt.

"Listen, friend—" Friend.

"Jack LeVine."

"Listen, Jack LeVine, if you wish to see me, speak with Miss Hamilton and make an appointment. I don't have meetings in hallways and I don't have meetings in elevators."

"It concerns the orchestra."

"Tickets have to be ordered by mail."

"That a fact," I said, lighting up a Lucky. "Maybe I'll order up a few. Make nice Chanukah presents. Thing is, actually, I need to speak with you concerning a problem you've got in that orchestra, and it's something you better address pronto."

Now Aaron turned all the way around. It was the first time his body had actually faced my body.

"What are you talking about?" His voice had dropped a full octave.

I took out my wallet, flashed my license.

"I'm a private investigator."

"Lobby," said the jockey. "Enjoy your lunch, Mr. Aaron."

The doors opened. Aaron and I walked out into the lunchtime melee.

"Gorgeous girls in this lobby," I brayed.

"If you don't get away from me right now," Aaron muttered, "I'm going to call security."

"That's your right, Mr. Aaron, and in fact I don't blame you. I'll admit I've been more than a little pushy—"

"Good afternoon."

Aaron started walking away from me. I took my hat off and inspected the sweat band. Not surprisingly, it was stained with sweat. "The thing is," I called out, "some people in the orchestra are convinced that Toscanini is missing."

Aaron stopped walking. He turned around and wiped his mouth, as if he had just ingested a large meal. Then he took one large step forward.

"What did you say?" His voice had dropped to a hush.

"Toscanini. Some of the musicians think that he's a missing person."

Aaron looked around the lobby.

"I think the security cops are by the desk."

Now the NBC honcho walked back to me.

"Who told you this?"

"A member of the orchestra."

"Who?" Aaron stepped closer. I could smell his breath, warm and sour, with a distant hint of colon problems.

"Sorry. That's a professional confidence."

Aaron stared at me.

"Be in my office at six-thirty sharp."

Aaron turned and walked away. He moved quickly, favoring his left leg, as if he had suddenly willed himself a limp.

"This is a hell of a view."

Sidney Aaron's office faced east; standing at the window, you could take a large bite out of New York, all the way from St. Patrick's, where rich and poor alike knelt and prayed for the end of communism, across the dark and briny East River, to the matchbox vistas of my beloved Queens.

"Not bad for a poor kid from Brooklyn." Aaron walked toward me holding two tumblers of scotch. "Flatbush, to be precise." He smiled. The guy was a real democrat; he had sent Miss Hamilton home prior to our meeting and was playing the host.

"Flatbush," I said. "Dodger fan, huh?"

"You bet, Jack. Tried and true. I think we'll go all the way this year."

"I'm not so sure. The pitching's only been so-so."

Aaron laughed heartily. If this guy was a baseball fan, I was a Hottentot. Nobody laughs when you say the pitching's so-so.

"Here we are." Aaron handed me my drink in a cut-crystal tumbler. "Cheers."

We clinked our glasses. Aaron sat down in a leather chair and gestured for me to sit in a facing leather couch. I sat down and kept on going; the couch was deep enough to hold a rhino. Aaron's desk was parked at the other end of the room, on a raised platform; behind the desk was a wall covered from top to bottom with various awards of a civic and humanitarian nature—B'nai B'rith, Catholic Charities—as well as photographs of Aaron, frequently in black tie, posed with everyone from Cardinal Spellman to Vladimir Horowitz. His capital-*c* Credentials, just in case you might forget you were in the presence of a Great Man.

Aaron had closed his eyes and was resting his ice-filled glass against his forehead. "I've been working too goddamn hard, Jack. You have to excuse me if I was a little curt with you this afternoon."

I spread my hands in an ecumenical gesture.

"Not to worry. I'm sure I could have been a little more diplomatic in my approach."

"This job, special programming—every culture vulture in town gloms on to you."

"Sure. . . ."

Aaron sat up and loosened his tie. I observed a mole on the back of his right hand. "Every hustler and phony-baloney, every bozo with a one-act play in his closet or under his bed. Sometimes real crazies, Jack—dispossessed, embittered, rejected artists of all stripes who might just lunge at you or cut your throat."

"You're not just speaking metaphorically?" I asked.

Aaron blinked. He clearly hadn't expected me to utter any word that contained more than two syllables. "Metaphorically" was a word I liked to roll out of the garage every couple of weeks, like an old lady's Ford Coupe.

"You'd be surprised," Aaron said. "Bruce Howard, an associate of mine, got his nose broken by a Negro actor who claimed that Canada Lee was systematically stealing all his parts."

"Why didn't he break Canada Lee's nose?"

"That's my point, Jack. The irrationality . . ."

"Mr. Aaron—"

"Call me Sidney. Everybody does." Fat chance.

"Sidney—"

Aaron abruptly got up and walked toward his desk. "Now, who on earth told you that Maestro is missing?"

"I really can't tell you that."

"I believe you said it was a member of the orchestra?" He shuffled through some papers on his desk. What a busy guy.

"That's right."

"One member?"

"One member, who told me he represented about a dozen musicians, all kinds—strings, horns, kazoos—who felt that by the end of the cross-country tour last spring—"

Aaron whirled around. "The most extraordinary public relations triumph in the history of classical music, Jack." Aaron walked forward swiftly, his right hand extended, spilling some scotch on the carpet. "People heard this orchestra in the boondocks, people who had never heard good music in their lives—rednecks, apple-knockers, yahoos, and hayseeds of all descriptions. Suddenly Beethoven and Brahms and Wagner entered their miserable lives. Wagner in Atlanta, Jack. Can you imagine?"

"The mind boggles."

"The mind boggles. No shit." He sat down. "And now some demented musician tells you that Maestro is missing."

"Apparently some of the guys feel the real Toscanini vanished before the end of the tour."

Aaron leaned as far forward as he could without landing on the floor. "So who conducted this orchestra, Jack? Mortimer Snerd? Kay Kyser?"

"A stand-in. A double. That's what they think."

" 'They.' How many?"

"A dozen."

"You met with a dozen?"

"No. I met with one."

"So how do you know he represents a dozen musicians?"

"I don't. But I've been in this business long enough to recognize a bullshit artist. I don't think this guy is a bullshit artist."

"Who is he?"

I shook my head. "Can't."

Aaron got up again. This was not a relaxed man.

"We've had labor problems recently. I'll bet this is the start of some negotiating move. Jesus."

"I doubt that."

"You doubt that?" He stopped in his tracks. "What the hell do you know about it, a private dick? This is labor trouble; I can smell it." He tapped his well-developed nose.

"So you don't think—"

"That Toscanini is missing? What are you, joking? I spoke to Maestro this morning. He's up in Riverdale, like always, preparing for the new season. How can you even think he's missing?"

"I don't think anything. I was hired to look into this."

"Well, you looked into it. Tell this *meshugenah* musician that Toscanini's up at Villa Pauline and he's fine. He should find something else to get hysterical about, and maybe he should seek out some professional help."

"So as far as you're concerned, there's no merit in his claim."

Aaron stared at me as if I had just peed on his oriental carpet.

"No."

"Then let me ask you something."

He started to pick his nose, but thought better of it. "What?"

"If you're so positive this claim is bullshit, why did you want to see me?"

Aaron swirled the ice cubes around in his scotch, soothing himself with that tinkling boozy sound.

"Curiosity. And that curiosity has now been satisfied. I have nothing else to say, except that if there really are a dozen musicians who think Maestro has disappeared, I suggest they come up here and discuss it with me. I'd be more than happy to meet with them and answer any questions they might have, or deal with any doubts circulating among them. There's no reason for them to have any uncertainty on this score."

"My impression is they felt there might be reprisals."

Aaron's brown eyes got very hard.

"Reprisals? In 1946 I was the B'nai B'rith Man of the Year. It's a humanitarian award. They don't give it to dictators. That's my answer to that. Good evening, Mr. LeVine."

I was all alone on the elevator going down, just me and a Cuban elevator jockey. He was lost in his tropical thoughts, as I was lost in my detective thoughts.

I didn't have a doubt in the world that Arturo Toscanini had disappeared.

THREE

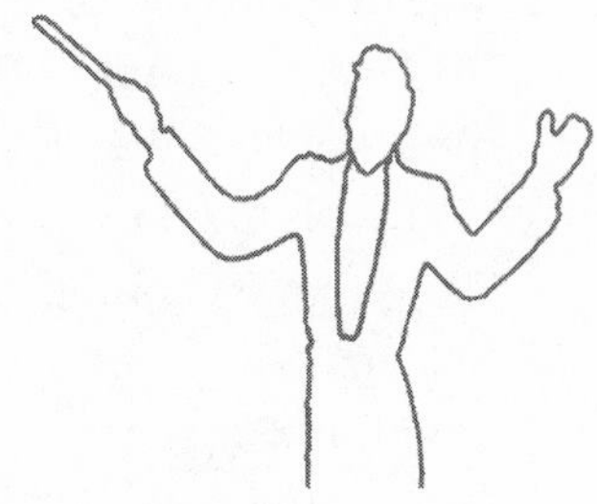

The sun was streaming through my bedroom window the next morning and, although it was September, at seven o'clock the street had the hazy, slow-motion look of a summer day. Two garbagemen were playing catch with the metal cans outside my building, making sure that the last sleeping citizens in Sunnyside would capitulate and tumble cursing from their beds. I brewed up some strong coffee and fried a couple of eggs and when the clock hit eight-thirty, I got on the phone and dialed Fritz Stern. He picked up on the first ring and sounded less than enthusiastic when I told him I wanted to take a drive over to Toscanini's house.

"Maestro's house," he said. "Maestro's house."

"It's in Riverdale, right?"

"Yes. Independence Avenue. They call it Villa Pauline."

"You know how to get there?"

"Maestro's house," he said.

"Am I getting an echo here?"

"It's Riverdale, yes." Stern sounded panicky, as if he had just heard the bootsteps of the Gestapo clacking down his corridor. "But Mr. LeVine, I don't think, really . . ." I could hear him breathing.

"You don't think what?" I was still in my boxer shorts, holding a mug full of Chase and Sanborn. I didn't look anything like a private detective.

"Maestro's house."

"Am I speaking to you or your parrot, Mr. Stern? I think it's an obvious move, going over there. All I want are the directions, although it'd be extremely helpful if you came with me."

"To Maestro's house."

"Well, you've added a 'to.' We're making genuine progress."

"You wish to go to Maestro's house with me."

"Now, that's a complete sentence. Yes I do."

"When?"

"Right now."

"Gott in Himmel."

"I live in Sunnyside, in darkest Queens. I can pick you up in about forty minutes. Just take the Harlem River Drive, right?"

"Maestro's house."

"Mr. Stern, with all due respect, we're not going to see Heinrich Himmler, for crissakes. The guy's a conductor."

There was a long beat. I heard more breathing.

"Hello?"

"I'm at 540 Fort Washington Avenue. The apartment is 1-C. Ground floor."

"Great. If you're hyperventilating, Mr. Stern, I recommend holding a paper bag over your mouth. Works for me sometimes."

Fritz Stern's suntan seemed to have faded overnight. He stood in the foyer of his apartment, already wearing a khaki windbreaker and a cap; my guess was he had put them on right after hanging up the phone. Germans like to get ready early. Standing behind him was an agitated woman in a housedress who studied me as if I were for sale.

"My wife Hilde," he said in barely audible tones, as though speaking louder would set her off like a guard dog. Hilde Stern had thin lips and worried blue eyes; her features were delicate but ravaged by anxiety. Her hair was black, but her face was gray.

"So this is the private detective." Her voice was huskier than I had expected. Not quite Marlene Dietrich, but throaty all the same.

"That's right." I looked around the apartment, if only to escape her unwavering and semi-hostile gaze. "Terrific place," I told her. It wasn't. The Sterns had five rooms and furniture enough for ten. Sofas, chairs, hassocks, and breakfronts were jammed together like the treasures in Charles Foster Kane's warehouse. There were numerous places to be seated, but no place to sit down. The blinds were drawn behind closed draperies, so there wasn't a ray of natural light in the joint. To make things even more oppressive, the upholstery on the couches and chairs ranged from St. Louis brown to mustard-gas yellow.

Mrs. Stern watched me check the place out. "The furniture is all from Germany."

"It's very impressive. Solid."

"In this country I don't think they are made this well."

"You may be right," I told her. "But there are a few things we do better over here, cheeseburgers and free speech for openers."

Stern was having trouble standing still. I could hardly blame him. His bride was not a relaxing presence.

"We should go," he said.

Frau Stern kept eyeballing me, then turned and swept a pair of framed photographs from a side table.

"My daughters," she said, as if challenging me to an arm-wrestling match. She handed me the tinted "poses."

"Beautiful girls," said Ambassador LeVine. The younger daughter was frail and bespectacled and already looked, at age thirteen, like she was going to marry a guy with a heart condition; the older daughter ("twenty-two next month") was dark and complicated and a one-round knockout. I stared at her picture for about five seconds too long.

"We should go," Stern repeated.

Hilde Stern turned to her husband.

"And you'll be back when?"

"Soon."

"Soon is when?" She was really murder.

"When we're done, Hilde. I really can't say this for sure." Stern turned and walked out the door.

I turned to Mrs. Stern. "A pleasure to meet you."

"I don't understand this at all," she said, looking past me to the door.

"Well . . ."

"He is paid to play the violin, not to hire detectives."

"I understand your feelings—"

Stern reappeared in the doorway. "Enough," he shouted. "Enough with your doubting! Mr. LeVine!"

"We won't be long, ma'am," I said to Mrs. Stern, then sped out the door before the happy couple started hurling *weisswurst* at each other.

Stern said next to nothing during the fifteen-minute drive to Toscanini's residence. He offered laconic directions—"left here," "at the light, right"—but otherwise listened mutely as I described my meeting with Sidney Aaron.

"He has a lot of power," Stern said, gazing out the window of my '48 Buick Roadmaster. Although the day had begun on a promising note, with blue skies and an engaging mugginess, it was turning gray and the breeze out of the north hinted at the shorter and colder days to come.

"It certainly appeared that way to me," I told Stern, one hand on the Roadmaster's faux-ivory steering wheel. "Swanky office, English secretary. All the comforts of home."

"Oh yes. And he enjoys the power. Too much."

"No such thing as too much, Mr. Stern. Power to those guys is like oxygen to a fire."

Stern sighed. He seemed genuinely troubled. "It's funny . . . maybe not so funny, actually, but I thought that Mr. Aaron, Mr. Sarnoff, the chairman, that they were *landsmen,* you know, Jews, and therefore they'd be what in German we call *simpatisch,* which is like both sympathetic and empathetic, but . . ." Stern shook his head.

"Forget it. Over a certain price range, they're all killers."

"You said it. Here you bear right." Stern leaned forward, rubbing his hands as nervously as a squirrel.

"You ought to relax."

"Maestro's house."

"Not again."

"No," Stern said. "This is it."

The Villa Pauline was not quite the Mediterranean-style palazzo I had anticipated, but rather a large Tudor-style house, badly in need of a paint job and surrounded by five lush acres of lawn and very well established plantings. It wasn't hard to figure out why a European émigré would feel very much at home here. In the distance one could see the cliffs of the Jersey Palisades and a suggestion—just by the valley of light—of the venerable and mighty Hudson River.

I stopped the car. We were on the corner of Independence Avenue and 254th Street.

"Nice setup the old man has here," I said to Stern.

He wasn't listening.

"Look," he said, pointing out his window.

Two men were crossing the grounds. They walked swiftly in our direction.

"Friends of yours?" I asked Stern.

"No. Of course not."

I stepped on the accelerator and headed toward the Villa Pauline. Stern was appalled.

"What are you doing?"

"Relax."

I drove onto a long graveled driveway that led to a porte cochere on the south side of the house.

Stern gripped his door handle.

"Mr. LeVine, please . . ."

"What's to lose?" I told him.

The two men picked up their pace. They were now running toward the car. And the closer they got, the larger they appeared. Neither of them resembled Jascha Heifetz.

"Lieber Gott," said Stern.

They reached the driveway and held up hands the size of porterhouse steaks, signaling me to stop the car. I did so and poked my head out the window.

"What's up, fellas?" I asked, friendly as a pup.

The larger of the two men—the one who was six-foot-five rather than six-foot-one—approached the car, walking very deliberately. His blond hair was cut short, very Aryan, and he wore sunglasses and a brown suit that looked to be the only one he had ever owned. "This guy isn't Toscanini, is he?" I asked Stern. "Maestro's a smaller man with better clothes, right?"

"Lieber—"

The big man bent over and peered into the car, like King Kong gazing into the windows of the Third Avenue El.

"What do you want?" he asked in a surprisingly thin and disembodied voice.

"We're here to see Toscanini," I told him. "A private matter."

The Aryan stared at me, then at Stern. He wheeled around and addressed his partner.

"They're here to see the old man."

His partner had bent over and was filling his fists with gravel. He stood up, let the gravel fall to the ground, and patted his hands clean. The partner had shaggy black hair, wore corduroy pants, a leather jacket, and a tweed cap.

"What do they want with him?" he asked.

The giant turned back to us.

"Why do you want to see Mr. Toscanini?"

"We're with the American Baton Company. We understand the Maestro is in the market for our new Excalibur model, which is extremely lightweight."

The giant examined us again. God only knows what he was looking for.

"He's asleep," he finally said.

"Really." I made a big show of checking my watch. "It's ten-thirty. You might want to think about getting him up."

"Can't be disturbed."

"He's gonna be pissed when he finds out that you shooed away the guys from the baton company."

"Maybe we should be going," Stern mumbled, but I kept yapping away.

"This is a really first-class piece of goods we're talking about. It's not just a stick, you understand?"

The big man shook his big head.

"Sorry. We got orders from Walter Toscanini. His father is not to be disturbed."

"The old guy feeling all right?" I asked.

"Orders from Walter," the giant repeated. "No visitors. So beat it."

His partner started walking toward us; now I could see that he had a glass eye and a scar than ran the length of his left cheek.

"Mr. LeVine . . . ," Stern muttered.

"What do you think?" I said cheerily to Stern. "Ready to go?"

"Please . . ."

I threw the Buick into reverse. "A pleasure meeting you fellas," I said to the two large men. The partner was waving at something off in the distance. "Let's all have lunch sometime soon."

"Please," Stern said again.

"We're gone." I backed the car out of the driveway onto 254th Street and then turned onto Independence Avenue, which is where the blue Chrysler began to follow us. I wasn't surprised. Not even a little.

"So what do you think, Mr. Stern, was the Maestro sleeping?"

Stern was wiping his face with a bright yellow handkerchief that looked suspiciously like a linen napkin.

"Those men," he said. *"Shrecklich."*

"Not the musical type. He wasn't there, I'd bet my life on it."

"You don't think so?"

"Oh, you got me into a doozy, Mr. Stern. I've handled doozies before, but they always crept up on me. This one appears to be an immediate, direct-hit doozy." I lit up a Lucky and rolled my window all the way down. "By the way, just as a point of interest, we're being followed."

Stern started to turn around.

"We don't turn around. That's rule number one," I told him.

"Lieber, lieber."

"No reason to fret; I'll lose them before you can say Johann Sebastian Bach. For twenty-five a day, you get the deluxe package."

I slowed the Buick down to about ten miles an hour.

"You go slowly?" Stern started to turn in his seat again. "Why do you do this?"

"I repeat—don't turn around." I checked the rearview mirror. The Chrysler was trying to blend into the scenery and slipped in behind a taxi. When the taxi stopped to pick up an elderly couple with shopping bags, I immediately accelerated and crossed the double yellow line to get around a pair of buses that were lumbering down Independence Avenue in tandem.

"Lieber!" Stern crouched down in his seat.

"Here we go," said Captain Jack. I completed the maneuver by running a red light, hooking a left on 252nd Street, and then beating a garbage truck that was backing into the middle of the block. I sped down to Broadway, catching a green light, took a right, and sailed off unencumbered. There was no way the Chrysler could make it up, but I ran two more reds just to play it safe.

"Now you can look around."

Stern straightened up and peered out the back window.

"This is like one of those gangster pictures," he said.

"Like? It is a gangster picture, but unfortunately we're not the gangsters."

I got Stern home in about ten minutes. He got out of the car and stood on the sidewalk, understandably reluctant to go back into his apartment.

"I probably don't tell Hilde what happened."

"I would say that's an extremely sensible idea."

"Yes." He fidgeted. A light rain had started to fall. "So what do you do next?"

"That's an excellent question, Mr. Stern. I guess I play detective. That's always a start."

"Good luck."

"Thanks. To you, too."

I pulled away. In the rearview mirror, I could see Stern watching my car. Finally, he stared up at the rain as if for a sign, then turned and walked into his building. As for me, I had a slightly queasy feeling.

No. Make that a very queasy feeling.

FOUR

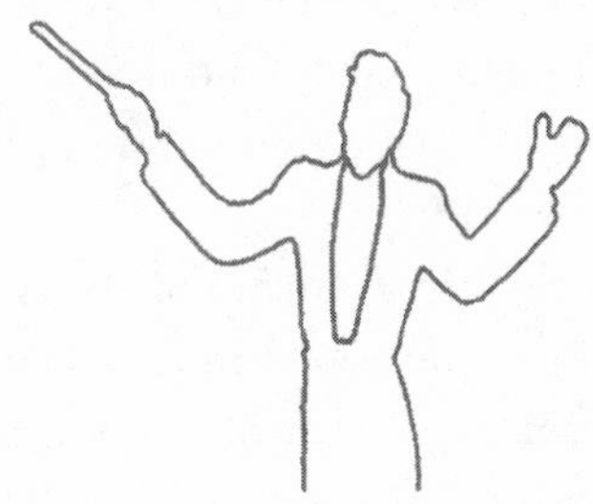

The telephone began to ring at three-thirty in the morning. I recall the precise time because it didn't wake me up. I was seated in my living room, wearing a seersucker robe and reading an Ellery Queen mystery, my stomach on the blink after a midnight bowl of canned chili. I looked at the phone and checked my watch. If there is anything worse than being awakened at three-thirty in the morning by a call, it is being wide awake at that hour and hearing your phone begin to ring. There is no way on earth that it can be good news.

It wasn't.

I picked up after the third ring. "Hello?"

"Mr. LeVine, I woke you up?"

"Actually, no."

"No? You are not sleeping?" The accent came into focus, but the voice seemed disembodied.

It was Hilde Stern.

"Mrs. Stern? Is this Mrs. Stern, Hilde Stern?"

"He is killed."

My blood cooled to an Arctic blue.

"Wait . . . Mr. Stern was killed?"

"The police, they came here, to the door, at half past one o'clock. Shot in the street. On the West Side, near the piers and the ocean liners. What is he doing there? I was worried to death, of course, where is he, he told me he had a late meeting with some of the other musicians, but by one o'clock, I said to myself, this is not Fritz, he would have called if it was going to be so late. My daughter Linda is here, of course; Barbara is coming down from Cornell, can you imagine, she is driving all night, she has wonderful friends and they drive her, so soon she is here, thanks God. You have children, Mr. LeVine?"

"No, I don't." She was in shock, talking to keep reality at bay, to keep the world in an eternal Present Minus Two Hours Ago. The ordinary speech of the average day—comings and goings, it isn't like Fritz, he would have called, friends are driving her . . . Life goes on, keep the conversation going, please, and then comes the moment when Death walks in, takes off his coat and hat, begins unlacing his shoes, and makes himself comfy. But Mrs. Stern was still weeks, maybe months away from that devastating, final moment. She still lived in Two Hours Ago.

"You worry and worry about them, and then something like this. I don't even know if it was musicians he was meeting with—"

"Mrs. Stern—"

"He got a phone call around nine-thirty and said he had to go out, a call from a colleague—"

"Did he say who, by any chance?"

"And then he puts on his jacket, it was still raining; I said to him, Fritz, you have to put on your raincoat, sometimes with him you don't know what he's thinking, it's like the weather is for other people, not him—"

"Mrs. Stern—"

"And he leaves, it is almost ten, I say to him, Fritz, this can't wait? He says it can't wait, he'll call if gets too late, but I should go to sleep. And then . . ." And then. It was all she could get out this time around.

"I'll be right over. Are the police still there?"

"No. They left. It's just us now. Just the family."

* * *

Sunnyside, Queens, is a beautiful village at four-thirty in the morning. The buildings seem rooted in some cheerful domestic and commercial history, the streets are clean and quiet and without memory. I picked up a scalding container of coffee at the Bickford's on Broadway and balanced it carefully between my legs as I headed toward the Queensboro Bridge. Cool air blew in through the window; trucks bearing milk and bread and the latest editions of the *News* and *Mirror* made their predawn journeys through the dense and varied neighborhoods of Queens. On the radio, Symphony Sid was playing Lester Young. Symphony Sid. What about Symphony Arturo? The sky began to lighten; there was no stopping this day, much as I would have liked to.

They were seated in the living room when I arrived—Hilde Stern and her two daughters, all wearing black dresses and the bewildered expressions of accident victims. Hilde arose and introduced her children.

"This is Barbara, the college student, she just got here . . . and our baby is Linda." Linda was quite petite at age thirteen, maybe five feet tall, with curly black hair and a prepubescent body. She was pale and deeply sad and totally unapproachable. Barbara stood about five-eight in flat shoes, and her funereal duds could not conceal a body that Jane Russell would have been proud to call her own. She had thick black hair, brown, almond-shaped eyes, a beautifully sculpted nose, and a mouth you couldn't look at for very long without becoming thoroughly ashamed of yourself. "And this is Mr. LeVine," Mrs. Stern told her children, "who Papa had hired to help him." I had been transformed from a Broadway shamus into an angel of mercy.

Barbara shook my hand. The warmth of her long fingers went through me like a low-voltage shock.

"I'm so terribly sorry," I told her. And I was. Linda, the little one, turned away from me and began to cry. Hilde took her in her arms. Barbara just stared evenly at me.

"What's going on?" she said quietly. "Who the hell would shoot my father?"

“I really have no idea.”

“He hired you to do what? The thing with Toscanini?” She looked back over her shoulder toward Hilde, who was now leading Linda out of the room, presumably back to her bedroom.

“He told you about it?”

She stepped closer to me and lowered her voice.

“He could confide in me a lot more easily than he could in my mother.” I’ll bet he could. This was a girl you would confide the secret of the atom bomb to without a second thought. “My mother was always on him, castrating him, doubting him. . . . He told you his theory?”

“About?” I answered, Mr. Neutral.

“About.” She was not patient, this fabulous girl. “About Toscanini being missing. About the double conducting the orchestra.”

“Yes he did.”

“And do you think it’s a completely nutsy notion?”

“It appeared to be, at first blush.”

“What about second blush?”

“I just started on this yesterday. The first thing I find out about it is that your father’s been murdered.”

“Which means that it’s probably true. He wasn’t shot down like a dog for no reason.”

“I agree.”

“You do.”

“Yes. But that doesn’t necessarily confirm that Toscanini is among the missing.”

“So you think it’s a *coincidence*? Come on.”

“I didn’t say that. Listen, you’re an Ivy League girl—”

She rolled her eyes. “What does that mean? That I’m a goddamn prodigy? I’m not.”

“Okay, I stand corrected. You’re of average intelligence—”

“Mr. LeVine—”

“All I’m saying, Miss Stern, is that I’m sure you realize that while the death of your father is highly suspicious, it's still a giant leap in logic to say that it necessarily follows that Toscanini's been snatched."

"So you don't think he's missing? I don't follow."

"I have no idea. Right now I'm principally concerned with who killed your father."

"I understand, but my father hired you to find out what happened to Toscanini. Maybe I'm just a chump, but in his memory"—her eyes teared up—"I'd like you to keep doing that. . . ." Tears now flowed. "Shit. . . ."

"I can do both. It's not an either-or situation. In fact, everything says that there is a connection. So if Toscanini is in fact missing, then figuring out what happened to your father will lead me to what Sherlock Holmes used to refer to as the final solution."

"We don't talk about final solutions in this house," she said. "Too many dead relatives. And now this goddamn thing." She wiped away more tears. "Jesus God, of all the people, my father."

"I understand."

Barbara dried her eyes and pointed to the pack of Luckies in my jacket pocket.

"May I?"

I handed her a cigarette and lit her up. She took a very deep drag, sighed, and walked toward the hallway, in the direction of her younger sister's heart-rending wailing. I followed at a discreet and gentlemanly distance, until I could see Linda's bedroom, still a very young girl's bedroom, with photographs of Vaughn Monroe and Perry Como adorning the circus-themed wallpaper. Stern's youngest daughter lay sobbing on her bed, her thin legs sticking storklike from her black dress, a helpless kid at the most exposed moment of her just-started life, knowing that her protector and keeper has been blasted out of the world forever. Hilde sat beside her daughter, stroking her hair and saying words I wasn't able and didn't need to hear. Barbara turned back toward me. Smoke streamed from that gorgeous nose.

"You'll stay on this case, Mr. LeVine."

"I will."

"There will be a lot of pressure on you, as I'm sure you realize. There's some very tough sonsofbitches over at NBC—"

"I said I will. That's the end of it. And call me Jack."

She managed a grim smile. "Not yet, Mr. LeVine. Not yet."

We sat in the living room until around six A.M., drinking coffee and exchanging fragments of conversation. Mrs. Stern made rye toast with butter and orange preserves and we ate it without thinking. Two neighbors had joined the vigil—Kurt and Ilse Weissman from apartment 3-C. Kurt Weissman was a dry cleaner in Washington Heights, a fact he repeated to me several times, along with the establishment's precise address on St. Nicholas Avenue. Weissman was a pallid, heavyset man in his late thirties whose brains seemed to be receding along with his light brown hair. His blond, intense wife never took her eyes from me, even when contradicting her husband, which occurred nearly every time he opened his mouth.

"In this country I would never expect such a thing," he said.

"What does that mean, Kurt?" she barked. "For God's sakes. Such crap you talk. This is the Garden of Eden? Please. In this city the criminals run free like wild dogs. Has been true since we got here. I have no illusions about such things. Even in our store"—she looked to me—"you have to be careful."

Barbara just stared at me, faintly amused. The Weissmans were a distraction from the numbing fact that at this moment her father's body was laid out like a haunch of beef on a cold steel table in the police morgue. Hilde emerged from the kitchen with a fresh pot of coffee and tray full of butter cookies.

"Linda is sleeping, I am happy."

"The best thing," said the dry cleaner, then looked at me intently. "You agree with this?"

"Thousand percent," I assured him.

"If she sleeps," he added, "for a while at least, this horrible thing is out of her mind."

Ilse instantly cracked her whip. "Kurt, for God's sakes, it's never going to be out of her mind. How can you say such an idiotic thing?" The dry cleaner cringed at her attack. Weissman was a major league nitwit, but still you had to feel for him.

I took another cup of coffee from Hilde Stern. As I was spooning in some sugar, the intercom buzzer sounded with the sudden force of an air raid siren. Hilde gasped.

"Even money it's the cops," I told her.

"They were here already," Barbara said, straightening her dress. She went into the foyer and buzzed back.

"That was just to break the news. This time they'll bring their paper and pencils."

A voice could be heard squawking over the intercom. "All right," Barbara said, then looked to me and nodded.

Kurt Weissman leapt to his feet; he looked ready to scurry into Anne Frank's attic. "We should go, Ilse. Soon . . . now."

And then the doorbell sounded.

They were plainclothes, Homicide. Lieutenant Eddie Breen and Sergeant Dick O'Malley. I figured Breen to be about forty, although his bland pockmarked kisser could have been ten years older or younger than that. It just didn't matter. O'Malley thought he was a young blond dreamboat, and would have qualified but for a left eye that wandered and some persistent acne on his forehead. He wore a handkerchief in the pocket of his houndstooth jacket, which he straightened as soon as he got a good look at Barbara Stern.

Breen cleared his throat. "I apologize for the intrusion; I realize it's terribly early in the morning and you folks have been through a great deal already."

The Weissmans introduced themselves, Kurt again emphasizing his bona fides as a dry cleaner, his concern for the welfare of the Stern family, and his need to get adequate rest before another day of Martinizing. He and Ilse backed out of the apartment like Abbott and Costello in a ghost picture, Kurt never taking his eyes off the cops. Ilse shook her head at me as if we had a secret compact, then loudly shut the door. I could hear their footsteps echoing down the hallway, and then Ilse's raised voice as she railed against her overmatched mate.

The two cops took their coats off and helped themselves to coffee, before seating themselves in a most gingerly fashion on the cane-backed chairs that flanked the couch. The chairs appeared fragile; the two homicide bulls did not. Hilde and Barbara huddled close to each other on the couch, and I remained standing, as I usually do in the presence of trained law enforcement professionals.

"We know this is a terrible ordeal for all of you," O'Malley added. He and Breen were playing good-cop/good-cop. "So we don't want to overstay our welcome. We'd just like to pull together a few facts to help us get started on our investigation and then we'll be out of your hair and on our way as quickly as possible."

Hilde shrugged. "Who can sleep anyhow? You ask what you ask."

The cops didn't quite know how to play that, so they simply nodded. O'Malley looked over at Barbara and nervously rubbed his wedding band, as if hoping it would disappear. Breen straightened the crease in his pants and eyeballed me.

"And you're . . . ?"

"Jack LeVine, capital *V.* Private investigator, 1630 Broadway. If you'd like my card . . ." I fished through my sports jacket.

Breen threw an inquiring look Hilde's way.

"Mrs. Stern, there was really no need to hire an investigator."

"She didn't hire me," I told Breen. "Her husband did." I found a card and handed it to the pockmarked cop. "Earlier this week."

"Why?" Breen asked me, then regretted it. He looked uneasily at Hilde, as if assessing, and immediately dismissing, the possibility of marital hanky-panky.

"He had a professional concern."

"Things were good between you and your husband?" O'Malley asked Hilde.

"Things?" Hilde looked as blank as if O'Malley were speaking in Swahili.

"Your marriage."

"He was my husband. Of course I loved him."

"Recent arguments, disagreements?"

Barbara jumped in with both feet.

"Are you joking?" she asked the hapless homicide dick. "My father was shot to death! This wasn't some domestic squabble, for cris-sakes!"

"Barbara!" Hilde was clearly appalled by her daughter's fear-lessness. She glanced nervously at the door. Like her late husband, she was always on the alert for the sudden, spectral arrival of storm troopers.

"You see my mother," Barbara continued. "I mean, do you actually think for *one instant* that she's capable—"

"Certainly not"—O'Malley wanted to stay on Barbara's good side, which was every side—"but there's a certain routine we have to fol-low. . . ." He looked hopefully toward me for confirmation of his meth-odology, but I just examined my tie for gravy stains.

Breen continued applying the soft soap. "No matter how outra-geous or obvious the questions may appear—"

Hilde finally tuned in to the line of questioning, as if she had just located her favorite radio station. "You think I have something to do with this?" she asked. "With a *shooting*?" She wasn't angry; she just couldn't comprehend what they were talking about,

I grabbed a jelly-filled cookie off the tray. "No they don't, Mrs. Stern. Everybody knows what kind of a marriage you and Fritz had. They wouldn't suspect you in a million years." There wasn't a nicer guy than me, not anywhere in New York at six-eighteen in the morn-ing. "The police just have a certain protocol they have to follow. But I think, fellas, I'd wrap up the domestic strife angle pretty quick."

Neither Breen nor O'Malley appreciated my analysis, but you could tell they weren't going to call me on it, not right now.

"As the man said, it's basically just a matter of protocol," O'Malley said, glancing over at me with no great affection. "Now." He flipped through his spiral notebook. "You mentioned earlier that your husband received a phone call at approximately nine-thirty last night and he stated that it was from a colleague. He didn't say which colleague, did he?"

Hilde shook her head.

"No."

"Didn't make any indication? A name, nickname?"

"No. Nothing. He said . . ." Hilde looked a little vague. "It was something like, 'Hello? Yes. Okay. If it has to be now, it has to be now.' That he said, I definitely remember."

" 'If it has to be now, it has to be now.' " O'Malley looked my way, as if I might have something to add. I didn't. I rubbed my jaw and realized that I had never gotten around to shaving. The cop forged on.

"Now, it wasn't generally a habit of your husband's to go out at all hours, was it?"

"Fritz?" Hilde just waved her hand. "Of course not. He worked nights, naturally, when the orchestra played. But when he was home, he was home."

"He wasn't the type of person to just step out at night, like for a walk, or to get the paper?"

"No."

"He would usually come right home and stay home."

"Yes," Hilde said with some force. "That's what I thought I said already."

O'Malley abruptly put his coffee cup down and rose, as if suddenly restless.

"How did he appear when he left?"

"Appear?" Hilde asked.

"His manner," Breen added helpfully. "Was he maybe a little nervous or agitated?"

"I would say he was generally a nervous individual," Barbara said.

"Ach!" said her mother impatiently. "He wasn't always nervous. Come on, Barbara."

"Maybe a little subdued, then. Maybe that's what I meant."

"Subdued?" asked Breen. "Like down? Something troubling him recently?"

"Not down." Barbara brushed her bangs back from her forehead. O'Malley leaned forward, his hands gripping the back of a chair; he was just hypnotized by this girl. "And understand I hadn't seen him since I went back to school at the end of the summer. He just sounded on the phone recently . . ." Barbara thought better of it, sat up, and straightened her dress. "I don't know. Stick with subdued."

"Your father have any enemies that you know of?" Breen continued.

"Enemies? Fritz?" Hilde was incredulous. "Please." She arose somewhat abruptly and walked into her bedroom.

"My father," Barbara told Breen, "was really not *capable* of making enemies."

"So you think this was just an accidental—"

"Let me finish." It came out a little rougher than Barbara had intended, and she knew it. "I just mean I want to complete this thought while it's fresh in my mind, because I'm awfully tired and upset. . . . I wasn't trying to be sassy."

"We understand," Breen said, and checked out his partner. O'Malley nodded with the dumb frozen attention of a farm animal.

Barbara crossed her legs and sighed. "Mr. LeVine, could I trouble you for another cigarette?"

"I got one," O'Malley said automatically, pulling a pack of Pall Malls from his jacket. Breen instantly reached for matches, and together they serviced her, like a pair of chorus boys doing some half-assed number in a musical. She really was awfully good, I had to say, and not just for a twenty-one-year-old.

"You have to understand something about German Jewish refugees," she began, taking a drag on her cigarette. "As far as they're concerned, they've *made* all their enemies already, okay? Made them for life. From an accident of birth. The ones who were lucky enough to get safely out of Europe never wanted to make another enemy again in their lives, sometimes to a fault. In fact, often to a fault, I would say."

Hilde came out of the bedroom holding a photograph and a glass of water.

"Here." She handed the photo to the two cops. "Here is the big criminal with all his enemies."

"We didn't want to imply . . ." O'Malley sat back down and examined the photo with Breen. I walked over and eyeballed it over their wide shoulders. It was a snapshot taken somewhere in the country, the rolling hills in the background indicating a Catskill or Berkshire setting, and it showed Fritz Stern seated in an Adirondack chair, a small and wary smile on his face, his right hand wrapped around what looked like a glass of lemonade.

"That's fresh lemonade," Hilde said, as if reading my mind. "I made it every afternoon. It made him so happy, why not do it."

"Looks like a very fine man," Breen said.

"I can vouch for that," I said. "He was modest, mild-mannered. An Old World gentleman. Described himself to me as 'high-strung,' his little joke being in that he was a fiddler."

"He was too good," Hilde said, taking the photograph from the cop's hands. "Too good for his own good."

Fritz Stern's widow headed back to her bedroom, walking more quickly than before. This time she closed the door, and then we heard some crying. Not wailing, nothing too operatic or Mediterranean; just an icy gust of misery blowing across Hilde Stern's life as this new and altogether frightening day began. Barbara listened in silence for a few moments, as if considering whether or not to go comfort her mother, then just sighed and continued her narrative.

"What I'm getting to is that these people, these refugees, are virtually incapable of making enemies because they're incapable of any kind of confrontation. Their experience of anger and what it might bring was so terrifying, so *permanently* terrifying, that they can only think this: 'If I make someone angry—' Forget that. 'If the wrong person *even knows I'm alive,* I could get myself packed into a boxcar and sent off to a concentration camp.' "

"I know it was rough," O'Malley offered. "I saw the newsreels."

Barbara stared at him as if awaiting a translation. "Yeah," she finally said. "It was very rough. So there's no way most of these people wanted to get themselves even *noticed,* much less start pissing other people off. That's what I'm getting to in terms of enemies. My father was not a mouse, that's not what I'm saying, far from it"—her eyes started brimming over again—"but he was not a man who could go out and actually make an enemy. Okay?" The tears ran down her cheeks. From her bedroom, Hilde's crying grew louder; in the other bedroom, Linda lay in her own grief. There wasn't much that either I or the two homicide dicks could say to make any of this better. I turned to the two bulls and made a clerical gesture with my hands.

"Fellas . . . this has been a very long night for these folks."

Breen and O'Malley shook their heads solemnly and stood up.

"Yeah," said Breen. "Ma'am, this is where we can be reached. Anything comes up, anything you need." He handed Barbara his card. "Anything," he repeated significantly.

"We both can be reached there," O'Malley added, patting Barbara's hand. He was about as subtle as a rash, but Barbara didn't seem to notice.

"Thank you." She took the card and dried her eyes. The two cops went to the door and looked at me as if I were supposed to leave with them; when I didn't make a move to go, Breen threw me a little nod and I walked over to him and his partner. They both held their hats in their hands and spoke in the general direction of the floor.

"I don't expect you to tell us everything you know, pal," Breen said, "but let me remind you that this is a murder case."

"Hey, I'm as anxious as you to find out what the hell happened," I told them. "This was a good guy with a good family. But I just got here myself, believe me. Maybe you can help me—where exactly was he shot?"

"They found him in a stripped Mercury coupe on Tenth Avenue and Forty-sixth Street," O'Malley told me. "Two shots in the head at close range."

"Sounds like a professional job."

"Most likely." Breen raised an eyebrow. "Any mob connections here? Somebody he knew, an associate . . ."

"Fellas, far as I know the guy was as clean as my grandmother. Maybe cleaner. He was a *violinist,* for crissakes."

"What he hired you for . . ."

"Wouldn't lead me to think about a mob hit in any which way."

"But it wasn't a domestic thing."

"Guys . . ." I tried to shrug helplessly.

"Okay," Breen said. "You can play this as cute as you want right now. But sooner or later you have to help us."

"I'll say what I always say in these circumstances—and you can ask around about me, call Joe Egan in the Sunnyside Precinct—I'll help you when I have something to help you with. Okay?"

The two palookas looked at each other and put their hats on, just like they learn to do in police school.

"Okay," said Breen. "You'll be hearing from us."

"I'll put out my best china."

They reluctantly exited on their own, taking a last longing look at Barbara Stern. When the door closed, I walked toward the living room window.

"I'll be on my way shortly," I told Stern's daughter. "I just want to make sure those two yokels aren't hanging around outside."

"No rush," Barbara said. She reached around and tied her hair into a ponytail, fixing it with a rubber band. I was always awed by how easily women could do that. "You don't feel like jousting with them any further?"

"I'm not sure that was jousting. It was more like free-style wrestling." Breen and O'Malley were down the street now, stretching their arms and backs, as if they had just completed some enormous physical task. O'Malley opened the door to a black Ford; Breen, the senior of the two, took the shotgun seat, after taking a final peep at Fort Washington Avenue. "I'm too tired to play with them. Also, I have nothing to tell them."

"Nothing you're *willing* to tell them," Barbara said.

"If you want to be a stickler about it . . ."

"You don't want to tell them about Toscanini?"

"Those two? It would only confuse them."

She managed a smile, a small one, but still sufficient to reduce any heterosexual male to eternal servitude.

"Trust me," I told her. "I'll handle the musical end of this."

"Mr. LeVine . . ." She started to speak, then bit her lip, strolled over to the window, and stared out onto the street, holding on to a lace curtain.

"What?"

"I'm just thinking, and maybe this is stupid . . . should we stay in this apartment? My mother's going to be frightened, and Linda, too. Frightened to death."

"You can't blame them," I told her.

"But is there any reason *in fact* . . . ?"

"No."

"You really don't think so."

"If I thought so, I wouldn't let any of you stay here. I recommend, however, that you *know* as little as possible."

"Because what I don't know can't hurt me."

"Precisely. Ignorance is your shield at the present time. You're going to have enough on your plate here; your mother, your sister, they all need your strength."

"I know." Barbara looked tired and I told her so. She nodded, a little absently. "I better take something or I'll never sleep. My mind is so *crowded,* is the thing. Every time I feel tired, these images appear in my mind, these thoughts. . . . I can't stop them."

"I'm sure . . ."

"What was he thinking those last few seconds, what did he look like when he saw the gun, what was his exact expression, was he terribly frightened, did it hurt?" She took off her shoes. "It's just so goddamn unfair, that's what I can't stop thinking about. Of all the people, my poor father. . . ."

"It stinks, no question. But it happened, so we have to deal with it." I walked to the door, hat in hand. "Get some rest."

"You'll keep me posted?"

"How long are you going to be around?" I asked her.

"Till you figure this out. No way I go back to school until you do."

"Well, that's an incentive for me, then. You gotta get your degree, right?"

She stood up, her shoes in her hand, a gesture that stirred both lust and longing: a woman, a home, a hearth.

"I suppose. College seems really irrelevant right now."

"I'm sure, but that feeling won't last forever. What are you, a senior, a junior?"

"A sophomore. I took a few years off after high school; there was a big world out there and I wanted to see it as soon as possible." I had the feeling there were volumes left unsaid, with copious illustrations. "I was in a hurry, I suppose. I don't regret it."

"You were born in Germany, I take it?"

"Yeah. No accent, I know."

"None. I never would have guessed."

"I took acting lessons for a few years, got rid of whatever trace there was." She pretended to yawn. "I'm awfully tired."

"So get some rest. You need it. Your family needs it."

"Yeah. I know."

I opened the door and exited, taking one last look at Barbara as she turned and walked slowly toward her mother's room, her stocking feet silent on the parquet floor. The apartment suddenly seemed as quiet as a museum. Which, in a way, it was.

FIVE

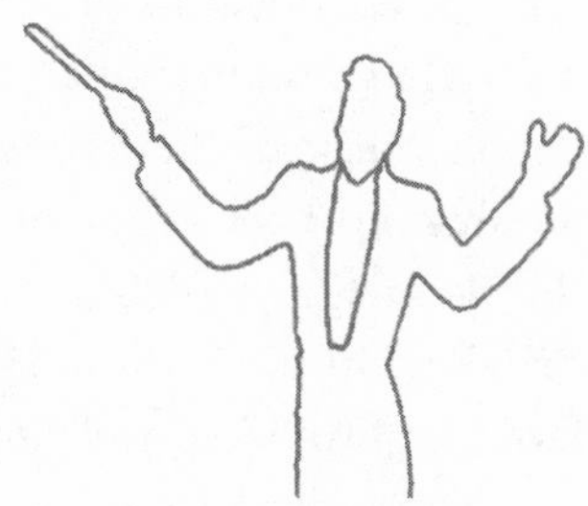

Fritz Stern's funeral was held a day later at the Riverside Chapel, a gray and suitably cheerless edifice on Amsterdam Avenue in Manhattan. It was raining hard when I arrived, fast-moving streams backing up around sewers clogged by soda bottles, cracker boxes, and pages from yesterday's newspapers. I hurried inside the chapel; the service was scheduled for eleven and I had cut it pretty close, thanks to a stalled moving van and resultant tie-up on the Queensboro Bridge. I followed some other stragglers toward a reception room, which was filled with guests waiting to embrace the family and offer empty words of hope and reassurance which at times like these somehow never seem empty at all. Each visitor is transformed into an emissary from the world of the living, a sentient and physical reminder of continuity. When my old man died, I was shocked by how poignant the smallest gestures of kindness became, how moved I was by the dressed-up and well-barbered appearance of even the most ill-tempered of his associates from the hat trade.

I hung my raincoat on a coatrack tightly packed with soaked foul-weather gear. The humidity in the room was at the saturation point and I could feel sweat starting to bead my extensive forehead. The Stern family was somewhere across the room, surrounded by dozens of crouched, whispering people. There was a great deal of hugging and crying. At one point I saw Barbara rise and nuzzle a white-haired woman who was leaning heavily on a pair of canes. I waved in Barbara's direction, but she never saw me and I realized I was just a guy for hire with no real business in this room, so I walked out, grabbed a black yarmulke from a basket, and strolled into the chapel. It was a very large room, but already nearly filled by close to three hundred people, most of them looking as dazed and stricken as survivors of an air raid. They sat or stood, whispering in groups or just staring at the floor. I spotted Sidney Aaron seated about six rows in back of Fritz's plain pine coffin. He was wearing a midnight-blue suit and a fancy embroidered yarmulke. He was speaking with great animation to a short, deeply tanned man to his immediate right, a man who looked like he'd never been anywhere near Riverside Chapel before. On Aaron's left was a tall redhead in an ermine stole who looked like she'd been to a lot of places.

The short, tanned man turned around again and my aging brain started laboring. I knew this guy from somewhere, and it wasn't anywhere good, but I couldn't pin the name or face down. He had a slight facial tic, a nervous blinking of his left eye. Blinky somebody? Who the hell was he?

The short man turned back around and I began studying the other mourners, trying to ascertain who among them might be Fritz's fellow musicians. It wasn't difficult. Musicians are used to wearing either tuxedos or sports clothes, so I guessed that the middle-aged men in shiny or off-the-rack suits had to be them. Almost to a man, they appeared to be wary and disoriented. A colleague had been murdered, that was bizarre enough, but I wondered how many of them were also wondering if their Maestro had been snatched, and if he was dead or alive.

A door opened at the front of the room and we all stood up as the family entered, trailing a massive, pink-skinned rabbi who wore the imperious and implacable expression of a Jewish Mussolini. His name was Ludwig Strauss, seemingly past sixty and even balder than I was. As he marched toward the lectern, he gazed across the room as if daring anyone to speak or even relieve an itch in his august presence. The family walked in Rabbi Strauss's wake like frightened ducklings: Hilde, Barbara, and Linda, followed by a peroxide blond and a plump gray-haired man whose hawklike features marked him as a likely brother of Hilde's, only after a prefrontal lobotomy. He wore a terrible cocoa-brown jacket and even worse yellow checked pants and his movements were slow-motion and oddly abstracted. I didn't think he was out of sync due to grief; this guy looked to be pretty much out of his skull. The bottle-blond held the poor slob by the arm until they reached his seat and then she sat him down very carefully and lovingly. There was no reason for me to have known that Hilde had a damaged sibling, but here he was and I found it totally unsettling. Then again, dealing with physical and mental disabilities has never been my strong suit; even that blind albino who plays the accordion outside of Macy's makes me queasy.

Fritz's family sat down, and we all followed obediently. The Rabbi silently surveyed the room for what seemed like a full minute, during which nobody moved a muscle or so much as coughed, then abruptly and loudly launched into a Hebrew prayer. My Hebrew was pretty rusty, but I knew he was talking about God and it didn't sound like good news. The Reb vigilantly watched the crowd as he chanted; he was a mightily intimidating presence, a broad-shouldered six-footer who looked like he could crack walnuts with his bare rabbinical mitts. He finished the prayer and then opened a black loose-leaf binder.

"My dear ones," he intoned, gazing down at the family like holy Moses himself. Strauss had a thick German accent, so I figured him for a refugee, but most definitely not of the submissive variety; this Reb was about as meek as Killer Kowalski. "We are told when we are growing up that there is time for every purpose unto heaven." The rabbi spoke very deliberately and with enormous measured weight, enunciating each word as if it were worth its weight in platinum. "Today, as we say good-bye to our beloved Fritz, perhaps some of you might question what that purpose was, might question what *purpose unto heaven* did it serve to take this good and talented individual from us and from his family in such a sudden and horrible fashion."

I stole a look at Sidney Aaron, who was surreptitiously unwrapping a Smith Brothers cough drop and slipping it into his mouth. His swarthy, blinking seatmate was staring down into his lap; I had the feeling that he was reading something, and I had the feeling that it wasn't the Holy Bible.

"I wish I had a satisfactory answer to all our doubts and all our questions," the rabbi continued. "I wish I could say that I understand why our dear Fritz, who managed, like so many of us, to escape Hitler and the Nazi terror, was unable to escape terror here in the adopted city and musical capital he had come to love so much." Strauss gripped the lectern with both hands and gazed around the room. "I know that our Fritz was . . ."—and here he took a dramatic pause—*"a curious man."*

Sidney Aaron just stared straight ahead. The redhead to his left was studying her left hand for a chipped nail, but the jockey-sized man shot Aaron a curious glance. The NBC veep didn't even acknowledge the look; he just gave the slightest, tick-tock shake of his head.

"A curious man always," Strauss continued. "Curious about music, curious about *world events,* curious about the many people and personalities and places he encountered here in the America he loved so much."

Was the rabbi speaking in code? Had Stern told him his theory of the missing Maestro?

"Perhaps it was his curiosity that got the best of our Fritz," the rabbi continued. "Perhaps he tried to help someone, someone in *danger,* that night he walked out of his home for the last time. Maybe it was this that brought about his terrible end." The rabbi cast a slow look around the room, as if challenging the assembled mourners to come up with a better theory.

"I do not know," he resumed in a lower voice. "He was always looking to aid his fellow man, this I know from the stories that his beloved Hilde and his dear Barbara and Linda have told me. He was always looking for a way to give. Maybe, as is often the case, we are looking to God for a quick and reasonable answer when there is no answer yet available. God is not an Answer Man, like on the radio. God is a scheme of nature, God is a spirit, God is a code of law and moral behavior. But God owes us nothing. We owe Him everything." He raised his voice again. "Does this mean that what happened to Fritz was senseless, that there was no *purpose unto heaven* in his passing? No. It just means that we do not know it yet, or we just don't *get it yet*. It just means that this purpose *has not yet been revealed to us*. But"—and here he looked again to the family—"I have no doubt that there is a divine plan, however mysterious and *aggravating* and heartbreaking it may seem at times, and I know that we did not lose our dear Fritz for no purpose unto heaven."

Rabbi Strauss seemed to study each kisser in the room with his unblinking blue eyes, and the temperature seemed to drop about fifty degrees. There was enough coughing and clearing of throats to shame a TB ward, and then the rabbi introduced no less a dignitary than Jan Peerce to sing two songs by Schubert, favorites of the deceased. Peerce was a stocky tenor who looked more like a guy who sold sports jackets at Wallach's than someone used to the opera spotlight. But he didn't sing like a salesman; he sang like a portly angel. But as beautiful and melancholy as the music was, I'm not sure anyone was listening. I certainly wasn't. I was thinking about a poor dead fiddler and the mess I knew I would get myself into before this was all over.

Outside the chapel, the rain had slowed to a faint drizzle, and the temperature was turning positively balmy. The sun was breaking through and the mourners looked slightly discomfited by the physical brightening of this appalling day. Just another reminder that God Held the Cards and that the hand one was dealt, however dismal, was never really surprising. Whatever happened in life was always somehow inevitable: cancer, twins, a flat tire, you name it. So the sun breaking through on this horrifying day seemed every bit as appropriate as the downpour had been before. I was smoking a Lucky and contemplating these cosmic issues when I felt a tap on my shoulder. When I turned around, I was in no way surprised to see Sidney Aaron standing before me.

"Jack . . . terrible tragedy. Terrible day. I looked at his poor wife, those girls. . . . What's the oldest's name?" he asked oh so casually.

"Barbara."

"Beautiful kid." Kid. You knew he had taken one look at Barbara Stern and had begun peeling off her clothes, layer by silken layer, visions of a DO NOT DISTURB sign dancing in his head. Just like your faithful correspondent, but at least I had the decency not to refer to her as a "kid."

"How are they all holding up?" he asked with heartfelt concern.

"Like you'd imagine," I said helpfully.

"Makes me sick to my stomach, the whole goddamn thing. . . ."

The redhead stood a couple of feet behind him. He turned gallantly to her.

"Sweetheart, this is Jack LeVine. A really sensational private investigator. Jack, this is Carol DeAngelis. She works for Texaco."

"Texaco, no kidding," I told her. "You ever work at the station on Northern Boulevard and Forty-sixth Street?"

Aaron pretended to laugh, but the redhead didn't bother. Carol DeAngelis appeared to be in her late thirties, with the exquisite facial bones and long legs of a model. My guess was that under the right circumstances she could be plenty of fun, but it would take a lot of work and a lot of money.

"I'm in cultural affairs," she told me with no irony.

"Which is where Sidney comes in, I guess."

"Texaco's spent millions on opera and symphony broadcasts over the years, Jack," Aaron told me. "They've been fantastic." He put his arm through mine, and turned to Miss DeAngelis.

"Sweetheart, I need a couple of seconds with Jack," he said, then led me toward the street, away from the mourners crowding the sidewalk.

"In answer to the question playing on your full firm lips," I told him, "I don't know a thing about his murder."

"You're sure it's murder?"

"I believe we just attended his funeral."

"You know what I mean. There's no chance it was some sort of bizarre accident?"

"I can't say no chance, but I wouldn't bet a nickel on it."

"You wouldn't."

"No." I flipped my spent Lucky toward the gutter. "Now I get to play: Why the hell would you bring a monkey like that to the funeral?"

"What are you talking about?" He looked back over his shoulder. Carol DeAngelis had flipped open her compact and was freshening her lipstick. "You can't be referring . . ."

"Not her, obviously; I mean the chimpanzee who was sitting beside you. Small, swarthy guy; built like a jockey."

Aaron's expression remained blank.

"The man on my immediate right? Him?"

"Him."

"I have no idea. I sat down and five minutes later he came in, looked around, and took the space next to me."

"You never met him before?"

"No. Why?" Aaron bit his lip, pretended to think about it. "He seemed a little out of place, didn't he?"

"I would say he'd be out of place in many of our finer establishments and institutions."

"Well, who the hell is he?" The NBC veep feigned agitation "You seem to act like you know."

"His name escapes me at present, but I believe it's Italian in origin and if I'm not mistaken, he worked for Lucky Luciano before Lucky got deported."

Aaron brushed his hand across his eyes, as if a bug had just flown into them. "You're joking," he then said. "Worked for Luciano?" He was playing this pretty well. Not Academy Award quality, but I'd seen a lot worse.

Carol DeAngelis tapped Aaron's arm.

"Sweetheart, I have to get back."

"We're going," Aaron reassured her, then turned back to me. "You like the fights, Jack?"

"The fights? Sure."

"Any interest in the one tonight?"

He was being oh so coy. "The one tonight" was nothing less than the aging Joe Louis defending his heavyweight title against Ezzard Charles up at Yankee Stadium. The odds had been moving against Louis; Charles was a smart if unimaginative heavyweight with quick hands and feet, and there was a growing feeling that the older man might not be able to keep up with him. The prospect of witnessing Louis's demise gave me heartache, but nothing on this earth made the blood race like a heavyweight title fight. The last one I had attended was in 1941; both Louis and I had been a great deal younger and I stood and hollered as he pounded fat Tony Galento's kisser into steak tartar.

"They're ringside," Aaron told me.

"I would expect nothing else, and I'd love to go. But why me?"

The NBC honcho just shrugged.

"Carol has an aversion to grown men bleeding in public, and I'm sick of going to sports events with these corporate stiffs. You strike me as the kind of guy who would enjoy the evening. Prelims start at eight, main fight at ten. You need a ride up to the stadium?" He was heading for the street, his arm out, flagging down a green Checker cab.

"No. I'll drive myself."

"Then meet me at the press gate at half past eight." He held the cab door open for Miss DeAngelis and waved cheerily, then got in. The Checker pulled out of sight. I turned around and observed a hearse slowly backing up on Amsterdam Avenue and then Fritz's coffin rolling out of the chapel like a very impractical and cumbersome piece of furniture. Four black-suited men guided the coffin over the irregular sidewalk, as if worrying about the bumps disturbing the fiddler's slumber. Then Linda Stern appeared, taking the smallest steps imaginable, her little face buried in her mother's coat, following the coffin and her own uncertain future, and then I just couldn't watch anymore.

One hour later, I found myself seated in the *Daily News* clipping morgue, sorting through a huge pile of photographs and yellowing articles dealing with that much-beloved dope dealer, smuggler, and all-around player known as Lucky Luciano. The *News*'s clipping morgue was a long and dingy room up on the twelfth floor of the *News* building on east 42nd Street; it had the sour smell of disintegrating newsprint, stale cigarette smoke, and hours of wasted time. I was there courtesy of my old comrade Toots Fellman, formerly the house dick at a Broadway fleabag called the Hotel Lava. When the Lava was mercifully torn down to make way for a parking lot, Toots decided, at age forty-five, to dye his hair brown and try his luck as a crime reporter. He had made countless friends and done numerous favors, most relevantly for a married editor at the *News* who had stashed a Copa girl at the Lava for a passionate year and a half, during which he had occasionally been spotted wearing the Copa girl's lingerie. When Toots decided to change careers, the editor in question—not surprisingly—hired him on the spot. Toots surprised everyone except me by becoming an ace reporter, befriending every cop in Midtown and having a gift for the terse written word. And he was a generous and lonely soul, always available when I needed assistance, which was most of the time. In this case, what I needed was the opportunity to do some free research.

Toots unearthed the *News* clipping file on Luciano and rolled it over to me on a kind of shopping cart. It was that extensive. Toots was about five-foot-eight and weighed close to two hundred pounds. But he carried it well, as they say, with the broad shoulders and muscled arms that had served him well in his years as a house dick. He was still dying his hair a kind of otter-brown, but his features were freckled and boyish, so the dye job wasn't that hard to take.

"Twenty folders' worth," he announced, dumping half the folders on a metal table before me. "Truman's file is probably bigger, but not by much. You want to tell me what you're looking for?"

"A short guy with dark hair and a blinking left eye. Looked mob, looked familiar, like from the Luciano era. Ring a bell?"

"No." Toots lit his pipe and headed for the door. "But let me think about it."

It took two and a half hours and a dozen folders, but I finally found what I was looking for. It was a photo taken in 1936 at Lucky's trial for pimping, which was a small-potatoes charge, but the feds had been so determined to jail him that pandering was good enough. After all, they had managed to put Al Capone in the slammer for tax evasion, which was like nailing Hitler for running a stop sign. In the photo I held in my sweaty paws, Lucky was walking into a Manhattan courtroom looking as modest and utterly middle-class as a Queens barber. Five steps behind him, younger but no better-looking, was the mug I had spotted at Stern's funeral. The caption did not identify him, except as one of many "friends and supporters of Mr. Luciano."

I put the clipping into a manila envelope and hotfooted it downstairs to Toots, who was seated in the bullpen of the city room, pounding a Remington typewriter with so much force I thought Pearl Harbor had gotten bombed again. He had his pipe in his mouth and his hat on his head and looked just like one of those motormouthed reporters from the movies.

I handed him the clipping. "You have any idea who this is? The guy five steps behind Lucky."

Toots gave it a glance. "Frank Sinatra."

"Sinatra's taller. Seriously."

"Seriously you want," Toots said. "Then seriously you'll get."

He put the clipping on his desk and stared at it. Smoke plumed up from his pipe and he contemplatively scratched his bare arms; Toots was the kind of guy who would wear a short-sleeved shirt in Antarctica.

"The suspense is killing me," I told him.

"Shh." He took his hat off and placed it on his desk, then studied at the photo for another three minutes—I counted—before turning to me and saying, "Giuseppe LaMarca, alias Joey Little, alias Joey Big, alias Joey Blinks."

"You're sure?"

He looked at me with something like pity.

"Sorry I asked," I said.

"What do you want to know about him?"

"Anything. I know zip."

"I know slightly more than zip, but not much. I know that after Lucky got deported, LaMarca got involved exclusively with the Brooklyn docks."

"He had an abiding interest in the sea?"

"He had an abiding interest in extortion, shylocking, and smuggling of all kinds. He worked for Anastasia, but the word was that he always stayed close to Lucky."

"Lot of drugs go into that port."

"I would say drugs would also be of great interest to him. He was never a boss, never wanted to be. He stayed a couple of levels below the captains, but just above the button men."

"A utility guy."

"Exactly. More of a go-between, a fixer. Lucky liked and trusted him, which accounts for his long-term survival." Toots picked up his hat and twirled it in his hand. "Now would you like to tell your Uncle Toots why you're interested in this scumbag? Off the record, of course."

"Because I just saw him at the funeral of a German refugee violinist who was a client of mine for about a day and a half, and I can't imagine what he was doing there."

"The guy shot on Tuesday night? Guy who played for Toscanini? He was your client?"

"Yes, yes, and yes. Not only was LaMarca at the funeral, he was seated next to an NBC vice president."

"Named?"

"Sidney Aaron. That do anything for you?"

Toots shook his head. "I've heard the name, that's about it. No matter what the connection, hard to figure LaMarca showing at the funeral."

"I'm totally mystified. Aaron said he just sat down next to him and he had no clue who he was."

"Which is horseshit."

"Which is probably horseshit. But he's taking me to the fight tonight, so I'm feeling a little charitable toward the guy."

"Aaron, not LaMarca."

"Correct."

"Big fight." Toots relit his pipe. "That's not a casual invitation, Jack."

"He did it casually—'my girl friend can't go . . .' "

Toots shook his head.

"No. He wants to talk."

"I agree."

"What was your client like?"

"German refugee. Quiet, shy. But troubled."

"About?"

"That I can't tell you yet."

"Something he got killed over."

"Probably. This one could go very deep."

"You always like the deep ones. Nothing light for you."

"True, but this one is special. And no fun at all. Poor bastard left two kids, one of them thirteen years old."

Toots sighed.

"Stinks." He looked away, then back at me. "Okay, back to work." He tore a sheet of paper out of his typewriter, inserted another. "Who do you like in the fight?"

"I have a really bad feeling about Louis," I told him. "I think my glorious youth ends tonight."

Toots shook his head. "Charles doesn't have enough meat on his bones. I say the old guy puts him away before the sixth. You'll buy me lunch tomorrow and tell me all about it." He turned back to his afternoon's work, resuming his rapid-fire typing. I took the elevator back upstairs and returned the file to the morgue, then took my leave of the *News* building and strolled across town on 42nd Street. It was four o'clock and the temperature had climbed to near seventy degrees; a beautiful early autumn afternoon, one that should have made me cherish all the pleasures and promises of daily life. All the sunlight and warmth in the world, however, couldn't make me stop thinking about that little girl with her face buried in her mother's coat, following her dead father and clouded future out onto Amsterdam Avenue.

SIX

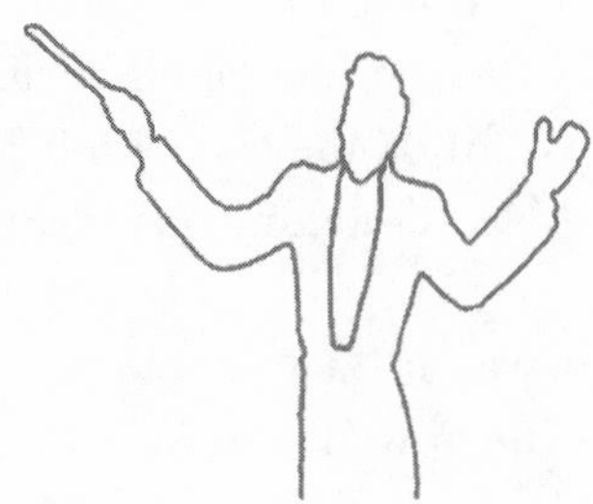

According to the newspapers the following day, the crowd at Yankee Stadium for the Louis-Charles fight was just over twenty-two thousand, but I thought it was smaller than that, and God knows how many tickets had been given away by the promoters. While the ringside was packed and the bleachers had partially filled up with the plebeians, the upper deck was nearly empty and the mezzanine only about half filled. It was depressing and somehow ominous to behold all those ghostly seats in the big ballpark.

"It's being carried live on CBS, that's the problem," Aaron shouted over to me during a prelim between two clumsy heavyweights—Elkin Brothers, which sounded like a moving company, and Dutch Culbertson, which sounded like Dutch Culbertson. Both pugilists were pretty awful, but Brothers was stronger and the Dutchman was en route to a quick demise. "We've created a monster with television. I hope it doesn't kill live sports." Aaron was wearing a brown houndstooth jacket, dark wool slacks, a white monogrammed shirt, and a silk necktie from Sulka featuring pheasants in flight that alone cost more than my suit. But he sipped his Ballantine ale from a bottle, just like a regular working stiff.

"I don't think television's the whole story," I replied. "I think a lot of people stayed away out of fear. The possibility of Louis falling on his ass is just too goddamn depressing. Like Bing Crosby singing flat or Fred Astaire stumbling over his shoelaces. Each one is another milepost on the way to the cemetery."

"Cheery thought, Jack."

"I have my dark side."

Aaron took another slug of beer.

"Well, the hell with it," he said. "Too bad for everybody who didn't show. It's a gorgeous evening for a fight."

It was in fact gorgeous, a perfect autumn night to be seated three scant rows from the brilliantly lit ring, watching various luminaries file in as the time for the main event approached. Governor Dewey waltzed by, shaking every hairy hand in sight, followed by Acting Mayor Impelliteri, Judge Pecora, and a gaggle of city councilmen, commissioners, and other assorted parasites. A heavyweight title fight was a force field of power, and it drew politicians as irresistibly as Mecca draws Muslims.

"So you really don't know Joey Blinks?" I said without warning to Aaron, half a hot dog stuffed in my mouth.

My calculated remark didn't get the anticipated result. The NBC exec appeared to draw an actual blank.

"Who?"

"Your seatmate at the funeral. Giuseppe LaMarca. He runs with two other aliases, Joey Little and Joey Big. Take your pick."

"He introduced himself as Joe Lane."

"That makes four aliases. Do I hear five?"

"What's his real name again?" If Aaron was faking, he was doing an absolutely first-rate job of it.

"Giuseppe—" I began, but then a sound began to arise from above and behind me, a mounting, agitated roar, and I knew without even turning my head that the gladiators had appeared. Aaron and I stood up and gawked like everyone else as Louis and Charles emerged from the stadium dugouts, Charles dancing nervously and Louis as stolid as ever, walking slowly and tapping his gloves together as tentatively as if he had never worn them before. As I watched the two men approach the ring, my heart began to sink into my Florsheims. The champ looked closer to forty than thirty-five: there were bags beneath his eyes, his face looked sallow and puffy, his dark hair was thinning into lonely patches. What he retained, however, was that implacable, impenetrable stare, devoid of anger or fear. Charles, on the other hand, appeared skittish and eager, fairly racing toward the ring. He was jet-black handsome, with bright eyes and marcelled hair, and looked like a flush busboy out for a night on the town.

Sidney Aaron groaned, *"Oy vay,"* as Louis climbed gingerly into the ring. "He isn't getting any younger, is he, Jack?"

"If I was Catholic, I'd say a Hail Mary for him. What do Jews say, a Hail Murray?"

"He'll be okay if he can get rid of this guy fast."

He didn't.

In the first round, Charles sped out of his corner like an Olympic sprinter and immediately began belting Joe with a series of disrespectful lefts and rights to the body, including a solid and inadvertent hook to Joe's nuts that made me clench my teeth and cross my legs. Joe tried to stalk him in that familiar, deliberate style, but his jab kept missing; his thought processes were unchanged, but not his reflexes. In the second round, Joe managed to knock Charles back on his heels with a straight left and the crowd stood as one and started screaming for blood, but the blood never came. Charles danced around the ring until his head cleared, and then started banging the old man's ribs again.

And so the fight unfolded, round by round; it wasn't a massacre, but it wasn't close. Charles was outweighed by thirty pounds, but his speed more than compensated for his lack of bulk; he insouciantly flicked his jab into Joe's kisser, and moved the older man around the ring like a housepainter walking a ladder across a room. When Louis made the younger man's knees buckle in the tenth with a short left to the jaw, Charles gathered himself smartly and foxtrotted out of danger. When the bell rang ending the round, Aaron and I just looked at each other.

"It's over," I said. "That was his best shot."

Aaron nodded. "Makes me want to cry. We all used to be so young, Jack. The world lay before us like presents under a Christmas tree."

"We didn't have a Christmas tree in our house."

"You know what I mean."

I did know; we were witnessing the end of the era that had ignited all of our youthful dreams.

In the fourteenth round, Charles simply kicked Joe's ass around the block; by the fifteenth, both fighters were pretty well spent and when the final bell sounded Joe looked like a man who had just lost his wallet. The decision was unanimous and one-sided. The ref, Mark Conn, had it ten-five Charles, but he was just being polite. The judges really stuck it to the champ—thirteen-two and twelve-three. The two men shook hands politely and left the ring. People applauded Joe, but he kept his head down all the way back to the dugout. Then the lights came up in the big ballpark and we all filed out.

The silence was deafening.

I felt like I had attended my second funeral of the day.

Throughout the evening, Aaron had maintained his peculiar reticence about the events that had brought us together—we were just two guys at a fight—so I was not surprised that when I offered him a ride back to Manhattan he readily accepted. I knew this had not been a casual invitation; Aaron knew hundreds of other people he could have brought to this fight and at least half of them had better legs than I did. At some point I knew he was finally going to get to the point: He would try to buy me off or, failing that, threaten me.

I was ready, and, as usual, I was dead wrong.

No sooner had I pulled the mighty Roadmaster onto Jerome Avenue than Sidney Aaron, vice president for special programming at NBC, put his head against the passenger-side window and began to cry. And these were not wistful tears; these were great, heaving, gulping sobs.

"It's so te . . ." he began, and then he dissolved, his shoulders shaking, his breath ragged. I hadn't seen a grown man bawl so openly since my Uncle Irving had watched his button store go up in flames on Rivington Street, and even he hadn't carried on like this. It was all I could do to keep my eyes on the road.

"You okay, Sidney? Want to pull over somewhere, maybe get a drink?"

He just shook his head, then blew his nose with considerable force into a monogrammed, snow-white handkerchief.

"I'm so sorry," he finally managed to say.

"Hey," was the best I could do.

"It's just . . ." Some more tears rolled down his cologne-scented cheeks.

"Just . . . ?"

"Just so difficult."

A fire engine raced past, its sirens and horns at full cry, followed by an equally noisy hook and ladder, so I had an excuse to pull the car over and stop.

Aaron dabbed at his cheeks and took deep noisy breaths. "I feel like such an idiot."

"Hey, even Lou Gehrig cried. Want a smoke?"

"No."

I fired up a Lucky and rolled down my window. "You are going to tell me why you were crying, right?"

Aaron honked his sizable nose one more time, then stuffed his handkerchief back into his pocket.

"You can't believe the pressure," he said. "I haven't slept in three weeks."

"Okay, let me take a wild guess—Toscanini really got snatched, didn't he? And you're the monkey in the middle."

Aaron stared at me for a few pregnant moments.

"You must swear—"

"I won't tell a soul. That's part of the package. I told Fritz that and technically I'm still working for him. His daughter wants me to stay on the case."

"I see. Would it be a conflict to work for me?"

"Probably."

"Why?"

"Because her interest is in finding out who killed her father. I don't know what your interest is yet. Was he snatched? Let's start there. A simple yes or no will suffice."

"Yes," Sidney Aaron said. "He was snatched."

"Okay. Question two: Where was he snatched?"

"Sun Valley."

"Sun Valley, Idaho?"

"On May twelfth. Here. Look at this and then we'll talk."

Aaron handed me a newspaper clipping. As the Woodlawn elevated train rattled above me, throwing sparks down onto the street, I studied the clipping. It was an Associated Press wire photo of Toscanini riding a chairlift, waving happily, jaunty in a beret.

"I remember this shot," I told him.

"It was picked up everywhere." Aaron dried the remaining tears from the corners of his eyes.

"And this was taken in Sun Valley?"

"Yes."

"And it's him? In this picture, it's him?"

"I'm not completely sure. It was him going up the chairlift, but evidently it wasn't him coming down. It was a double."

"He got snatched at the top of the lift?"

"Yes."

"He was alone? How could this have happened without anybody noticing?"

"There were orchestra members all over the place, but nobody saw a thing. The lift apparently goes into this little shedlike structure, where it turns around and then comes out the other side. That's where it must have happened."

"In a flash."

"In a flash. He's a very strong man, but, Christ, he's eighty-three and quite diminutive, actually. No more than five-foot-three."

"Makes no difference how strong or how short. This is a world-class professional snatch, a top-shelf operation all the way. This double they got, there's gotta be significant plastic surgery involved; this is something that gets planned for at least a year, maybe two." I checked the picture again. "How do you know for sure that Sun Valley is where it happened? You guys played over a dozen cities."

Aaron took the clipping back.

"That's our information."

I pulled the car back into traffic and turned on the radio. Kay Starr was singing about lost love. I pretended to listen and drove in silence for five blocks before Aaron spoke up.

"What's the matter?" he asked.

"You're jerking me around."

"What are you talking about? I just told you—"

"You just told me something I suspected, something you figured I already knew. So you didn't tell me anything, maybe you bullshitted me entirely."

"Jack . . ."

I killed the radio and turned up my own volume.

"Here's what you can't do. You can't tell me you know it happened in Sun Valley and then say 'That's our information' when I ask you how come you're sure. Doesn't work that way. You want to do business with me, you have to give me straight answers, because if you don't, I'm going to wind up like Fritz Stern and I promised my mother I'd never let anybody shoot me dead. So if you tell me 'That's our information,' I assume you've been in touch with the kidnappers, maybe there's ransom involved. And why, then, I ask myself, do you need me except to play me for some kind of sucker, which I have no intention of being played for? Now, I'm not sure that's actually an English sentence, but I think you get my point."

Aaron sighed.

"Yes I do. This is unbelievably complicated."

"Spare me the horseshit."

"You have no idea. . . ."

"I can't believe NBC doesn't have their own security. This guy was snatched over three months ago. What the hell's been going on all that time? And then you say you need me? For what? There's no logic to it except Stern got to me first and now you're trying to keep me in the room by feeding me these little cocktail weiners of information, one at a time."

"I can understand your paranoia. . . ."

"Mrs. LeVine, who is actually Mrs. Levine, didn't raise any paranoids. I'm just a run-of-the-mill scared Jew."

"Well, so am I, in case you didn't guess." Aaron allowed himself a smile. "Jack, obviously NBC has its own security, but the problem goes much deeper than that, and it's why I need to go outside the company."

"What's the problem?"

Aaron looked into my eyes with as much soulfulness as he could muster. I felt like I was on a date that was about to get really dramatic.

"The problem is, Jack, and this is why it's all gone on so long . . ." He paused and sighed. "The problem is, I'm not sure NBC wants the Maestro back."

I started to move my lips, but for once I was speechless.

"Holy shit."

"Yes," Aaron said. "Holy shit."

I drove over the 155th Street Bridge and then down the Harlem River Drive, the radio off, my brains starting to overheat.

"When you say you're 'not sure . . .' " I began.

"Running the NBC Symphony costs a bloody fortune," Aaron began. "Our chairman, General Sarnoff, while a visionary, is also a deeply conservative man, concerned, naturally, with profit and loss. The whole business is in flux, Jack; it looks like television could really be the end of radio. Nobody's sure yet, but it seems like a strong possibility. At the very least, radio is going to be greatly diminished. The audience will never, ever be the same. We expect dramatic decreases in its size over the next five years."

"And what's watching an orchestra on television compared to watching a wrestling match?"

"Exactly. Or even compared to watching a good drama. So do we continue spending millions on something that's geared for radio? It's a real issue. When the orchestra was put together in 1937 it was a tool to sell radios and phonograph records and record players. But things are changing. Even before this happened there were discussions about the efficacy of keeping the orchestra in a television age. People aren't going to run home at night to watch a hundred middle-aged men playing fiddles. That's just reality; we've done studies. Television is the future, period. We have to deal with the changes it's going to bring."

"Is there ransom involved?"

Aaron reflexively straightened his tie. "Yes."

"How much?"

"Three million bucks."

"Yikes. And General Sarnoff doesn't want to pay?"

"I've gotten mixed signals."

"What does that mean?"

"Exactly that. I'm not sure. The ransom was at five million this summer. It's down to three."

"Sarnoff thinks he can just work them down to nothing?"

"I don't know what he thinks. He's devoted to the Maestro, there's no question about that, but he's been getting more and more heat from stockholders and some of our big advertisers about the cost of this orchestra. NBC isn't just Sarnoff's candy store. Before he writes a ransom check for that kind of money, there's people he has to deal with."

"Don't you guys carry insurance on the old man?"

"Sure, but then what happens? The insurance company gets its investigators involved, and if you think our guys are knuckleheads . . . Maestro would be dead in twenty-four hours."

"I agree. Too risky."

"And then there's the factor of precedent," Aaron continued. "What does it say to the world if we submit to this kind of blackmail? Do people get ideas? What happens if Jack Benny or Bob Hope gets snatched? We just open the treasury? You see where this could lead, Jack."

"But NBC knows that these people will kill the old guy eventually. You can't dick around forever."

"We all know that, Jack." And then Aaron shrugged, indicating that it was out of his hands.

"Holy Christ," I said. "You mean there's people who wouldn't mind? You guys really play some hardball. . . ."

"It's not as simple or as crude as that. Like I said, there is serious concern about the issue of setting a precedent."

"I understand that, Sidney. But correct me if I'm wrong—I'm hearing that there's people at NBC who feel if Toscanini gets croaked, what the hell, he's eighty-three and he's costing the company a fortune anyhow—"

"Drop me here," Aaron said suddenly. We were on Park Avenue in the eighties.

"Which is your building?"

"Down two blocks between Park and Madison. But it's probably better if I get out here."

"They're watching your apartment?"

"I think so."

I stopped the car. Aaron looked out at Park Avenue. Two couples paraded past in formal clothes, the men looking more than a little drunk, puffing cigars and laughing much too loud.

Aaron turned and faced me. "Can you be in my office tomorrow at noon?"

"Sure. You don't mind if I'm seen there?"

"It's widely known that Fritz hired you. That's no problem." Aaron got out of the car. "One other thing," he said before slamming the door shut. "You have a valid passport?"

"Yeah. Why?

"I think you're going to need it."

SEVEN

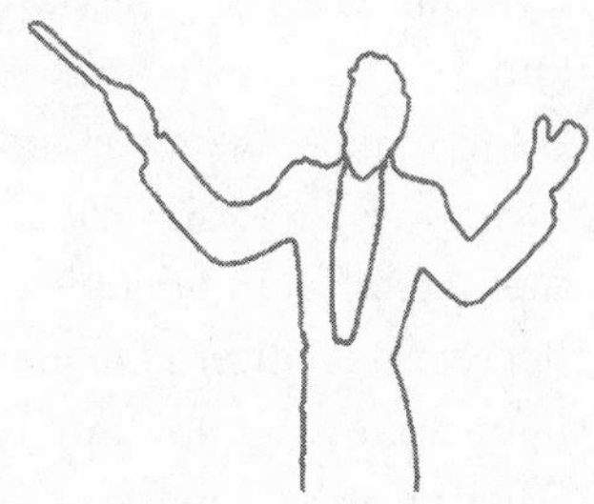

When I got into the elevator at 1630 Broadway on Friday morning, José, the new elevator jockey, gave me a big wink. José was a forty-year-old hunchback who sported a thin mustache and wore cowboy boots under his gray elevator togs. I thought he added real style to the building.

"Nice," he said, and winked again for emphasis. Subtlety was not his strong suit.

"Nice? What's nice?" I was holding a cardboard container of coffee that wasn't any hotter than molten steel.

"You'll see." He stopped the elevator at nine. "Have a good day, Señor Detective." He laughed and opened the door.

José was still chuckling when I stepped out of the elevator and saw Barbara Stern leaning against the wall outside my office. She was wearing a black beret, a dark skirt, and a black cotton sweater—casual mourning attire.

"Good morning." She waved as I ambled down the hall, my hand beginning to melt like an object in a Dali painting.

"Good morning." I placed the coffee container on the floor and fumbled for my keys. "You want some coffee? I'll put on my asbestos mittens and go get another cup."

"No thanks."

I opened up the office and turned on a couple of lights. She followed me in without being asked, which I liked very much. I'm a person who thrives on female companionship and the past year had been spent entirely too much without it. Various old flames, like Kitty Seymour, had gotten married and weren't available even for social dinners; a fiery romance with a funny and hot-blooded English professor named Susan Handelman went kaput after three exhausting months because she couldn't believe she was actually banging a private detective and decided to return to her husband, a humorless but successful pediatrician named Ronnie. She continued to call from time to time, complaining about Ronnie's long hours, and the sound of her voice still made me adjust my slacks, but if I have learned one thing in my chosen profession, it is this: Sleeping with married women is not, in the long run, a worthwhile endeavor. But I sure as hell missed the short run.

So despite my awareness of her tender years and recent tragedy, it gave me a warm and cuddly feeling to watch Barbara Stern unhesitatingly enter my renovated headquarters. She looked around and sniffed the still-pungent aroma of Little Dutch Boy.

"It's spiffier than I thought it would be," she said. "I was expecting more of a Sam Spade kind of deal. Fresh paint?"

"I redecorated a bit this past summer. The end of a crisis of confidence."

I unlocked the inner office and she followed me in.

"Crisis of confidence? Like a breakdown?" Scary, when someone twenty-one years of age can look inside you with the speed and accuracy of an X-ray machine.

"I would refer to it as a breakdownette." I pulled the window open and sat down behind my desk.

"Occasioned by middle age?" She made herself comfortable in the red leather chair that faces my desk. "Am I being incredibly nosy? Just tell me. I have that tendency."

"Doesn't bother me. Nosy is what I do for a living." I carefully opened the coffee lid and a volcanic cloud of steam billowed out. "Yes, my breakdownette was occasioned, in a general sense, by middle age, divorce, a general uncertainty as to the meaning and purpose of my life. The immediate trigger, you may be interested to know, was the death of my father."

"Really." She crossed her legs as I blew into my coffee.

"Yeah."

"Of natural causes, I take it."

"Listening to Jack Benny, which is about as natural as it gets in the twentieth century. His heart just stopped. There was a glass of seltzer next to him, the radio was on, and his head was back in his favorite chair. A Jewish still life."

She nodded. "Very well put. And you loved him?"

"How much time do you have?"

"I understand," she said. "It's always complicated."

"I did love him. He was a brusque little guy, but his heart was in the right place. Started working when he was like thirteen, spent his life in the hat trade, made a buck or two, enough to rise to the very bottom of the middle class. Not an amazing story, you won't find a biography of him in your school library, but good enough. He didn't have a lot of free time. He worked, he retired, he died. It's very simple, then again nothing's so simple. There's misunderstandings, things you never said that you should have, things you did say that you didn't mean. But, add it all up, and I loved him, yes. That's the short version."

"He was your pop, what the hell, it hurts. Hurts a lot." Her eyes got misty, then she sighed and sat up, straightening her sweater across her lovely chest. This was a girl I could easily get tired of after forty or fifty years.

"But that's old news. How are you doing?" I asked.

She looked at me for a long beat, as if wondering whether she trusted me enough to really talk; then I saw something switch off in her.

"I'm doing," she finally said, and reached into her purse. "I found this on my father's desk last night and I thought, you know, that you should take a look at it."

She slid a slip of paper across the desk. When I picked it up, it appeared blank; a closer examination revealed the tracing of an address scrawled across it.

"I couldn't quite make it out, but it looks like, what, eleventh . . ." She leaned across the desk toward me and our faces were mere inches apart. I could feel the heat radiating off her.

"Yeah," I mumbled. Stern had written down an address, then torn off the top sheet. It looked like, "11th Ave., 46."

"Eleventh Avenue and 46th Street?" I said. "That ring a bell?"

"No," she said. "That's near the piers."

"Yeah. Your father was found a block away."

"His body, you mean." She took the slip of paper and sat back in her chair. I missed her already.

"Yes."

"You don't have to be delicate with me."

"I'm delicate with everyone," I told her. "So he gets a call, your mother says from a colleague, goes to the piers at nine-thirty at night."

"Peculiar behavior for anyone, isn't it? But especially for my father; he was about as impulsive as a clock."

"Which of his colleagues was he really close to? Who would call him and tell him to go down to the piers that he would listen to?"

"He didn't really have any close friends in the orchestra."

"He didn't? He told me he'd been with the symphony since 1940."

"You have to understand that my father, like most refugees, basically had no real buddies in the American sense. No 'pals.' His social life was built around his family. Whoever called him up was obviously one of the musicians in on this Toscanini thing."

"But you don't know who that might be."

"I could guess, maybe. He hung out with a bassoonist named Frank Rosenberg, a violist named Georg Lukas, another refugee, a Hungarian, but I really have no idea if they were among those who thought Toscanini was missing."

"Okay. You also might consider this—the fact that he told your mother it was a colleague on the phone doesn't necessarily mean that it was."

Barbara Stern thought that one over.

"My father was compulsively honest."

"Yeah, but I'm sure he wanted to protect your mother and maybe protect himself: She was certainly less than enthusiastic about his hiring me, or getting involved at all in this mess."

She raised her eyebrows. "And as it turned out . . ."

"She was right."

Barbara got up from her chair, jumpy, suddenly not totally comfortable in her own wondrous skin.

"So what have we found out?" She walked in back of me and stared across the air shaft; the clerks at Fidelity Insurance were sipping their morning coffees and beginning their actuarial tasks.

"We?"

"You. Come on, you know what I mean."

She sat down at the edge of my desk, thought better of it, went back to the window.

"Well, I know next to nothing about your father's death, but a little more than that about the Toscanini business."

"What do you know?"

I lit up a Lucky.

"Jesus, this is just like the movies, isn't it?" she said. "The cigarette, the whole goddamn bit."

"I'm a walking cliché," I told her happily. "And proud of it. Okay." I blew out the match, took a dramatic pause. "He's missing."

"Toscanini."

"He was snatched in Sun Valley. Your father had it right on the button."

"Jesus Christ." She sat back down in the chair and pointed to my pack of Luckies. I extracted one and lit it up for her. Who walked off with him?" she asked. "Any idea?"

"No, not yet, but this is where it gets really dicey." I handed her the lit cigarette. "Between us, and when I say, 'between us,' Barbara—"

"You're still working for my family, correct?"

"Yes I am, but what I'm going to tell you now can't go anywhere, including your mother's ears, and if it does, I'm going to quit the case immediately. Is that understood?"

Barbara looked at me with something resembling pity. "Yes. It's understood."

"I'm serious."

"Okay."

"Fine. Here's the curveball: I'm not sure that NBC really wants Toscanini back. They may let him get knocked off, save the ransom, and reap some sort of public relations wave of pity."

She stared at me without moving a muscle. "What are you talking about?"

"The orchestra costs the company a fortune every year and apparently there are some in the top brass who think television is going to totally kill public interest in longhair music."

"You must be joking."

"That's what I'm told. You can believe it or not."

"They would let Toscanini get killed?"

"There are evidently some powerful individuals who don't want to pay the ransom."

"Which is?"

"Three million. They may also believe they can call the kidnappers' bluff. Toscanini's been missing for three months and, as far as we know, he's still alive. Maybe they're on to something; the old man's no good to the kidnappers dead."

"No, but if he does get killed and anyone gets wind that NBC did anything but move heaven and earth to save him . . ."

"It would be a catastrophe. I understand. That's why they're trying to handle this as carefully as possible, which is where my bald head figures in. I'm as low-profile as they come."

"Where did you get all your information?"

"I believe it's reliable."

She took a long draw on her Lucky. "You're not going to tell me."

"There's no reason to tell you."

She bounced out of her chair again.

"Mr. LeVine, I don't know if you think I'm just some innocent coed, but let me assure you that I'm not. I've seen a lot already in my life, too much." She paced across the room. "I left Germany with my parents when I was ten years old and I'd already had my fill of Nazis parading outside our house and my little schoolmates throwing stones at me during recess—"

"Listen, I understand."

"You can't understand."

"Of course I can understand! I don't want to hear that crap that because I wasn't running around Dusseldorf or whatever—"

"Essen."

"Fine, Essen. Because I wasn't running around Essen wearing a yellow star, I can't understand what went on. I do. The reason I'm not telling you who told me is I don't see the point of endangering you. Knowledge is, as you know—"

"A dangerous thing," she fairly moaned. "Please."

"It's the truth. It won't help you to know who told me these things and might, in fact, hurt you at some point. This is what I do for a living. Trust me. Plus, it's just raw information at this point, and totally uncorroborated. Now let me ask you something—two things, in fact."

"Shoot." And now she did sit on the edge of the desk. "Do I look like Lauren Bacall?" she asked with a smile.

"Better," I told her in all honesty. "First question: What's the story with . . . is it your uncle? At the funeral he seemed . . ."

"That's my mother's brother Otto."

"Last name?"

"Feuerberg. He was a lawyer, very brilliant. One night he's on the East River Drive, going way too fast, loses control of his beautiful black Chrysler, and smashes into the wall of an underpass. You know the one, beneath Gracie Mansion?"

"Very well. That's a nasty curve."

"Nasty curve and Otto always drove in a fairly reckless manner and this particular night he might have had a couple of cocktails, which was pretty unusual for him. He was in a coma for two weeks; when he came out of it he had, as they say, 'reduced brain function.' That was 1947, and they've had a nurse living in ever since, he and my Aunt Gretl."

"Live-in nurse? That's pretty expensive."

"It certainly is. What's the other question? You said you had two."

"Question number two is—and just think about it for a second before you start ranting and raving . . ."

"What?"

"Does anybody in your family or in the circle of your father's acquaintances have any connection to the mob, or familiarity with people involved in organized crime? That may seem like a nutso question, I know. . . ."

Barbara Stern slid off the desk very slowly, keeping a hand on it to retain her balance. She looked a little green.

"You okay?" I asked her.

"Yes. Fine." She sat back down in the chair. "Little too much stress right now." She stubbed the cigarette out. "And smoking's no help, that's for sure. Gives me this buzz sometimes. So, gangsters in our family, is that the question?" She tried to smile, but it was a near-miss. "Let me think."

"I don't necessarily mean in your immediate family, you understand. I mean people who might have run into situations—"

"Relatives who might have had ties, because of business or whatnot. I understand."

The dead man's daughter gazed at the wall behind me, put a graceful hand to her chin. I didn't want to be thinking what I was thinking, but I was thinking it all the same—she was stalling.

"I mean, I can't account for everybody," she said. "Obviously I'm just limited to what I'm told, but I don't think anybody was ever involved with anyone, you know, nefarious or anything. Certainly not that I can remember, but I'm trying to think, you know, of all our family and even acquaintances, what they did for a living . . ." She was talking way too much. I tried to chalk it up to shock.

"So the answer is no?"

"As they say, to the best of my knowledge. Now let me ask you: Why in the world would you even think that? I mean, my family? They're all scared of their shadows." Some color was returning to her face.

"Because a man named Giuseppe LaMarca attended your father's funeral and I can't figure why."

Barbara shook her head. "LaMarca? That name I've never heard. Who is he, like a mobster?"

"Used to work for, maybe still works for, Lucky Luciano, which makes him a mobster in my book."

"Indeed it does. Giuseppe LaMarca . . ."

"Alias Joey Big, alias Joey Little, Alias Joey Blinks, alias Joe Lane. A regular basketball team all in one, except he's about five-foot-two."

She didn't bat an eye. "Doesn't ring a bell, by any of those names." She stood up. "I really should go; I promised my mother I'd be home by lunch."

"Sure." I arose with her. "Anything else you want to tell me, Barbara? Anything at all?"

For an instant, something like a wild, uncontrollable fear flew into those big brown eyes, but then flew right out again, like a barn swallow.

"No, Jack. Not right now." Then she turned and left the office.

She called me "Jack."

I noticed them the instant I left my building. They were standing a half a block down Broadway, feigning interest in the menu displayed outside Jack Dempsey's Restaurant. One was looking over the other's shoulder, which wasn't all that easy because the guy closer to the menu stood about six-foot-five. No big surprise—they were the same pair of bookends who had chased Stern and me from the missing Maestro's villa up in Riverdale.

I started walking in their direction, which momentarily threw them for a loss; they backed up, at which point I turned and began hotfooting it south down Broadway. They started right after me. I glanced over my shoulder; they were double-timing it down the sidewalk. This was no tail; they were after me. I started running; they started running.

They were faster.

I reached 50th Street and already my heart was pounding. Frick and Frack were about thirty yards behind me and gaining, pushing civilians freely out of their way. When the light turned against me on Broadway, I crossed, the traffic bearing down on me. I dodged a cab.

"Hey, fuckface!" the cabby screamed at me. I looked around; the two apes were stepping off the curb onto Broadway. One held up his beefy paw, bringing a *Daily Mirror* truck to a rubber-burning halt. I stood in the middle of the street. A bus was about fifteen yards from me and accelerating. The bus driver honked; I faked indecision, headed back toward the two mugs, who came racing toward me. I stood my ground, then backed up in the center of the street, into the path of the speeding bus. The bus driver honked frantically. I turned, saw the bus ten feet away, and put on a burst of speed, racing toward the east side of Broadway. The two apes came right after me, their vision blocked by a double-parked parcel van, and stepped directly into the path of the oncoming bus. After that, the laws of physics were in play.

I had reached the sidewalk when I heard the awful thud. I turned around to see the larger of my two pursuers flying through the air like a punted football before landing on the roof of a Silvercup bread truck. He wasn't bleeding much more than a slaughtered cow. The smaller of the two was attempting to crawl back to the sidewalk when he got hit once again, this time by a blue Packard. People were racing toward the scene of the accident; the bus had stopped and the driver was getting out, his hat in his large Irish hand. I felt badly for the poor slob, but I wasn't about to hang around; I straightened my tie and made my way to Sidney Aaron's office.

"Jesus Christ," said Aaron.

"Yeah." I was seated on the couch in his office. Miss Elizabeth Hamilton had led me in with the hushed respect usually accorded a British viceroy in India; when I informed her that I had just witnessed a tragic pedestrian accident, she scurried off to fetch me a cup of herbal tea that smelled better than the Brooklyn Botanical Garden.

"Very good for the nerves," she told me, and then retreated back into the outer sanctum.

Aaron watched the door close. "You think they're both dead?" he asked.

"The ape who landed on the Silvercup truck, if he wasn't dead when I left, will be within ten minutes. The way he was bleeding—"

Aaron held up a hand.

"Please . . . I have a weak stomach."

"No you don't, but I'll spare the details because that's the kind of guy I am. Now, the other thug, I don't know. That was like a two-cushion shot—the bus, then a Packard with tired brakes. If he's alive, I'd say his gun-slinging days are certainly over. He must've broken half the bones in his body."

"And you're sure they were after you."

"No. They could have been training for some Olympic event—a human steeplechase through live traffic."

Aaron sat back in his chair. "Jesus Christ," he said again.

"Yeah. Ditto."

"And you say these same two characters had pursued you up at Villa Pauline?"

"Correct. But I don't believe they're going to represent much of a problem in the future, like I said, due to the fact that they're both either dead or disabled."

Aaron got up and went over to his desk. "If I was a drinker, I'd start drinking now," he said.

"Don't let me stop you."

"Just joking." Aaron looked as a grim as a funeral director—grimmer, actually; funeral directors are by and large a cheerful bunch. He opened the top drawer of his desk and extracted a sheet of paper, then walked back to me holding the sheet between his thumb and forefinger as if it were radioactive.

"The most recent demand," he told me. "As of yesterday." I took the sheet of paper from his two fingers and held it about a foot and a half away from my eyes. Sooner or later, I would have to invest in either a well-trained baboon or a pair of reading glasses.

The document, once it swam into focus, was a typed letter on the stationery of the Hotel Nacional in Havana, Cuba. The letterhead art depicted a large double-winged hotel surrounded by tropical flora and high-rollers of all ages. A sunny gamblers' paradise. The terse note read:

"We expect THREE MILLION cash by next Friday or you will receive TOSCANINI'S right hand by registered parcel."

That was it.

"Nice touch, the hand."

Aaron remained standing. "Can you imagine?"

"Yes I can."

"Me, too. Makes me dizzy, just the thought." Aaron walked back to his desk. "Have you ever been to Havana, Jack?"

"No. Miami's as far south as I've traveled. I did once date a Cuban dancer. . . ."

"Havana's quite fabulous, quite decadent." He opened another desk drawer.

"You're not about to pull out an air ticket, are you?"

Aaron smiled thinly. "There's a nonstop flight out of Idlewild at nine-thirty tomorrow morning that'll get you into Havana at a quarter to three in the afternoon."

"That's just great. Then what am I supposed to do, rent a couple of bloodhounds and a magnifying glass? Or do I go to plan B and assemble a mercenary army?"

Aaron shrugged. "You're the detective."

I jumped out of my chair, more than a little irritated. "Listen, I just got chased across Broadway by two gorillas intent on extreme physical harm. Now you want me to storm into Havana like I'm Teddy Roosevelt, six-guns blazing, and carry the old man out on my back? Blow it out your ass. That's point A. Point B, I'm still working for the Stern family and not for NBC."

"I spoke to the widow this morning."

"To Hilde?"

"I asked her if we might share in the expense of Mr. LeVine."

"And she said yes, of course."

"She said she and her daughter were very fond of you." Aaron scratched his cheek. "Particularly the daughter."

"Stop it."

"She's unbelievable, Jack. I haven't seen a body like that—"

"Enough. So Hilde's willing to let me do this?"

"She was very supportive of the idea."

"Does the daughter know?"

"I have no idea. Now, I'm not sure what Fritz was paying you, but we'll give you two thousand dollars just to go to Havana, and ten thousand more if you bring Maestro back alive."

"Who's 'we'? I thought the top brass didn't want the old man returned."

"I have a budget to play with. There's funds in there for what we call development," Aaron explained. "Okay?"

"So you're out on your own on this?"

"I want him back. Period." I was starting to think this guy was maybe a little nuts, but I also was starting to like him. "Now, I don't expect you to go in there like the Rough Riders."

"But you expect me to bring him back?"

"I didn't say that. But obviously that would be the optimum result."

"What's the minimum result?"

"I want to know who's behind this."

"You really have no clue?"

"None."

"And all the NBC gumshoes . . . ?"

"They're idiots. Security here is mostly ex-army. They strategize and bullshit, but mostly what they do is cover their own asses, in the time-honored tradition of the military. That's why I feel it's time to go outside the company." Aaron pulled the air ticket from his drawer.

I got up and walked over to his desk. He held the ticket toward me.

"I want twelve thousand if I bring him back alive," I told him. "Not ten."

Aaron didn't blink. "Done."

"What would you have said if I asked for fifteen?"

Aaron smiled. "Given it to you."

"That's what I thought." I took the air ticket from his hand. "I used to be considered very bright."

"You still are. Have a good trip."

"Guess I'll stay at the Hotel Nacional."

Aaron's phone started ringing. "You're already booked," he said. "Ocean view." He picked up the phone and I left the office.

With a knot in my belly.

José had another greeting for me when I returned to 1630 Broadway.

"Two cops," he told me, and slammed the elevator door shut.

"Sure they're cops?"

"Definitely. They got that stupid look. Too much hair."

"Never a good sign."

"No." José touched his own disappearing coiffure. "Us baldies, we stick together, right, Señor Detective?" He opened the doors to the ninth floor. "Don't take no shit from them."

No surprise—it was O'Malley and Breen, holding up the wall across from my office.

"Now my day is perfect," I greeted them.

They grunted in reply and watched me unlock my front door as intently as if I were performing a magic trick, then followed me inside.

"Lights are on," O'Malley observed. "You were here already."

"That's sound detective work."

"Then you went running some errands?"

"Now you're two out of two," I told the younger of the two cops. "Want to go for the hat trick?"

"Why are you giving him shit?" Breen asked huffily.

"He's seen too many Bogart pictures," O'Malley said. "That's how the shamuses talk at the Roxy." Now they followed me doggedly into my inner office. I took my hat off and tossed it onto the antlers of my moosehead.

"Cute," said Breen.

"I like to think so," I told them, then sat behind my desk and yawned. It was a quarter past twelve, but I would have been very happy to go back to bed.

"Busy day so far, Jack?" Breen sat down without being asked. O'Malley pulled the other chair over and sat down beside him.

"Have a seat, boys," I told them.

"Don't mind if we do," O'Malley said. "Shall we continue jesting at each other?"

"Fine with me." I lit up a Lucky. "I'm good at it."

"I'm sure you are," Breen said. "Busy day so far?"

"You asked me that already."

"Yeah, but you didn't answer."

Now the two buzzards just stared at me.

"Is this what they call a significant pause?" I asked them.

O'Malley grunted, while Breen reached into his pocket and pulled out a small brown notebook. "About an hour and a half ago," he began, flipping through the book, "there was a serious vehicular accident a block from this office involving a city bus and two pedestrians. It resulted in the death of one individual and the serious injury of the other. The injured party is at Roosevelt Hospital; his prognosis is about fifty-fifty."

I pulled a bit of tobacco from my lower lip. "Do tell."

"The dead man was identified as Michael Carbone, otherwise known as Mikey Blond or Mike the Kraut, on account of his blond hair pigmentation."

"Should I be taking notes?"

Breen rolled on. "The injured party is one Vincent Galliano, who also goes by the name of Vinnie Meatballs."

"Not very imaginative. Must of been an off day in the nickname department," I said.

"I have to agree," said Breen.

"That's not really the point," O'Malley added helpfully.

"Both these guys are out of Brooklyn and they're in the Anastasia crew. Used to work for our old pal Lucky Luciano."

"No shit."

"Yeah." Breen put the notebook away. "So how come, Jack, how come they're chasing your fat kosher ass up the street?"

"And don't even try to deny it," O'Malley said. He took his hat off and placed it in his lap. "We got three eyewitnesses."

"Am I denying it?"

"You're not?"

"No."

"So they were pursuing you."

"Correct. But God's blessed truth is, I don't know why."

The two cops looked as pleased as if I had just puked on their shoes.

"Jack," Breen began, his voice tightening to a nasty whisper, "I'm starting to lose my fucking patience here."

"You can lose your patience here or in the lobby, that's not my concern," I said cheerfully. "The fact is, I didn't know who these guys were, nor did I know that they were mobbed up."

"You never saw them before."

"I never said that. I said I didn't know who they were."

"So you had seen them on a prior occasion?" asked O'Malley, using his meaty thumb to pick his nose ever so subtly.

"Once. In Riverdale."

"Riverdale." Breen opened his notebook again.

"Where in Riverdale?" O'Malley asked.

"That I can't tell you."

Breen's eyes turned to ice chips. "Jack, stop pulling this coy shit. We have a homicide case here."

"I thought we were discussing a traffic accident."

"We're talking about the Stern case, for crying out loud," O'Malley interjected. He crossed his legs and looked at his partner in exaggerated dismay.

"You're sure they're connected? Listen . . ." I got up and opened the window. "I'm really not trying to make your life more difficult, but Stern hired me on a matter that's shaping up as a lot more complicated than I originally thought."

"So try to help us out, Jack," said Breen. "And maybe we can help you out."

"Guys, don't play dumb, you know the drill. I'm a licensed PI. Confidentiality goes with the territory." Breen opened his mouth, but I ran right over him. "I know you're going to say this is a homicide, but that still doesn't mean I'm gonna share every half-assed lead I have with you. I can't."

I sat back down. The two cops looked glum.

"I will share one thing with you, however, because there's no confidentiality associated with it. You say the guys who got whacked by the bus were out of the old Luciano mob. Well, there was another of

Lucky's cronies at Stern's funeral, a squirt named Giuseppe LaMarca, and nobody can figure what he was doing there."

"I know that name." Breen said. "Why was he—"

"I just told you, I have no idea. But there it is."

Breen looked befuddled.

"This is a mob case, Jack? Some little fiddler gets shot? What the fuck?"

"Exactly," I told him. "What the fuck?"

Breen got up. O'Malley sat for a second, like he was thinking about something, then realized he wasn't thinking about anything, so he got up, too.

"We'll be back," Breen told me.

"How did I know you'd say that?" I told him, but he was already out the door.

EIGHT

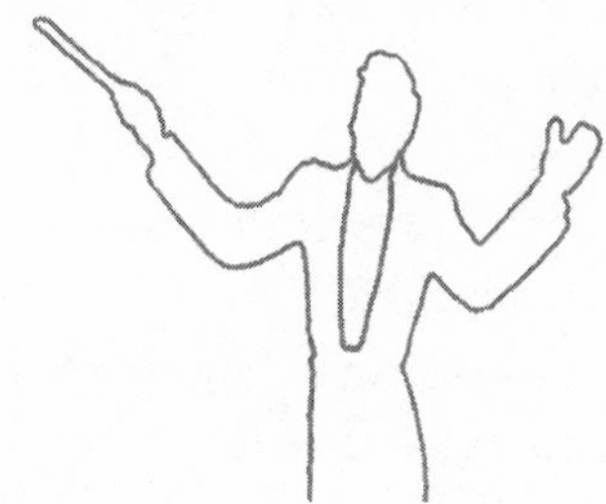

The National Airlines flight to Havana featured a red carpet stretched across the Idlewild tarmac. It was a gray, windy morning when I boarded the DC-6 with about forty other passengers, about half of whom were dressed entirely in white. Some looked to be legitimate businessmen, down for sugar or cigars, but most looked like gamblers, particularly the parties in white. There were maybe six women on the flight, none of them a day over twenty-five, and they were all accompanying the gamblers, none of whom was a day under forty-five. You will probably not be surprised to learn that the women were a great deal thinner than the men and that none of them appeared to be deeply in love.

The plane was remarkably plush, with navy blue carpeting and thickly padded seats; "We're in the Money" played through a Muzak system hooked up to speakers recessed in the ceiling. The plane also featured an area dubbed the "Starlight Lounge," where one could have a drink and read a magazine or just sit and dream of hot roulette numbers. This was like no other airplane I had ever been on and resembled more of a flying cathouse than anything Lucky Lindy had ever imagined while he was winging his way to Paris. I liked it very much.

My seatmate was a dour Cuban in his sixties who introduced himself as Alfonso Logart, Jr. He told me that he ran a soft drink business outside Havana and was attempting, without much success, to make cream soda a popular beverage among the Cuban people.

"They know beer, they know Coca-Cola, Pepsi-Cola. That's it. And fruit juices, of course. But I had to make this attempt," he told me, tapping my arm with his chubby fingers, "because I believed in cream soda."

"Maybe if the Cubans ate more pastrami, they'd get the hang of cream soda."

Logart, Jr., shook his large graying head. He couldn't have been more than five-foot-three, but more than compensated for his lack of height with his girth, which was well over three hundred pounds. He carried his weight right above the belt, like a large and placid pet.

"You are a Jew?" he asked, smoothing his tie over his gut.

"Yes."

"So you understand cream soda."

"With all my heart."

He nodded. "We are a people who love pork. Pastrami, this does not exist in Cuba as you know it. You are quite right, though. Maybe it would be of help." He sighed and tugged at his pendulous earlobe. "What brings you to Cuba? You are in the smoked meat business, by some chance?" He smiled and revealed some fabulous gold bridgework.

"No. Just going to see the place."

"You have been before?"

"Never. I hear the Nacional is fabulous."

Logart shrugged. "It will all end one day."

"End? What do you mean?"

"There is much poverty and much corruption. There are many people looking to line their pockets and then get out. It is not a stable situation."

"By 'not stable' you mean what, exactly?"

He looked around the plane, lowered his voice. It was an hour into the flight and we had hit some choppy air.

"There are forces in Cuba, and individuals, who are not so desirable, if you understand what I mean. Not native Cubans."

"Is Luciano still hanging around down there?" I asked him.

Logart tightened the seat belt around his wondrous gut.

"Not these days. I understand he is back in Italy. But he is not the only one of his sort, believe me. And Batista, he is still running things from his seat in our senate."

"And he's a flat-out crook."

Logart smiled and shrugged, the picture of innocence.

"So you think, what, the place will go up in smoke?" I asked, somewhat mystified.

"This I do not know. I am just saying that it is not a place that should be taken for granted. Is not like the movies, just mambo and rum. Lot of poor people down there." He yawned prodigiously. "And now, if you do not mind, I will take a little nap." Logart plumped a pillow behind his head, turned with no little difficulty on his side, and within two minutes was fast asleep, snoring like he had a rack of pool balls rolling around his sinuses. I yawned and opened my *Daily News*. Governor Dewey was getting involved in the Harry Gross bookie probe, that was the front page; Sinatra was getting divorced on page three. Mrs. Sinatra was entitled to three hundred and fifty grand a year, so she was smiling through her pain, but Frankie looked pleased also, a feeling much enhanced by having Ava Gardner clinging to his bony right arm. Down the page, a small item informed me that Al Jolson had returned from Korea, declaring that "this is a much tougher war than the last one, believe me." I turned the page and found what I was looking for:

BUS ACCIDENT KILLS MOBSTER

It was a one-column headline in the middle of the page. The three-paragraph story informed me that Vincent Galliano was now fully conscious and expected to recover. Both he and the deceased Michael "Mikey Blond" Carbone were identified as members of the Anastasia clan, but the story was otherwise sparing on details. Police were said to "believe this was simply an accident." Eyewitnesses told the *News* that the two men appeared to be pursuing a "stocky man in a brown suit." I resented being called stocky and the suit was glen plaid, but I considered myself lucky that no one had gotten a decent peep at me. There was nothing in the article to indicate that the cops thought this was anything worth investigating, which meant that Breen and O'Malley were keeping it buttoned up, and that was just fine with me.

Much more importantly, the Yankees had clinched a tie for the pennant, and the Dodgers had fallen three games behind the Phillies, which made me feel warm all over; you just couldn't inflict enough pain on the Dodgers to suit me. I was halfway through a sidebar item about Phil Rizzuto when the words began to blur, so I shut my eyes. The next thing I knew the captain was speaking over the PA system and I learned that we were one hour and five minutes from the island of Cuba.

Stepping off the plane in Havana was like walking fully dressed into the St. Marks Place baths. The temperature was close to ninety and the humidity wasn't far behind. I took my suit jacket off the instant I reached the terminal, but by the time I saw my black leather suitcase come rolling corpselike into view, my shirt had turned from white to sopping gray. The taxi ride from the airport didn't help matters at all—my driver kept his radio tuned at high volume to an all-mambo station ("El Voce de Mambo!") and puffed on a pungent cigar not much smaller than a Louisville Slugger. Between the smoke and the heat, the music and the gas fumes, by the time the taxi rolled up to the chandeliered porte cochere of the Nacional, I had a blinding headache and my stomach felt like I had swallowed the contents of a guppy tank.

I stumbled into the long and narrow lobby, following a white-jacketed bellman to the front desk. Palms abounded inside and out; a set of double doors were opened to a pillared veranda facing the ocean and a grassy expanse that rolled down to the seawall they call the Malecón. There was a steady breeze, but the thick tropical air, scented by a mixture of gas fumes and sewage, only made me queasier.

The bellman waited for me at the front desk, a toothsome grin on his face; the sicker I felt, the more he smiled. He gestured toward a beaming and pomaded gentleman behind the desk.

"Welcome to the Nacional," the man behind the desk said brightly. "I am Rolando. At your service." Rolando at my service wore his hair slicked back and sported a dapper little mustache that appeared to have been purchased from a novelty shop.

"You have had a pleasant journey?" he asked in all sincerity.

I just nodded in reply, fearful of barfing on his lovely marble countertop.

"I speak the full English," the deskman said happily. "So there is no the need for be shy with me."

"Great," I belched. Rolando reeked of bay rum, which wasn't helping my nausea one little bit. "The name is LeVine, capital *V*." When Rolando lowered his head to find my reservation, I checked myself out in the mirror behind the desk. What I saw wasn't pretty: a green-complexioned spook wearing a wet shirt and a crumpled seersucker suit.

"Mr. Levine—"

"LeVine."

"Of course . . . You are in a beautiful room, 804, that will face the ocean." He rang the bell on the desk, even though the bellman was standing two feet away. "Edgardo will take you, have a pleasant stay at the Nacional, and there is . . ."—he stuck his hand into the cubbyhole for room 804 and extracted not only a gold key, but an envelope—"there is for you, yes, an envelope. Again welcome."

I took the envelope and shoved it in my pocket, then followed the happy Edgardo down the hall to the elevator. He gestured for me to get on board, which I did, stifling a bile-filled belch. Edgardo smiled at the tall and very broad elevator jockey, who slammed the gate shut and rocketed us up to eight.

The elevator stopped with a shudder. I knew I wasn't going to last much longer. Edgardo beamed. *"Señor?"*

The bellman gestured for me to exit the elevator, then I tailed him down the air-cooled corridor to my room, which was near the fire exit at the end of the floor. There was a lingering scent of disinfectant in the air, which further roiled my unhappy stomach. I followed Edgardo inside the room, slipped him a buck, for which I earned many more exclamations of *"gracias"* than I needed to hear, and watched gratefully as he exited, so I could run to the bathroom and toss my cookies into my very first Cuban toilet. I'm sure I'd been sicker in my life, but off the top of my bare head I couldn't remember when. I peeled off my clothes, washed my face, and, feeling too weak in the pins for a shower, lay down on the king-sized bed and was asleep before I could say Giuseppe Verdi.

I awoke about an hour later, groggy and disoriented. I felt chilled from the air-conditioning, so I arose and opened a window and welcomed the warm late afternoon breezes blowing in off Havana Bay. I took my first deep breath, then checked my watch—it was a quarter past five. My stomach had settled, although my mouth still tasted like I'd gargled with battery acid. I decided that a shower would do me all the good in the world, so I pulled off my socks and underpants and was parading to the bathroom in all my natural splendor when it occurred to me that I had never opened the envelope given to me by the deskman.

I picked my still-damp seersucker jacket up off the chair I had draped it across and extracted the envelope from the side pocket: It was hotel stationery. I tore open the envelope and removed an elegant cream-colored card, likewise bearing the Nacional's insignia and address. There was a note written on the card in a hurried scrawl. The message was brief, but it had the approximate impact of an atomic bomb:

LeVine—

Meet me in the hotel bar at 6:30.

Meyer Lansky

I took a very long shower.
And then a very long shave.
At six o'clock I started laying out my clothes.

I'd heard about Meyer Lansky my entire adult life, my entire youth for that matter, even though he was only four years my senior. He was the Henry Ford, the J. P. Morgan, the George Washington Carver of the Syndicate, the man who had put the "organized" in "organized crime." He'd been helping run Havana for a good long time, carefully working its casinos like a plantation owner working a sugar field. He was meticulous and ruthless, which both impressed and unnerved me; sitting down with Lansky to discuss a shakedown was like going to the park to have a catch with DiMaggio. My heart raced with anticipation.

How he had known I was coming to Cuba was a question that barely occurred to me. Lansky knew everything about everything—he could have found out via Sidney Aaron, via the homicide dicks, via Joey Blinks via Sidney Aaron or Joey Blinks via somebody else in the know. Astounded as I was to receive this card from Lansky, I was far from surprised. I was dealing with a high order of criminal mind here, one eminently capable of engineering a snatch of Toscanini or the President of the United States or anyone else he cared to grab.

I got down to the bar at six thirty-five, stalling five minutes so as not to look like the eager chump; he was already there, seated in a corner banquette, sipping a glass of soda water and picking at a bowl of nuts. He didn't rise when I approached the table; he just raised his eyebrows and flashed a sour half grin.

"You're LeVine?" His voice was higher than I had expected.

"Yes. You're Lansky."

"We should start a law firm together," he said, gesturing for me to sit across from him. "Has a nice ring to it."

The second my ass hit the chair, a waiter was at my side.

"What do you want?" Lansky asked me.

"Same as you," I told him. "Glass of seltzer."

"Aqua mineral," Lansky told the waiter, who at once sped off to the bar. "They don't know from seltzer down here, the dumb fucks. They need educating."

"Well, you're the guy to do it," I told him.

He smiled and popped a cashew into his mouth. Lansky chewed with his mouth closed, like his mother had taught him; he was a compact, dark-haired man of forty-eight with a prominent nose and the impassive, wary expression of a certified public accountant. Except for the eyes, his was a most ordinary face. But the eyes gave him away; they were piercing, evaluating, and beyond all mercy.

"Aqua mineral," he said again. "I feel like a schmuck every time I say it." He grimaced, suppressed a belch. "Obviously you got my note."

"Obviously."

"What, you take the National flight this morning, with the lounge and the music and all that fancy shit?"

"Yes. It was a lot more relaxing than the cab ride in from the airport."

"Should've told me you were coming; would've had you met. The cabs down here are from hunger."

"If I knew you were here I would have written weeks ago. Just to say hello, wish you a happy new year—"

"You didn't know I was here?" Lansky asked. He seemed genuinely surprised.

"No. I don't even know you. You're not confusing me with someone else, are you?"

He popped an almond into his yap and shook his head. "No. You're the guy I want. You're looking for the missing Maestro, right?"

My *aqua mineral* arrived. I took a sip—it was almost like seltzer, but without the enthusiasm.

"Am I right?" Lansky repeated. "You're down here to find the old man?"

"Yes, I'm down here to find the old man. Now let me ask you what might appear to be an extremely naive question."

Lansky raised his eyebrows and munched placidly on his nut.

"What's your involvement in this?" I asked.

Lansky nodded, stopped chewing. He waved at someone crossing the room. I turned around to see who it was and found myself staring at Tyrone Power. Power walked over to Lansky and shook his hand.

"How are you, Meyer?" he said in a resonant actor's voice.

"Fabulous," Lansky said. "And you?"

"Having a helluva time down here," he said. Power smiled at me with blank sincerity. "Tyrone Power," he said, sticking out his paw. He was extremely handsome but appeared somewhat less than manly.

"Jack LeVine," I told him.

"Great to meet you, Jack." Lansky just stared at Power, without asking him to sit, so the movie star got a little jittery and started backing off. "See you later in the casino, Meyer?"

"Me?" Lansky said with a sour laugh. "I don't gamble." Power chuckled and walked backward for about three yards before having the nerve to turn and walk away.

Lansky shrugged. "I think he's a fag, but he doesn't know it yet."

"Really."

"It's his business. Nice kid, though. Dresses the place up, having him around." Lansky rubbed his nose. "You asked me something."

"About your involvement with Toscanini."

"Involvement," Lansky said. "That's a good word, 'involvement.' Not too specific." He sipped some more *aqua*. "I'm an interested observer. You buy that?"

"Maybe. What's it going to cost?"

"That might be negotiable." He smiled, but it was strictly a ten-watt smile—his mouth twitched, but his eyes didn't play along. "We both like to banter, am I right? I can see between us a whole lot of witty fucking banter."

"That's very likely. You live down here now?"

Lansky shrugged. "I live here, I live in Miami, I live in New York. I'm semi-retired, in a fashion."

"How semi?"

"Semi-semi. Sometimes I work, sometimes I sleep late. It's too much strain to work all the time, and what's the point, really? Monetary gain?" He shook his head. "Hardly worth it anymore. Taxes have taken all the fun out of it, am I right, Jack?"

"I was never in your tax bracket. Doesn't affect me all that much."

"Taxes go against everything that made America great—enterprise, intelligence, business savvy. The politicians have turned all those virtues into shit." Now his eyes shifted and he looked past me, over my shoulder toward the entrance to the bar.

"Here she is," he said quietly, almost to himself. Then he raised his hand and snapped his fingers. "Sweetheart!" he called out.

I turned around and you could have knocked me over with a bubble of *aqua mineral.*

Standing at the entrance to the bar, looking quizzically around the room, was Barbara Stern.

I turned back to Lansky, my mouth dry. There was no little merriment on his features. "You know this girl, am I right?"

I arose and watched as she slowly crossed the room, fully aware that everyone in the joint was staring at her, not only because she was approaching the great man's table, but because she was wearing a flowered chiffon dress cut just below her knees that clung to every perfect bend in the road. As she neared the table, Barbara looked at me with a serene and bemused expression that said, *Surprised to see me?*

I was not only surprised, I was numb. My legs felt like concrete posts.

"Hello, Miss Stern," I said in as firm a voice as I could muster.

"Jack." She held out her hand and I shook it. "Meyer."

Lansky patted the banquette.

"Sit by me, darling," he said.

Barbara smiled at me cryptically and sat down beside Lansky. He pecked her on the cheek; she responded by patting his arm, still keeping her eyes on me. If she had kissed Lansky full on the lips, there's a strong chance I would have broken down and cried, which is something I rarely do in hotel bars.

"When did you get here?" I asked casually, Señor Composure himself.

"Late last night." Our waiter came trotting up to Barbara Stern's side. One thing you had to say for Lansky, the guy commanded some fabulous service. Speaking fluent Spanish, Barbara ordered herself a local beer and requested some limes on a dish.

"The lime peps up this local beer," she explained to me.

"You've been here before," I said.

"Oh yes. A couple of times."

"So you came down last night," I repeated. I felt like I was speaking to her in code.

"Yes. There's a flight that gets in around nine."

"She was smart enough to let me know," Lansky interjected. "No cabs for this little girl." He put an arm around her and gave her neck a little squeeze.

"And you, Jack?"

"Just got in a few hours ago." I sucked on a pistachio, trying to feel my way. "How's your mother doing, and your sister?"

Barbara shrugged. "About the same. I told Mom I'd be away for a day or two. She was okay about it. She understood."

"She did."

"Sure."

Her beer arrived at the speed of light, and the accompanying slices of lime. The waiter placed another bowl of nuts on the table, this one large enough to feed a family of squirrels for the winter. Lansky happily grabbed another handful.

"I probably shouldn't be eating these," he said. "I don't think they're so healthy. But I never could lay off them."

"Oh, Meyer. Enjoy yourself." Barbara spoke to him like he was her uncle. Lansky smiled at her and I sat sipping my Cuban seltzer, trying to get a fix on their relationship. I had no doubt that they had been lovers at some point—no way Lansky was going to restrain himself from *shtupping* someone who looked like Barbara Stern—and maybe it was just wishful thinking on my part, but what I saw passing between them now indicated that the heavy breathing was most likely a thing of the past. What remained was just the good-natured affection of a beautiful Cornell undergraduate for a murdering sonofabitch.

Lansky beamed in my direction.

"He's trying to figure this out, our friend Mr. LeVine. Am I right?"

"Oh, Meyer, don't play games," Barbara said. "It gets tedious."

" 'Tedious,' " he repeated. "The mouth on this kid. The problem is, she's overeducated. That's one thing nobody ever accused me of."

I was starting to tire of all the chitchat, Lansky or no Lansky. I guzzled my *aqua,* cleared my throat.

"I'm not trying to figure you and Barbara out," I lied. "Not at the moment. All I want to know is where Toscanini is stashed, what, if anything, you know about it, and why you wanted to talk to me. Not necessarily in that order." I looked to Barbara. "Am I correct in assuming that your father got involved in this business because of you?"

Barbara looked daggers at me. "And therefore I'm responsible for his death?"

"Watch it," said Lansky, his eyes turning as lifeless as a pair of ball bearings.

"I didn't say you were responsible for his death."

Barbara was no longer listening to me. Her eyes puddled up with tears.

"No, he did not get killed because of me, nor did he get involved in this because of me. He never knew about Meyer and me. But when my mother called me Tuesday night and told me what had happened, my first instinct was to call Meyer. That was the order of events. I called him from Ithaca right after I heard."

"Which you neglected to tell me."

"I hardly *knew* you. Christ. What did you think, the first thing I'm going to say when we're introduced is, 'By the way, I used to date Meyer Lansky'?"

Lansky watched all of this with great amusement. "You can't browbeat this girl, LeVine, believe me."

"I'm not trying to browbeat anyone," I told him with a little heat, then turned back to Barbara "So your parents never knew that you and Lansky had been involved."

"No. And they never will. I mean," she took a breath, "my mother never will."

Lansky stroked her hair with the back of his hand, threw me a rueful smile. "She's ashamed of me."

Barbara shook her beautiful head. "It's not that. She just wouldn't understand." No kidding. Hilde Stern would be as enthused if Barbara had started dating Goebbels. I wasn't too keen on it myself. The thought of Barbara Stern's long slender legs wrapped around Lansky's naked little body was, to say the least, dispiriting.

"Okay," I forged ahead. "So you find out about your father and place a call to Havana." I turned to Lansky. "That was the first you'd heard of it?"

"Of what?"

"The snatch. Not the killing."

Lansky shook his head. "No."

"You knew about the snatch."

"I'd heard rumors to that effect."

"What effect?"

"I'd heard there were parties who had taken Toscanini and were apparently looking for a major score. I wasn't sure about the numbers involved, but I understood they were sizable."

"Three million bucks," I told Lansky.

He smiled. "Then I understood right." Now the little gangster snapped his bony fingers, prompting the waiter to practically fly back to our table. "More Cuban seltzer, *por favor,*" Lansky told him.

"Que?" asked the waiter.

"Aqua mineral," Lansky repeated. *"Por todos."*

The waiter nodded furiously—*"Sí, sí! Por todos"*—and disappeared again.

"This fucking place is starting to get on my nerves," Lansky grumbled.

"He's been saying that forever," Barbara said to me, squeezing Lansky's arm affectionately.

"All right," I said. I was losing my patience. "You'd heard about the snatch. Any idea who's involved?"

Lansky shook his head. "No."

"You have no idea."

"You're talking facts or guesswork?"

"For openers, let's say guesswork."

"That's a waste of time." Lansky rummaged through the nuts as if looking for a missing diamond. Barbara took a long swig of her beer.

"Then what are we doing here?" I was starting to feel like a participant in the world's worst scavenger hunt. "You sent me a note, you want to see me. Fine, I'm here. Now, do you want to help me out or just play these little verbal games, because if it's the second, I'm getting way too old for it."

Lansky gave me an empty stare, as if I were a stranger who had just stopped by to ask directions.

"I want to help you, and I want to help the girl." Lansky patted Barbara's hand and leaned forward. "What happened to her father was a terrible thing—for a civilian to get hit like that, particularly a person of culture and breeding, an artist. The whole thing is so unnecessary."

"So you're a bystander here, that's your role," I said to Lansky.

"Basically."

" 'Basically.' Meaning if there's some sort of payoff and Toscanini gets delivered in one piece, you'd like a taste of it."

"I don't think that's what he's saying," Barbara interjected.

"No?" I asked.

Lansky shrugged in a rabbinical manner. "I would just want some consideration."

"That would be up to NBC," I told him.

Lansky blinked innocently. "I completely understand."

"Good. So let me ask you, is Toscanini down here or not?"

"He might be," Lansky said. "I'm not certain."

"The ransom note was written on Nacional stationery." I told him.

He scratched his nose. "Doesn't mean a thing."

"Someone could just have taken the stationery," Barbara said.

"I understand that," I said. "But do you have any reason to believe that he's either here now or was here?"

"Yes I do. Otherwise I wouldn't be wasting your time, Jack. I can call you Jack?"

"You can call me Rosemary Clooney; I'm just desperate for information here. What's your reason for thinking that the Maestro was or still is in Havana?"

The waiter returned with a tray full of the green bottles of *aqua mineral.* If I drank much more, I might as well sleep in the bathtub tonight.

Lansky waited for the waiter to leave. "I've come to believe that my friend Charlie Lucky may have wanted him here, for his safety."

"Luciano?"

Lansky nodded. "Yeah."

"When you say Luciano wanted him here for his safety," I continued, "you're referring to Toscanini's safety? Or Lucky's?"

"Toscanini's," said Lansky.

"And you base that on what?" I asked him.

Lansky smiled. "I base it on knowledge, let's leave it at that. Not *facts,* okay? I'm not saying I know facts." The little man leaned forward. "I have some knowledge of possibilities."

"Okay," I plowed ahead. "Next question: Is Lucky still around here?"

"In Havana?" Lansky looked surprised. "No. Not for years."

"He's in Italy," Barbara said reflexively, and threw a sort of *oops* look at Lansky, who just shook his head like a forgiving parent.

"He's in Italy, yes."

This made no sense to me. Why the hell would Lucky Luciano be protecting Toscanini—and from whom?

"So if Toscanini is being snatched for his protection," I said, speaking as quietly as was possible in the increasingly crowded and noisy bar, "I don't figure the ransom, except to throw people off the scent."

"That would make sense," Barbara said. "It sells the kidnapping."

"He's missing for a while, right?" said Lansky.

"Since the end of May."

"It's September, Jack," he said helpfully.

"How does NBC explain that?" Barbara asked.

"Poor detective work," I told them.

Lansky shook his head. "I don't think so. I think they wanted him back, he'd be back, big fucking company like that. I think they pay up a long time ago."

"Maybe they don't want to set a precedent—paying big ransom for kidnapped stars."

Lansky just shook his head, unconvinced.

"You don't buy it?" I asked.

"I don't buy it."

"You think they want him missing?"

"I think they want him dead," Lansky said, then arose. "I gotta pee. You two don't talk behind my back."

Lansky slid out of the banquette and crossed the room toward the lavatories, which were just beyond the bar. Barbara watched him go, then smiled the demurest of smiles at me.

"I guess you're a little surprised," she said.

"Surprised? I'm speechless," I said. "How the hell—"

"I was never in love with him, Jack. It was just the excitement. It was all kinds of things, actually."

"Where'd you meet him?"

"First a cigarette." I shook a Lucky out of a fresh pack and played the gentleman, lighting both of us up.

"I had graduated high school," she began, taking the lit cigarette. "Thanks. . . . It was the summer . . . 1947. Some friends and I went to the Copa to hear Dean Martin sing, one of his first big engagements, I think. We were there maybe ten minutes when this man approached our table, started talking to us, said that a friend of his wanted to meet me. The friend of his turned out to be Meyer. Not sitting ringside or anything. Near the back, that's his style. He likes to sit by the exits."

"You knew who he was?"

Barbara shook her head. "He was just a name, I didn't really know much about him. But he was very polite and very funny and he had a kind of force to him."

"No kidding."

"I don't mean it in that sense. Listen, obviously, I don't condone what's he done in his life. But you have to understand, I had grown up in this refugee world where timidity was basically like a code of conduct. To meet a man who didn't live like that, to meet a man who felt in complete command every second of his life, that was just a revelation. And he treated me very, very well."

"So you didn't go to college."

"No. I told you, remember? Back in New York? I took a couple of years off. My parents didn't care all that much; they didn't think a girl necessarily needed a college education anyhow."

"So what did they think you were doing?"

"They thought I had a job. Which I did, sort of. Meyer got me hired by this printing concern he had an interest in, but the deal was, I could show up or not. When I traveled with Meyer, I would tell my parents the boss needed me to go with him and take dictation. He was almost seventy, the boss, a nice old Polish Jew, so they didn't give it a thought. My mother would help me pack, in fact." Barbara smiled. "Although she didn't much approve of my clothes, I have to admit."

"So you and Lansky traveled together."

"Yes. We came down here, we went to Rome once or twice, Miami. We weren't together all the time, understand; I was still living at home and he's married, after all."

"In a fashion."

She nodded. "In a fashion. He was separated when I met him, then he got remarried, but it didn't change anything. That's the world he lives in. People are sort of married, but it's not in the way that most of us know. He and his associates live in a world of laws, but it's *their* laws. It's not like anarchy. It's their code and they get married in a certain way. So yes, Meyer was married, but we saw a great deal of each other, and the life he lived and the way he treated me . . . it certainly opened my eyes."

"I would think so."

"But there's a big downside, of course, because there's no future in such a relationship, or such a life, really. After two years, I'd had enough; I didn't want to be possessed by someone, which is what it is with Meyer—you're essentially owned by him. I wanted to continue my life, go to school. So I told him I wanted out."

"How'd he take it?"

"He was great about it. Said he wasn't surprised, it was time for me to go on with my life, I deserved it, he would never stand in the way. Said all the right things."

"You were what, then, twenty?"

She nodded. "Yeah. But an old twenty. I'd been through a great deal already, remember, in Germany—getting kicked out, the whole deal." She watched her cigarette smoke rise to the ceiling. "It wasn't love, Jack; Meyer's not capable of love and I certainly could never feel love for him. Genuine affection, yes, but not anything deeper than that. It was just an episode, a totally fascinating episode. Maybe one day I'll look back on it and have my regrets, but I doubt it. I'm a fatalist."

"So it was meant to be? You and Lansky?"

"Yes. I think so." Barbara looked off, drifting into thoughts I would never know, home movies I would never see—of hotel lobbies and nightclubs and terraces overlooking oceans, of men in fedoras having whispered conversations in sitting rooms, of putting on make-up and overhearing monosyllabic phone calls. Then she smoothed her hair and returned to the present tense, to this clamorous bar in Havana. "Anyhow, when it was over, he told me to remember that he'd always be there for me if I needed something."

"So when your father got hit, you thought of him."

"Yes. Even before then. When my uncle got brain-damaged in that car wreck—"

"Otto, from the funeral."

"Otto from the funeral. Very good." She nodded at me, flashed that brilliant smile. God, she was a heartbreaker, and the more I listened to her, the more I learned of her history, the hotter I got for her. "After that accident, I called Meyer, because the expenses were just horrific—the hospital, the private nurses. Brutal. He came through for me immediately and never said boo about it, no self-congratulation, none of that crap. And he's still paying for Otto's care."

"Nobody ever asks where the money's coming from?"

"I told my Aunt Gretl, Otto's wife, that I had a rich boyfriend who was paying and she shouldn't tell my mother. That was fine with her—she barely speaks to my mother anyhow."

"And she loves knowing something your mother doesn't. Puts her one up."

"Exactly. She told my mother that Otto's law firm had established a fund to pay for it." She stubbed out her cigarette in an ashtray the size of a catcher's mitt. "Families."

"Yeah."

Barbara took another sip of her beer and studied my face.

"You know, you're a good-looking man."

"Please . . ."

"I'm serious."

"I look like fifty thousand other slobs. You see them every day in the subway, chewing Juicy Fruit and reading the *Mirror.*"

"Stop it. . . . No, there's something really . . . *strong* there." She looked right into my eyes and was holding her gaze when Lansky returned from the john. At that moment, Abe Lincoln could have walked over in his stovepipe hat and I wouldn't have noticed, but Lansky got my attention, clearing his throat loudly behind me.

"I gotta make a couple of calls," he announced.

"No dinner?" I asked.

He waved his hand as dismissively as if I'd suggested we go folk dancing. "Dinner doesn't mean anything to me. I got jumpy insides. We'll meet later." He looked to Barbara. "Eat with her, she's better company."

And just like that, he turned and started walking away. I got out of my chair and followed him across the room.

"What's the problem?" he asked, without turning around.

"I don't know where we stand."

"Stand? I met you, you met me. It's called a meeting."

"I understand what it's called. . . ."

Lansky stopped and faced me. I could see Barbara watching us. She was drinking her beer out of the bottle now.

"Listen," Lansky said, his eyes narrowed to the size of baby peas. "I understand you want the Maestro back. I want to help you and I don't want anybody hurt."

"You have any idea who bumped off her father?"

"No, but obviously I have an interest in finding out, right? I have a history with this person. Sounds to me, from what I heard, like a screwup."

"Please. Two shots in the head?"

Lansky looked at me like I'd just described the theft of a bag of doughnuts.

"Happens. Human error." He looked back to our table. "Have a nice dinner."

We had a nice dinner. A place near the water, La Habañera, nothing fancy. Yellow stucco walls, paper lanterns, some cheerfully rotten local art. The very relaxed patrons included local businessmen and some families out for a long easy dinner. There were no obvious tourists to be seen, except for me. I had *pollo asado*, a salad, some beer, and a couple of cups of Cuban coffee strong enough to race King Kong's heart.

"This coffee could wake the dead," I told Barbara.

She looked at me wistfully over her coffee cup. "If only . . ."

How clever was I, making references to the deceased to a girl whose father had been dead for all of four days. When you lose someone close, you lose a layer of skin; it grows back in time, but there is a period when every allusion to death, no matter how glancing or oblique, causes an immediate and stinging pain.

"Sorry. Blame it on travel fatigue."

She shook her head. "Don't start editing yourself." Barbara looked around the room and took me off the hook. "I love this place," she said. "Don't you?"

"It's very comfy."

"Comfy, lively, but not crazy. Meyer didn't like it too well. But he hates most restaurants. Hates to eat. I'm not sure what he lives on."

"Greed."

She smiled. "Possibly. He's a complicated guy; there's a lot going on that he keeps to himself. His first wife was seemingly quite religious, wanted their son to become a rabbi, and I think she gave him a very hard time about his . . . *career,* shall we say. Then apparently she went a little nuts, or maybe a lot nuts; I never got the full story. He's a very hard man, but I think there's a huge amount of guilt lurking not far below the surface. He'd have these nightmares and sort of wake up, but not really? He'd be sweating, his eyes would be wide open, and he'd be shouting, but not words, just sounds. I'd have to cradle him back to sleep. In the morning, he'd have zero recollection of it. I'd tell him that he was yelling and perspiring and he'd just laugh it off, or say he must have been dreaming about being a kid in Poland."

"He grew up in poverty," I said. "but what else is new? How many Polish Jews grew up in the lap of luxury?"

"But he was *seriously* poor, at least as he describes it." Barbara sipped her coffee. "Lived on the Lower East Side in a slum that was like one of those old Jacob Riis photographs. Spent his whole life fighting with anti-Semites, in Poland and then here. You know he met Luciano when he was just a kid? They were both about six or seven, actually. They've spent their entire lives together."

Our waiter brought over two snifters of brandy and pointed to the owner. *"Con los complementos de Señor Alvarde."*

Señor Alvarde, gray-haired and elegant, was standing next to the bar, attired in tan slacks and a snow-white guayabera shirt. He bowed and waved at Barbara.

"Muchas gracias," she told the waiter. *"Es muy generoso."* The waiter left and Barbara took a sip of her brandy. "It's not the greatest, but if we don't drink it, he'll be terribly insulted. The Cubans are very big on these gestures."

"So I'll drink it," I told her.

She looked at me with an expression I couldn't quite read. It was as if she were trying to remember something, but couldn't quite retrieve it.

"Yes," she finally said. "Then I'd like to get out of here."

We went back to the Nacional without exchanging a word—not during the brief, helter-skelter taxi ride, not as we crossed the lobby, not as we got into the elevator. When I asked her what floor she was on, she looked into my eyes with a bemused and patient expression, and only then did I realize I was on a train that had already pulled out of the station, and I lacked both the power and the will to stop it. Barbara followed me down the quiet, carpeted corridor, staying two steps behind me. A waiter pushing a room-service trolley stopped and bowed as we passed; I nodded back to him like a general reviewing his troops. I unlocked the door to 804; as we entered the room, I went to turn the lights on, but Barbara put her hand over mine.

"No," she said in a midnight whisper, "no lights." She took the DO NOT DISTURB sign and hung it out in the hall, then locked the door and turned to me, cupping my face in her long smooth hands. "I'm going to shower. You get into bed."

And then she was gone, into the bathroom, and I heard the shower taps turned on and imagined her taking her clothes off and stepping into the tub, closing the curtain behind her. I thought of that smooth young body standing behind the shower curtain, the water running in rivulets down every sculpted inch of her, and I wondered, as I do at such moments—was it me she was thinking of as she soaped herself up, or was there some other agenda?

It wasn't the age difference. That didn't faze me in the slightest; she was no child and her supple mind had already absorbed enough information and pain for a lifetime. When a woman is that beautiful, she learns to make a great many choices early on; the world comes at her like snowflakes in a storm, exhilarating and relentless. Barbara was not yet twenty-two, but she might as well have been forty-two.

But she didn't look forty-two when she stepped out of the bathroom fifteen minutes later. I was lying beneath the top sheet of the bed, having pulled the blankets down and opened a window to the tropical night air. The bathroom door swung open and the light behind her went out. Barbara was wearing a bath towel and I could see drops of water glinting in her hair as she crossed a narrow shaft of moonlight in the middle of the room. And as she crossed that band of light, at that very theatrical moment, she allowed her towel to drop to the floor.

"Hello," she whispered.

It was all I could do to keep from just crying out. It was not simply the harmonious beauty of the parts; it was the ease of her revealed body, her delighted acceptance of its perfection, her total lack of self-consciousness. She was just a happy naked girl.

"This is an awfully big bed, isn't it?" she said, then took one step backward and jumped, landing next to me, face-to-face.

"Good evening," I said, "and welcome to the Hotel Nacional." She put her hand over my mouth and giggled. When she removed her hand, she kissed me on the lips very lightly. I kissed her nose, her eyes, inhaled the clean, dense fragrance of her hair.

"You taste good," she whispered, and then she began to kiss my neck and work her way south and when she got halfway down my body she stopped to survey my throbbing parts with the enthralled gravity of a botanist in a garden. She began to kiss and lick and nibble in earnest. I heard a moan and it was me and then I heard another moan and it was her; when I looked down, she had me in her mouth and was touching herself and her eyes were closed and her head was moving ever so slowly and then my eyes were closed and I was lost in an overrun tropical garden of damp sensations.

I remained that way until the door to the room went flying off its hinges. I looked up but I never saw a thing, just two dark shapes and then the back of my head exploded. And then I remember nothing.

NINE

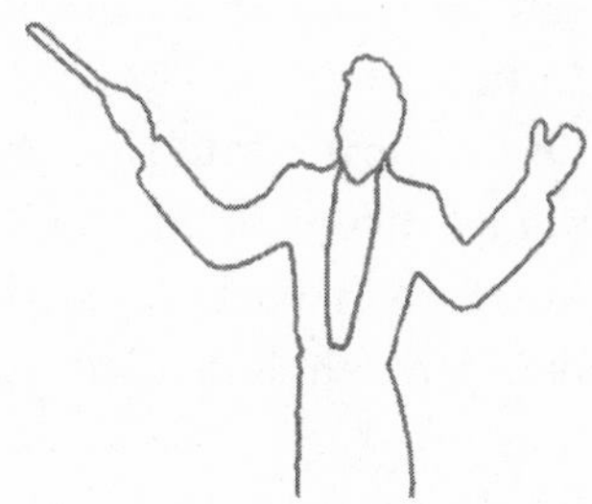

I thought I heard music, then I didn't, and it was dark again, and I spiraled away. Time passed, I'll never know how much, and then I heard it again, that music, except it was sort of woozy and distorted, like someone humming off-key. Though my lids were still shut, I entered a new state of consciousness and I thought I made out shapes somewhere around me; my head was pounding and I felt a rocking motion beneath my body. The humming got more insistent; it sounded almost like groaning, but it had rhythm and force. I tried opening my eyes, but the light flooding my retina made my insides turn like a frightened animal, so I shut my eyes once again. The rocking continued, and so did the humming. Two possibilities presented themselves: I had either been tied to a rocking horse, or I was on a boat. The humming I couldn't figure.

More time crept by. I endeavored to sit up and was successful on the second try; I pulled myself upright, moving ever so slowly, my eyes still shut. Every bone in my manly body ached and cracked. Once again I tried to open my eyes and this time I managed to keep them open, at least for a couple of seconds. Yes, I was on a boat, in a small cabin on a top deck, lying on some sort of daybed; through a window I could see the ocean and a cloudy day at sea. Thank God for the clouds; full sunshine would have blown my circuits entirely. I turned and found the source of the insistent humming. Across the cabin from me, perched on a sofa and singing along to a musical score, was Arturo Toscanini.

The score Toscanini gripped in his small, smooth hands had WAGNER written across the top and DIE MEISTERSINGER below in Gothic lettering. The Maestro held the score very close to his face, like a mirror, studying the notes with eyes set so deep they were almost like a blind man's eyes. And as he examined the score, he hummed in a hoarse, nearly tuneless voice—"Dah, dah, dah-dah, dah-dah-dah-dahhhhh." The notes ascended and descended, music of genius croaked in the accents of a fish peddler. I leaned forward, my head beginning to clear, and the bed creaked loudly. The Maestro stopped his singing and gazed curiously across the room, putting the score down on the sofa beside him.

"Awake?" he said, looking at me with some curiosity. *"Alla fine."*

"Yes."

"Was a noisy sleep."

"I snored, did I?"

"Ma! For too long! I took a walk, for the air, and to escape your noise, *signore."*

"I apologize, Maestro."

He nodded, an amused smile on his lips. He really was a beauty, this Toscanini, with a baby's alabaster complexion and the white hair of a biblical prophet. His eyebrows were dark and his nose was slightly bent, but these slight irregularities only made his appearance all the more arresting. The Maestro didn't appear to be much taller than five-foot-three, but he radiated the power and authority of a head of state. When he looked at you he made eye contact, yet he seemed to be also looking through you, to some other place, and you got the feeling that you didn't really matter all that much, that he had much bigger fish to fry, that his real intimates and soulmates were Beethoven and Brahms and Verdi.

I tried to stand up, but got instantaneously light-headed and sat right back down. I was somewhat surprised that I hadn't been restrained, but then again, we were at sea, and whoever had smashed the back of my skull had probably calculated the odds of my jumping from the boat and swimming to Havana to be long indeed.

"Maestro, may I ask how long I have been here?"

Toscanini took a pocket watch from his black jacket. He was wearing a white shirt with a blue silk necktie, formal gray-striped pants, and a pair of black slippers that looked to have cost as much as my car. He looked spic and span, ready to mount a podium and start the music. I didn't know what he had been through over the past couple of months, but it obviously had not involved any rough treatment. The old man appeared serene and unscathed.

"You were here, *signore,* since dawn. They brought you out."

"Brought me out."

"*Sì.* On a little . . ." He looked for the word.

"A skiff? A little boat."

"*Sì.* You were lying on a little boat. I was up already, like every day, up when the sun is up. Five o'clock, six o'clock, I am up. I am outside and they are bring you in and you are lying there like a *pesce.*" He chuckled. "Like a fish."

"I don't doubt it. I had gotten a nice whack on the head and probably a few pharmaceuticals as well. So you were here already on the boat?"

Toscanini looked at me blankly, which was when the obvious fact penetrated my addled brain.

"You've been on the boat for a long while, am I right? For a couple of months."

"Yes. Was necessary, *sì*? But soon it is over. Today, *a la mossa, sì*? On the move!" He arose. "Time for a walk."

"The boat usually hasn't been moving?" I asked.

He made a circular gesture with his right hand.

"Around and around, like *carosello* . . ."

"Carousel?"

"*Sì.*" The old man leaned forward. "You? You are who?"

"Jack LeVine. I'm a private investigator from New York. Excuse me, Maestro, for not introducing myself earlier. I'm a little off my feed."

"You are detective?"

"Yes."

"Like Boston Blackie."

"Something like that."

He smiled. "*Molto bene.* Now it gets interesting." Toscanini arose and clapped his hands. "*Molto bene.* Time for a walk. Come, Detective, we take a walk!"

"I'm not sure if I can."

"Maestro is old man, not walk so fast. You come."

Toscanini walked to the door. I arose, and had a wobbly moment, put my palm flat against the wall.

"I don't know. . . ."

The old man clapped his hands again.

"You come. Is good for your head."

There was no turning this guy down. He had been a virtual dictator for his entire adult life; if you contradicted him, he didn't even hear it. Toscanini lingered in the doorway for a moment, stroked his mustache, then stepped outside and took a deep breath.

"Bella! Aria del mare!"

I made my way outside on legs of sand. It was a hot, gray morning, with a steady breeze coming out of the west at about ten or fifteen miles an hour. Or knots, whatever the hell they were. I couldn't grasp the concept no matter how often it was explained to me, which, in truth, wasn't all that often. "We don't need to know that," my father used to say, to explain his avoidance of any technical knowledge that didn't involve the manufacture of hats. Over the years I had come around to his point of view—I didn't need to know about knots. It was breezy, that was enough.

The vessel on whose top deck Toscanini and I were standing was a substantial and costly pleasure boat, about a hundred and twenty feet in length, freshly painted white with three decks and teak fittings everywhere. A nearby life preserver indicated that the name of the boat was *Four Aces* and that its registry was Key Biscayne.

Toscanini placed both his hands on the railing and looked out over the ocean. In profile, his head looked like it had been carved out of marble.

"*Bella,* eh, Detective?"

"*Bella,*" I replied.

"*Parle Italiano*?" he asked hopefully.

"Just enough to get through a menu," I told him. "How's your Yiddish?"

Maestro beamed. "Not bad. Is like *Germano,* yes? But more messy." He took a handkerchief from his pocket and delicately mopped his forehead. "Still they are after me, five years after war."

"Who, the Germans?"

"No. *Fascisti.*"

"The fascists are after you? Is that what you're saying?"

Toscanini looked at me like I was a bassoonist who had just played a wrong note.

"You are detective? Why you think I am on boat? For sightsee?"

My mind went slightly blank, as if I had fallen asleep for a half second. Whatever drugs they had slipped me had obviously retained a hefty residual kick. I haltingly attempted to process what the old man had just told me.

"I wasn't sure what you were doing out here, Maestro. . . . Staying clear of the fascists, is that it? Personal threats were made?"

Toscanini looked at me, then returned his gaze to the ocean.

"I refuse to play fascist anthem in *La Scala* for years; then, 1931, there is *fascisti* riot, screaming, try beat me to pieces, so I leave *Italia,* come to New York, tell the world I will not conduct in homeland until *fascisti* are gone. I stay to my word. Not until war is over and no Mussolini." He loudly smacked his right fist into the palm of his left hand. I looked around the deck—there was nobody else in sight, and for one lost and druggy moment I thought perhaps the old man and I had been cut adrift.

"So you received an actual threat?"

"Always threat—letter, *cartolina*. . . . Then in spring, big threat, *molto serio*. FBI come."

"The FBI got involved?" I took a deep breath and hoped to get some oxygen headed in the general direction of my brain.

"During tour. You hear about tour?"

"Yes. On the train across America. A great triumph."

The old man clapped his hands in great, almost childlike satisfaction. "Toscanini train! All over. Bravo everywhere! Do Beethoven *Eroica,* Schubert *Incompleto,* Brahms, Dvorak, Strauss. In South of America . . . Richmond is called . . . ?"

"Richmond, Virginia?"

"*Sì.* There we play 'Dixie' song, people are jumping from seats! Everywhere we go, sold out. People on streets looking for tickets, money in their fists! Everybody happy, even me." He allowed himself a small smile. "And, Signore Detective, I am not so happy all the time. Music is big suffering for me. I love too much."

"That's the way I've always felt about baseball."

The old man shook his head. "Baseball I no like. Is *morto,* boring. Wrestling I like." He raised his small hands and made a gripping, choking gesture. "This Rocca, is *Italiano*—he kill people!" He laughed happily. "Watch the television, is *miracolo.* Every night, wrestling, *pugliato*. . . ." He assumed a boxer's stance.

"Boxing."

"*Sì.* Marciano, eh?" Toscanini raised his right fist, his eyes suddenly ablaze, a wild, crooked grin on his face.

"He's a brute," I said.

"*Sì! Bruto! Un toro*—a bull! Then . . ." The Maestro sighed, his expression turned dour. "Then we go San Francisco, FBI come on train, say to me, 'Maestro, is danger from *fascisti.*' "

"Danger of kidnapping."

The Maestro shook his head. "No kidnap." He raised his right hand, cocked his thumb and index finger. "*Assassinio!*"

"The FBI came to you and said there was a plot to shoot you."

"*Sì.*"

"During a concert?"

"Shoot during concert?"

"Yes."

The Maestro shrugged. "During, before, after . . . *no conosco* . . . this they don't tell me."

"And you saw their badges, you were sure these guys were really FBI?"

"My son Walter brings them in, says, 'Papa, these are FBI, have to talk to you.' " Toscanini looked down at those fabulous slippers, then threw me a sideways glance. "Why you ask that, Detective? Who you think they are?"

"I have no idea. I'm just asking."

"Because you are good detective."

"That's right. So then what happened, they arranged for you to disappear?"

"They tell me when we get to this place, Sun Valley, yes? You hear of this?"

"Sure. Sun Valley, Idaho. Big skiing town."

"*Sì.* There, they say, they take me off this . . . *macchina.*"

"The chairlift."

"*Sì.* They will take me off *macchina,* then they will say Maestro is sick and since tour is almost over, they get someone else to finish last few concerts. I say get Cantelli or maybe Leinsdorf." I didn't know who the hell he was talking about, so I just nodded. Obviously, they hadn't informed the old man that they had cooked up a double. And the FBI? I was highly dubious that the Bureau could have been involved in what seemed, at least thus far, to be a remarkably heady and sophisticated operation. Most G-men I had met couldn't find their asses with a five-minute head start.

"So they told you that after Sun Valley, NBC would just move in a new conductor and announce that you had taken ill."

"*Sì.*" The old man turned and looked over my shoulder. "*Ecco!* My friend."

I turned around.

Walking toward us was none other than that man of multiple nomenclature, Giuseppe LaMarca.

"Who's this guy?" I innocently asked the Maestro.

"This," said Toscanini, "is my friend, Signore LaMarca."

"Using your real name," I called out to LaMarca. "That's a sign of respect, I take it."

LaMarca was wearing a lightweight tan suit and a Panama hat and looked to be passing himself off as a plantation owner. He grasped Toscanini's hand and kissed his ring finger.

"You know this man?" Toscanini asked LaMarca. "Signore Detective."

"I haven't had the pleasure." LaMarca's voice was thin and raspy. "Giuseppe LaMarca, but everybody calls me Joey."

"They call you a lot of things." I said to him. "I'm Jack LeVine."

"Yes." LaMarca nodded, leaned closer to Toscanini. "Maestro, I need to talk to Mr. LeVine here for a couple of minutes. Are you all right, or should I send someone up?"

"No, *grazie.* I take a little walk."

"You want me to send Walter up?"

"No Walter. Am fine." Toscanini smiled at me. "You feel better, Signore Detective?"

"Yes," I told him. "Thanks for asking. I have to say that it was a very great honor to meet you, sir."

Toscanini just nodded. There was no false modesty; he knew it was an honor to meet or even to be in the same room with him. The old man didn't bask in his glory, he just lived in it. Like the Mona Lisa, or Michelangelo's David, he was a work of art. He perspired, he breathed in and breathed out, but that was where his resemblance to mortal humankind ended.

Toscanini jammed his hands into the pockets of his jacket and took off for his stroll down the deck. I was left standing alone with LaMarca, or whatever the hell he was calling himself at this particular instant.

"Beautiful morning," he began. "Little cloudy, but I like the clouds sometimes. If the sun was out, we'd be boiling to death out here."

"You always dress like this, Joey? Or you just impressing the Maestro?"

"I gotta say, he's like a god to me, the old man. I don't give a rat's ass about music, but he's the real goods. Two minutes you talk to him, you'll follow him anywhere. Reminds me a little of Lucky in that regard, you know? That same type of dynamic personality."

"And you're out here protecting him from the forces of fascism, that's the story?"

LaMarca placed a short stout cigar in his mouth and lit it up, turning the stogie slowly and with great ceremony, the smoke billowing out to sea like a genie escaping from a bottle.

"Something like that," he finally said.

"The old man thinks the FBI is protecting him. He just told me that."

"He did?"

"He can't think *you're* with the FBI."

LaMarca chuckled, the laugh turning into a wheeze. "He don't ask who I am. I'm Italian—that's good enough. He knows I'm looking out for him."

"And his son Walter? He really thought that it was FBI agents who showed up at the hotel?"

"They did come, FBI agents. That was the truth."

"To tell the old man he was in danger from some fascist lunatics still holding a grudge from the war?"

"That's right."

"I don't believe it."

"You don't."

"No. And I don't think the FBI whacked me on the head and

doped me up and brought me out here, and I don't think they killed Fritz Stern, either, although I'm not saying it's impossible. God knows the FBI's done a lot worse."

LaMarca took the cigar from his mouth and studied it as if appraising an uncut diamond. "These go for two bucks a pop, can you believe it? But they're worth every fucking penny. Best thing about Cuba, far as I'm concerned, the cigars and the hookers, who are out of this world."

"I didn't have a chance to find out."

"Next time," LaMarca said amiably, as if discussing a favorite restaurant. "It's not just that they're gorgeous and hot and know every trick in the book, but they're *friendly.* They don't make you feel like they're doing you a favor. There's some heart to it."

"You want heart from a whore."

"I do. Absolutely. I always had a romantic streak, which makes me different from most other mugs. Although the Yid has one, too. A romantic side."

"Lansky?"

"Yeah." LaMarca looked at me with no expression at all. "He was really nuts about that fiddler's daughter. Talked about her all the time."

"She's quite the young woman."

"Certainly is. In every respect." He placed the priceless cigar back in his yap, looked back over that restless, roiling ocean. "Can't imagine the Yid would be all that happy about you boffing her."

"I didn't boff her, Joey. The festivities got broken up pretty early."

"Sorry to hear that."

"It was quite the coincidence, I must say—those apes breaking the door down at that particular moment in time. Educate me, Joey, because so much of this seems out of kilter—was this whole thing a setup? Did Lansky ask Barbara Stern to lead me along until he could smash my skull in? It doesn't really add up. He could have had me jumped the minute I walked into the Nacional. Why bring her into it?"

"Doesn't seem logical, does it, Jack?"

"Couldn't have been Barbara's idea, could it?" That hardly seemed possible, even to a garden-variety paranoid like me.

"That's hard to buy, Jack, but, tell you the truth, I can't say for sure." LaMarca shook his head, demonstrating heartfelt confusion. "I been out on this boat since Thursday night. Flew down right after Stern's funeral."

"How come you were there?"

"At the funeral? Meyer asked me to. He didn't feel he could make the trip."

"Because of the girl's family."

"Maybe. I didn't ask. He's not the type of individual who invites a lot of questions."

"I can imagine. How long have you worked for him?"

"I work for me, Jack."

"No you don't. You worked for Lucky, then you worked for Anastasia, and now it looks like you're with Meyer, unless you're just on loan from Anastasia. Or are you still with Lucky?"

LaMarca pulled a stray bit of tobacco from his tongue.

"You're making this very complicated, Jack."

"*I'm* making this complicated? As far as I can see, *none* of it makes a goddamn bit of sense. NBC flies me down here to find the old man. Fine, I come down. No sooner do I check in than Lansky invites me to share a couple of gallons of water with him. I do so, and after maybe ten minutes of chitchat, Barbara Stern waltzes in, and the next thing I know, Lansky is on his feet excusing himself and I'm off to dinner with possibly the most beautiful girl in the Western Hemisphere. We have a quiet, friendly, sober dinner and then I proceed, against all dictates of common sense, to crawl into bed with her. The party has barely begun when a grand piano falls on my head, followed by what I presume was enough morphine to keep Man O'War quiet for the weekend. When I come out of my stupor, I find myself I don't know how many miles at sea, headed I know not where, strolling the decks with Arturo Toscanini. Given that everyone was clearly lying in wait for me, why in the name of God was I brought down here in the first place? Why not let me just chase my tail in New York?"

"We have too much respect for you, Jack."

"That's a total crock of shit. You're trying to distract me, that's all this cockamamy trip is about. You want me out of New York and out of circulation. You snatched the old man and now you snatched me. I feel like a grade-A nitwit."

LaMarca puffed on his cigar. "Jack, think about it a little—we didn't fly you down here, did we?"

"NBC did, ostensibly."

"So there you are. There's your answer"

"You're saying that NBC brought me down here to get me out of the way?"

"I'm not saying anything, Jack. I'm just talking."

"You were sitting next to Sidney Aaron at the funeral. I gotta presume you two cooked this up."

"Too much presuming, Jack. I know Sidney from way back. Whenever he has a labor problem, he knows to give us a call."

"He told me he never met you before."

"That doesn't surprise me." LaMarca smiled. "I'm a nefarious character, right? Why should a guy like that admit he has knowledge of me? Those guys use us because they have to, Jack, not because they want to. I'm sure he's embarrassed he ever met me."

I was getting more befuddled by the second, and I didn't think it was the drugs.

"Listen," I told LaMarca. "If you, or you and NBC, or you and NBC and Lucky Luciano or the fascists and the FBI, or whoever is behind this fucking insanity—if one of you thought I was getting in the way in New York, why not just plug me like you plugged Fritz?"

"We didn't plug Fritz."

"Give me a break."

"Why should we? Nice gentleman like that, the father of Meyer's ex-girlfriend? Does that make any sense, that we would hit him? Think about it."

"I did think about it. So if not you, who? NBC?"

"That I wouldn't know. I doubt it."

"You do."

"Yeah."

"But they're involved in this snatch."

LaMarca's eyes narrowed. It didn't make him any better-looking.

"There's no snatch. I thought you understood that, Jack. We pulled the Maestro off the tour for his own protection. There's plenty of these Mussolini-lovers still running around and they hate the old man's guts. He's on this boat for his own best interests. I don't know why you can't see that, Jack. Instead of ranting and raving about NBC and saying me and Sidney Aaron bumped off this fiddler, why not consider the possibility that it was these fucking fascists who went after Stern and things got out of hand?"

"Joe, why the hell would the fascists kill Stern? He's looking for Toscanini, they're looking for Toscanini. There's no reason for them to bump him off."

"I agree, not unless things got out of hand. That's what I think happened."

"You do."

"Absolutely. These fascist bastards get wind—I don't know how but they do, probably they still got spies everywhere—they get wind that Stern suspects the old man is missing. They call him that night and set up a meet; they're looking to pick his brain. He goes down there to the West Side, suddenly finds out who he's dealing with, Nazi lovers, and of course, a Jewish fella like that, he panics. Maybe he tries to run, they plug him. They're animals, you know that, Jack. They'll plug anybody."

I stared at LaMarca. The story he was telling me was entirely plausible, but I didn't believe any of it.

"You're not buying it, I can tell," he said.

"I'm no genius, Joey, but I'm totally lost right now. I feel like I'm watching a ball game, except there's three teams on the field. It's like I don't even know what the rules are here, except I'm pretty sure nobody's been straight with me so far, with the probable exception of Toscanini, who thinks he's under the FBI's care. Let me ask you two questions. You can answer them or not."

"Go ahead, Jack. I got no reason to bullshit you."

"You probably have two dozen reasons to bullshit me. No matter. Question one: This bogus Toscanini, that's a major undertaking—train a guy to swing and sway like Sammy Kaye, the plastic surgery . . ."

"Took over a year."

"I would think at least that."

LaMarca nodded his head gravely.

"So the FBI telling the old man it's the fascists suddenly on his tail has to be a load of crap if you consider that this bogus Maestro's been in the works for over a year."

LaMarca permitted himself a small smile. "That's a good point, Jack. Except the fascists been after the old man since the late 1920s. Maybe certain individuals planned this other Toscanini long ago out of their love and respect for the old man."

"A backup Maestro?"

"Exactly."

"Guy in the bullpen, for times of crisis."

"Think about it, Jack: The old man's worth a bunch of money to a bunch of people, plus he's a political target practically his whole fuckin' life. Wouldn't it pay to have a double for emergencies?"

"This is science fiction, Joe. You're telling me that Lucky and Meyer had this ersatz Toscanini in the works for years?"

"What's ersatz?"

"A phony, a stand-in."

"I don't know about that, how many years. There was planning involved, leave it at that, Jack. What's your other question?"

"Question two is more mundane: Where are we going?"

"Now?"

"Now."

"We're on our way to Miami, Jack. Should get there by about four o'clock."

"And then?"

"Then we get in a couple of limos and drive to the airport."

"The airport. Great. I don't suppose we're all going back to New York, are we? 'Cause there's twelve grand in it for me if I bring the old man back alive."

LaMarca shook his head. "Wish I could say we were, Jack. But you be a good citizen with us and you could walk home with a lot more than twelve grand."

"I could."

"Definitely." The clouds were breaking up and, predictably, the temperature was beginning to soar. The back of my shirt was rapidly getting soaked. "You play straight with us, you could walk home with some very serious money." LaMarca blew a few smoke rings in the general direction of the equator. "You ever been to Las Vegas, Jack?"

"Never."

LaMarca squinted into the horizon. "Well, you're in for a real treat."

LaMarca patted me on the arm with his left hand, then tightened his grip and quickly brought his right arm around. I felt a stinging sensation in the area of my right biceps.

"Sorry, Jack," he said. "Got no choice." I saw him depress the plunger on the syringe he had stuck into my upper arm. "This'll just make the trip go smoother for everyone concerned."

TEN

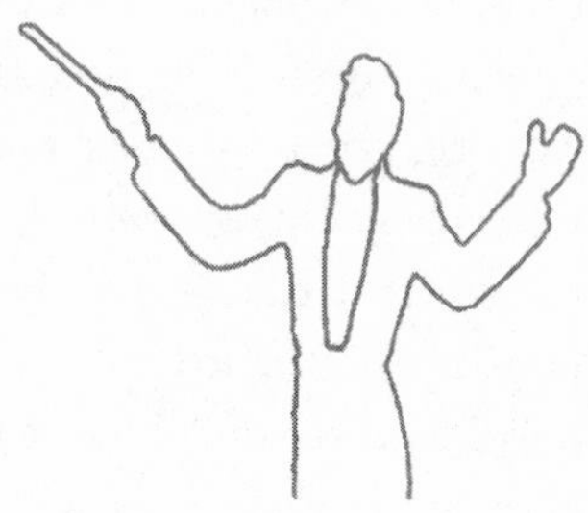

This time it was dark and as I arose into the beginnings of consciousness I felt myself perspiring like a guy in a *shvitz*. The pillow behind my head was drenched and sweat ran down my forehead and across my closed lids; it formed little streams on the back of my neck and dripped onto my shoulders. My eyes felt as though they'd been glued shut. When I tried to move my legs, I could feel water puddling behind the backs of my knees. Groggy and disoriented, I attempted to sit up and realized that this time I'd been restrained; my arms and legs were tied to a mattress or air cushion of some sort. I breathed as deeply as I could and concentrated on getting my bearings. The steady drone of airplane engines reminded me of my curious location, fifteen thousand feet in the air above the southern United States, flying toward a mysterious and synthetic city that I had only read about. The air currents were remarkably smooth and I had little sense of being airborne; if I hadn't been drugged and roped down like a calf, I might have enjoyed the trip.

It took several minutes—maybe five, maybe twenty, I was still totally muddled—before I could muster the strength to open my eyes. When I did, everything was out of focus, so I shut them again, as tightly as I could. My nerve endings were like so many downed power lines, sparking and then bursting into low spastic flames. Evolving shapes illuminated my brain, swirling kidney-shaped blobs in hues so vivid they made my stomach turn and forced even more sweat through my wide-open pores. I sighed, maybe too loudly—I had lost all awareness of my own volume—and then I sensed a cloth on my forehead. Someone was patting me down, cleaning me off. When I opened my eyes, I thought I saw Toscanini before me, but he was wearing green fatigues and an army hat. I shut my eyes, certain that I was hallucinating and not liking it one little bit. I felt the cloth on my neck; it was strangely comforting and made me feel happily infantile. I was ready for a warm bottle of milk and for a can of talcum powder to be sprinkled across my ample behind. After another deep breath, I forced my eyes open; again I saw Toscanini, still wearing his military costume.

"You had quite the snooze," the old man said, speaking with a pronounced Brooklyn accent.

"Excuse me?" I said. This was straight out of *Alice In Wonderland.* I had obviously been injected with enough high-octane opiates to scramble a hippo's consciousness.

"You were out like a light," said Toscanini. "We're almost in Vegas. Another half hour."

"Really," I mumbled. I lifted my head, looked around the small plane. I could see nobody else. "Where's everybody, Maestro? Where's Signore LaMarca?"

"Joey?"

"Yeah. Joey."

"He's in the other plane," Toscanini said.

"There's two planes?"

"That's correct."

I shut my eyes again. When I opened them, Toscanini was still in the green fatigues and army hat. No matter how many times I opened and closed my orbs, this bizarre fact remained the same. Maybe I had just snapped, or maybe . . . It finally dawned on me.

"You're the other one," I said. "Jesus Christ, how dumb can a guy be? You're the double."

What I could only presume was the ersatz Toscanini leaned back in his chair. He was seated directly across the aisle and I realized that I was lying not on a mattress or cushion, but on an airplane seat that had been forced all the way back, so that I was virtually prone. Leather straps bound my arms to the rests and my legs were strapped tightly to the seat.

"Double?" Toscanini said with a smile. *"Che fantasia!"*

"Too late to *parle Italiano,* Charlie; I already met the genuine article," I told him, then began coughing. And coughing. My saliva tasted like lighter fluid. The faux-Toscanini thoughtfully produced a spittoon, which I immediately utilized.

"Jesus," I muttered. "What did they give me?"

"Drug cocktail. A highball."

"I can't stop sweating."

"Wait till you get to Vegas, you want to know from sweating. Hits about a hundred ten, hundred fifteen at midday. But it's a dry heat, that's what the locals like to say. Hundred and ten and dry. You leave a wet bathing suit outside for over an hour, you can fuckin' break it in two."

"I assume you've been there."

"Lots of times. Tremendous place."

"Really. Never read about it in the papers. Toscanini in Vegas. Must've been a sensation."

"Papers don't print everything." He smiled shamelessly and took off his cap. Beneath, he had the same pink dome as the old man.

"They did some job on you, unbelievable," I told him. "What was it, some clinic up in the Swiss Alps? Or was it in Sweden, some joint hidden away in the fjords? Blond physical therapists catering to your every need?"

"I don't know what you're referring to," he said, and put the cap back on.

I closed my eyes again. My head was slowly beginning to clear.

"Why play this half-assed game?" I said, my eyes shut as if speaking to a silent psychiatrist. "Just say who you are. Who am I going to tell, ten thousand feet up in the air and tied down like a magician's stooge?"

"As far as you're concerned, I'm Toscanini, okay? That's all you need to know."

I opened my eyes. The man in the army fatigues smiled.

"Everything's going to be fine. Just keep the questions to a minimum." With that he arose and walked to the front of the plane. I lay back and stared out the window at the night landscape. There was nearly a full moon out, casting a spectral light across the vast cratered desert. A lone highway unspooled below, looking largely unoccupied; as I gazed out the oval pane of glass I observed a car, then a truck, slowly moving west. That was it. There was no other sign of what we like to call civilization. I could have just as well been flying over Saturn.

As I studied this moonlit void with a child's fascination, I felt a tap on my knee. When I turned around, Lansky was leaning against a seat across the aisle.

"Enjoying the view?" he asked.

"Not in the slightest," I told him. "Why the hell do you keep drugging me? Is this some goddamn medical experiment?"

Lansky nodded. "We're studying the effects of certain pharmaceuticals on circumcised detectives. Sending the results up to Yeshiva." He shook his head. "Sorry, Jack. I didn't think it was really necessary. But others disagreed."

" 'Others'? Come on, Meyer, let's stop playing footsie. You're calling the shots here; it sure isn't LaMarca or this department-store Santa you got pretending to be Toscanini."

"Me?" Lansky shook his head in exaggerated innocence. "I never give the orders. That's why I've survived this long."

"Please . . ."

"I'm serious, Jack. Don't overestimate me." Lansky sat down in the seat the surrogate Maestro had just vacated. "People always try to give me credit, like I'm some fucking mastermind arch-criminal. I don't need that kind of credit." He smiled. "It's bad for the health."

I just sighed and shifted in my seat. Lansky leaned over and untied my legs.

"We didn't want you to hurt yourself while you were knocked out."

"You could have avoided the trouble by not knocking me out."

"Well, that's a moot point, isn't it? Fact is"—and now he undid my arms with sure and quick hands—"it probably was overcautious, but it's over and done with and that'll be the last time."

"Until the next time."

Lansky rubbed his substantial nose and smiled. "Yeah."

"Where's LaMarca?"

"On the other plane."

"With the old man?"

Lansky nodded. "With the old man and the old man's nurse."

"Nurse?"

"Just in case. He's eighty-three, Jack." Lansky smiled. "Nurse is about thirty-five and the old man handpicked her. From what I hear about him, he's probably slipping it to her. Horny old guinea, loves the ladies. Lot of stories about him and they're probably all true. He's still got the pizzazz, am I right?"

"Certainly does. Magnetic old bastard."

"Yeah." Lansky stared evenly at me. His lips pursed, as if he were sucking on a sourball. "Speaking of ladies, I understand that you and Barbara started to develop something of a relationship."

I couldn't think of anything very cogent to say, so I stayed mum.

"Who's gonna fault you, Jack?" Lansky sat back down. "You're a single man, she's one of the great pieces of ass of the twentieth century. You're only human. Smoke?" He offered me a Lucky and I took it. "I'm sure you're aware of the fact that we were together at one time, but that's strictly in the past. I'm happily married now, which I'm sure you're very glad to hear."

"I'm delighted, Meyer."

"I appreciate the sentiment." He lit both our cigarettes. "Barbara only came back to me because she was in need of assistance."

"Which is why I got poleaxed thirty seconds after I got into bed with her? What was the point of that?"

"She had nothing to do with it."

"She didn't?"

"No." Lansky shook his head. "Jesus, you're more paranoid than I am, and that ain't easy."

"Is she on her way to Vegas?"

The little hoodlum shook his head. "Sorry, pal. I told her she oughta be with her mother and baby sister right now. She would have liked to come, I think. She's torn, you know—her devotion to her family, knowing how much they need her on the one hand, her desire to do justice for her father and be with you on the other."

"She said that?" I wasn't too much of a sap. Even the hint of a nice word from Barbara Stern and I rolled over on my back like an Airedale.

"She likes you. God knows why. Obviously, she's got a thing for old men."

I felt a chill and shivered.

"Freezing in here."

"It's the drugs, Jack; air-conditioning's barely working in this fucking crate." He rubbed his eyes, looking weary. "Anyhow, she hopes to come out in a few days."

"A few days? How long are we going to be out there?"

Lansky now took his jacket off and folded it over the seat.

"That's a good question. Depends on how long it takes to bring this to a head."

"You mean the payoff."

"Sure," Lansky said vaguely. I was still so hammered I didn't trust myself to gauge mood and meaning. I just fumbled my way forward.

"You mean the three million," I said.

Lansky scratched his nose. "Jack, this is a whole lot bigger than three million. You're a smart guy, you can understand this—I'm telling you, this is the dawn of a new fucking civilization."

"In Vegas?"

"In Vegas. We're talking about something that's gonna make history—hotel history, entertainment history, economic history. We're talking about amounts of money that's gonna make Monte Carlo and Havana look like crap games in Harlem." He smiled as broadly as a survivor of Lower East Side tenement life ever could. "This Toscanini, he's gonna be the foundation of the greatest thing that ever happened to business in this country. Mark my words, Jack, you're in for an eye-opener."

"I am?" I was still feeling pretty woozy. "How's that?"

Lansky measured me with his eyes, as if calculating how much of the truth he would share before he ran out of it, like a stretch of road, after which he would continue alone and on foot.

"He's gonna lead an orchestra in Vegas, Jack. Just imagine."

I closed my eyes and tried unsuccessfully to imagine such a thing, then opened them again. "You've gotta be shitting me."

Lansky slowly shook his head.

"Arturo Toscanini in Las Vegas. At the biggest hotel ever constructed. Welcome to the second half of the twentieth century, Jack. It's gonna be money like no one ever dreamed of before, and all clean as a whistle." He smiled, but not with his eyes, and I knew at that instant that he had ordered Fritz Stern's death. It was clear that the snatch of Toscanini was only the tip of the proverbial *Titantic*-crushing iceberg and that the little fiddler's curiosity had been an enormous threat.

"Can you comprehend what this means?" Lansky asked.

"The beginning of the legitimization of your businesses. That's why the old man is so important."

"There's nobody in the world more legit than him. Nobody. Maybe Einstein, but Einstein can't play a casino." Lansky smiled. "Not yet, at least."

"So Vegas becomes a cultural center?"

"An entertainment center. One day it could be the entertainment center of the whole goddamn country. The old man comes, then the biggest names in show business come. They attract the customers. The customers have a wonderful time in the most beautiful hotels ever built on the face of the earth and they're happy to lose their money. They're entertained. They're dazzled. They leave happy and they mainly leave broke."

"So Maestro's a front man. Nice way for him to go out. From Carnegie Hall to this."

"He's more than a front man, Jack. Don't belittle what we're doing here. Toscanini spreads culture across the whole country. It's not just confined to rich society broads in New York or old-money German Jews. He beings it out West, to where ordinary people can hear him."

"Hear his double, you mean. He's not going to conduct some cockamamy orchestra in Vegas."

"Fuck do those yokels know? And in the end, does it make a difference which one they heard? I don't think so, long as they leave happy." Lansky tapped my arm and arose. "We'll talk more after we land." I felt yet another wave of fatigue about to engulf me.

"They gave you too much dope," I heard Lansky said. "They wouldn't listen to me," and then I was asleep again.

I was awakened about twenty minutes after we landed, or at least that's what they told me later. The ersatz Toscanini fed me a cup of double-strength coffee, which enabled me to at least disembark the plane unaided, although I descended the small portable stairway in a most gingerly and tentative fashion. It was a windy night in Vegas and the air was blast-furnace hot. When I looked around the airport, it appeared to be a small and somewhat jerrybuilt affair; in the distance, I could make out a blaze of light, which must have been the casinos. There didn't appear to be any other signs of life in the surrounding area and I felt like I had landed on a distant and much-overheated planet.

A cream-colored Cadillac was parked on the tarmac. A uniformed driver with shoulders no wider than a subway car stood by an open back door, his arm extended to guide me. He stared at me with an odd mixture of deference and disdain, like I was some sort of VIP drug addict. I looked over my shoulder and saw Toscanini's double bouncing down the stairs behind me, mutely chewing gum. He was wearing dark glasses and a *Hollywood Stars* baseball cap and he slipped very quickly into the front seat of the car.

"Where's Lansky?" I asked the driver.

"I don't know nothing about any Lansky," he answered, then hooked his arm under mine, steered me into the backseat, and slammed the door.

The red plush interior of the Caddy was air-conditioned sufficiently to transport an ice sculpture. My teeth were chattering as the driver pulled out and exited the airport through a steel gate trimmed with barbed wire. This airport had all the charm of the death house at Sing Sing.

I leaned back and took a deep breath; I was starting to feel slightly less muddled. The ersatz Toscanini sat quietly in the front seat, stirring only to lean over and switch on the radio; he fiddled with the dial until he located Artie Shaw bopping from the rooftop of some nameless hotel in Hollywood.

"No Mozart tonight, Maestro?" I asked him.

The faux-Toscanini just grunted and hummed along with the music. The driver said very little, except to bemoan his poor state of health every time he blew his nose, which was frequently.

"I'm dyin' here," he grunted.

"It's the air-conditioning," I told him.

"Tell me about it."

"Why don't you turn it down?" I told him. "You could store a side of beef in here."

"Nix. This fancy piece-of-shit car, it's all or nothing." He sneezed again, louder.

"Can't shake it," he said to the ersatz Toscanini. "Two weeks this fucking cold." The Maestro's double just shook his head and tapped his finger on the dashboard in time to Artie Shaw.

I looked out the window and saw a sign indicating that we were passing the site of the future Las Vegas Racetrack. From the looks of it, nothing had been accomplished at the site except for a sizable accumulation of Nevada trash. Then we passed a series of cupid-and-heart-adorned wedding chapels with names like Wee Kirk in the Heather, Gretna Green, and Chapel de Amour. The lights above the chapels glowed in fluorescent greens and pinks; the buildings looked to have been designed by thirteen-year-old girls. My head continued to clear, which was both the good and the bad news. I'm a city boy, but Las Vegas didn't look so much like a city as a kind of candy-colored amusement park for dipsos and fly-by-nighters.

"We're getting close to what we call the 'Strip,'" the driver announced. "That's where the major hotels are located." We passed some dingy motels and a handful of near-empty restaurants and pizza joints. This looked like a great town to commit suicide in, except you might not realize you were dead.

"That where we're headed?" I asked. "The 'Strip'?"

"Sure is, chief," he replied.

"And what about Toscanini here?"

"Why don't you ask him?"

"He seems kind of quiet tonight." I waited a beat, then asked him directly. "What about it, Maestro—you headed for the Strip?"

The faux-Toscanini just chewed his gum and nodded.

"Any idea where the real Maestro is staying?" I asked him.

Not surprisingly, there was no reply. The driver sneezed yet again, rubbed his wet nose with the back of his hand. "Fuck me," he muttered. The car seemed colder than ever.

Suddenly the Caddy slowed; we took a sharp right and passed a festive and high-class establishment called El Rancho Vegas. It looked to be a sprawling one-story hotel spread around a large illuminated swimming pool; EL RANCHO VEGAS was spelled out in orange and green lights that blinked in rapid sequence, and a spotlit sign indicated that Tito Guizar was the star attraction in the nightclub.

We rolled on, now approaching yet another large hotel-casino, the

Thunderbird by name. According to a massive sign in front of the hotel, Mel Torme and Betty and Jane Kean were starring in the Royal Stardust Room. As we neared the Thunderbird, the cream-colored Caddy abruptly braked, then pulled directly into the parking lot.

"This is where I'm staying?" I asked.

"Stay put," the driver said.

The ersatz Toscanini pulled his cap low over his head and got out of the car without even saying good-bye. A gray truck bearing no identifying marks of any kind was idling in the Thunderbird lot. I watched as the Maestro's surrogate raced across the lot and pulled himself up and into the truck, which took off the instant he slammed the door shut. The truck accelerated and doubled back onto the highway and out of sight, a ghost vehicle in the night.

"Should I stay back here?" I asked the driver.

"Why not?" he replied. "We're almost there."

"There" was the Flamingo, the extravagant resort that had become Bugsy Siegel's last will and testament to the world. It was located, appropriately enough, on Flamingo Road, just off Las Vegas Boulevard, and the glowing red neon sign out front indicated that Vaughn Monroe himself, "Star of the Camel Caravan," was currently appearing with his orchestra. As we drove through the main entrance to the hotel's parking lot, I took off my necktie. The driver checked his rearview mirror.

"Thought you were freezing."

"Started sweating again," I told him. "They doped me up six ways from Tuesday. My whole system's haywire."

The driver chuckled and as he did I leaned over and wrapped my necktie around his throat. He made a few croaking noises and reflexively lifted his hands from the steering wheel. The Cadillac swerved onto a strip of gravel adjacent to the parking lot. As the driver pawed at his neck, I pulled harder on the tie, then wrapped it tightly around my right hand, which allowed me to lean across the front seat and shut off the ignition. The car came to a shuddering stop and so did the driver. He toppled over to one side and his jacket opened, revealing a shoulder holster and the cutest little .44 tucked inside it. I grabbed for the .44. The driver opened his eyes and pawed at the gun, but I pulled it out and smashed him on the back of the head in one fluid and elegant motion.

This time he was out for keeps.

I got out of the Caddy and opened the front door. The heat of nighttime air outside the Flamingo was absolutely volcanic; the temperature had to be at least ninety, stoked even hotter by a desert wind that blew grit and dust straight into my eyes. Cups, handbills, and sheets of newspaper swirled wildly around the parking lot. Breathing heavily, I leaned the driver carefully across the front seat, then opened the glove compartment and discovered yet another gun, this one a .38, and a half-empty fifth of Ballantine scotch. I pocketed the .38, then opened the scotch and poured a capful over the driver's clothes. Anybody spotting him would only have to take a passing whiff to guess that he was loaded and, thus ignore the growing, reddening lump on the back of his head.

I returned the booze to the glove compartment, slammed the car door, and began walking toward the main entrance of the hotel. I walked as quickly as my delicate condition would allow, scanning the crowd for unfriendly faces, but saw nobody who looked even remotely familiar. It was a motley throng that stormed the barricades of the Flamingo this late September night, and it was easy to see why Lansky was so pumped up about Las Vegas—this was Mecca for suckers. Chumps of every stripe and persuasion were streaming toward the Flamingo's glass doors with the anticipation and excitement of kids heading toward a circus tent: servicemen in uniform, cowpokes in ten-gallon hats, Ohioans in short sleeves, and Los Angelenos in sunglasses and tight pants. There were fancy and unfancy women of every description. As the mob got closer to the doors and the first icy zephyrs of the casino's arctic air-conditioning blew outward, some of the suckers actually began to run, the way I did as a kid when I would first lay eyes on the outfield grass of Yankee Stadium from the steps of the elevated train platform. The Flamingo was nothing if not a child's dream of gaudy and imminent riches.

As I entered the lobby along with the rest of the surging multitudes, I was stunned by a tidal wave of color and noise: the tutti-frutti hues of the slot machines and roulette tables, the hoarse shouts of the crap players, the relentless metallic chinging of the slots. I had never seen a casino this large or this frenzied; the California gold rush of 1848 had nothing on the human stampede inside the Flamingo. I stood and watched as the suckers darted past me like schools of fish, and suddenly realized, in a moment of startling and air-conditioned clarity, that for the first time in forty-eight hours I was a free man.

The trick would be to remain that way. I figured I had a limited amount of time before Lansky and LaMarca recognized that something had gone awry, and in that time I would have to make a radical change in my appearance. To that end I waylaid an elderly bellhop.

"There a barbershop in this dump?" I asked him.

The hop stared at my gleaming head.

"I'm not asking for an editorial opinion," I told him. "A barbershop, yes or no?"

"Downstairs," he said. "Concourse A."

I took an escalator down to Concourse A, a brightly lit corridor dizzyingly carpeted with pink flamingos on a black background. The concourse was the hotel's shopping area; it featured clothing and jewelry stores aimed at the visiting chumps, a souvenir and art shop overflowing with "authentic" western and Indian artifacts, and Angelo's Men's Hair Styling. Angelo's was an elegant little establishment, with blinds on the door and a curtained window festooned with dozens of signed photographs of the show business luminaries who had honored the shop with their presence and shorn hair. A cardboard clock hanging on the door indicated that the place stayed open for business until eleven o'clock at night. I checked my watch—it was a quarter past ten.

When I opened the door to Angelo's, a little bell tinkled melodiously, and despite the lateness of the hour, three barbers smiled at me like I was a long-lost relative.

"Good evening," said the barber closest to the door. This had to be Angelo—with his thinning black hair and Sacco and Vanzetti mustache, he could have posed for a mural depicting Italian immigration.

"You're Angelo?"

"I am Angelo," he said in lightly accented English, then smiled and gestured toward a row of unoccupied leather chairs arrayed against the wall. The other two barbers—one a gray-haired gentleman with rimless steel spectacles, the other young and deeply tanned, were giving haircuts. Angelo was administering a shave to a nearly prone customer in the first chair whose face was covered with a luxurious snowfall of foam.

"You want a trim or shave?" he asked.

"I want to know if you sell hairpieces," I told him. "Like a temporary thing, but of decent quality. I don't want to look like I'm wearing a coonskin hat."

"Sure. Have a seat. Frankie, he's gonna help you; he almost done." Angelo waved his razor in the direction of the tanned barber, who nodded at me and indicated with five upraised fingers how much time he had left with his mute, crew-cutted customer.

I took a seat and picked up a copy of *Look* magazine. General MacArthur was on the cover, staring majestically and myopically into the future with the look of a guy who has spent most of his life posing for photographs.

"How was the first show, Mr. Monroe?" I heard Angelo say.

"Beautiful," rumbled a basso voice from beneath the shaving cream. It was Vaughn Monroe, in the flesh, getting a shave between shows. "Except I find out two guys in the band and one of the Moonmaids got the clap."

"No!"

"Can you believe it?" Monroe continued in those richly upholstered tones. "I warned everybody before we got here, I said this is a town that plays hard. . . ."

"Sure," Angelo cooed.

"But you gotta watch who you play with, guys and gals, and make sure you wear a little raincoat, *capisce*? So what happens? Two of my horn players start banging chorus girls bareback and one of the Moonmaids, Cissy, thinks she got a dose from that pig Jackie Lane."

"The comedian?"

"Can you believe it? Her boffing that fat slob?"

" 'Atsa terrible, Mr. Monroe."

"It gets worse. Eddie, he plays tenor, he comes and tells me he can't do the midnight show, 'cause he's gotta go to the doc. Every time he takes a leak he says it feels like he's pissing lava."

"Oh my God . . . lava. Sonofabitch." Angelo clucked and started shaving the crooner's prominent chin.

"Hey, I can play the sax," I heard myself say.

Monroe tilted his head. Angelo abruptly stopped shaving, to avoid slicing the singer's chin in half.

"Who's that?"

"Buddy Barrow," I told him.

"Barrow?"

"Barrow as in Berkowitz."

"You're a sax player? For real?"

"Well, I'm better than no sax player, let's say that." It was the truth; I had played the tenor sax in high school. Once a month, I played scales. "Just don't give me any solos."

"You have the clap?" Monroe asked.

"Not yet," I told him, "but I just got here."

The velvet-voiced singer roared with laughter, and the barbers and other customers joined in. It was a regular laugh riot in this place.

"All I need is a room here, Mr. Monroe. Like I said, I just got into Vegas. Need to change, get organized. . . ."

"My road manager will take care of it. And call me Vaughn." The crooner settled back in his chair and Angelo resumed work on his much-adored kisser. "Good thing for me I came in for a shave, boss."

"You betcha," Angelo said, as cheery and uncomplicated as a character in a Sunday comic strip.

Fifteen minutes later I was staring at the mirror as Frankie, the young barber, rotated a curly brown hairpiece till it sort of fit on the top of my head.

"What do you think?" Frankie asked.

I thought I closely resembled a springer spaniel, but the overall effect wasn't quite as monstrous as I had anticipated. And the very good news was that I was nearly unrecognizable: I hadn't had a full head of hair since I was nineteen, and had been truly, legally bald since I'd turned thirty. I couldn't say the rug was an improvement, but it did the job for which it was designed: concealment.

"Pretty good," I told him. "Could you take a bit off the sides? Make it look a little less toup-y."

"Sure. This is just for sizing."

He took a tape measure and made the appropriate marks, then lifted the rug off my head and put it on a white dummy head and made the minutest of snips. Monroe arose from his chair, as clean-shaven as a newborn. He had a very large head and broad shoulders; from a distance he looked like the actor Lee J. Cobb, but when he got closer he looked like a bandleader, all white teeth and shiny surfaces.

"How much longer, Frankie?" he asked my barber.

"Fifteen minutes."

"When you're done, Buddy, you go to the desk and check in, then get to the club by eleven-fifteen." Monroe looked me over. "Where are your clothes?"

"In a locker," I lied.

"Great," he said. "Thanks for bailing me out, Buddy. Bad news is I can only give you twenty-five bucks for the show."

"I've worked for less," I told him.

* * *

Fifteen minutes later, I hit the shops and purchased a cheap valise, as well as socks, underwear, a couple of white shirts, two pairs of slacks, and two blazers—one blue, one burgundy. I told the shopkeepers that my name was Buddy Barrow, that I was a novice member of the Monroe orchestra, and that I wanted to charge the purchases to my room, a necessary strategy since I was walking around with less than sixty dollars in cash. The God of the Hebrews was on my side: A call to the front desk ascertained that I had indeed been registered to room 207, but had yet to check in. The purchases were cleared without further inquiry. I was genuinely starting to like this town—try and pull a stunt like this in a Manhattan hotel and the house dick would drag you through the lobby by your nose hairs.

With my brand-new valise filled with brand-new clothing, the newly coifed LeVine followed a diminutive but muscular bellhop across the still-riotous lobby toward the first bank of elevators. A tag on the hop's white-braided uniform identified him as HAPPY. He looked to be no more than twenty-three years of age.

"That's quite a moniker," I said to him as we waited for the elevator.

He stared blankly. "What?"

"Happy."

"Oh yeah," he brightened. "My real name is Ronnie. But I thought I would get farther in Vegas if I identified myself as Happy. The guests get a kick out it. They say, 'How come you're happy when I'm feeling so bad?'—stuff like that."

"A lot of snappy patter."

"That's right, sir."

"Where you from originally?" I asked, Mister Congeniality.

"Canton, Ohio. But this place is the beans."

"You think so?"

"I know so. It's whatever you want however you want whenever you want." The elevator arrived and a half dozen giddy Americans emerged, roaring drunk and eager to lose their life savings. "If you need any assistance in that area"—he gestured for me to get in the elevator—"don't hesitate to ask for Happy."

"Are you by any chance referring to the possibility of good-natured female companionship?" I asked him.

"Yes sir, I am." The doors closed and Happy pressed a large white button for the second floor. "Just call the bell desk and ask for Happy."

"And get lucky."

He smiled. "No luck involved, sir." The elevator started with an unsettling jerk. "And the girls are the best—beautiful and stacked and clean as a whistle. Have to be, the kind of clientele we get."

"You guys draw plenty of celebrities, I would guess?"

"Always, sir."

"I hear that Lansky stays here sometimes."

Happy's face turned into a slab of marble.

"Don't know any Lansky, sir." He turned to the front and that was pretty much the end of our conversation.

Room 207 was a nice-sized double with a shower and a tub and real bath-sized soap in the bathroom. I handed Happy a buck and tried to win myself back into his good graces by telling him I'd let him know if my hormones started acting up.

"Most gorgeous girls in the world, sir," he said, warming up to me once again. "Any age, any shape, any color."

"I believe you, kid."

Happy winked at me, I swear to God, then he left the room and I sat down on the bed and started wondering how the hell I was going to get out of Vegas alive. I started by taking the .38 I had lifted from the Caddy driver and placing it just behind the Gideon Bible in the top drawer of the night table. It was a start, but I had the feeling it wouldn't be nearly enough.

ELEVEN

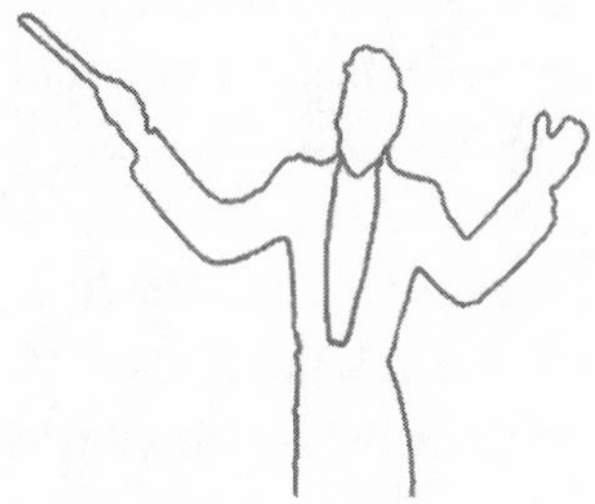

I changed in a large dressing room backstage at the Flamingo's nightclub. Monroe's band played in white shirts with black pants and red cummerbunds and there was a lot of comic byplay as I got into my outfit, particularly when the group found out I was filling in for Eddie Jonas, the clap-afflicted tenor sax man.

"I know who he got it from," said a long-faced bass player. "She was just a little heavier than Kate Smith." The room rocked with the musicians' laughter.

"He's hopeless," said a trombonist. "This is like the third time in the past two years. Plus he's got a wife and two kids in Jersey."

"Not for long," I told them, and there was more hilarity in the room—slapped thighs, wiped eyes. Musicians weren't all that different from private dicks: They maintained a naturally suspicious view of mankind, and, deep down, they were all patsies.

The midnight show began promptly at five past the hour. The opening act was Les Charlivels, an allegedly French dance troupe, made up of three painfully thin, rough-looking dames and four guys who looked about as French as the Pittsburgh Pirates. I peered out from behind the curtain and checked out the room—it looked to be pretty well filled, with only a few unoccupied tables near the back. A quick look around the room revealed no recognizable kissers, and that bothered me more than if I had spotted someone. I wasn't comfortable with my ignorance of Lansky's and LaMarca's whereabouts, because I knew that once they found their driver knocked ga-ga in the front seat of the cream-colored Caddy, they were going to get very busy very fast. As long as I was on stage, I was safe. Once I got off, I was going to be the proverbial sitting duck. A sitting duck with a twenty-dollar toupee.

I hustled back to the dressing room and studied the tenor sax charts for the midnight show. Nothing looked especially complicated. Ten minutes before show time, Monroe came into the room and threw his arm around me.

"I really appreciate this," he said in that luscious baritone. Listening to him was like slipping into a hot bath.

"Hey, it's my pleasure, Vaughn . . . and I can always use a job, however brief."

"Who've you played with, Charlie?" he asked.

"A whole shitload of hotel bands in the Catskills," I told him. "Lew Brown, for one."

"How is Lew?" Monroe asked.

"The usual," I said.

Monroe chuckled. "Still cranky as hell?"

"Maybe more so." I was shameless. Once I started lying, it was like running red lights—go through one, might as well go through them all.

"Who else?" the singer continued. He wasn't letting me off the hook so easy.

"Some other smaller bands," I vamped. "Sy Glotzer, Irv Tapp . . . house bands in the mountains."

"Don't know them." He looked into my eyes for a scary moment. "But I'm sure you'll be fine. Any screwups, the boys'll cover for you." He started picking through the charts. "We'll start with 'Let It Snow.' "

"Sure." I nodded.

"Then go to 'Ballerina.' I like to start with the *very* familiar. Particularly with these yokels. Then we'll do 'Trolley Song,' 'Tallahassee,' and 'Haunted Heart.' "

"Great," I mumbled, and jotted the titles down on a slip of paper.

"Then I just bullshit for a couple of minutes, tell some lousy jokes, kiss the audience's butt, tell them they're the greatest crowd I've ever played for." Monroe smiled. "Actually, the audiences here are pretty damn good. Love almost everything; I think half of them never saw a live band before."

"Lot of shitkickers out there," I said.

"Mucho shitkickers, but hey, that's not their fault. Gotta play like you're playing for the king of England." I liked this guy; he had very little pretension to him, show biz or otherwise, and after the collection of assassins and con artists I had run with for the past week, he seemed as honest and pure as Gary Cooper in a mountain stream yammering about the Spanish Civil War.

"Then I finally stop my spiel," Monroe continued, "and we do "Racing with the Moon,' and 'Red Roses for a Blue Lady.' I introduce the Moonbeams individually, pretend to look down their dresses; that kills a couple of minutes. Then we finish with 'Riders in the Sky' and 'Mule Train.' Then I come back and do 'Ballerina.' "

"Again?"

"Again. And they go apeshit. This is the Wild West, Charlie. It's all news to them." He clapped me on the shoulder. "Thanks again." He turned and walked out of the room, as square-shouldered and upright as a general. I was ready to marry the guy.

The show went without a hitch, and it was just as the crooner had predicted. When he did the encore on 'Ballerina,' the yokels were jumping out of their chairs with delight and a couple of fortyish women rushed the stage. I played my charts and only got lost once, during a key change on "Haunted Heart." Otherwise, I admirably faked my way through the set and Monroe smiled at me a couple of times and even gave me a thumbs-up during a little run on "Let It

Snow." It was oddly therapeutic; for the hour or so that the show lasted, I was lost in the music, blissfully ignorant of the increasingly bizarre and perplexing mission that had brought me to Vegas in the first place. The show ended to a standing ovation, the first one I had received since my bar mitzvah. I bowed with the rest of the band, keeping a steadying hand on my toup, and walked off the stage and out of my brief but exhilarating show biz career.

Backstage, I changed out of my show clothes and into my new blue blazer and slacks, received profuse thanks and twenty-five dollars from the band manager, then walked out the stage entrance and into the swarming hive that was the Flamingo casino. At one-thirty in the morning, the place was as overrun and noisy as Times Square at noon. I gazed over the rabble but saw none of my playmates, so I turned and headed in the general direction of the elevators. I was eager to give Barbara a ring, but loath to dial Hilde Stern's number at four-thirty in the morning East Coast time.

As I was calculating how many hours would have to pass before I would feel comfortable placing the call to New York, I passed a particularly boisterous crap table. The excited shouts of the gamblers slowed me down to a curious crawl and finally I just stopped in my tracks to watch the game. I instantly noticed a sober and bespectacled gentleman with graying hair and a salt-and-pepper beard who sat quietly placing bets and stacking chips. The bearded gentleman was conspicuous for two reasons: One, he was the only person at the table not screaming at the top of his lungs, and two, he was Lucky Luciano.

The beard was Lucky's cover, but I hoped my toupee worked better as concealing foliage, because the instant I laid eyes on him, my middle-aged heart started pounding like the beat-beat-beat of the tom-tom. There was no mistaking the steel in those brown eyes, the arch of those furry eyebrows, the Roman in that nose, or the meat in those lips. It was Charlie Lucky, live and in person, and it took all of the restraint I could muster to continue on and walk past his table without giving him a second glance. If anyone had staked a valid claim to paranoia, it would be Lucky, given his status as a government-certified deportee whose mere presence in Vegas would be enough to send a battalion of immigration officers marching into the Flamingo. It was therefore more than a little startling to see him not only in the United States, but hanging out so brazenly in a Vegas casino.

Maybe it shouldn't have been: Lucky had recently been earning a reputation for world-class chutzpah. The rumors had been all over New York that while residing illegally in Havana, he had been very much out and about and in the public eye, with the eager and most certainly well-paid cooperation of the local authorities. I would wager that he had greased more than a few outstretched palms in Las Vegas; still, it seemed wildly audacious of Lucky to be shooting craps out in the open at one-thirty in the morning.

And it was now impossible for me to leave the casino. There was no way that Luciano's presence in Vegas was unconnected to the Toscanini snatch. The way this case was going, I half expected the shade of Mussolini to come waltzing through the front doors.

There was nothing for me to do but hang around, so I sauntered over to a neighboring crap table and converted my recently acquired twenty-five bucks into chips. Keeping one eye on Lucky's table, I started rolling dice for the first time since the war, and within half an hour—to my amazement and in proof of the oft-disproved dictum that God protects the ignorant—I had turned my meager opening stake into five hundred American dollars. I did fairly well when I held the bones in my own sweaty paws, but earned most of my winnings during a logic-defying run by a four-hundred-pound crapshooter whom everyone called Sonny. Attired in a Hawaiian shirt and size-ninety shorts, a rum crook jutting out of the slit that was his mouth, the gigantic Sonny enjoyed fifteen breathtaking minutes before inevitably crapping out. When he was done, I pocketed most of my chips and bet very lightly for the next few games, not wanting to erode my earnings but unwilling to exit the casino so long as Lucky still graced the tables. I started to get bored, so I arose and walked over to the roulette tables, staying even on red and black bets until I turned and saw Lucky pick up his modest stack of chips and slowly make his way toward the cashier's window. He was unaccompanied—no muscle, no gunsel, no anybody; just a modest Italian gentleman finishing up an evening's entertainment.

I carried my chips to a neighboring window, cashed them out for a grand total of four hundred and seventy-five dollars, and then strolled ever so nonchalantly behind Lucky as he made his unhurried exit from the casino tables. I stayed back about thirty feet; Lucky pushed his way through the glass doors and out of the hotel and I did the same, lighting up a smoke to look ever so disinterested. The desert air assaulted me once again; even though it was now just past two in the morning, the temperature still stood in the mid-eighties. Fortunately, the wind had faded to a mere breeze, which was extremely good news for my hairpiece.

As quickly as if Lucky had rubbed a magic lamp, a black sedan pulled up scant moments after he emerged from the Flamingo. The passenger's-side door swung open and Lucky ducked inside; the door slammed shut and the car pulled away. As casually as I could, I waved my hand in the direction of a battered lime-green taxi that stood at the head of a short line of hacks. Producing a foul eruption of oil smoke, the cab lurched in my direction. When it stopped in front of me, I climbed inside and sank deeply and uncomfortably into the chewed-up backseat.

"Just follow that dark sedan, please," I said to the back of the driver's head. "And don't get too close."

The driver whirled around. He was a painfully thin man of about fifty, with prematurely white hair, rheumy blue eyes, and a purple and red explosion that passed for a nose. The odds were that he could be talked into having a drink just about any old time.

"Playing cops and robbers?" he asked with immediate suspicion.

"Just cops," I told him.

The driver shook his skinny head. "Nix, buddy. I don't get involved in that shit."

I shoved a ten-dollar bill at him and he stopped talking.

"What the hell," he said, and stepped on the gas. "But any rough stuff . . ."

"You've seen too many movies," I told him. "Just follow the car. When it stops, you stop. Simple as that. And stay at least a hundred feet in back of him."

"I know how to do it," he mumbled.

"Glad to hear it," I told him, trying to find a way to sit without getting a spring up my ass. "This is some swell car. My compliments."

"You don't like it, go fuck yourself."

"Fair enough."

Lucky's car pulled out onto Las Vegas Boulevard and after all of three or four long desert blocks, it hung a right and passed through the entrance to a glittering new edifice called the Desert Inn. I peered out through the filthy passenger's window.

"Pretty swank," I said. "Much as I can make out through this window."

"Oh, it's swank, all right," the driver said. "You're new in town, right?"

"You can tell."

"I can tell a lot of things," he said with very little conviction. This guy spoke like a B-actor. "Desert Inn opened up early this year. Hottest joint in town."

"Wish I would've known," I told him. "Maybe I'll switch hotels."

"No chance. It's sold out almost all the time. The high rollers, they want to stay only there."

"You drive a lot of high rollers in this junk heap?"

The driver had no nifty reply, so he just stuck his thumb into his ruin of a nose and rummaged around for artifacts. As he did so, I watched Lucky's sedan pull up to the front of the Desert Inn, stopping under a huge overhang that displayed enough wattage to light up the Polo Grounds. The back door of the sedan opened up and Lucky got out. He was still flying solo.

"Stop here," I told my driver, and handed him another five. The fare on the meter was a dollar twenty-five.

"I don't have change," he lied, but I was already out the door and walking toward the Desert Inn. Lucky disappeared inside the hotel and I picked up my pace.

The Desert Inn made the Flamingo look like a Bowery flophouse. It was ultra-deluxe, with a multichandeliered ceiling, thick burgundy carpeting, and first-class appointments all the way around. A jazz combo noodled tastefully from an open lounge in the rear of the casino. Where the Flamingo was raucous and jangly, the Desert Inn had more the ambience of an ocean liner and consequently appeared to draw a more affluent crowd than Bugsy's place. There were fewer hayseeds and rodeo clowns, fewer fat ladies in funny hats. The tables were surrounded by manicured guys with expensive haircuts and well-tailored suits, accompanied by women who looked like they commanded top dollar for the privilege of their brief but intense company. I took an instantaneous liking to the place; it seemed to be several expensive cuts above the rest of this raw and incomplete city. I could understand why it drew Lucky's attention and patronage.

However, it looked like Luciano had completed his gaming for the evening. He was walking toward the front desk with the slumped and red-eyed look of a man ready to call it a night. I circled the other way, then turned and walked past the desk as if I were coming back from the elevators.

And then I had a stroke of very good fortune.

As I sauntered by the front desk, a dark-skinned room clerk with the taut cheekbones and piercing eyes of a full-blooded Navajo uttered the following words to Lucky: "Have a good evening, Dr. Horowitz." Lucky grunted in reply and then walked away toward the elevators, yawning prodigiously. Even gangsters got sleepy. I walked back across the casino, keeping on eye on Lucky as he waited for a free elevator. He rubbed his eyes and checked his watch. An elevator opened its doors and Lucky got in. I proceeded to recross the casino and walk oh-so-casually past the elevators, noticing that Lucky had stopped at the fourth floor, which, at this low-slung resort, was the top floor.

I walked back around the casino, past the front desk, and toward the coffee shop, at which point it occurred to me that I was as hungry as an escaped prisoner. The coffee shop, according to a sign hanging on its perfectly washed window, was open twenty-four hours, which was the best news I had gotten in the last two days. A twenty-four-hour coffee shop is like a surrogate mother, a warm-hearted source of nourishment attentive to your every whim. I was starting to like this town very much, which goes to show how much of a pushover I really am—make me an omelet at two-thirty in the morning and I'm yours forever.

The coffee shop was enormous but quiet as a tomb; there were maybe twenty people spread out across a hundred tables and booths, in varying states of anticipation or digestion, so conversation was at a bare minimum. If the customers had lost at the tables, they were naturally apt to be quiet. If they had won big, the odds were they would either be at the bar feeling expansive, or in their rooms with some hookers feeling whatever they had paid to feel.

I wanted to blend into the woodwork as much as possible, so I took a booth near the back. A mid-fortyish blond waitress with dark roots and a name tag identifying her as Charlene came over at once and asked if I wanted some coffee.

"I need all the coffee you have," I told her. Charlene nodded and strolled toward the coffee station, while I scanned the multipaged plastic menu, nearly drooling all over it. I was ravenous. Another fifteen minutes and I'd be getting the shakes.

"You ready to order?" Charlene asked, pouring my coffee.

"Here's how hungry I am," I began.

"How hungry, darlin'?" asked Charlene. Her accent was Georgia or northern Florida.

"If you can get a salami omelet with hash browns and two orders of *very* buttered toast to this table in under five minutes, I'll give you ten smackers."

She smiled. "You're going to lose that money."

"And rolls now, please, or I'll pass out right here on the floor."

She smiled. "You're scarin' me, darlin'."

Five minutes later, I was scarfing down my food like a hobo let into the kitchen of the rich folks' house. I couldn't remember anything ever tasting as good as that salami omelet. The salami had been cut into perfect cubes, the onions were sliced to mere gossamer clippings and perfectly browned, and the hash browns were enough to make a grown man cry. If I was on death row, this might be the way to go out.

Charlene came over and surveyed the ruins of my meal.

"You just get off the chain gang?"

"That was scary, it was so delicious."

"The night chef's the best, I swear. And I recommend the rhubarb pie. And of course you want more coffee, don't you, honey?"

"Any chance of you adopting me?" I asked Charlene.

"None," Charlene said, and laughed. "Got two already." She picked up my plate and looked at it and her smile turned a little thin. "Plus a third, my oldest, William, lost him on D-Day."

"I'm very, very sorry," I told her.

"Yes sir. Nineteen years of age. Believed in what he was fighting for and that's the important thing, I suppose."

"It certainly is, ma'am. What he was doing on that day couldn't have been more important to the world."

"Yes sir." She nodded. "I'll get you that pie." She started away, then turned back to me. "Could I say something to you, mister?"

"Sure. Anything."

"It's sort of personal."

"Go ahead. I can take it."

"Okay. It's just . . . you have a real good face. You'd look a whole lot better without that toupee."

I left the coffee shop, a toothpick stuck in my mouth, and walked toward the house phones, my eyes still peeled for Lansky or LaMarca or anyone who looked like they could be their playmates. All I saw were happy gamblers.

The house phones were white and they were located on a marble table across from a row of unoccupied pay booths. I picked up a phone and an operator instantly answered.

"Desert Inn. Good morning," she said huskily. "How can I help you?"

"I need Dr. Horowitz in room 204, please?"

There was a pause.

"There is no Dr. Horowitz in room 204. There's a Dr. Murray Horowitz registered in room 401."

"That's him. Could you ring me through, please?"

She paused again. I heard a sheet of paper rustle on her end.

"I'm sorry, but there's a 'do not disturb' on that line."

"No problem. Thanks for your time." I hung up and hustled over to the elevator bank, just as an elevator opened its doors. A gray-haired man rolled out in a wheelchair pushed by a painfully thin Pakistani wearing a turban. The gray-haired man held a silver walking stick across his lap and was puffing on a meerschaum pipe. You had to love this town. I slipped into the car as soon as the duo wheeled out of the way and banged the button for four, keeping a finger on the DOOR CLOSE button. I didn't want company. The elevator crept to the fourth floor. Its doors opened noisily. I got out and followed the arrows toward rooms 400–410. The corridors were relatively short, making a complete circuit of the floor in a series of angles. When I passed room 405, I made a left into another short corridor. At the end of it, I observed a folding chair set up directly across from what had to be Lucky's room. Next to the chair was a table holding a radio, a thermos, and a paper bag; perched on the chair and eating a sandwich was a young red-haired man who was as tall seated as I was standing.

He looked up at me with no particular curiosity.

"Room 415?" I asked him.

The giant pointed past me and waved his hand, signaling that I should turn and walk the other way. He probably didn't want to speak with his mouth full. I thanked him profusely and started back around the other way, circling back down the short corridors until I turned the final corner and reached the elevator once again.

The giant was standing in front of me.

When he was upright, I saw that he wasn't exactly a giant. He stood about six-foot-four and wasn't all that much wider than a brownstone. I guessed him to be about twenty-five.

"You got here pretty quickly," I told him. "You ever play football?"

"High school," he said. "Guard."

"You go to high school out here?"

He looked at me, his eyes narrowing. "Near here. Elko."

"Really. And now you're working for Dr. Horowitz?"

He didn't know quite what to do with that. The kid was just local talent, subcontracted out to work the night shift. Lucky was getting very casual in his old age; one would have thought he'd have brought his own muscle from Naples or New York. Maybe he was saving on air fare.

"This is a VIP floor," the red-haired kid said with all the importance he could muster. "What are you doing here?"

"I guess I got lost. How do you like that for an answer?"

"Not very much," he said, and he blinked a couple of times, kind of a nervous tic, the kind that made me think physical violence was not all that far away.

I glanced over the redhead's right shoulder and nodded at an invisible stranger. It's an ancient ploy, taken from *Captain Jack's Big Book of Detective Tricks,* but the kid went for it just long enough to throw a glance over his shoulder, at which point I jerked my knee directly into his crotch. He groaned and bent over in pain; I raised both my arms and smashed the meaty portion of my right hand directly onto the bridge of his nose, breaking it immediately. Blood sprayed across his face like water from a busted pipe, and the kid instinctively raised both his hands to cover the wound. As he did so, I ran out the fire door and started hustling down the stairs. I have to admit that I felt badly for the kid. Not terrible, but pretty bad.

I took the fire stairs two at a time. The kid began lumbering after me, but that knee to his crotch had taken most of the spring out of his step. When I ran out of stairs, I pushed open the fire door and walked out into the never-ending din of the casino. A new combo was playing in the lounge and new suckers were hitting the tables. Lansky was right on target—this was the dawn of a new era, the creation of the most perfect machine ever designed for the continuous extraction of money. Adjusting my toup, I crossed the floor with all deliberate speed, keeping my eyes fixed on the front doors.

I exited the Desert Inn into the relative stillness of the night. It was just past three in the morning, but the heat never quit in this town. Maybe this was what hell was like—twenty-four hours of flames and lounge comedians. I took a deep breath to slow the pounding of my heart and scanned a line of cabs that stood in front of the hotel. At the head of the line was a candy-apple-red Chevrolet in considerably better shape than the junker I had arrived in. Its driver waved at me to get in.

I slid into the front seat and closed the door behind me. The cabby turned around.

"Where are we going?" she asked. I had never seen a woman cabby before, but the smoky register of her voice, as well as the sinuous musculature of her upper arms, indicated that she was just a chromosome or two away from switching teams. Her brown hair was combed back over her ears and she wore no makeup around her bright blue eyes. All in all, she was pretty hot stuff.

"I guess we're going to the Flamingo," I told her.

"You guess?"

I looked out the window. Lucky's night watchman was stumbling out through the Desert Inn's front doors, his right hand pressed to his still-gushing nose.

"Yeah. Let's move, sweetheart."

The driver accelerated.

"My name's Kim," she informed me. "That guy with the busted beak, he a friend of yours?"

"He's my son. I cut his allowance and he got mad."

Kim laughed. "You gotta be strict with kids these days," she said. "Actually, I know that guy."

"My son?"

"Yeah, your son. Be careful, mister. At first you might think he's just a garden-variety nitwit, but the fact is he's pretty much of a psycho. He started coming on to me one night at the bar over by the Thunderbird, obviously not clued in to the fairly obvious fact that I'm a devout lesbian. Or that my friend was, Cheryl, who dances in the show there. She's less butch than I am, so she can pass. Not that I'm *all* that butch, really. I'm not shocking you, am I?" She glanced up into her rearview mirror. "I just guess that you have a certain amount of sophistication, given that you came waltzing so casually out of the Inn having turned Wally's nose into chitlins."

"You're not shocking me," I told her truthfully, "although I can't say I'm used to people being so forthcoming."

"Well, that's who I am. Also a motormouth, but you probably figured that out already. We still going to the Flamingo, by the way? You seemed unsure."

"We're going there, but take your time. I'll pay for it." My head felt sweaty under the toupee. "Wally, that's his name?"

"That's what he told us. He's like a freelance goon; I've heard rumors that he strangled a couple of girls out here."

"On whose behalf?"

"On behalf of whoever paid him, I guess. That part's not so clear," Kim said. She stuck a cigarette in her mouth and lit up with one hand; this girl was like a lesbian Dead End Kid. "Maybe people who thought they might get shaken down. Some of the hookers out here are seriously brain-impaired, stupid enough to try a little amateur blackmail on the wrong people."

"Were those killings investigated?"

"Not in what I would call a terribly rigorous fashion. There's a certain Wild West quality to life here. Dodge City with slot machines. So if a couple of working girls disappear it's not exactly a cause for civic alarm."

I settled back in my seat as she cruised down Las Vegas Boulevard. "How long you been driving here?"

"Since the war. I was stationed in South Carolina as a WAC, which was pretty much heaven for an eager little girl of my persuasion. Lot of wonderful women, many of them straight, who just figured, what the hell, it's wartime, let's give girls a try. Then their fellas came back." She shook her head. "But they'll still have their memories, right?"

"I'm sure they will. Those humid nights down South."

"Way down South. God, don't get me started." She laughed. "Anyhow, that ended and I went back to LA, which I never really cared for terribly much. Too heartless by half. So I figured I'll start fresh and you can't start fresher than Vegas. This place is a blank page. Gets a little more filled in every day."

"You know pretty much everybody here?"

She again looked up at the rearview mirror; this time she made eye contact.

"You a private dick? Somehow I get that feeling."

"Yeah."

"New Yorker?"

"Right again." I lit up a Lucky. "I get a feeling, too. That I can trust you."

" 'Cause I'm a dyke?"

"No, because you strike me as both intelligent and ethical. God knows I've dealt with enough lesbians in New York, and some of them were totally disreputable."

"Tell me about it." Kim blew a cloud of smoke out her window. "That's what I love about Cheryl, actually: her honesty. That and her tits." Kim laughed loudly.

"Well, that's two major attributes."

"Yes sir. You want me to double back to the airport while you decide where you actually want to go?"

"Sure."

"Somebody waiting for you at the Flamingo that you don't particularly want to see?" Kim asked, half turning around. "Pardon my curiosity, but that rug you're wearing looks like a very temporary measure."

"It's still alive," I told her. "I can feel its little heartbeat."

Kim laughed again. "You're funny, pal. Really. Very."

"Call me Buddy."

"That's your name?"

"It is tonight."

She nodded and blew more smoke across the Nevada desert.

"You don't look like a Buddy. Try another name."

"How about Lassie?"

"Now you're getting warm."

We were getting near the airport. I looked at my watch; it was a quarter to four.

"What the hell," I told her. "Let's go to the Flamingo."

"You're ready."

" 'Ready' isn't the right word. 'Resigned' is probably more like it." I leaned forward. "Listen, there's gotta be a service entrance over there, right?"

"You don't want to march through the lobby."

"Correct." I was ready to take this girl on as a partner.

"Okay. I have a friend in the back. Dorothy Washington. She'll take you up the freight elevator. She's a dyke, too, a Negro one, talk about two strikes and you're out."

"Is she someone who keeps her eyes open?"

Kim looked at me in the mirror again.

"Believe me, Lassie, there's nothing happening inside that hotel she doesn't know about."

Ten minutes later Kim was leading me from the cab to the service entrance of the Flamingo. It was now nearly four in the morning, and kitchen and casino workers were arriving for the dead-of-night shift. They walked alone or in friendly chatting groups across a parking lot that was about a quarter-filled with cars and trucks and a large green bus that had VAUGHN MONROE ORCHESTRA painted in white script across both of its sides. The Flamingo—like all of Las Vegas—was an enterprise that never stopped, and Kim acted as if she owned the joint.

I followed Kim through the service entrance like a kid she was taking to kindergarten. She marched straight to the house phone, picked up, and asked for Dorothy Washington. I flattened myself against the wall, but it was an unnecessary precaution—the Flamingo employees were parading past me as if I didn't exist.

Kim listened for a couple of silent seconds, then hung up.

"She'll be right down." She studied me. "You look awful tired."

"I've had a busy couple of days."

"Maybe you'll tell me about them sometime." Kim raised her eyebrows. "Right? When you're in the mood? I've always liked private eye stories." Even under the fluorescent lights, Kim had high color in her cheeks. We were standing face-to-face, maybe a foot apart; I studied her small and sensuous mouth, long and inquiring nose, observed the startling blue of her eyes.

"By the way, you're a knockout," I told her.

"Thanks," she told me. "I bet you're pretty cute when you take that beaver off your head and hang it back on the wall."

"I'm adorable."

We both smiled at each other, had an intriguing flicker of eye contact, and then she laughed and shook her head.

"Uh-uh. No more guys for me. Not worth the trouble."

She squeezed my arm in friendship. I rewarded her trust and

affection with an immediate hard-on, but that tumescence wilted the instant that Dorothy Washington came into view. Wearing the black and whites of her profession, Dorothy was built roughly along the lines of Jersey Joe Walcott, with wide shoulders and a massive high-cheekboned head. Her skin was cocoa-colored and she had dyed her brush cut into a copper-coil red.

Kim made the introductions.

"Dorothy Washington, meet Lassie."

"Buddy," I offered.

"That's not his name, either."

"Pleasure to meet you," Dorothy said in a delicate soprano totally at odds with her imposing physique. "You're staying here?"

"In 207."

"But you want to keep out of the mainstream, is that the point?" she asked.

"That's exactly the point."

"He's a private dick, but he's a good guy, has that wicked New York sense of humor," Kim said, then leaned over and kissed my cheek. "I have to go back to my chariot." She then handed me a card, which identified her as Kim West of the Royal Flush Cab Company. "You need any help, I can play Nancy Drew." Then Kim kissed Dorothy on the cheek and went racing out the back door.

"She's something," I said.

"She's everything," said the maid.

Service elevators, like service entrances, are all the same; from the swankiest establishment to the rankest, they all stink of moldy bedsheets and rotting cheeseburgers, and the Flamingo's was no exception. Dorothy and I stood shyly on opposite sides of the drab green elevator car, like two people on a blind date.

"When you check in?" she asked.

"This evening. Listen, I'm going to have to trust you completely, Miss Washington, because I'm on my own in this town, and there's a great deal of very strange stuff going on."

"Always is in Vegas," she said. "And call me Dorothy."

"You born here, Dorothy?"

She smiled. "Nobody was born here. I'm from Chicago."

"You like this town?"

"It's a new world, mister. That's what I like. For people like me, people like Kim . . ." she didn't elaborate and didn't have to. "It's easier, y'know? People don't ask any questions 'cause they all got their own secrets. That's why a lot of folks come here. To start from scratch."

"How long you been at the Flamingo?"

"Since the week before it opened."

"Really. So you knew Bugsy?"

She smiled with a certain reserved pride. "Yessir. I remember Mr. Siegel, all right. Everybody thought he was just so handsome, but he wasn't handsome when you looked in his eyes, know what I'm saying? In his eyes he was just plain crazy. I wasn't surprised he wound up with a bullet in his head. Not at all. That man was put on this earth to get himself shot up."

"So then you must know Lansky," I said just as casually as all get-out. Dorothy's expression never changed. She just smiled. That was it; there was no elaboration. When I took out my wallet, she waved it off.

"Don't even think about it," she said.

"About giving you some cash if you help me out?"

"You can do it later if I do help you out. I don't want to owe you nothing."

"Fair enough. So what about Lansky?"

"What about him?"

"When's the last time you saw him?"

She checked her watch. "About an hour ago. He's in 406. Looked like he was turning in for the night. I can check if you'd like."

"I'd like," I told her.

The elevator stopped. Dorothy got out and gestured for me to follow. We stepped into a dun-colored cubicle that held a half dozen ghostly room service carts and some lidless trash cans.

"Room 207 is right across the hall. Hang on." She picked up a house phone, but this one wasn't virgin white like the ones in the lobby. This one, for the enslaved class, was industrial gray.

"Hey, it's me," I heard Dorothy say to her unseen comrade-in-dust-rags. "There a 'Do Not Disturb' on 406?" She looked over at me, listened, then nodded. "And he got his night service? Okay, thanks." The chambermaid hung up. "He closed up shop for the night. That going to help you sleep better?"

"It's a start. Thanks."

"No problem. Any friend of Kim's . . ."

I looked out through the window of the service door. My room, as advertised, was directly across the way. I pushed the door open, then turned back to Dorothy Washington. She was ringing for the elevator.

"Dorothy, do you know who Toscanini is? Arturo Toscanini?"

Dorothy stopped and stared at me. For the first time, there was a flicker of unease in her eyes.

"No." The elevator doors opened.

"You never heard of him? The most famous symphony conductor in the world?"

"Heard the name maybe. Sure. Once or twice."

"He's staying at this hotel, Dorothy, isn't he?" I walked toward the chambermaid and she backed into the elevator. "You couldn't miss him in a thousand years. He doesn't look like anyone else in the world, particularly anyone living west of the Mississippi. Came in sometime yesterday."

"I don't know," she mumbled. "Haven't heard the name."

Dorothy reached for the buttons in the elevator, but I held my finger on the down button, keeping the door open.

"Gotta go back to work, mister," she said with a little quaver in her voice. It was a little unsettling to see this strapping woman so discomfited.

"They told you to play it deaf and dumb? If you see him you don't see him?"

"Let go of the button, please."

"He's about five-foot-three, snow-white hair, and pink, luminescent skin. You'd miss Teddy Roosevelt checking in before you'd miss this guy."

"I'm asking you nice, let go that button," she said, her voice getting firmer.

"Fine. You don't know a thing, you never saw him. You're doing your job, I respect that. But here's the problem, Dorothy—I've also got a job to do, which is to save the old man, because the fact is he's been snatched and I don't think he'll ever get out of this town except in a fancy Italian box."

Dorothy's eyes opened very wide.

"Mister, I don't know anything about this." She said it very slowly, so I would understand that further questions were pointless.

"I'm sure you don't, and there's no way I'm going to put you at any sort of risk. You could do me one favor, though."

Dorothy continued staring; I knew she was real sorry she'd ever been introduced to me, Kim or no Kim.

"The favor is this: I need a waiter's uniform. Forty-four regular. After that, I won't bother you."

The elevator bell rang downstairs.

"You'll let go of that button?"

"Yes, ma'am."

"And I get you a uniform, you'll never say how you got it?"

"You can trust me with your life. I mean that."

"Okay." The elevator bell rang again. Someone was getting impatient. "Just let go, mister. Now."

I did so. The doors started to close, then abruptly reopened. Dorothy stuck her head out.

"What kind of waiter?"

"Room service."

"That's what I thought. Be careful, mister."

"Don't worry. I know my way around a hot plate."

She didn't smile. The doors closed.

* * *

I got out my key and entered room 207. It was dark and I fumbled for the wall switch. I half expected to be jumped the instant I came through the door, but the room was happily free of stalkers. I had not been spotted coming back to the hotel and there was no reason for anyone to connect me to someone named Buddy Barrow. But this was a very small town and I had no illusions that I'd be able to continue this charade much longer. I was going to have to find the old man and find him fast.

After fifteen minutes, there was a delicate knock at the door. I checked the peephole: Dorothy was outside, looking up and down the hall as fearfully as if a pack of yelping Alabama bloodhounds was tearing up the carpets after her. I opened up. She handed me a black plastic garment bag.

"I need this back by nine A.M.," she whispered. "No later."

"You'll have it. Thanks a million." She walked away before I ever finished the sentence. And never looked back.

Five minutes later I had the uniform on and was examining myself in the bathroom mirror. It was not a pretty sight. Between the bad toup and the monkey suit—white shirt, black bow tie, red jacket, shiny black pants—I looked depressingly like half the foul-tempered Yids who enjoyed dripping matzo ball soup onto my lap at the Stage Deli. I sighed and checked my watch; it was now four-thirty in the morning and I had sailed past fatigue into a sort of altered and anxious consciousness. I felt like a long-distance truck driver with a belly full of pills and Minneapolis still four hundred miles away. It was a tad too early to start making my rounds, so I decided to call Hilde Stern.

The prolonged process of placing a New York call through the hotel operator gave me more than enough time to check my impeccable nails; in fact, I could have gotten a manicure and a facial in the time it took the Flamingo to hook me up to Manhattan. Finally, the call went through and after three rings, Hilde picked up.

"Mr. LeVine," she said. The connection was filled with light static and a kind of distant jangly distortion, as if somewhere in the middle of the country a telephone lineman were swinging from the wires.

"*Lieber Gott,* where are you?"

She sounded as if she hadn't gone to sleep since the last time I'd seen her.

"I'm out West, actually." I suddenly felt an almost physical chill of paranoia. "And just call me Buddy."

This threw her for an immediate and predictable loop.

" 'Buddy'? *Vas* is 'Buddy'?"

"It's just better if you call me that or call me nothing at all, you know? Just don't use my name."

"*Lieber, lieber . . .*" I could hear the phone on her end begin to clatter like a percussion instrument; she had obviously gotten the shakes. Placing this call was shaping up as the dumbest idea I'd had since taking the case in the first place.

"There's nothing to worry about, Mrs. Stern."

"*Lieber, lieber, lieber.*" The clattering got worse. Much worse.

"Please, relax. Listen, everything's really going very well. How are you and Linda doing?"

I heard a sigh on her end. The clattering slowed down as she tried to pull herself together. "How should we do?"

"I know. It's a very difficult time for you all," I said inanely. "But I'm sure Barbara's been a big help. She seems like a wonderful girl."

There was a pause as I waited for God to strike me dead.

"Barbara, she's not here," Hilde said.

"She's not." My mouth went dry.

"No. She left since two days; she said, 'I go find who did this to Papa.' I said to her, this is the detective's job and the police's job, but she is very stubborn like her father. She says she knows people from when she was working who could help. I don't know who or what. . . . I told her I needed her here, and she said she'd be back in two or three days. Now she called yesterday and said she is in California and will be here on the weekend, and I shouldn't worry. She sounded good, thanks God."

"California," I repeated like a mynah bird.

"*Ja.* She has friends there. She has friends everywhere. Always she has been very popular."

"Yes, I'm sure," I said, and suddenly I felt genuinely sorry for Hilde Stern. It must have been an enormous burden to produce a daughter as dazzling as Barbara, a girl who would so effortlessly attract men and trouble. There was no doubt that she'd be a handful for any mother, but for someone as anxious as Hilde Stern it must have been as unsettling and mystifying as if she had given birth to a mermaid.

"If she calls here again, and I'm sure she does, Mr. . . ." Hilde remembered my warning and stumbled. "If she calls, I tell her you phoned. Is there anything to tell me? You have some news?"

"I'm making progress."

"All right," she said. "That's good. I tell Linda." I heard her voice break and I knew she was crying, crying pretty hard, and I was able to remember why I was still involved in this.

"I'll see you soon," I told her.

"Yes," she said softly. "But you will please be careful."

"I'm always careful," I said, then I hung up and left room 207 and took the malodorous service elevator down to the kitchen of the Flamingo Hotel.

TWELVE

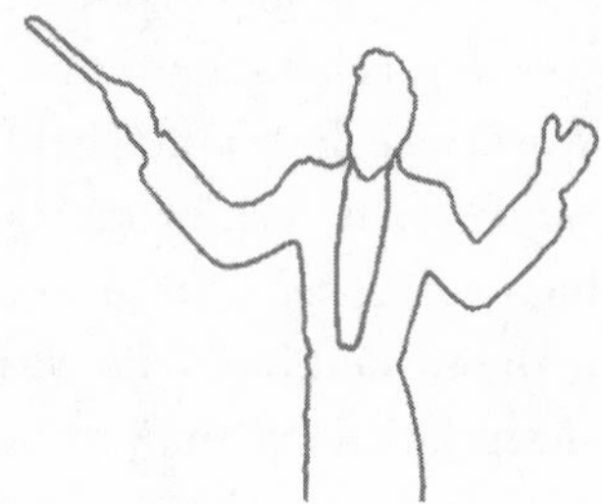

The Flamingo's kitchen was predictably enormous, and even at five o'clock in the morning, its black-and-white-tiled expanse was vibrant with activity. Fruit was being sliced and diced, oranges were being pulped into juice, acres of bacon were being spread across acres of griddles, and immense coffee urns were being filled with Niagaras of water. All this busyness was fortuitous, making it easier for me to get lost in the crowd of still-sluggish employees. I moved through the kitchen keeping my head down as much as possible, but also attempting to look like a man perfectly at home in the world of order slips and steam tables. When a couple of passing waiters threw me quizzical looks, I winked and greeted them.

"Filling in for Joe, he's got the flu," I informed them. The waiters nodded and shuffled on. I circled the kitchen and picked up a tray, then strode purposefully to the silverware station. I was backing and filling, stalling for time. Having remembered the Maestro's informing me that he arose at dawn's first light, I was looking for any sign that the great man's breakfast was being prepared. I obviously had no way of knowing whether Toscanini was even staying at the Flamingo, but given Lansky's presence in the hotel, it seemed like a very good bet. If the old man wasn't here, I would have lost nothing but time.

I was starting to load up on butter when the aroma of a particularly pungent blend of coffee wafted my way, and then I heard a voice say, "Okay, pal, come and get it."

I turned around and observed a compact and thick-necked man in street clothes picking up a silver breakfast tray from a horse-faced gent sporting a chef's toque and whites. The silver tray was topped by an Old World lace doily and it held a plate of freshly washed fruit that Cezanne would have been proud to paint, a basket of rolls and danish, and a highly polished espresso pot. The thick-necked man picked the tray up with one deft hand; he was graceful and light of foot but also had the sharply defined upper body of someone who had spent significant hours lifting barbells over his head. From the look of his well-cut suit and highly polished footwear, he appeared to be professional and well-trained muscle; if the redhead at the Desert Inn was any indication of the local talent, then I guessed this guy to be strictly an import.

The man in street clothes walked swiftly toward a service elevator located at the far end of the kitchen. I grabbed a bowl of fruit and box of shredded wheat, placed a glass of orange juice and a coffeepot on my tray, and followed him over. When the elevator arrived, I followed him on board, yawning ostentatiously.

"Too goddamn early," I said in a collegial manner.

He looked at me and smiled thinly, then pushed a button for the third floor and shot me an inquisitive glance, his finger still poised over the buttons.

"Same for me, amigo," I said, then made myself busy straightening the silverware on my tray.

The man in street clothes pressed the button to close the door, then stared at his black shoes. He wasn't much for small talk. When the door opened to the third floor, he mutely gestured to me to get out first.

"Thanks," I told him. "Have a good day."

He nodded again. I got out, pushed open the service door, and took a left; the man in street clothes followed behind me and took a right. I walked ten feet, turned a corner, then put my tray on the floor and started creeping back around on tiptoes, my size-ten loafers silent on the thick carpeting. The man in street clothes was marching inexorably toward a set of double doors set at the very end of the hall. I slipped into a dimly lit alcove that housed an ice machine not much larger or noisier than a garbage truck. When I stuck my head out again, like a house dick in a B-movie, the man in street clothes had reached the double doors. He knocked once, then twice, then repeated the sequence. From the same B-movie.

The door swung open.

Sidney Aaron stood in the doorway.

Aaron was wearing a blue silk robe over a pair of gray slacks and a white shirt. Behind him, I could see Toscanini seated on a red velvet couch, wearing dark slacks and a black smoking jacket, and engrossed in a score. He started to rise when the man in street clothes entered with his breakfast, and then Aaron swung the door shut and the show was over. I sidled out of the alcove and began to creep down the hallway. I got close enough to the room to see that it was identified in pink script lettering as the Royal Valencia Suite, and that it bore number 300–301. I also got close enough that when the door abruptly reopened, I had a terrific view of Sidney Aaron's pupils dilating as he registered who I was.

"Well," he said, then cocked his head toward the man in street clothes. "Gino."

"Gotta run," I told Aaron. "The penthouse just ordered a sturgeon omelet." I turned to go, but it was a fool's mission. Gino put his hand on my shoulder and started gripping it so tightly that my entire right side began to go numb. When I turned back around, Gino's jacket swung open and I could see a .38 revolver tucked into his pants. I decided it would be better for all concerned if I stuck around.

Toscanini didn't even look up when I entered the suite; he had started enthusiastically wolfing down his breakfast, which had been arranged before him on a marble-topped coffee table. The suite had been set up like an apartment: There was a bookcase newly jammed with musical books and scores, and side tables adorned by gold-framed photographs of Toscanini posed with family, musicians, or just by his own legendary self. The most casual glance around revealed that there were at least two other rooms in the suite and a peek at their memento-filled confines confirmed what Lansky had already implied—this was not intended as a quick layover.

I walked toward the old man and greeted him loudly.

"*Bon giorno,* Maestro."

Toscanini lifted his head and peered at me nearsightededly.

"Yes?" he said absently, and then I lifted the toupee off the top of my head. The great man's eyes widened and then he began to laugh heartily. *"Que cosa!"* he exclaimed. "Boston Blackie!" He extended his hand and half rose to greet me. *"Come va?"*

"Never better. Had a helluva couple of days. And you, Maestro?"

Toscanini shrugged and gestured vaguely around his strange new living quarters. He suddenly looked small and vulnerable, like an exquisitely dressed immigrant asking for directions.

Aaron glided over.

"Maestro's doing splendidly, considering all that's been going on," he said, as smooth as Mother's own chicken fat. Aaron put his arm through mine. "Maestro, you'll excuse me and Mr. LeVine. Enjoy your breakfast in peace."

"Sì," the old man said. *"Bene."* He sipped the coffee. *"Bene.* They finally get it right." He looked to me. "Yesterday, coffee was *infamia*! *Vergognoso!"*

"Well, we got that straightened out, Maestro," Aaron crooned. "If nothing else, now they know how to make coffee in Las Vegas. So we've accomplished something, haven't we?" Aaron chuckled with the oily bonhomie of an uptown art dealer, then led me to an adjoining room dominated by a Steinway grand piled high with yet more music scores. The minute we walked through the door, he dropped the Mister Continental routine.

"What are you, nuts, Jack?" Aaron whispered fiercely. "You have some kind of a death wish, running around the hotel like this? You know it's not safe."

"It's not?" I said, whispering back. You really had to admire Sidney Aaron's total duplicity. This guy did nothing halfway.

"You may or may not believe me," he continued to whisper, "but right now I'm the only thing standing between you and the noon show at Riverside Chapel. Do you know the kind of people you're dealing with here?"

"You, for one, unfortunately."

"Jack, you really have no idea—"

"I have a very good idea," I told him. "I know you shipped me to Havana just to get me out of New York and into the loving arms of Lansky. If it wasn't for Stern's daughter, I'd probably be lying in a Cuban morgue with a machete sticking out of my butt."

"That's completely fanciful," Aaron said. "The fact is, I told Meyer point-blank I wouldn't tolerate any more bloodshed."

"You did."

Aaron raised his right hand as if taking an oath.

"So by 'any *more* bloodshed' I can assume that Meyer did have Stern killed," I said. "As if I ever doubted it."

Aaron looked away and sighed theatrically. "The reality is, it was an accident. A tragic accident. They sent a button man to scare him, but Stern didn't scare, so this hothead took the path of least resistance and gunned him down."

"On Meyer's orders."

"Meyer doesn't give those kind of orders."

"You know that for a fact?"

Aaron just stared at me. No part of his face moved.

"So it had to be Luciano."

Now he nodded, almost imperceptibly. Aaron was doling out gestures like Christmas pennies at an orphanage. "That's right, my friend. That's who we're dealing with, and let me tell you, it is far from a day at the beach. Luciano's a highly intelligent man, but not nearly as clever as Meyer and much more cold-blooded."

"Really? Luciano cold-blooded?"

Aaron nodded ruefully. "Call me naive, but it's been much worse than I ever expected. Meyer's a hoodlum, but at least he thinks like a businessman. Lucky likes to fancy himself a businessman, but he thinks like a hoodlum. And that's both the big difference and the big problem, Jack; it's made life extremely difficult for us."

"And by 'us,' you're referring to the esteemed National Broadcasting Company."

"Correct." Aaron lowered himself onto the piano bench and rubbed his eyes. "I haven't gotten up at dawn in a long goddamn time. Can't say I like it."

"So NBC set up this snatch, then contracted it out to Luciano and Lansky? That's some bedtime story."

The NBC honcho shook his head vigorously. "No, Jack. We would never do something so disgraceful, on the one hand, or audacious, on the other."

"It was Lucky's idea?"

Aaron nodded. "Totally. He planned it for two years. Apparently he got the idea in Italy one night, while listening to *Abduction of the Seraglio*. Mozart. You know it, Jack?"

I shook my head. "Not even close."

"Lucky says he suddenly had a vision of the whole thing. He can be very dramatic; claims he actually had a dream about it, how it would all work. He told Lansky, who was visiting him in Naples, and then they filled in the details. One night over dinner, in a private room in a restaurant, as he tells it. From that point, it took six months to find the double, a year to train him, and then six weeks for the actual surgery and the healing process."

"Where'd they do the surgery, Switzerland?"

"Denmark."

"And who's the double? When he lets down his guard, he's got an accent like a guy who toasts frankfurter buns at Nedick's."

"They never told me his name. Born in the Bronx but grew up in Utica, New York, had extensive musical training, played in some small orchestras in upstate New York and Pennsylvania. A cellist."

"He doesn't talk like a cellist."

"Most cellists don't talk like cellists."

"How did they find this guy?"

Aaron shrugged in a rabbinical fashion. "How does Lucky find people? He asks around, he gets messages to people who get messages to other people. God only knows what the process is."

"Okay. Then what?"

"Once they found him, they brought him to study conducting privately in Italy; Lucky hooked him up with someone from the Rome Opera. Then, of course, this guy watched all the film on Maestro he could get his hands on. Came to New York and studied him in performance; learned all the gestures. He's a quick study, I'll say that. Something of an idiot savant, in fact."

"I've been called that," I said. "Except they leave out the savant part."

Aaron smiled grimly. "This guy's quite astonishing, I have to say, for the degree of *nuance* he was able to absorb."

"He's obviously fooled a lot of people."

"Except for poor Fritz and a few others."

"So he gets Maestro down pat, returns to Europe, and gets the full-bore facial surgery. After the weeks of healing, Lucky and Meyer then just go ahead and pulled the switch in Sun Valley, with no advance word? The blackmail notes come after the fact?"

"Right."

"So you're saying you had no warning of any sort. It was just, 'Pay us three million and avoid a public embarrassment.' "

"Right again."

It didn't add up at all.

"You look skeptical, Jack."

"I'm way past skeptical."

"Why?"

"*Why?* For one thing, what the hell are you doing here? Why send me to Havana to track down the old man if you could find him yourself?"

"Because LaMarca called me yesterday and told me they were

bringing him out here and wanted to conclude the negotiations." Aaron pretended to get agitated. "How the hell was I supposed to contact you? I called the Nacional, they said you'd checked out."

"I don't buy it," I told him.

"You don't. You think Toscanini is here on vacation?"

"No. I think he's here against his will, no question. But I also think that if there is a snatch, you're part of it; otherwise, why would you be sitting around this suite like the hired help?"

Aaron crossed his legs and ran his hand across his brow. When he started to speak, he sounded like a man trying to explain the family business to his idiot nephew.

"Because I'm trying to protect Maestro, who I love more than I love myself, and because this is no ordinary snatch. Jesus Christ, Jack, I already told you what the problem was, I told you back in New York."

"That NBC wasn't in any hurry to get the old man back because the orchestra was becoming a financial headache. Fine. But I still don't buy that they'd just let him get killed, nor do I think that Lansky or Lucky would be dumb or disrespectful enough to kill him; Lansky because he's too smart and Lucky because the old man's like an Italian treasure. Bumping him off for three million bucks makes absolutely no sense; they can earn that moving heroin on a slow afternoon."

"So you're saying this whole thing is a sham?"

"I don't know what the hell it is. But I think this snatch has zippo to do with ransom and everything to do with the hotel business, and here's another wild guess—you boys are in for a piece of the action, which is why you're lounging around here in that lovely silk robe."

Aaron manufactured a look of disbelief. "NBC is in for a piece, that's what you're telling me?"

"That's what I'm telling you. I think the ransom notes were bullshit, manufactured to leave a phony paper trail. The reality is that Lansky and Luciano want the old man to front a hotel they're going to build which will legitimize this cow town forever."

Aaron unsuccessfully simulated laughter. "Is that what Meyer told you? Toscanini is going to front a Vegas hotel? *Please.* I thought you were an intelligent man, Jack."

"Why else would they *schlepp* him out here? To work on his tan?"

"No, Jack. Maestro was brought to Vegas because Meyer has almost total control over the press here. He and Lucky didn't feel they could keep the lid on in Havana much longer."

"Word would get out."

"Of course. One thing about this god-awful place: You want something locked down, it gets locked down."

I looked around the room. "Fine, I can believe that. But from the looks of this suite, Maestro's set to hang around here for keeps. I have less furniture in my apartment, not that that's any standard."

Aaron waved his hand impatiently. "Jack, we're talking about one of the great artists in *the history of the world,* okay? What he wants, he gets, at least as long as I'm around. If he's here for a day, a week, or two weeks, I make sure he has his comforts, his music, his *ambience,* okay? In the meantime, I'm trying to negotiate him out of here."

"So that's why you're here, to negotiate? I thought it was to protect him."

"It's all the same, Jack. Jesus Christ! I'm just a middleman with a commitment to protect the life of a great man. Believe me or not, that's what's going on. When I sent you to Havana, I was desperate. But I'm glad that I did, because I think you flushed them out, forced their hand."

"I got bopped on the head, that's what I did."

"You were a catalyst for all this activity." Aaron rose from the piano bench. "You'd be well within your rights to ask for the twelve thousand bucks right now."

"I would be?"

"Yes."

"So you're saying you want me to go home?"

"I think your work is pretty much done."

"What about Lansky?"

"I'll tell him to lay off you."

"Promise?"

Aaron smiled and raised his hand. " 'Swear to God,' as we used to say in Brooklyn."

"Great. And you're just going to stay here and bargain for the old man to get out?"

"I'll do my best, within the constraints I'm under."

"What if NBC says it doesn't care if he gets knocked off?"

"I believe I can persuade my superiors otherwise. Principally on a public relations basis. If Maestro gets killed because of our inaction, Lansky and Luciano could run corporate blackmail on us that would be unbelievably destructive. They own reporters all over the world; that's the ugly reality."

"So you think Sarnoff will pay the three million."

Aaron bowed his head, took a breath.

"What . . . ?" I said.

"That's where I misspoke, Jack. As of last night, they want seven million."

I almost whistled. "That's a lot of cabbage."

"It's an unimaginable amount of money. But I think I can persuade the general of the consequences if we don't pay off."

"Good luck."

"I'll need it," said Aaron. "Do you want me to call you a car to get you back to the airport?"

I shook my head. "I'll handle my own arrangements, but thanks. First I gotta get back to the kitchen and return this outfit."

"It's not a flattering look for you, Jack, I have to say in all honesty." Aaron smiled and held out his hand. "Thanks for a tremendous job, pal; you were the right guy in a very tough jam."

I shook his hand. It was not a dry hand.

"Appreciate it, Sidney. Thanks."

"Anytime," Aaron said. "How about I give you half now in cash and then have Elizabeth mail you a check for the remainder?"

"Six thousand in cash?"

"That's right. Too much?"

"No. It's the least you can do."

Aaron chuckled. What a terrific guy. "Hang on. Let me get at it." He headed toward the second bedroom and I turned and walked into the living room. Toscanini was contentedly *shmearing* jam on a roll.

I knelt beside him. "Maestro, I have to run."

He looked at me quizzically.

"Boston Blackie," he said gently. He looked around the room, then leaned closer to me. The look in those myopic yet infinitely expressive eyes flickered from contentment to uncertainty. "Is *necessita*?"

"You mean, do I have to go?"

The street-clothes muscle was sitting on a chair leafing through the morning paper. He turned a page and yawned.

"Yes, I do. But I'll be back."

Now his eyes registered a flicker of fear, for the very first time. "Is not right here. *Capisce?*"

"Yes. And you're correct; it's not right here."

"Is not *fascisti,* I think."

"I agree."

"I want to go home." The Maestro's eyes misted over a bit. "To Villa Pauline."

"I'll get you home."

Aaron was reentering from the next room. I patted the old man's hand, gestured for him to lean toward me, and then spoke quickly and softly. "Whatever happens, try and stay on the grounds of the hotel. Okay?"

The old man nodded. "Sì. I try and wait for you, Boston Blackie."

"Hang in there, Maestro." I got up and started for the door. The plainclothes man put down his newspaper and began to rise, but Aaron waved at him to sit back down. He walked toward me holding a thick envelope.

"Again," Aaron murmured, standing close enough to me so I could smell his stale morning breath, "thanks for some brilliant work."

I mumbled my gratitude and took the envelope, sticking it in the inside of my jacket. "See you back in New York."

"You bet, Jack. Let's get some dinner when this is all over."

"That's a great idea," I told him, then walked to the door and opened it. When I turned around, I saw the three men in the room sitting and standing as stock-still as if they were having their portraits done, their eyes fixed on my departing self.

I waved jauntily and took my leave. I figured that if I remained in Vegas I had maybe an hour to live.

THIRTEEN

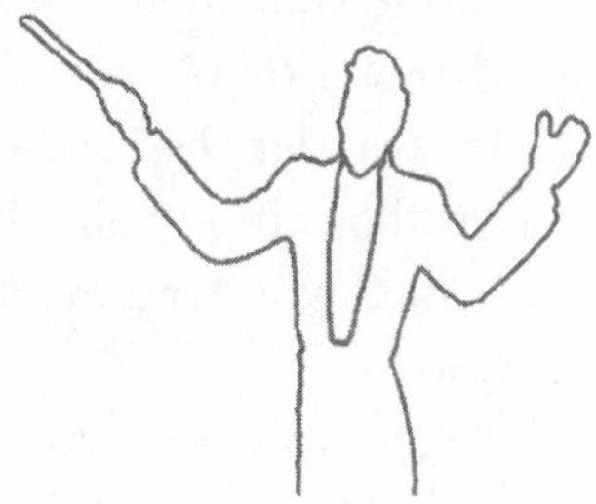

I rushed noisily down the fire stairs and was panting like a spaniel by the time I reached my room. I cautiously opened the door, then double-bolted and chained it the moment I got inside. The room was just as I left it, with two significant differences.

There was a fine leather valise on the bed and it didn't belong to me.

The shower was running.

I walked quietly to the night table, pulled open the top drawer and removed the .38 I had pilfered from the driver, then crept toward the bathroom, finally nudging the door open with my left hand. I was instantly rewarded with the gratifying sight of soapy water cascading down Barbara Stern's lustrous body. She screamed, of course, at the very sight of me.

"Jesus!" she said, and yanked the shower curtain all the way shut.

"I won't bother asking how you got in the room," I said, closing the bathroom door and pocketing the gun.

"It wasn't terribly difficult," she hollered over the running water. "The bellhops here respond very well to minimal offerings of cash. Plus, I batted my eyes a little."

"I'm not registered under my name."

"Somehow 'Buddy Barrow' spoke to me. Sounded like something you'd dream up. Then I described you, and this kid—"

"Name of 'Happy'? On the short side? With overdeveloped shoulders and imagination?"

"Happy, yes. Said there was a gentleman who fit the description, except the gentleman was wearing a cheap hairpiece."

"I resent that."

Barbara laughed and shut the water off, then poked her beautiful wet head out from behind the curtain.

"Could you hand me a towel?"

"No."

"Okay, you want to be like that." She smiled demurely, then stepped daintily out of the shower, arching her leg high over the rim of the tub and affording me a momentary and heart-stopping view of the entirety of her. Barbara wrapped a bath towel around her waist and draped a face towel around her neck, leaving her full, elegant breasts exposed.

"I called your mother," I told her. "She said you'd gone to California. Imagine my less-than-delighted surprise."

"I had to tell her I was going to California." Barbara began toweling her hair dry. "She would've had a breakdown if she knew I was flying here."

"So you came here straight from Havana?"

"With a stop in Miami. I told Meyer I was going back to New York. Guess I've been lying to everyone."

"Including me that night in Havana."

She stopped drying her hair and looked directly into my innocent brown eyes. "No. I never lied that night. What happened to you was truly out of my control. You have to believe that."

"It's an awful lot to believe."

"I know it is. But as God or whoever's on vacation up there is my witness, I had nothing to do with it." She peered at me from under the towel. "That thing on your head, Jack, please tell me it's a disguise."

"You don't approve?"

"Looks like an otter pelt."

"I'm trying to avoid your old playmate."

"Well, a fella can't blame you for that," she said. She let the towel droop babushka-style over that magnificent head and took one step forward. "But it's gotta go."

She leaned forward and lifted the toupee off my head like it was a loose Band-Aid. "Much better," she murmured, then pressed her lips against mine. We kissed oh-so-softly, then she flicked her tongue up across my chin—don't knock it till you've tried it—and kissed me a lot harder, uttering a low and incendiary moan. I could feel myself short-circuiting and took a step back.

"Last time you made that sound, I got hit by a truck."

"You don't trust me, do you?" She brushed her knuckles against my cheek. "How could you, after what happened?"

"I don't know what I think. You're so gorgeous it really isn't a fair fight."

"That night was totally mortifying." She now took the towel and began to dry her breasts; I would describe what that looked like if there were words adequate to the task. "Those guys dragging you out of there, staring at me the whole time . . ." She sighed. "I think Meyer flipped is what really happened."

"Out of jealousy? Come on, he left us together, for crissakes."

"Obviously he didn't think we'd get physical."

"Because why would you go for a moldy old Hebe?"

She smiled. "You're mature, not old. Big difference." She lifted the towel off her head and wiped my sweaty forehead. It was plenty steamy in the smallish bathroom. "Fact is, I don't think Meyer even *considered* what I might be feeling about you—no big surprise there. I'm also sure he figured you wouldn't have the gall to seduce his old girlfriend." I was sufficiently a sap to feel my robust heart ache at the mere use of the word "girlfriend." It took Barbara approximately the speed of light to see inside me.

"Don't look so miserable, Jack. I was never in love with him, I told you that." She put her arms on my shoulder and kissed me again. The towel fell from her waist and she ground herself up against me.

"Baby, we can't . . ." I told her while I could still form English words.

"Afraid you're going to get clobbered again?" She kissed my nose, my eyes, brushed her lips against my cheek.

"I have to get out of Vegas. . . ." I stepped back, held up my hands. "We gotta stop." I opened the door and walked out of the bathroom. Barbara followed.

"You want to get out of Vegas? Let me call Meyer and arrange it." She walked to the phone.

"No."

"Don't panic, he'll listen to me." She picked up the phone.

"Put it down!" I yelled.

She stood holding the phone, wearing only that little towel around her shoulders. "First time you ever raised your voice, Jack."

It was now all of seven-fifteen in the morning and I was trying to gather my wits before those wits got scattered to the desert winds. I wasn't at all sure that I could trust Barbara Stern, nor could I trust my judgment when I was around her. I realized that for my protection, and probably for hers, I would have to hurt her very badly.

"Sweetheart, Meyer's not our friend here."

"I know he has schemes. He always does."

"No, baby, I'm not talking about schemes. Meyer had your father killed."

Fritz Stern's daughter pursed her lips as if she were about to say something, then sat down on the bed and stared at her bare feet.

"Whether he or Lucky gave the actual order is moot," I told her. "He's responsible." Barbara didn't lift her head. "Sidney Aaron's version is that the intention was simply to scare your father, but the button man got carried away. I don't believe that for a second. I don't believe anything Aaron says. It was a hit, pure and simple."

"Meyer did it." She mumbled this to herself in the form of a question that supplied its own answer.

"It's a nightmarish thing to consider, I realize that, given your history with him, but there's really no time to dwell on it. Right this second, there's gotta be a half dozen guys looking for me, and seeing how easily you tracked me down, I don't have high hopes for getting out of here with my arms and legs still attached unless I start right now. And I don't think there's any way Toscanini gets out, either, not unless we do it—literally, you and I physically transporting him."

Barbara looked up at me; tears coursed down her cheeks.

"They're going to kill Toscanini. That's so totally impossible for me to conceive."

"I didn't say they're actually going to kill him. I think the idea is to keep him in Vegas until he dies a natural death, at which point, or shortly thereafter, they kill the double. Or maybe they just stick the old man in a freezer for a while and continue the scam."

Barbara stared at me, not yet comprehending.

"Why . . . ?"

"Did Meyer ever tell you about the hotel he wanted to build here?"

"He mentioned something about it in Havana, said it was going to be gigantic."

"Beyond gigantic. He told me it was going to change the gambling business forever. And the live entertainment business."

"La Scala," Barbara said. "That's what he said it was going to be called." She paused and then her entrancing mouth opened in full amusement-park wonder. "Holy smokes, how could I be so stupid? La Scala—like the opera house."

"Precisely," I told her. "The Old World comes to the New World. Meyer's front men erect Hotel La Scala and announce that the world's greatest orchestra will be organized to perform here, none other than Maestro himself to conduct it. That's what Meyer told me."

"Toscanini in Vegas."

"The faux-Toscanini leading the Hotel La Scala Orchestra. Except, of course, the old man would never agree to it; he just wants to get back to New York and lead the NBC Symphony. He's up on the third floor, a prisoner in the Valencia Suite."

"So you're saying this kidnapping is all about this La Scala Hotel?"

"Totally. Lucky and Meyer build their hotel and this fake Toscanini is the big drawing card, plus NBC is in for a piece—probably a big piece through a phony corporation—and just like that the company's out of its obligations to the symphony, which costs a fortune and isn't worth it now that television's here to stay. Aaron admitted as much, although he was pretending he was on guard against the barbarians. In fact, he's the middleman here."

Barbara lay back on the bed, oblivious to her nakedness. I wasn't.

"Jesus Christ," she said. "Even I'm surprised, and I don't surprise easy."

"It's a huge deal, with giant consequences for Vegas, which is why Meyer and Lucky had your inquisitive father eliminated. He was just the wrong curious guy at the wrong time."

"It's entirely my fault." Barbara lay unmoving.

"No. It's a hideous coincidence is all it is. Maybe your father gets killed earlier if it wasn't for you. But we really don't have time to discuss this. Get your clothes on. I never thought I'd say that, but I mean it from the bottom of my heart."

While Barbara started to get dressed, I opened my wallet and fished out the card that Kim the lesbian cabby had handed me.

"What's that?" Barbara asked, hopping into a pair of tan slacks.

"I gotta make a call," I told her, and picked up the phone.

"To who?"

"To the only person I've met out here who I'd trust with my life."

"What about me?"

"I didn't meet you out here."

"True, but I hope that's not just a technicality." She started getting into her brassiere, turning her back in a sudden show of modesty. I dialed the number on the card and after three rings, a very sleepy voice answered.

" 'Lo?"

"Kim, it's Lassie. I know I'm waking you." Barbara threw me an appropriately disbelieving look.

"Las . . . ?" Kim mumbled.

"The private dick from New York. I hate to do this to you, but I'm in a spot."

"Really." I heard coughing on her end. Barbara strolled over to me, pulling a sleeveless white sweater over her head. Her arms looked very long and very brown.

"What's with 'Lassie'?" she whispered. "That some kind of joke?"

I covered the phone. "Long story."

"Another girl, Jack?" Her eyes flashed with amusement, but also some concern, I was gratified to note.

"She's a woman, she's a cabby, and she's gonna be a lot hotter for you than she is for me. Please, get your shoes on. We gotta get moving."

"Such a bully." She strolled over toward her valise.

"What time is it?" I heard Kim say, then I detected some mumbling beside her. Probably her dancer pal, Cheryl.

"Almost seven-thirty," I told her. "The day's practically shot."

"Jesus H. Christ."

"Listen, I'm in the middle of an extremely dicey situation here and I need a very substantial ride."

She coughed some more. "I gotta quit smoking."

"Yes you do."

She wheezed a little, then cleared her throat. "So where do you need to go, Lassie?"

"You can call me Jack."

"That's the real?"

"That's the real. Jack LeVine. And I need to go to New York."

There was a brief, pregnant silence.

"New York by taxi."

"Correct."

"When do you need to go?"

"Five minutes ago."

"Really. It's like that."

"It's more than like that."

"Dangerous."

"Very."

"I'm just taking you?"

"No, there's two others—the daughter of a violinist who's been murdered, and a musician. A very eminent one."

"How eminent?"

"You can't imagine."

There was a pause. Kim was trying to wake up and process this locust-plague of information at the same time.

"Shit," she said. "This some sort of musical crime in progress?"

"You're very warm."

"What are you willing to pay me?"

"A lot."

"Define 'a lot.' "

"Five hundred bucks."

"Really. Plus gas?"

"Plus gas, oil, water, and sandwiches."

"That's a bunch of money, Jack. Should I be terrified?"

"Yes."

At this moment a large shadow fluttered rapidly past my window. My stomach turned over; seconds later I heard a dull wet thud. Then silence.

"What the hell was that?" Barbara asked, looking up from her valise. But she knew. "A person?"

"Kim?" I said into the phone.

"Yes?"

"Can you do this?"

"What the hell . . . sure."

"Meet me at the Flamingo service entrance in fifteen minutes."

I hung up the phone. There was the beginning of a commotion outside, an almost slow-motion perception of disaster: voices, distant at first, then closer, then some yelling. I walked over to the window and pulled it open.

"What's going on?" Barbara said from in back of me. I poked my head outside, into the early morning heat. "Should I look?"

"No," I told her. People were gathering around a concrete fountain set in the middle of a triangular walkway. Sprawled across the fountain, his head hanging limply in the water, was a man wearing gray slacks, a white shirt rapidly turning red, and a handsome silk robe.

Sidney Aaron was as dead as yesterday's headlines.

I slammed the window shut and headed for the door. "Stay here," I said to Barbara, just like a big strong man.

"Why?" she asked. "Where are you going?"

"Upstairs."

"To Toscanini?"

"Yes."

"Then I'm going with you."

"Barbara, listen—"

"I'm not staying here," she said emphatically, pulling on her shoes. "What happened out there?" There was now a growing and continual static of activity from outside—racing footsteps, overlapping shouts, car engines turning over.

"Guy got air-mailed out a window." I opened the door. "Could you just give me five minutes? If I'm not back—"

"You're not listening to me, Jack. I'm coming with you."

I paused at the door. She picked up her valise

"If you're coming, at least leave the valise here."

She shook her head. This was some stubborn gal.

"We're not coming back to this room ever, Jack, I just know it. All my stuff is in this bag, all my makeup—"

"You don't need any makeup."

Barbara smiled tightly. "Silly man."

The two of us left the room and went creeping down the hall like Nick and Nora Charles in *The Thin Man Goes to Las Vegas*. I opened the steel door to the fire exit and immediately saw a pair of scrawny house dicks hustling up the staircase to the third floor.

"What the hell's going on?" I asked. "Guy can't sleep around here with all this racket."

"Accident," the first dick said breathlessly.

"Accident, my ass. Sounded like somebody got tossed. What kind of a dump is this?"

"Can't talk right now, chief." The two dicks continued hot-footing it up the stairs.

I waited a beat, then signaled Barbara to come back out to the corridor. I hustled over to the elevator and pushed the down button. Barbara stared at me in some bafflement.

"Why the elevator and why down?"

"Because if those two monkeys are running up to the third floor, it's my guess that our friend in the Valencia Suite has already vacated the premises and is either going to be in this elevator or in the lobby."

"Our friend being Toscanini?"

"And his keeper, Gino, who probably did the tossing. The good news is the old man isn't exactly Jesse Owens. It's going to take a while to go anywhere with him."

Barbara looked at me anxiously. "Who was it, Jack?"

"The guy who got tossed?"

"Yeah."

"Sidney Aaron."

"From NBC Sidney Aaron?"

"Yes."

"Jesus Christ." She bit her lip. "And you're sure it's Meyer behind all this?"

"I have to think so."

"Goddamn," she said, quietly but urgently.

The elevator doors opened. The car was empty save for a seventy-year-old woman carrying a sack full of nickels. She had bluish hair and wore steel-rimmed spectacles. We entered and I impatiently pressed the button for the door to close.

"I won eleven dollars last night," the elderly woman informed me.

"That a fact," I said.

"Yes indeed." She smiled warmly at Barbara, then at me. "You have a lovely daughter. You must be very proud."

I nodded gratefully. "I've done my best with her. Thanks so much." The elevator doors opened and I gallantly let the blue-haired lady out onto the casino floor with her cache of small change. Barbara shot me a devilish look.

"Don't say a word," I told her.

"Me? Wouldn't dream of it."

Even at seven-thirty in the morning there was action in the casino. Slot machines were ringing and about a third of the blackjack tables and crap tables were in operation. The only intimation that someone had just been hurled out of a window was the sight of two maids scurrying toward the front doors, their arms filled with bath towels.

Barbara raised her eyebrows.

"To clean up the mess, you think?" she asked.

"I would say so." I stopped and looked around the lobby. Barbara took my arm and squeezed it with some force.

"Jack, do you have like a *plan*? Or do you think we're just somehow going to find Toscanini and drive away? Because that seems like a highly unlikely—"

"I don't disagree. But I can't think of anything more systematic, and I'd hate to have gone through all this trouble—getting whacked on the head and doped up—for no reason at all. Plus, I owe it to your old man and your mother."

"And me?"

"And you. And your sister."

"That wasn't exactly what I meant. . . ."

There was a stir across the casino. I heard a voice raised and then I saw Giuseppe LaMarca, in a gray silk suit, yelling at Wally, the red-headed thug who had been guarding Luciano's room at the Desert Inn. Wally's broken nose was purple and bandaged, and he didn't look to be in any better mood than he'd been in last night. The red-haired lout threw up his hands and started jogging toward the front doors.

"You know him?" Barbara asked. "The little guy?"

"He works for Lucky. Giuseppe LaMarca, also goes by Joey Little or Joey Big, depending on his self-image when he gets up in the morning."

"Very funny. Why was he screaming at that thuggy-looking guy?"

"God only knows. The thug's name is Wally; he's local talent and he's apparently killed a couple of hookers in his time. He was guarding Lucky's door at the Desert Inn when I made his acquaintance. Why Joey's screaming at him, I don't know. But nothing that's happening this morning falls under the heading of good news. Tossing Aaron out the window could mean any number of things. Mainly, I think it means he must've gotten greedy; started lobbying for a bigger piece of the new hotel, either for NBC or maybe for himself."

"You mean make his own deal?"

"Exactly. Decided to freelance, which is never a great idea when you're dealing with Lucky or Meyer."

Now Barbara looked off, and her eyes got very wide. She mouthed, *Jack,* but no sound came out.

I followed her gaze. Toscanini and Gino were getting off the elevator. The old man was wearing a raincoat and a tweed cap and was almost unrecognizable. He looked frightened and disoriented.

"Where is Walter?" I heard him ask.

"Went back to New York," Gino told him.

"Perche?"

"To get things nice for you there."

"I go back?"

"Soon."

Gino took the old man under the arm and they started for the front doors. Across the casino floor, I could see LaMarca recognize the two men; he started running across the room.

"Get ready. The shit's going to hit the fan very fast now," I told Barbara.

"Let me talk to that Gino." She extracted a cigarette from her bag.

"I really don't think—" I started to say, but she was already in motion. Barbara pulled her sweater tight, to emphasize what hardly needed emphasizing, and strolled over to Gino, cigarette in hand. She tapped the goon on the shoulder and smiled; Gino turned to her, as did Toscanini. Neither of them knew where to look first. Toscanini gazed at her chest, Gino looked into her eyes. She was evidently asking Gino for a light, moving clockwise to force him to put his back to me. Gino reached into his pockets and I stepped forward. LaMarca was halfway across the casino when he saw and yelled, "Gino," but I already had my gun out and was cracking the goon on the back of the head. Gino started to fall into my arms, but I stepped back and let him tumble very hard to the floor.

LaMarca was reaching into his pocket.

"Hit the floor," I yelled at Barbara, who ignored me, grabbing Toscanini and covering his body with hers, which bothered him not at all. I turned around and shot LaMarca high in his right shoulder. Not a great shot, but it did the trick. LaMarca's gray suit instantly started to darken. He grabbed at his arm and slumped slowly to the floor, while the patrons of the casino started scattering like geese.

"Okay," I said for no particular reason. I whacked Gino over the skull one more time for good luck, causing Toscanini to cry out with hoarse enthusiasm, "Kill him, Boston Blackie!"

"Not necessary to kill him, sir, but we do have to blow." I turned to Barbara. "Ready?"

"Yeah." Her forehead was shiny with sweat and her eyes bright with the excitement of the moment.

"Maestro, pardon the indignity," I told him, then picked the world's greatest living musician up and over my right shoulder. I turned and started running toward the coffee shop, Barbara at my side, lugging her valise.

"The coffee shop?" she asked. "I don't think we're hungry, right?"

"No, but it's the quickest way to the service entrance. There's only one kitchen in this joint; it handles the coffee shop, the restaurant, and room service. Leads right out of this dump."

"And you're sure your friend will be there?"

"I deeply hope so." I could feel the old man's weight bouncing on my shoulder. "Maestro, how are we doing?"

"Molto bene," he said.

I raced into the coffee shop. There were a couple of dozen gamblers consuming their breakfasts, having just arisen or getting ready to hit the sack. They watched curiously as Barbara, Toscanini, and I double-timed our way past the booths and tables. Barbara ran on her tiptoes, which created a great deal of body movement, which, in turn, produced a great deal of attention. We sailed through the double doors into the kitchen and never slowed down.

"There," Barbara said, espying the service door. She sprinted toward it and pushed it open, then peered outside. I stood and caught my breath.

"You are strong, Boston Blackie," Toscanini croaked.

"I used to be stronger."

"Like a bull." He looked toward the door. *"Chi es la bella figura, le bella donna?"*

"Barbara Stern, the daughter of Fritz Stern."

"No! *Incredibile!"*

"She certainly is, Maestro."

"You are making her?" A wicked smile crossed the old man's features. "Bravo, Boston Blackie! Bravo!"

Barbara came back inside and waved at me. "Cab's pulling up!"

I gathered myself together and *schlepped* Toscanini outside. The moment we stepped through the door, we hit an almost palpable wall of heat. At eight A.M., it had to be well over ninety degrees.

"Plenty hot, isn't it, Maestro?"

"Orrendo! Un inferno!"

I watched as Kim's red Chevrolet came rolling to a stop outside the service entrance. That was the good news. The bad news was the cloud of black smoke billowing out from under the hood.

Kim hopped out of the cab. I put Toscanini down on the ground.

"Morning," I said to the cabby. She was wearing dungarees and a short-sleeved white shirt with the name of a bowling alley embroidered in red thread across the pocket.

Kim walked silently to the front of the car and, oily rag in hand, lifted the hood open. It wasn't a pretty sight. The Triangle Shirtwaist fire might have produced more smoke, but not by much.

"What an effin disaster," she said, examining the smoldering ruin of her engine. "I thought the radiator was full." She turned to me. "We have as much chance of getting to Mars as New York in this piece of shit."

I felt a tug on my arm.

"Jack," Barbara said. A black car pulled up across the Flamingo service lot and three very large men emerged: Wally the redhead and two other goons. They didn't notice us and began running toward the hotel.

"We gotta blow," I told Kim, who was staring at Barbara as if she had just seen a vision of life eternal. "Kim, this is Barbara, and this is Maestro Arturo Toscanini."

Kim turned her head from Barbara for an instant.

"Holy shit," she said, registering who the old man was. "You're him. I've heard your records."

"Is my pleasure," the Maestro said, beaming at Kim. Then he turned to me. "Boston Blackie, this *macchina* . . ." He pointed at the useless cab.

"I know," I said, and then had another idea. Thirty yards away sat the large green bus with VAUGHN MONROE ORCHESTRA painted in white script across its sides.

"You ever jump-start a bus?" I asked Kim.

"I've jump-started a lot of things, sweetie pie. But heisting that bus would be a major crime."

"So's murder, which was just committed about fifteen minutes ago and is about to occur again if we don't get out of here. Maestro?" I lifted Toscanini up across my shoulder again.

Kim took another gander at Barbara. I could see her chest rise and fall with longing. "What the hell. Five hundred bucks?"

"That's what I said."

"Let's do it," she said, and started jogging in the direction of the bus.

We made our way across the molten parking lot. I felt like an ant being tortured by a kid with a magnifying glass.

"How do you stand this heat?" I asked Kim, loping across the lot, the Maestro bouncing on my shoulder.

"I only go out at night, unless some half-witted shamus calls me at seven-thirty in the morning."

We reached the bus, which loomed like an emerald mirage in the middle of the parking lot. Kim popped open the hood of the bus and called out to Barbara. "Honey, could you shield me here?"

Barbara threw me an inquisitive glance. I gave her a high sign, and she instantly positioned herself between the service entrance and Kim.

I put Toscanini down and gestured toward the bus. "Maestro, after you."

"Grazie," he said, and slowly climbed the three steps into the bus, his eyes never leaving the two lovelies hovering over the engine. *"Bella figuras,"* he muttered, totally enchanted. I boarded behind him. As the old man got to the top step, he stopped and took a long look at the interior of the bus.

"Mamma mia," Toscanini muttered. *"Che cosa! Che lusso!"*

The Monroe Orchestra bus was indeed a deluxe creation. The old seats had been ripped out and replaced with swiveling chairs upholstered in red velvet. Each chair had an individual footrest. Running overhead on both sides of the vehicle were highly polished chrome racks for storage and in the middle stood a cabinet containing all the latest magazines and trashy books. In the rear of the bus were two paisley love seats covered with throw pillows. The vehicle had the smell and aura of a very plush parlor car on the Twentieth Century Limited. It was totally fabulous, but it was about as inconspicuous as Moby Dick.

I sat Toscanini down in a chair near the back. The temperature inside the bus had to be over a hundred and the old gent was starting to wilt. He had taken off his raincoat, but was still wearing his Old World black smoking jacket. He mopped his beautiful head with a silk handkerchief.

"We'll try to get moving as quickly as possible," I told him, then looked out the window. The three large individuals, led by the redhead, had now emerged from the Flamingo's service entrance and were looking anxiously but blankly around the parking lot. I raced to the front of the bus and tapped emphatically on the windshield. Barbara looked up and I flashed her the hurry-up sign. She in turn whispered to Kim, who gazed up at me and gave me a thumbs-up and at that instant I heard the bus engine turn over with a roar of well-tuned combustion. Kim slammed the hood shut and never took her eyes off Barbara as the two of them climbed the stairs onto the bus.

I checked out the three gorillas and, as I had feared, the noise of the bus had drawn their undivided attention.

"Let's go!" I yelled.

The thugs had taken revolvers out of their pockets. They began jogging toward the bus.

"Is like Wild West," Toscanini shouted. He was glued to the window, watching the action as happily as a nine-year-old perched in the balcony of the RKO Keiths.

"Maestro, hit the floor."

He shook his head. "Is too exciting."

"It's too dangerous, sir."

He didn't budge, so I started racing toward his seat. Kim ran on board and enthroned herself behind the wheel. I could feel the interior of the bus begin to cool.

"This thing has air-conditioning?" I yelled back at her.

Kim surveyed the controls. "It has everything but wings." She put her foot down hard on the gas pedal and I staggered backward into a seat; this bus had significant acceleration. We went thundering out of the lot as Lucky's and Meyer's boys took a few potshots at us, but it's difficult to aim and run at the same time and their bullets sailed harmlessly over and past the bus.

They stopped and started hustling back toward the hotel, presumably in the direction of their car, but Kim had the band bus moving very fast. God knows what kind of engine had been custom-fitted into this baby, but it was moving a lot quicker than any bus I had ever stepped into in New York.

I pulled myself out of the seat I had tumbled into and sat down next to the Maestro. I was a little exasperated at his blithe disregard of danger.

"Sir, it is not, repeat *not,* a good idea to stare out the window while people are firing loaded revolvers, okay? Just a little bit of friendly advice, because I'm afraid this may not be the last time it happens."

"Boston Blackie"—he patted my arm—"I am Toscanini. Is all right."

"What does that mean? You think you're immortal, Maestro?"

He shrugged and stuffed his handkerchief back into his breast pocket. "I am *fatalista.* What happens, it happens." He fiddled with a button on his chair and it reclined. The great man smiled with childlike glee. *"Un miracolo! Molto bene!"* He rested his head and yawned. "Boston Blackie?"

"What, sir?"

"We are going home?"

"That's my intention. It may be a sort of roundabout route and I believe we'll have to switch modes of transportation quite frequently—"

"Because is dangerous."

"Yes. But we'll get there. I'm confident."

"*Sì.* You are *acuto.* Smart."

"Thank you, sir. I've been around the track a few times. But this particular track is very, very fast."

"Sì." He looked out the window. We were heading out of the center of this strange city-resort and into the desert. Kim had the bus doing about seventy. "Is not *fascisti*. For sure now I know this."

"No, it's not, Maestro. They have a double of you they're running around with."

"Double?"

"Yes, who they're passing off as you. And NBC is in on it. It's all about the hotel business."

Toscanini shook his head. I knew he did not completely get it, but there was just so much information I wished to burden him with. "And Signore Aaron?" he asked. "I was in bathroom. . . . hear him shout, yes? And then . . ."

"Then they threw him out the window."

Toscanini nodded and looked both sad and mystified. "I did not so much like him, Signore Aaron, was *insincero,* but to throw out window . . . Is like *fascisti,* but also like *banditi,* gangster. This whole place, this Las Vegas . . . *molto bizarro.*"

"I agree. *Bizarro* and very depressing. All those poor rubes pissing their money away day and night."

Toscanini shook his head to affirm his own thoughts. *"Sì. Molto bizarro,* but now we go home." He raised those thick dark eyebrows. "Will be adventure, yes?"

"Yes. These are serious people after us, with serious intentions."

"Banditi."

"It's Lucky Luciano, sir, and Meyer Lansky."

And now the old man looked impressed. He folded his hands in his lap, pursed his lips.

"E' vero?"

"Yes it's true."

For one instant, Toscanini's eyes seemed to glaze over and he appeared to age ten years, but then he wrapped his unlined and very white hand around my wrist and gave it a vigorous squeeze. His eyes brightened. "But you are smarter, Boston Blackie. You are number one detective," he said, and then he exhaled mightily and sat back in his seat. He looked toward Barbara and raised his eyebrows.

"Why you want to sit with old man? Go." I hesitated. *"Cretino,"* he said. "Go!"

I got up and took a seat next to Barbara. Kim had settled in behind the wheel and had us doing about eighty. This was some high-class machine. I kept expecting a pursuit car to appear in the rearview mirror, but either we were going too fast or our pursuers had encountered car problems. Or there were other options I couldn't or didn't want to imagine at this early hour in the desert.

We turned off Las Vegas Boulevard and followed a sign directing us toward Route 91. "Want to check out a map?" she called to me over her shoulder.

I told her that I did, so she extracted an Esso road map that was stuffed behind the visor over the driver's seat and tossed it in my direction. I caught it and observed that next to a drawing of the friendly Esso man washing some happy Christian's windshield was block lettering reading WESTERN UNITED STATES. That was a helpful start, because Nevada and Utah were about as familiar to me as the plains of Africa. I unfolded the map, while Barbara leaned over and rested her head on my shoulder. I had been divorced in 1941 and this moment, studying a road map with Barbara's glowing cheek on my shoulder, was the first time since then that I had felt stirrings of husbandship, or husbandry, or whatever you call that strange, oddly prideful feeling of mingled manliness and helplessness.

"So where are we going?" Barbara asked.

"Yeah," Kim echoed. "I was sort of wondering the same thing because it'll greatly affect how I turn the steering wheel."

"Very amusing," I grumbled like the beleaguered head of a raucous household. "Hang on." I studied the map and the most cursory glance indicated that our options were less than limitless. We were in the new and undeveloped American West and its highways and byways were few and far between. This map was as unlined as a baby's tush.

"We're heading toward Route 91, correct?" I asked.

"Correct, *mein führer.*" Kim took a cigarette from her pocket and lit up. "Although the complete sentence would be, 'Heading toward Route 91 in a stolen bus worth more than the Taj Mahal.'"

"Well, if we ditch this fabulous bus, what'll we do?" Barbara asked. "We'll just have to steal another vehicle, right? That seems completely nuts." She smiled at Kim. "I mean, doesn't it?"

Kim smiled back at Barbara. I could just imagine the slide show running in the back room of Kim's mind and wondered if similar visions of entwined sapphic bliss were taking shape in Barbara's fecund imagination. She was so entirely sexual that I didn't doubt the possibility for a second.

"I agree," I said quickly. "We have to keep moving in this baby, and moving fast. I suggest we head straight for Salt Lake and hope we don't run into any more unfriendly fire."

"Salt Lake is a real hike, Lassie," Kim said. "Close to three hundred miles."

I looked down at the map once again and traced the route, calculating distances with my PS 84 arithmetic skills.

"Looks to be three hundred almost exactly. But there's no place between here and there that looks like a better means to a route east."

"Which means what exactly?" Barbara asked.

I put down the map. "There's no way we can drive this Ferris wheel all the way to New York without getting picked up."

"You don't think so?" she asked. "It goes really fast, doesn't it, or am I missing the point?" She picked a little lint off my jacket, which moved me much more than it should have. "I am, right? Missing the point?"

I looked over my shoulder: Toscanini was staring out the window, seemingly enthralled with the landscape. He had donned a pair of sunglasses.

"I mean," Barbara continued, "what I'm thinking is, isn't the idea to get home as quickly as possible?"

"The idea is to get home alive, period. There's a chance Meyer could convince Luciano to keep you alive, but the rest of us, including the old man, we're dead meat if we're caught."

"Even her?" She pointed at Kim, who was happily smoking her

Lucky and looking as butch as could be with both her strong hands gripping the steering wheel.

I nodded. "Especially her. She means zip to them and she knows too much already. And maybe even you're vulnerable, sweetie. This is a very big and very delicate game they're playing. People with information are a big threat. Lucky doesn't want to get locked up again. That's why I say we go to Salt Lake, dump this bus, and grab a plane."

Barbara thought it over. "I've always had a gift for survival, Jack. Not that I treasure or respect it all that much right now. It's about my body, basically. Men want to keep my body alive, not me."

"I understand. But the point I'm belaboring is that no matter what they ultimately do with you, this bus is like a giant blinking sign. It's going to draw way too much attention. Once it's reported stolen, which could be any minute, its going to be a snap to track down. Fortunately, it's so unpopulated around here that there aren't many cops. I'm also banking on the fact that nobody with the Monroe band gets up much before noon, so maybe we get a decent head start. But we can't know that for sure." I looked out the window; we were getting onto Route 91. It was a wide two-lane road and we appeared to be the only vehicle on it.

"Salt Lake or bust," Kim announced, winking at Barbara. Barbara smiled back at her, then turned to me.

"Jack, if the cops do pick us up, would that necessarily be so terrible? With the old man and all. They'd protect us, yes?"

"We can't risk it. First of all, I would hazard a guess that highway patrolmen in Nevada and Utah don't know Toscanini from Elmer Fudd. Second, you know better than anyone how wired Lucky and Meyer are. They might own half the troopers out here; the cops could do their dirty work for them, or maybe just bump me and Kim off, leaving you and the old man to be picked up later."

"So we're sitting ducks if we stick with this bus."

"Totally. At some point we have to ditch it. Hopefully not before Salt Lake, but I wouldn't be surprised if we don't make it that far."

Barbara took my hand. "I don't scare easily, but I have to tell you—I'm definitely fearful."

"Good," I told her. "I was starting to worry about you."

She put her head on my shoulder and within five minutes, Barbara Stern had shut her eyes and was breathing rhythmically, a young girl's smile on her face. Some happy and faraway dream. I suddenly felt very much like a stranger, an old stranger at that, so I decided to stop looking.

FOURTEEN

I joined Kim at the front of the bus. She looked back toward her two passengers: Toscanini had tilted his head back and appeared to be catching a few winks, Barbara had shifted in her seat and now she slept facing the aisle, backlit by the morning sun. Kim watched her recumbent form with almost palpable longing.

"She's yours?" Kim's gaze returned to the empty road.

"She's nobody's."

"Figures."

"Can't imagine she ever will be, either," I told her.

"She's what my father used to call a 'humdinger.' " Kim brushed a stray hair back behind her ear. "My heart actually goes pitty-pat when I look at her."

"Yeah," I said, and slowly dug a cigarette out of my pocket.

"That's all you have to say on the subject?" Kim asked.

"Her old man was killed. That's how this whole mess began."

"Really."

"Sweet little guy. A fiddler."

"Which is how Toscanini fits in?"

"Exactly."

"Amazing. Me driving Toscanini around." She looked back at the sleeping beauty. "Look at her. The way the light hits her arm, the swell of her ass."

"I get the point." I lit up my Lucky.

She smiled. "Maybe you do. Not to tell you more than you want to know, but I've been sort of soaked ever since I laid eyes on her."

"That's plenty more than I want to know."

"I'm sure. But God, what a work of art she is." She looked at the dashboard. "I should distract myself. Think anybody'd wake up if I switched on the radio?"

"Not if you keep it low enough."

She turned the radio knob and we began to hear an oleaginous male voice crooning a tender ballad about the Lord Jesus Christ. Kim changed stations and we were treated to a feed report from Lubbock, Texas. Corn was evidently in for a very rough day.

"No real choice so far, is it?" Kim muttered, and turned the dial farther to the right. Now some old cowpoke was singing softly about corrals and doggies.

"Can you stand this, Jack, or should I keep looking?" Kim asked.

"I can stand plenty. It's fine." I stood and watched the desert fly past, my feet planted firmly on the floor, one hand on a chrome bar mounted to the rear of the driver's seat. The sky was a deep blue I had only seen in Westerns.

"This is a dazzling part of the world," I said, inhaling my Lucky. "But it doesn't seem real to me."

"You get used to it."

"To the unreality?"

"Yep," Kim said. "It just sort of seeps into your consciousness and then it becomes normal."

"Gives me the willies. I feel like I'm traveling across the moon. We've seen, what, four cars in an hour?"

"It's early yet." Kim smiled. "We might see five or six more."

"There's just nothing here. Red rocks, some bluffs, a few evil-looking birds."

"That's why Vegas is going to keep growing. Fills a vacuum out in these parts. Once the big shots figured out how to air-condition large spaces, Vegas was inevitable." She fell silent, considering something. "Toscanini himself," she finally said. "Goddamn."

"Can you see him leading an orchestra in Vegas?"

Kim looked at me with some amusement. "For real?"

"That was the general idea."

"Can I ask you something that you don't have to answer?"

I pulled a bit of tobacco from my lip. "Go ahead."

"Someone swore to me they saw Lucky Luciano walking through the casino at the Inn. Is that possible? Wasn't he deported, like forever?"

I nodded. "It's more than possible."

"Holy shit," she said. "Is that in any way related to this old guy leading an orchestra on the strip?"

"You're two for two." I cocked my ear. There was an increasingly loud engine noise of unknown origins. I listened and it only got louder. "Is that coming from this bus?" I asked Kim.

She listened. The noise deepened and widened. It had a different dynamic than the bus or the odd passing car or truck.

In point of fact, it was at a different altitude.

Kim stared into her side mirror. "Jesus . . ." I leaned over her shoulder and saw what she did: a single-engine plane about two hundred yards behind us traveling maybe four hundred feet off the ground.

"What the fuck is this, Jack, pardon my Italian?"

"Get off the road."

"What?"

"Get off the road. Now."

The plane was, not surprisingly, gaining on us.

"Get off where?" Kim asked.

"Right up there."

We were passing a bluff; a dirt road marked MOAPA TRAIL loomed a hundred yards ahead.

"There?" she shouted. The plane was really loud now. "The dirt road?"

"Yeah." Our airborne stalkers were closing the gap with comical ease. The dirt trail was ten yards away. Out the window I saw a small metallic object land on the road beside us and roll to a stop.

"Now! Now!" I bellowed at Kim. She yanked the wheel hard to the left and we went barreling off the road and onto the dirt path. Two seconds later, there was a deafening explosion.

"Holy Christ," I said to Kim.

"What was that?" She'd gone white under the gills.

"A hand grenade."

"You shitting me?

"No ma'am."

Barbara woke up. "What's happening?" she mumbled.

"A small detour, ladies and gentlemen," I told her.

We were raising a thundercloud of dust as we sped down the dirt trail. The single-engine prop had gone past us on the highway and was now skimming the air virtually on its side, beginning a slow turn to double back in our direction.

"Stay close to the bluff," I hollered at Kim.

"A grenade," Kim said. "Holy motherfucker . . ."

I looked into the side mirror. The plane was taking another pass. We accelerated, spraying dirt and pebbles across a sign pointing to the Moapa Reservation Market.

Barbara got up from her seat. "Jack . . ."

"Sit back down, sweetheart," I told her. "Please."

"This is *outrageous,*" she said, sitting down obediently.

"Now what?" Kim asked. The plane was getting lower and closer and *much* louder.

"Turn here," I hollered. There was a hand-painted, arrow-shaped sign by the side of the road that pointed to a tiny dirt trail that led back to Highway 91.

"This?" Kim shouted back.

"Yeah."

"You want to go back to the highway?"

"Yes!"

Barbara got out of her seat. "Jack, what the hell—"

"Sit down!" I bellowed.

We approached the dirt trail and Kim just shook her head.

"It's a little trail, Jack! Barely big enough for a car, much less this monster."

"Do it."

Kim turned the wheel hard to the left. The bus wobbled for an instant and Toscanini raised his head, clearly disoriented.

"Que cosa?" he asked foggily.

"We had a slight change of route," I told him. The plane was fifty yards behind and completing its turn, when its engine emitted a whining, scraping noise that even I could immediately tell wasn't kosher. I stared into the side mirror like a mad scientist as we went under an overpass carved from the bluff; the plane was now attempting to climb again when its engine stalled.

"What's happening?" Kim asked.

"You're doing great," I shouted. "Keep going."

Toscanini was now fully awake. "This is like war," he said almost gleefully. He started to pull his window open.

"Maestro, keep it closed!" I hollered.

The pursuing plane had restarted its engine; the familiar drone had resumed. The small craft began to climb, but then the engine began to sputter once again, before finally falling silent.

"Now what?" Kim asked.

"I think they're in major trouble," I told her.

They were in worse than major trouble. The plane veered to the left and started sinking. Barbara opened her window and stuck her head out.

"Put your head in!" I yelled, but she waved at me to pipe down. Now Toscanini followed suit, rising from his seat and pulling his window all the way open. Kim accelerated, but the two of them didn't budge, gawking like a pair of yokels taking the *Maid of the Mist* under Niagara Falls.

The small plane made another pass at restarting its motor, but to no avail. It fluttered left and right and then started to sail toward the bluff with the doomed inevitability of a kamikaze.

Kim watched it develop in her mirror. "Oh my God," she said, more to herself than to me.

I threw open a window and watched the catastrophe unfold. The single-engine craft sailed like a runaway skier into the side of the bluff and instantaneously exploded.

"*Mamma mia,*" exclaimed the Maestro.

It was as if Zeus himself had hurled the plane into the bluff. Bits of wing and engine and fuselage went flying everywhere. I thought I saw a pair of legs soar up and back, but that might have been my childlike imagination taking flight. Whatever the particulars, it was more than evident that our pursuers had been turned into so much cream of wheat.

Kim guided us back onto the highway. Despite the polar air-conditioning in the bus, her face was bathed in sweat.

"Yikes," she said.

"You were unbelievable," I told her.

"Thank you. I couldn't agree more." She wiped her forehead with her slender but well-muscled arm. "Now what?"

"On to Salt Lake, with *mucho allegro.*"

"Means fast?"

"Means fast."

"So you don't think we're in the clear?"

"Not even close."

I walked to the back of the bus. Toscanini and Barbara had lowered their windows, but there had been a change in the seating arrangements: Maestro, unsurprisingly, had taken the chair beside hers.

"*Que cosa,* Boston Blackie?" he asked me.

"We were pursued by air and it was resoundingly unsuccessful."

"Who do you think was in the plane?" Barbara asked, and I detected a weird note of concern in her voice.

"You mean was it Meyer?"

She stared at me and I was certain I had struck a nerve. I'm sure she was feeling a lot of things at once—shame, guilt, and leftover affection all vying for first position.

"I'd be very much surprised if he was in that plane. Aerial pursuit in a single-engine tomato can like that falls under the heading of *'goyische kopf,'* which certainly eliminates Lansky."

Toscanini smiled. "I know this, *'goyische kopf.'* Horowitz say this sometime. *Molto comico.* But not always true." Toscanini looked a little nearsightedly into my eyes. "They drop bomb, Boston Blackie?"

"A grenade."

He let that sink in.

"They are serious men," he finally said.

"Very," I told him.

We drove the rest of the way to Salt Lake without incident. It took well over six hours and despite the tedium of the drive, I was unable to nap or relax or even take a deep breath; I never had a sense that we were in the clear. To distract myself, I took the wheel for a couple of hours, driving through the rocky beauty of Zion National Park and the spooky moonscape of the Diamond Valley Volcanoes. It was hard to believe that all this natural splendor existed on the same planet as Newark, New Jersey. While I drove, Toscanini dozed and Kim took the opportunity to chat with Barbara. During the time they were together, I adjusted the front mirror and checked it at depressingly regular intervals, like a jealous high school kid. Kim frequently touched Barbara's thigh—for rhetorical emphasis, I'm sure—but it didn't get any more physical than that. At one point, Barbara tousled Kim's hair and Kim turned and seemed to blush; shortly after that, she returned to relieve me of my driving duties.

"That was amazing," she whispered to me, as I pulled the bus over to the shoulder of the road.

"She's very bright, isn't she?"

Kim looked at me with a kind of pity.

"Jack, when she touched my hair, I had an orgasm." No one could accuse this gal of pulling her punches. "That never happened to me before, just like that."

"Are congratulations in order?"

Kim climbed in behind the driver's wheel. "Yeah. I think they are," she said, and stepped on the gas.

We got to the Salt Lake airport a bit after five o'clock. The days were still long enough so that the sun had not yet dipped behind the mountains. We circled the terminal and I checked off the names of the airlines—American Air, National, Trans World, PSA, Frontier, Ozark, and then some smaller ones, like Utah Air, Salt Lake Air, Mountain Air, North Central Air. Barbara came up beside me.

"What do you think?" she asked. "Which one do we take?"

"Beats the hell out of me," I told her.

"Where are we going exactly?"

"I'd like to get to St. Louis, then grab a car and drive to Chicago. From there we have other options—take the Limited, say. But first let's just worry about St. Louis."

"Figure American Air would go there, to St. Louis. Right?" Barbara bit her lip in a girlish and perplexed fashion. I had rarely seen her puzzled and it was very appealing.

"Or Trans World." I thought about it. "What the hell." I turned to Kim. "Go around again and we'll get out at American Air."

"Then I just put the bus in the lot?"

"Yeah. I'll ring up the Flamingo and let them know where it's parked. You can either spend the night here and rent a car in the morning, or go back tonight. Whatever you like." I dug into my pocket. "In any case, here's your five hundred."

Kim shook her head. "Oh no. That was for New York."

"I insist. You've been fantastic. Take it."

"Geez." The cabby took the money, looked at it with the wonder usually accorded a gold nugget, then stuck it in her jacket. "Gonna miss you, Lassie. You and your stimulating pals."

"Yeah," I said. "Me, too. I'm keeping your card."

"Okay." She ran a nervous hand through her hair, looked more than a little wistful. Barbara went over and put her hand on the cabby's shoulder as she drove around the airport, and Kim's eyes welled up a bit.

I walked back to the Maestro. He was watching Barbara and Kim with great interest.

"Lesbica?" Toscanini's eyes glittered as he whispered. "She is too beautiful, her bosom too fantastic just for men. Needs *tutti*!" He lightly clapped his hands. "Is a lot for you, Boston Blackie. *Coraggio!"*

"Thanks," I told him. "But I'm not principally concerned with my sex life at this moment. We have a hell of a trip to figure out." I sat down beside the old man and explained my plan.

He sagged with fatigue. *"Mama mia,"* he said.

"I know."

"But you think is important we go this way—plane and then drive."

"I think if we can get to Chicago in one piece, we'll be all right. We'll be more visible."

His ever-penetrating eyes measured me. "There you can say, *'Ecco,* we have Toscanini.' "

"Something like that. Out here in the boondocks, it's too scary. Too much space, too few people. The farther east we get, the tougher it gets for Lansky and Lucky to operate in the open."

The old man patted my knee. "You go, I follow. Is not the usual for me, you know, Boston Blackie. My whole life I lead."

"I know, but you've been a model client, I have to say. You listen a lot better than most of the furriers and garment monkeys I've worked for." The Maestro smiled with childlike pride at his accomplishment. "Just hang in there for another couple of days. Then you can lead all you want again."

He lightly banged my knee again. *"Molto bene,* Signor Detective."

The bus slowed and I could see that we were nearing the terminal doors; they were marked AMERICAN AIR in blue lettering. My whole body tensed as Kim pulled the bus over to the curb.

"Okay, Maestro, let's get your raincoat on," I said to the old man. He rose somewhat shakily to his feet and I helped him slip into his Burberry. Barbara got her valise and pecked Kim on the cheek. Kim rose and embraced her, holding her for a long yearning moment.

"I know," I thought I heard Barbara whisper.

"Yeah," Kim said. Then she turned and kissed me, then Maestro.

"Brava," Toscanini told her.

"Thank you, sir," she told him. "Would it be terribly rude if I asked for an autograph?"

"My honor, *signorina."* Toscanini smiled and bowed.

Kim handed him the road map and the old man inscribed his name across the face of the friendly Esso man. *"Bona fortuna,"* Maestro told her, then kissed her sincerely and with no little force on the lips.

"You, too, handsome," Kim told Toscanini, then pulled a metal handle and opened the bus doors, which is when I saw the man in the leather jacket step from behind a pillar in front of the terminal. He turned and walked away from us and began conversing with a porter, but my heart was pounding.

"Stay close to me," I told Barbara and Maestro, "but not *on* me, okay? Keep a little air between us."

"Why, sweetie?" Barbara asked.

"Just do it. And keep the old man between us."

We stepped down off the bus, and my hand went snaking after the .38 in my jacket. While the Salt Lake airport was not exactly bustling, there were a fair number of citizens walking toward and away from the terminal portals, an even mix of businessmen and cowboy-hatted shit-kickers. I started in the direction of the terminal doors and threw a glance over my shoulder: The man in the leather jacket was still chatting amiably with the porter. The porter picked up a duffel bag and began to tie a tag around its cloth handle; the man in the leather jacket tossed him some change. My heart rate slowed back down. I turned and made sure that Toscanini and Barbara were just a breath behind me; past them I saw Kim take a step off the bus to record one last look at us, or rather, at Barbara, to memorize the image of her departing form. Then I saw Kim's expression change and she opened her mouth to shout and then everything began happening in slow motion.

"Jack!" Kim cried out, at which point a man toting a briefcase and wearing a string tie blew her clever brains out with a single shot from a sawed-off shotgun. She stood for a terrible moment, already dead, before toppling backward into the bus. The gunman turned toward me and I unhesitatingly fired my .38, managing to put a hole right through his string tie. He dropped to his knees and then fell over, spritzing blood like the Trevi Fountain.

It had all happened in a double heartbeat, but now there were shouts and the beginnings of civic panic; I turned to Barbara and Maestro, who stood paralyzed behind me.

"Walk toward the doors!" I yelled. "Quickly, but no running!"

"Run?" asked Toscanini. He seemed to be in shock.

"No, no run!"

"What happened to Kim?" Barbara asked.

"She's dead, sweetie. Let's go."

"You sure she's dead?"

"Honey, we've gotta move." I heard shouts and screams behind me, calls for help. Barbara and I hustled toward the American Air doors, holding Toscanini under his arms. I took the .38 and jammed it down my slacks, tucking it deep into my undershorts; the barrel was still piping hot but the effect was far from arousing. Not surprisingly, I began to sweat profusely.

We pushed through a revolving door into the terminal and walked with all deliberate speed toward the ticket counters, which were about a hundred yards away and on a diagonal to the right. The terminal was brightly lit and air-conditioned and I could feel the perspiration chilling to icy pellets on my forehead. Barbara was crying without making a sound and Toscanini was looking around for more shooters. People were walking toward the windows to see what was going on. I heard the distant whoop of a siren.

"Maestro, keep your head facing front, okay?" I told him. "I think we're in the clear now."

"Sì." The old man was badly frightened. "The girl . . ."

"Gone, Maestro."

He pursed his lips and I could see them begin to tremble. I patted his shoulder.

"I know, sir."

"Vergogna."

"Yeah." I observed a small newsstand standing in the middle of the floor and squeezed Barbara's arm. "Sweetheart, go get a paper, then sit the old guy down, give it to him to read."

"Okay." She was wiping her tears with a hanky. "I feel numb."

"I know," I told her. "Believe me, it's just as well."

There was increasing commotion outside, but it was evident that no one had gotten a good look at me during the hysteria of the brief shoot-out. No one was pointing in my direction. Instead, people were running about in all directions.

I couldn't wait to get the hell out of Utah. I hadn't been there very long, but I didn't like it one little bit.

FIFTEEN

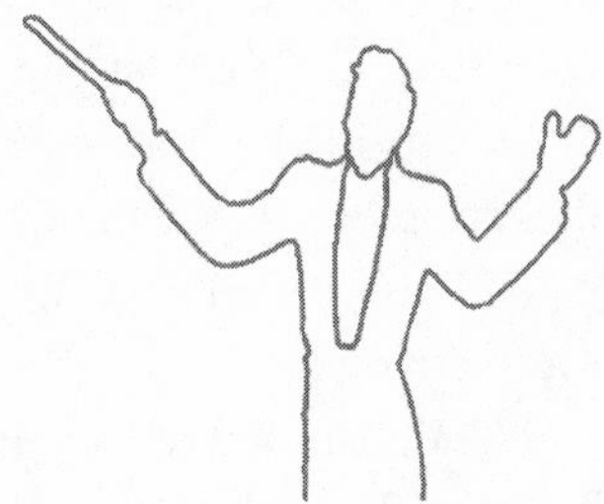

There was, thankfully, no line at the American Air counter. A petite blond ticket agent with a twitchy left eye informed me that a nonstop flight to St. Louis was leaving in forty-five minutes and would be boarding in fifteen.

"Seats available?" I asked.

"Plenty," she told me.

That was miraculously good news, because the prospect of hanging around the terminal and remaining incognito with Arturo Toscanini and the most gorgeous woman in Judeo-Christendom was, to say the least, daunting. It was easier to hide Toscanini than Barbara, although when she returned from the newsstand I noticed that she had donned sunglasses and wrapped a scarf over her head. She got the old man seated and handed him the *Deseret Sun-Times*; Toscanini pretended to read the first section while she scanned the sports pages. While they performed their pantomime, I purchased three seats on American Air Flight 106 for the sum of one hundred and seventeen dollars.

"What happened out there?" the little blond agent asked me. "Were those shots?" She said it in a casual manner, as if asking about the weather.

"I think so," I told her. "Happened just as we were walking in here."

"Goodness. This place is so soundproofed, sometimes I think they could set off an atom bomb and I wouldn't hear it." It was true—the drone of the air conditioners totally deadened the noise outside. I dried my neck with a handkerchief while the blond painstakingly wrote out the tickets; she looked to be around forty and was semi-attractive in the manner of a downtown cocktail waitress, but that flickering eye was a major distraction.

"Guess it's still the Wild West out here, huh?" she said, working ever so slowly.

At that moment, a very fat man in a plaid sports jacket pushed his way through the revolving door and started looking around the terminal. If he wasn't a homicide dick, then I was J. Edgar Hoover. I didn't want to rush the ticket agent, for fear of arousing her suspicions, but she was working at a maddening, arthritic pace. Like a pig sniffing a truffle, the homicide dick headed straight toward me, waddling past the seated Maestro and Barbara without so much as a glance.

"Evening," he said to me, whipping out his detective's shield. "Doug Douglas, Salt Lake Homicide."

"Yes sir." I can be extremely taciturn when I want to be.

"You witness what just happened out there?"

I scratched my ear. "Actually not, sir. As I was just explaining to Miss . . ."

"Barber," the ticket agent said. "Mrs."

"To *Mrs.* Barber, excuse me, I heard the shooting just as I came in through the doors."

Douglas surveyed me with eyes the approximate diameter and color of BBs, then looked over the counter and watched the ticket clerk painstakingly scribble. "Three tickets?" he asked.

"Yes sir." I gestured toward Toscanini and Barbara. "I'm traveling with my dad and his nurse. Trying to calm him down, actually; he got pretty alarmed when he heard the shots. I told him it was firecrackers."

Fatso looked over at my party. You could see him almost shudder with lust when he got a gander at Barbara, and he instinctively straightened his tie.

"That's his nurse?"

"Yes sir."

Douglas nodded and kept staring. "Maybe it's time I got myself sick."

The ticket agent giggled. "She's a stunner, isn't she?" she said, her left eye blinking.

"How'd you get to the airport?" the dick asked me.

"Took a taxi."

"You stay in town last night?"

"A motel about an hour from here." My mind searched for the names of places we had zipped past en route. "They all look alike to me. Mt. Zion Inn, maybe? About twenty units?"

"Yes, that'd be one," the fat homicide dick said, and glommed another peep at Barbara and Maestro. The longer he stared at Toscanini, the antsier I got.

"Here you go," Mrs. Barber said, and handed me my tickets. "Gate Two to St. Louis. It'll be boarding in just a few minutes."

"Thanks a lot." I turned to the Salt Lake gumshoe. "Well, my dad doesn't walk all that quickly. Better get a move-on." I was getting really good at this folksy chatter.

Douglas mopped his brow and nodded at me. "Yeah. Guess I better get back outside," the dick said. "Got two dead."

"Anybody you know?" I asked cautiously.

"Nope." The fat man turned his gaze from Toscanini and Barbara back to me. "Got a woman dead, looked to be driving a band bus of some sort. The other one seemed to be a professional shooter, judging by his weaponry."

"Well, good luck to you." I looked over to Toscanini. He waved at me feebly "Take your time, Dad," I yelled to him, then turned back to the homicide dick. "He's nervous, not used to flying."

"Yeah." Douglas was clearly unconvinced, but there was no direction he could go with me. Except one.

"You wouldn't have a problem if I patted you down, would you?" he suddenly asked.

"Not at all," I said, having a big problem, but not really having a choice. If I showed the slightest hesitation, I knew it would mean spending the rest of the day perched under a hot lamp like a rotisserie chicken, inhaling the cop's sour breath. I turned around and raised my hands in the air; Douglas began laboriously searching my exquisitely sculpted body. Barbara raised a quizzical eyebrow and I shrugged back like a helpless chump. Then she turned and started whispering to Toscanini, as if in explanation. She really was appallingly good at this.

Douglas patted my pockets, my legs, my shoes. Like ninety-nine percent of the manly cops on this planet, he never made a move for my pecker. After gripping my ankles, the homicide dick rose slowly out of his crouch, as breathless as if he had just carried a sofa up five flights of stairs.

"Sorry for the inconvenience," he wheezed.

"I understand," I told him. "You've got a job to do." I walked over to join my traveling group. "Good luck to you." I took Toscanini under one arm, Barbara clutched the other, and we started off toward Gate Two. The detective watched us go and then drifted back across the terminal, lumbering toward the growing assemblage of cops and curious travelers outside the doors.

"You had *pistola* by *testicolos*?" Toscanini whispered to me.

"Yeah. It's a safe place, usually."

The old man smiled. "Bravo, Boston Blackie."

Barbara leaned back and spoke to me over the top of the Maestro's head. "Anything get singed?" she asked in a low voice.

"Want to check?"

"I'll do a thorough inspection later," she whispered, inciting a small riot in my slacks.

Forty minutes later, we were in the air over Salt Lake City, climbing above the mountains and heading east in a DC-3 only slightly quieter than a pneumatic drill. Toscanini was parked by the window, and Barbara had the seat beside him; I had settled in across the aisle. The old man was gazing out over the clouds and Barbara looked morosely up toward the ceiling.

"Kim?" I asked.

She nodded. "When that fat slob was bracing you, all this adrenaline took over and I suppose I stopped thinking about what had just happened." Barbara's voice got very small; she took a red silk handkerchief from her bag and dabbed at her eyes. "Now it's sinking in and I realize that this person I was talking to and getting to know and 'let's write' and all of that, from one second to the next, she's just blown to kingdom come."

"It's a nightmare, but we're dealing in a very big-stakes game."

"Nothing's worth this." She was barely audible.

"It is to your old boyfriend."

She looked at me pretty hard and her voice regained its strength. "Don't call him that anymore."

"Okay."

"I mean it, Jack. Never again."

"I promise." She took my hand and kissed it. Her breath was moist and tropical. I squeezed her hand, then laid my head back against the seat and shut my eyes, trying to sort out the havoc I had just barely lived through. There must have been other gunmen in the airport, but they had likely panicked at the bloody demise of Kim's killer, or had been frightened away by the crowds and the impossibility of getting a clean shot at me or at the old man.

But I had no illusions that this was the end of the hunt.

It was breezy and cloudless when we deplaned in St. Louis at just past eight o'clock in the evening. The three of us crossed the tarmac with nervous haste, Barbara holding Maestro's arm, Maestro keeping his head lowered; in the distance, one could see the lights of the city in this flattest, plainest section of the USA. It was eerily quiet and the air was mild and smelled of soot. I looked around for a sign of any suspicious thing or body, but the people at the airport were polite and welcoming; nobody looked remotely ready to kill or kidnap any of us. It was all tranquil and low-pressure and easy, yet I had a large knot in my gut that wouldn't go away.

Arrayed in the drab lower concourse of the St. Louis airport were a series of counters fronting various outfits that rented cars to bewildered incoming travelers like myself. Most of the counters were quiet; in fact, more than half of them were shut down tight. St. Louis was obviously not a late-night kind of town.

I deposited the Maestro and Barbara on a bench and headed for one of the few open establishments, an outfit that called itself Prairie Rent-A-Car. The Prairie rental agent wasn't a day over twenty and wore a candy-red company blazer with a plastic name tag on the breast pocket that identified him as Buck. Young Buck had combed sufficient Vitalis into his hair to withstand typhoon winds and was afflicted with rampaging postadolescent acne. Looking into his mirror every morning must have been a cause of monumental heartache and anxiety; I decided to be very nice to him.

"Evening, Buck," I said like his favorite uncle. "I need a car pronto."

"Let me see what we can do for you." Buck automatically raised one hand over his face as he spoke; with his free hand, he leafed through some sheets of paper. "How long you need the vehicle for?"

"I've got to go to Chicago. As long as that takes."

"It's just under three hundred miles to Chicago, sir. About an eight- or nine-hour drive in normal traffic." Buck looked up from his sheets. "You'll be returning the vehicle when?"

"I have to leave it in Chicago."

The rental jockey's eyes went as wide as if I had asked permission to launch the car into outer space.

"Leave it in Chicago?"

"Can't be the first time that's ever been done."

He shook his head thoughtfully. "No sir, but it gets pretty darn expensive that way."

"How expensive is 'pretty darn expensive'?" I said in my most homespun fashion.

Buck checked his sheets again; when he lifted his head, his eyes seemed to bug an inch out of their sockets and I knew that Barbara must have slipped in behind me. "Just taking Dad to the men's room," she whispered, then smiled at Buck. "Hi. You have a nice shiny car for us?"

Buck blushed so deeply that his pimples seemed to rise up like tiny cities on a topographic map.

"I'm trying, ma'am. But your . . ."

"Fiancé."

"Your fiancé wants to leave it in Chicago."

"He tells me it's very expensive, honey," I told Barbara.

"Yes, ma'am," said Buck, his right hand now covering his right cheek. "That will be an additional . . ." He squinted at his sheet. "An additional seventeen dollars to drop it in Chicago."

"Really," I said. "And the daily rental is what?"

"I can give you a brand-new Mercury for seven dollars a day, plus sixty cents additional for your insurance. But it's expensive for us to bring the vehicles back, gotta send two men and a car, so we lose an additional car, you understand." The kid was explaining the seventeen bucks like it was a king's ransom. "We generally discourage it," he said to Barbara.

Barbara nodded as if she were giving the matter considerable and beauteous thought. "I'm sure you do, and it is costly, but we really have to get my dad to Chicago by morning." She squeezed my arm. "Let's go for it, darling," she said, then headed back toward Toscanini. Buck watched her every step of the way.

"Gol-ly," he said, like it was two words.

"I know what you mean."

He studied me, more than a little baffled, trying to match my kisser with hers.

"She's your fiancée?"

"There's hope for us all, Buck."

The clerk took his hand away from his face and smiled with genuine happiness.

"Gol-ly," he said again.

The Mercury was forest-green and had a burgundy roof. It was a very nice piece of goods. Buck walked me to the car and told me exactly where to drop it in Chicago, that being the Central States Garage, some three blocks from Union Station. He stole a last lingering look at Barbara and said a polite good-bye to me and to Toscanini, whom he didn't know from Harpo Marx, then handed me a map upon which he had kindly highlighted a direct route to Chicago in thick blue pencil.

"Thanks a bunch," I told him. "You've been a real prince."

He blushed again. "Well, that's why I'm here."

" 'Bye, Buck," Barbara fairly sang, as if it were the first line of a cowboy ditty. "Till the next time."

"Whenever you need a car in St. Louis, ma'am." He waved at her and was still waving as we drove out of the parking lot. For all I know, he stood there waving for the rest of the night.

"Is in love," Toscanini announced from the rear seat. "We are all in love, *bella signorina.*"

Barbara dimpled her features into the most demure of Mona Lisa smiles. Why deny the obvious?

The path outlined by honest Buck was fairly simple: Route 67 to Route 340 and on to Route 66, which would take us directly to Chicago. It was a fabulous plan, except that I immediately got stuck behind an arthritic lumber truck on 67 and stayed in his wake as he creaked along at thirty miles an hour. There was too much oncoming traffic to even think about passing.

"This is going to be some fun," I told Barbara. The old man had fallen asleep within fifteen minutes and was sprawled across the backseat. His mouth was open and he didn't look anything like the world's most famous musician. He just looked like an old guy.

"We can admire the scenery," Barbara said, studying the passing landscape of used car lots, bowling alleys, and liquor stores.

"Long as I'm trapped behind Paul Bunyan here, maybe I should pull over and make a couple of calls."

"Call who?" Barbara said with some alarm. "I don't really feature sitting alone in a car with Maestro. Not after Salt Lake. I don't want to be alone, period."

"I just need to find out about train schedules going out of Chicago and I have to call New York."

"Who in New York?"

"Are we playing Miss Marple all of sudden?" I said brainlessly.

"Not funny." She pulled her jacket tighter. She had put on a nifty little aqua jacket with a fur collar. "I'm getting cold."

"It's nerves."

"Stop knowing everything, Jack. It gets tiresome." I turned my head; Barbara was weary and cross and I realized that with all her experiences of life and lust, this was a twenty-one-year-old girl who had just witnessed a slaughter.

I spotted a pay booth right off the highway.

"Okay. Right over there," I said in my most conciliatory tone of voice.

The booth was located outside a boarded-up Sunoco station, beneath a flickering street lamp that cast a circle of sickly yellowish light. The scene resembled something painted by Edward Hopper's evil twin. I pulled over and stopped; Toscanini barely stirred when the car stopped. Barbara got out and attempted to make the old man comfortable, putting her coat under his head; he muttered something in Italian and licked his lips, then folded his arms across his chest. We watched him sleep, like adoring parents poised over a newborn's crib.

"Wish I had a camera," Barbara said softly, and then she climbed back into the front seat, while I approached the abandoned gas station. The wind blew the ghostly Sunoco sign back and forth in a rasping, blackboard-screeching rhythm. I pushed open the rusting doors of the wretched pay booth. It reeked of old and new pissings and was carpeted wall to wall with blackened newspapers and cigarette butts; bottle caps and smashed beer bottles crunched under my shoes. The urinous stench seemed to get worse as I picked up the phone, as if some drunk had peed all over the receiver. I started breathing through my mouth and fed enough nickels into the phone to call Shanghai. The first information I got pertained to the train schedule. It was pretty simple. The Twentieth Century Limited left Chicago for New York at eight o'clock in the morning. Another train departed at two in the afternoon. It was now nine-thirty and regardless of how quickly I drove, there was no way we were going to arrive in Chicago before five in the morning. I felt that for the sake of his health, it was important that we get the old man into a bed, no matter how much he snoozed in the car, and book the afternoon train. We could stop in a motel somewhere between here and Chicago—say, Springfield—get a couple of rooms, rest up, and then cruise into the Windy City as quietly as possible. I'd book a Pullman for the old man under a phony name and another for me and Barbara, settle in, and coast triumphantly into New York.

It was a thoughtful, well-considered plan and it remained in effect for precisely three minutes, when I called Toots Fellman at the *Daily News* and found out that I was in far worse trouble than I had ever imagined.

"You're where?" he hollered into the phone. The connection was patchy and shot with intermittent high-pitched crackling.

"Just outside St. Louis."

"St. Louis? Why the hell . . . ?"

"Long story. I need a major favor—"

Toots cut me off. "Nice, what happened to your friend, huh?" he asked suddenly.

"What friend?" I said, and the knot in my stomach tightened exponentially.

"The NBC guy. Whatisface . . ."

"Sidney Aaron? What about him?"

“Offed himself in Las Vegas. Came over the AP wire couple hours ago. Guess he had a bad day at the tables, huh?”

“He got pushed, Toots.”

There was a thoughtful, static-filled silence at his end. A yellow school bus from a Negro church rolled by, with kids leaning out the windows and waving. I felt like running down the road and jumping on the bus with them.

Toots finally spoke. “Jack, you know that for a fact?”

“I vas dere, Charlie. . . .”

“You were in Las Vegas this morning? And now you’re in St. Louis?” Toots asked wonderingly. “You got a rocket up your ass?”

“It’s the modern age of transportation. And here’s the reason I’m calling—”

“Wait a minute, I want to know what the hell happened with this NBC guy. You’re saying it’s murder?”

“Listen to me . . . remember the fiddler who got killed?”

“The refugee? There’s a connection?”

“I’m in a pay booth! Let me talk.”

“Then make it collect, putz!” Toots hollered. “Call me back!”

I hung up and dialed the operator, who put me through to the Murray Hill number of the *News*. Toots picked up precisely where he had left off, except this time we had a somewhat clearer signal.

“You’re telling me that Aaron was murdered in Vegas and it’s connected to your fiddler getting iced?” Toots asked.

“It gets better; what would you say if I told you Toscanini himself is sitting in the back of a rented Mercury fifteen feet from where I’m making this call?”

“I’d say you should be fitted for a clean white jacket with numerous buckles and straps.”

“It’s true. I brought him back from Vegas. He was snatched; that’s what all of this is about.”

“What the hell are you talking about? He had a heart attack, which they never told anybody about. When’s the last time you read a paper, Jack? It's in all the afternoon editions. He's due back tomorrow; Sarnoff himself is meeting him at the airport."

I could feel the blood pounding in my ears.

"A heart attack?"

"Here, I'll read it you. The *Telegram*—"

"How big a play?"

"Bottom of the front page. Not as big as you might think, but still plenty big. Three columns. 'Toscanini Comes Home After Heart Scare.' "

" 'Scare.' Not 'attack.' "

"You going to let me finish?"

Barbara looked at me quizzically from the front seat of the car. I waved at her encouragingly, but I could tell that she sensed my agitation.

" 'Arturo Toscanini, musical titan and conductor of the NBC Symphony,' " Toots began, " 'is scheduled to arrive at Idlewild Airport via private plane tomorrow afternoon at approximately four o'clock, having survived what NBC spokesmen described as "an extremely mild heart attack," quote unquote. The eighty-three-year-old Maestro was reportedly feeling extremely fit and was anxious to return to conduct this fall's slate of concerts with the orchestra. In a statement released this afternoon, RCA President David Sarnoff said that "Maestro Toscanini's doctors have given him a clean bill of health and we look forward to many years of great music-making." ' There's a little more, but that's the gist. So tell me, who's sitting in your car, Jack, some barber who can carry a tune?"

"*Toscanini* is, you fucking meathead, wearing a dark jacket and gray trousers. The guy Sarnoff is meeting at the airport is a ringer."

"A fake Maestro. Flying into Idlewild."

"Exactly."

"I don't know what to say, Jack," Toots said with some exasperation. "Up until now, you've always been a rational human being. No genius, maybe—"

"*I'm telling you, he's here.* And Sidney Aaron got pushed out a window over this guy. Listen, do you have the Salt Lake shootout story yet?"

"What shootout?" Obviously he didn't.

"At the Salt Lake airport. Two people gunned down. One of the dead was a lesbian Vegas cabbie named Kim West; she drove me, Toscanini, and Fritz Stern's daughter to Salt Lake in Vaughn Monroe's bus."

"Hey, you didn't tell me Vaughn Monroe was involved. Now it's starting to make sense!"

"Schmuck, you don't believe me, check the wire services!"

"Hang on."

I waited. Barbara opened the door of the car to stretch those fabulous legs.

"What's happening?" she asked.

"How good is your driving?"

"Good enough? Why?"

"Forget Chicago. We're going straight to New York."

She got out of the Mercury and walked over to the pay booth.

"Are you serious?" She looked back at the car and its celebrated passenger. "With *him*? It's a two-day drive."

"I don't see an alternative. We can't be out in the open anymore. Not till we get to New York."

"Why?"

"Because they're way ahead of us. It's all over the papers that the old man had a mild heart attack and is flying into New York tomorrow night."

Barbara put her fingers to her lips in shock. "Holy Christ. They're out front with the phony one? They're going to parade him in front of the press?"

"Meyer has to, because he knows we're running around loose with the real one. Which means, I believe, that we're all dead meat, unless we can sneak the genuine article in as speedily as possible."

"Jack . . ." I had Toots Fellman in my ear once again and held up a hand to quiet Barbara.

"Anything?" I asked.

"Yeah," Toots said. His voice was strained and I could hear him breathing. "Out of the UP bureau in Salt Lake."

"Saying . . ."

"Saying two people were shot dead in the Salt Lake airport. The girl, like you said, out of Las Vegas, and a local businessman—"

"What?"

"Let me finish. A local businessman named Fred Brancati—"

"He was a gunsel!"

"Are you going to let me finish?" I had never heard Toots quite so exercised. "A local businessman named Fred Brancati, and Jack . . ." Toots's voice quavered a bit. I heard a whistling sound over the line.

"Jack what?"

"According to this, you're wanted for the murders."

I took a slow, deep breath.

"Say that again."

"You're wanted—"

"For both murders?"

"Yes. The cabby and the businessman. 'New York City private detective Jacob LeVine.' Jesus Christ. . . ."

I stared at the road. A police car raced past and I felt my stomach fold up like a first baseman's glove. "I better call from another booth, Toots. I don't want to stand here much longer."

"Good idea. Call me in ten."

I hung up and ran toward the car.

Barbara ran after me. "What's going on, Jack? You don't look so hot."

"Nothing to worry about," I assured her. "I'm just wanted for two murders."

I drove carefully, filling Barbara in as best I could. She was shockingly calm about it.

"That's Meyer, all the way," she said. "Amazing the strings he can pull, particularly where his money can go a long way."

"In Utah, it can go a very long way. There's probably fifty cops in the whole goddamn state."

I pulled the Mercury up to a pair of pay booths outside an all-night Rexall. I figured I could make my call, then go inside for some aspirin or a bottle of arsenic.

I slipped into a booth and dialed O; after a dozen rings, a grumpy operator got on and placed my collect call through to New York. Toots answered immediately. I rested my hand against the top of the phone and attempted to form some coherent thoughts.

"Okay, Toots, what's going on is the following: I'm swimming in a shark tank with a bloody nose. And the sharks are named Lansky and Luciano."

The two names together—like Ruth and Gehrig, Dempsey and Tunney, Procter and Gamble—stopped Toots cold. "Holy Christ on a stick," was all he could muster.

"My sentiments exactly."

"They offed Sidney Aaron?"

"And then they tried to plug me at the Salt Lake airport, but killed the cabby instead. I nailed the shooter and made it out to St. Louis."

"And now you've got a target painted on your ass."

"Obviously. They plant this story, make me the suspect, means any cop between here and New York can get in Meyer's good graces by spraying my brains all over the road. I was originally going to drive to Chicago and then take the Limited."

"Forget that."

"I forgot it already."

"What can I do for you, Jack?" Toots asked. "Just tell me."

"When does the next edition go to bed?"

"In about an hour. You want to put something in?"

"Yeah. You running a Toscanini story, I presume?"

"Sure. Page three, on the bottom. It's pretty much the same as the *Telegram* piece. We all got it from the wires."

"And the wires got it direct from NBC?"

"I would imagine so. No one else is quoted."

"Okay. I need you to run a sidebar."

"Saying?"

"Saying that rumors persist that Toscanini's heart attack was more severe than is being reported and that the Maestro may have to end his legendary association with the NBC Symphony."

There was a pregnant pause before Toots started hollering. *"Are you fucking kidding? You want me to run with that?"*

"I do."

"What's my source?"

"Unnamed persons connected to the orchestra."

"Not good enough; my editors are gonna insist on the source."

"Tell them a person very close to Toscanini."

"How close?"

I looked over at the car. "I'd say about twelve feet."

"Jack, for the love of Christ . . ."

"It's the truth. Listen, don't shine me off—I'm about to hand you an unbelievable exclusive. . . . We're talking about corporate evil at the highest levels."

"Give me a hint."

"Use your imagination and let it wander out to Las Vegas."

There was a short beat. "NBC's in bed with Lansky and Lucky?"

"You win dinner for two at the Automat."

There was a two-second silence that seemed to weigh a million tons. "Swear on your father's grave you're not shitting me," Toots said.

"I'll swear on his grave and mine, because if you don't help me out, I'm gonna be the catch of the day at some morgue between here and New York."

"Okay, tell me again . . . slowly." I could hear the mechanical whir of a sheet of paper being rolled into a typewriter. "He may be so sick that he can't return to the orchestra? A source close to the Maestro himself told the *News*? That's the gist?"

"Correct. That edition should hit the street about when?"

"Midnight. But first I have to call NBC to get a reaction, Jack; no way to avoid that."

"That's exactly what I want."

"For them to know about this."

"Absolutely. They're going to go ape, but not right away. It has to percolate up to the top floor. No way the workaday flacks are going to know what this is really about."

"They'll just issue a flat denial."

"Which you'll run with the story, I presume. So you've protected yourself."

"And what good does it do you?"

"The higher-ups get wind of this and realize that I've figured out their game."

"Which is?"

"You'll love this. They want to get out of the Toscanini business—high cost and increasingly low return—while setting up this bogus Maestro in an ultra-hotsy-totsy Vegas hotel that Lansky and Lucky are going to build, with NBC as silent partners."

"That's what this is all about?" Now Toots wasn't whispering anymore. "Holy shit."

"That's what this is all about, and that's why my poor fiddler got hit. Now this story could only have leaked out from me, because obviously no one at NBC would spill this."

"Puts you further in jeopardy."

"No. It only accelerates their panic, because Meyer doesn't know where I am."

"What are you planning to do?"

"Drive straight to New York. I've got to get this out in the open as soon as possible. Should take, what, a day and a half if I push hard?"

"No chance. I did it once. It's almost a thousand miles. That's two days, unless you're Flash Gordon."

"What's the fastest way?"

"There's no fastest way. There's slow and slower. But you play your cards right, you could get to, say, Indianapolis by three, four in the morning, sleep over, then bust your hump tomorrow."

"How late you going to be working tonight?"

"I'm here till you get home, Jack. This is too big a story, plus I think I'm your only link to a kindlier universe."

I was touched by his friendship, even given the selfish motive of exclusivity on this most incendiary of stories. "I don't know what to say. Thank you, for openers."

"That's more than enough. Call me if you need anything." He started to get off, then thought again. "Jack, I have one other question. Something that doesn't figure."

"What?"

"Toscanini's family. He's got a wife, couple kids. What the hell do they think is going on?"

"That disgruntled, homicidal fascists are after him, still pissed about his anti-Mussolini activities."

"And that's why they think he's being kept out of circulation?"

"Exactly. And Meyer's guys will explain to them that the heart attack is part of the same cover story, to keep the fascists away. The reality is, it's all a holding action until they can get me out of the way and get the old man back to Vegas."

"The double."

"Correct. God knows what they do with the real one. Keep him in hiding till he croaks."

There was an admiring beat before Toots said, "You think about it, it's really a insidious, brilliant fucking plan."

"I agree," I told him. "They don't call him Meyer Lansky for nothing."

SIXTEEN

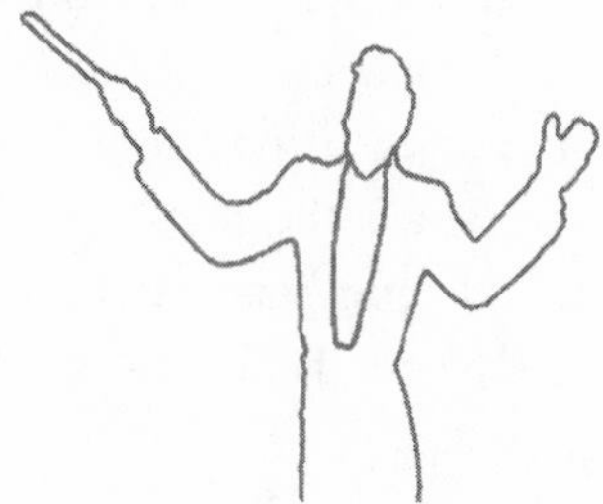

Barbara and I took turns behind the wheel for the next four and a half hours, until neither of us trusted ourselves to drive any farther. We were both punchy and more stressed than we wanted to admit. About an hour outside of Indianapolis, we stopped for the night at the Starlight Motor Hotel and booked two adjoining rooms. The night manager had a slight Castilian accent and identified himself as George Dobles.

"I am the owner of this motor hotel," he said. "So any problem, you can come right to me. There is not a middleman." Dobles had a thick Pancho Villa mustache and glossy black hair that reached the collar of his plaid shirt. His brown eyes glittered so merrily behind his horn-rimmed glasses that I suspected he had spent a significant part of the evening smoking reefer in his apartment. The door behind him in the motel office was shut tight. How a marijuana-loving Castilian had ended up in western Indiana might have made for a fascinating tale, but not at a quarter past three in the morning. All I wanted was to rest my bald head on a feather pillow.

Dobles opened the registration book and rotated it toward me. I signed in as Dr. and Mrs. Richard Abrams and registered the Maestro as Genaro Chusano, the name of my former janitor in Sunnyside. Dobles handed me the keys to rooms 14 and 15. They were attached to metal ovals with the room numbers engraved on them and didn't weigh much more than a pair of bowling balls.

"Just down the end here, Dr. Abrams," Dobles said with a soft smile that was either mocking or just plain wasted.

"Thanks," I told him. "I'll pull the car around." I went back to the Mercury, started up the engine, and threw the car into reverse.

"That's the night clerk?" Barbara whispered. Dobles had stepped outside and was watching us.

"Nope. That's the owner himself. Wish the hell he'd go back inside."

But he didn't. I drove our rented car thirty or so feet to our assigned rooms, and Dobles never moved a muscle. When Barbara got out of the car, he took his glasses off and cleaned them, then put them on again and just leaned against the office door.

"Just go about your business," I told Barbara. "Don't look at him." I handed her our room key. "Go to the room. I'll get the old man up."

Barbara walked over to room 14 and quickly opened the door. There wasn't a soul around and traffic on Route 36 had thinned to the odd truck rattling its commercial way to points east or west. Call me provincial, but the world outside New York seemed like a very lonely place.

I watched Barbara enter the room and switch on some lights, then I turned and lightly tapped Maestro on the knee. He grunted and shifted in his seat. It took two more attempts before I roused him and finally pulled him from the Mercury, limb by ancient limb. He was obviously disoriented and looked and smelled like any other geezer.

"Lean on my right arm," I whispered to him.

Toscanini just nodded and grasped my biceps for dear life. It was no act; the old guy had run out of gas. I fumbled with the key before opening the door to room 15. As I helped Toscanini inside, I saw that George Dobles still hadn't moved an inch. I nodded politely in his direction before closing the door behind me; Dobles nodded back and then began to slowly scratch his nuts. This was just a delightful spot all the way around.

I got the old man into his clean, sparsely furnished room and asked him if there was anything he needed. He just waved his hand and smiled. "Boston Blackie, are you crazy in head? I am in here." He pointed to the wall. "She is in there. You go now or Maestro goes!" He sat down on the bed and patted it. "Is soft, this bed. Maybe you will sink!"

"I just thought you might need some help."

"I need nothing but to sleep. You lock the door, Boston Blackie, make sure nobody take me away."

"Of course."

"*Bene.* And tomorrow, signore, we stop and buy . . ." he tugged at the waistband of his billowing briefs. *"Intima, sì?"*

"Underwear. Of course. Socks. We'll get you all fixed up."

"Sì." He nodded, yawned, pushed himself up off the bed, pointed to the door. "Go, *idiota*!" He smiled as I went to the door, waved a fist in the air in encouragement. I left Toscanini's room and locked the door, turning the knob twice to make certain it was secure. Dobles remained poised against the door of his office. He had ignited a short but pungent cigar, which I could smell as intensely as if he was standing beside me. He threw me a short salute and I waved back. Nothing about this guy seemed kosher, but it was too late to change our lodgings, and I chalked up some of my paranoia to the lateness of the hour and the bloody events of the day.

Barbara had left the door to our room unlocked. When I let myself in, I could hear the water running. "That creep is still standing in front of the office," I announced, then walked into the tiny bathroom. Barbara stood at the sink wearing only red silk panties and a toothpaste-covered smile; she rinsed her mouth and gazed curiously at our dual images in the mirror.

"Hey, there, sailor," she said.

I came up behind her and gave her a hug; my arms encircled her warm firm breasts and she pushed out her chest so I could feel every velvety inch of them. We both watched ourselves in the mirror. Talk about an unlikely couple.

"I haven't driven this much in one day since I was a pup," I told her. "I'm exhausted."

"How exhausted?" She pressed her exquisite bottom up against me and rotated it approximately fifteen degrees to the right and then back again. The results were immediate and obvious. "See? Not so pooped after all." She turned to me and kissed me full on the lips, her fragrant Ipana breath tickling my nostrils, then ran the back of her hand lightly against my cheek and kissed me again, ever so lightly—almost a phantom kiss, the tip of her tongue barely brushing mine.

"How can you be so frisky?" I asked.

Her reply was to kiss me once more, hungrier this time, while managing to wriggle out of her panties in one wondrous motion. Her girlish smile had been replaced by a look of womanly urgency. She took my hand and led me silently into the bedroom, then lay back on the bed with her arms outstretched, her toes curled up, and a look in her eyes than could have brought down a government. Any government.

I got out of my clothes with a good deal less finesse than she had, hopping around on one foot, struggling to pull off shoes and socks like Harry Houdini strapped to the submerged propeller of an ocean liner.

"How do you get undressed so easily?" I whispered to her, after I had finally disrobed and lay across from her on the lumpy double bed.

"It's a gift," she whispered, rapidly nipping my face with small darting kisses, all the while running the backs of her long warm fingers beneath my surprised and grateful balls. "I'm so hot," I think she said, although my power of hearing was rapidly disintegrating. Barbara rolled on top of me as easily as a jockey springing aboard a Derby winner, kissing my forehead, my lips, and my nipples in rapid succession. Kiss kiss kiss. She pulled her body down over mine, a kind of survey, grazing all of me with all of her, and then she pushed herself upward again, so that her breasts faced my wide eyes like a pair of beautiful twins. I nuzzled them, kissed them, sucked them ever so lightly, then not so lightly.

"Mmm-hmm," she crooned, from some place in the back of her throat, or her lungs, or her toes. God only knows. She leaned over and switched off the table lamp without seeming to move at all.

"How'd you do that?" I think I said. Her face was suddenly bare inches from mine, faintly illuminated by the dim light emanating from the fixture outside the motel room door.

"Do what?" She arched her back and I moved into her and she closed her eyes and began moving so slowly I thought we were underwater. I was both terribly aroused and deeply fatigued, as only a forty-four-year-old man inside a twenty-one-year-old girl can be; I drifted in and out of consciousness, as if fucking this wondrous soul at a dreamlike remove. She felt like some paradisiacal blend of feathers and gravy, and as we made our way across our joined terrain of skin and nerves, I knew I would do just about anything for Barbara Stern. It felt that good, and scarier still, it felt like we'd been doing it for years and years. We fit.

She moved a little quicker now, but remained ever in control. Barbara looked at me, then closed her eyes and tossed her hair; she ran her hands up across my chest, ducked down to kiss me, and then held out her breasts for both of us to feast on, taking increasingly fevered turns. It all moved at the speed of inevitability and when she got close, she reached back, wrapped her hand around me, and gave me a squeeze of ever so delicate force, like a plant enclosing me, and I shut my eyes as the two of us sustained our soft, sequential explosions.

After the event had subsided and we floated back to the middle of the sea, she tumbled into sleep, still attached to me like some fabulous appendage. We slept like that for a while, until I slipped out, but still I clung to her as if to life itself, and we negotiated the night that way, two loving near-strangers in a strange Indiana motel.

And then dawn arose in the Midwest and more hell broke loose.

We had gotten out of bed at first light and gathered up our belongings. Barbara marched sleepily into the shower and I went next door to check on Maestro. The old man had already bathed and looked pink and healthy as an infant.

"Today buy underclothes, Boston Blackie," he announced with gravity. "Is disaster."

"I agree. My shorts are no bargain, either. Only Barbara has a full complement of scanties."

He smiled at me and put on a smallish pair of gold-rimmed spectacles. "Was a good night for you?"

I returned the smile. "I slept very well."

Toscanini nodded. "You are gentleman. *Bene*. Men who tell *tutto*, everything"—he held up his black smoking jacket and I helped him on with it—"is *disgrazia, vergogna*." He buttoned the jacket, tapped his ear. "I heard nothing. You are very quiet, *sì*? Like mouses."

"It sort of happened in a dream."

He shook his head back and forth and made a kind of Italianate clucking nose. "A dream. *Sì*. With her would be *sogno umido* . . . a dream that is damp." He sat down and pulled on his impeccable black shoes; they looked to be made of kid, probably hand-crafted by some ninety-year-old Milanese cobbler in a shop filled with cats. The raincoat he had worn out of Vegas was laid out on a chair, along with the tweed hat.

"You want those?" I asked the old man.

"I take the hat. The coat is terrible. That person . . ."

"LaMarca."

"Was his. We leave here."

When Toscanini felt that he was sufficiently put together to face the day, he arose and looked around the room.

"*Addio a Indiana*," he said, and walked slowly toward the door. I opened it and we eased into the cool gray early morning. It had started to drizzle and the parking lot was already slick. I knocked on the neighboring door and Barbara stepped out, carrying her valise. She was wearing a brown leather coat and black wool slacks.

"Good morning, Maestro," she said, and then stared at something over my shoulder. I turned around and observed two tall men wearing sunglasses and brown suits emerging quickly from a gray Chevrolet sedan. They started walking purposefully toward me. George Dobles stepped from his office with a folded newspaper tucked under his arm. He silently observed the scene, then walked back into his office.

He had fingered me.

"Mr. Jacob Levine?" the first pair of sunglasses said, in a surprisingly thin and reedy voice.

"LeVine," I told him. "Capital V."

"You're under arrest for the murders of Kim West and Fred Brancati."

"It's not true," Barbara shouted.

"Che cosa?" Toscanini asked. "Who are you?"

"Indiana State Police, pop," the second pair of sunglasses said. He didn't sound much like a cop, nor, for that matter, like someone who lived in Indiana.

"Could I see some identification?" I asked.

The second pair of sunglasses took offense. "Hey, dickhead, you deaf? You're under arrest."

I didn't budge. "I have a right to know who's arresting me."

The first pair of sunglasses nodded at his partner. "He's correct," he said. "He's got every right." He took a step toward me and reached into his pocket for the badge I knew wasn't there and as he did so, I clutched at my heart.

"Shit," I mumbled, and sank to the pavement.

"Jack!" Barbara screamed like a Greek widow.

"Is heart attack!" Toscanini shouted.

"I have to get his medication," Barbara said, and started for the car.

"Wait a minute!" the second gunsel yelled, but she didn't listen and hurried toward the Mercury.

Toscanini began to pray in Italian. Very convincingly.

The second gunsel leaned over me. I was holding my breath and turning a deep red. When the gunsel got close enough, I grabbed a handful of his hair, pivoted, and smashed his head hard against the pavement. The gun fell out of his pocket. I picked it up and held it on his partner.

Barbara started the car.

"Mister," the first gunsel started to say. "We're Indiana State—"

"Cut the horseshit, for all our sakes, okay, genius?" I turned to Toscanini. "Maestro, get into the car."

"Bene." The old man started for the Mercury. The gunsel watched him go with the hollow-eyed anxiety of someone who knows he has screwed up royally and is going to pay for it. His partner was starting to come to, so I whacked him on the back of the head with his gun.

"You," I told the first gunsel. "Drop your weaponry on the ground, please, and kick it over toward me." He reached into his pocket, pulled a .22 from his pocket, let it fall to the wet asphalt, and kicked it in my direction. I took it, turned, and shot out the windows and tires of the gunsels' Chevy, then I arose and started walking backwards toward the Mercury. Barbara pulled the car closer to me. Dobles emerged from his office; for good measure, I shot out the windshield and tires of the blue Hudson I assumed to be his, then hustled into our rent-a-car.

"Go!" I told Barbara, and she floored the gas pedal flat. We went screaming out of the Starlight Motor Hotel and back onto Route 36. I looked into the side mirror—the gunsel whose head I had bounced on the asphalt was still lying on the ground, and his weak-minded compadre was leaning over him. It was a tableau that moved me not at all.

"Che cosa? Che cosa?" the old man said. *"Fascisti?"*

"They weren't cops, that's for goddamn sure," I told him. "I knew Dobles was a creep."

"You think it was him?" Barbara asked.

"Absolutely. I figure he saw my picture in the paper and called the state cops. The cops passed it right over onto Lucky and Meyer's plate. This is all their deal. The stories in the paper, the phony name of the deceased . . ." I turned to Toscanini. "See how important you are?"

"Too much with the guns," he said. His hair was tousled again and he was breathing hard.

"I couldn't agree more. We have to get the hell out of here."

Barbara looked at me. She was doing about sixty-five on a highway still empty at ten past seven. "Get the hell out of here meaning what specifically?" she asked.

I reached into my pocket and pulled out my wad of cash. I still had over five thousand dollars.

"Meaning we charter a plane and fly straight to New York. Screw all this driving. Sooner or later they're gonna catch up to me." I grabbed the road map out of the glove apartment and began to unfold it.

"You're talking about one of those little planes, right?" Barbara asked.

"I'll take whatever I can get—the *Enola Gay* or the *Spirit of St. Louis* will do fine."

"We fly, Boston Blackie?" the old man leaned forward and put his hands on the front seat, like a kid on the road with his folks.

"Yes. This way you won't have to worry about your underwear anymore. We can get there in four, five hours."

He clapped his hands. *"Bene!"*

"Those little planes don't bother you, Maestro?" Barbara asked him.

"No, *cara mia*. What bother me is to wear underwears for two day." He laughed. "Maybe I should borrow from you!"

"Right now?" Barbara smiled at the old man.

"Not while you drive, *bella mia*!"

"Okay." I had found what I was looking for on the map. "We're twenty-five miles from the Indianapolis airport. Stay on this road, there'll be signs."

"Which airport we go in New York?" the old man asked.

"We'll go to Idlewild if possible. It'll be very dramatic. Sarnoff will be there."

"Sarnoff?" the old man exclaimed. "At airport?"

"Yeah." I smiled at the thought. "Could be a hell of a payoff to this. Two Maestros, no waiting."

* * *

We made it to the Indianapolis airport in about forty-five minutes.

"What do we do with this car, Jack?" asked practical Barbara.

The answer was forthcoming; a billboard indicated that Prairie Rent-A-Car maintained an office half a mile from the airport. A couple of minutes later, we were pulling into a lot filled with cars being washed for the day's business. I dropped off the Mercury and did the paperwork as quickly as possible, paying out twenty-eight dollars in cash. The Prairie agent, a motherly soul of close to sixty wearing a University of Indiana team jacket and a kerchief over her hair, informed us that "a courtesy car" would take us to the airport in fifteen minutes. I thanked her profusely and went for a cab instead.

Within five minutes the three of us were getting out at an outfit called Hoosier Aviation, which the cabby had informed us was the hub of all private plane rental in Indianapolis. Hoosier Aviation was basically a massive hangar with some drab offices attached to the front. The double glass doors were unlocked and a sign indicated that we had arrived at the reception area.

We didn't get much of a reception, however. A bell chimed as we entered the fluorescent-lit, linoleum-floored facility, but the joint was empty. A threadbare banner hung over an unmanned oak counter at the far end of the room; it said HOOSIER AVIATION in block letters and featured a little silver plane cutting through some puffy pink clouds. I sat Barbara and Toscanini down on a pair of lumpy red chairs with chrome arms.

"Some setup, Jack." Barbara said. "Very reassuring."

"You rather be playing cowboys and Indians at motels?"

"No, but this gives me the willies." At that moment a broad-shouldered man of about thirty-five, sporting a blond crew cut and sideburns, sauntered out to the counter, wiping his hands on a paper towel. He was wearing a green jumpsuit with HOOSIER AVIATION sewn in red thread at the breast pocket.

"Morning," he said pleasantly. He smiled at me and looked over at Barbara and the Maestro. His mouth started to drop open, but then he remembered his manners and managed to close it. But he couldn't stop staring.

I approached the counter with my friendliest smile.

"Morning," I said. "We need a plane."

"Okeydoke." He kept staring past me, then lowered his voice. "Mister?" he whispered, "The gentleman back there, that by any chance be Arturo Toscanini?" In all our travels, this was the first person to recognize the Maestro, this jumpsuited flyboy at Hoosier Aviation. Go figure.

"Can you keep a secret?" I whispered back.

"Kept them all my life. That's what private aviation's all about—flying folks who got themselves all kinds of reasons for not flying commercial. Name's Vern Padgett. Who are you?"

"Jack LeVine, with a capital V."

He nodded abstractly. "And that's really him?"

"That's really him, and he has to get to Idlewild by four o'clock at the latest. Is that a possibility?"

"Sure, long as the weather holds up back East. Supposed to be pretty good today. Long ride, New York."

"How long?"

Vern popped open a box of Chiclets. "About seven hundred and forty miles. I'd recommend taking the new Piper, which is a Pacer PA-20. Has a cruising speed of about a hundred and twenty-five miles per hour. So if you do the math—"

"I flunked math."

"Be about six hours flying time, plus a stop to refuel. Figure we do that in Pittsburgh."

"So we're looking at about seven hours in all."

"Something like that." He shook out a pair of Chiclets and cracked them open in his mouth. I stared at the wall clock behind the counter, which had miniature Piper Cub wings as hands. The clock read ten past eight, which meant that we'd have to hustle to get into New York by four.

"We better get moving, then, Vern. Who's gonna fly us?"

"There's three real good pilots here, but I'm the best, and it would be my high honor to fly you good folks myself."

"Guess you're a music lover."

"Yes sir. Listen to that great man every weekend, listen to the opera Saturday afternoons." He smiled. "If I wasn't married to a former Miss Terre Haute, people 'round here would probably think I'm some kind of pansy." He looked toward Barbara. "Speaking of beauty contests, that young woman with the Maestro is quite a feast for the eyes."

"My fiancée."

"Okay," he said, without missing a beat. "So you must be a regular show dog yourself."

"A Hebrew terrier," I told him. "Born and bred. What will it cost me to fly to New York?"

Vern contemplatively chewed his gum. "You got some precious cargo there. This Pacer gives you a pretty comfortable ride. Four-seater. Virtually brand-new aircraft, just on the market this year." He nodded, as if to himself. "That'd be the one I'd like to take you all up in, and that would run four hundred and fifty dollars."

The amount was less than I'd feared and more than I'd wished for, but I had neither the time nor appetite to bargain.

"It's a deal," I told him.

"I get half now, and half when we land."

"What if we don't land?"

Vern cracked his gum and smiled. "Then you get a full refund."

"That's what I thought."

"Kind of a superstition, actually, the half up front." Vern looked over at Maestro and Barbara and waved at them. "Been doing it since I started flying. I ask for the second half the second the wheels touch the ground, that's the way I do it."

"What if I'm sleeping?"

"Way I fly, you won't be sleeping." Vern laughed. "That's pilot's humor."

"Hilarious." I leaned forward on the counter. "Realistically, how soon can we get out of here?"

"You're in a rush, I take it."

I decided that if I was going to trust him with my safety, I better trust him with the truth. "All of our lives are at risk, Vern. That's the way it is. The old man was kidnapped and at least two really good people have died because of that fact, and a couple of not-so-hot people as well. I've been hired to bring the Maestro back."

He stopped chewing his gum. "For real."

"For real. I also just had a phony murder rap hung on me in Utah, that's how rough this game is being played."

"So you're a private eye or something?"

"I'm a private eye *and* something, I'm that good. I also believe in leveling with decent people. You should know what you're getting into."

Vern nodded, ran a grimy hand through his hair.

"Flew over eighty missions in Germany, Mr. LeVine. Believe me, I know what rough is." He pushed himself away from the counter. "Give me twenty minutes."

Vern started walking away.

"One other thing," I called out to him. "Exactly where do we land?"

"You mean like what terminal?"

"Yeah."

"All private aircraft going to Idlewild have to use the General Aviation Terminal."

"All of them?"

"Yes sir. Now let me get to work."

Vern turned and pushed open a door that led out to the hangar. I strolled back to my fellow voyagers and informed them of the plan of action. Barbara was openly nervous, but the Maestro seemed to get younger with every eastward mile we traveled.

"Will be adventure," he said cheerily.

"Four seats," Barbara said. "That's *tiny*."

Toscanini took her hand and started to sing very softly and very badly. *"Che gelida manina,"* he croaked. "Means 'what a cold hand.' "

"La Bohème," Barbara said. "I know it well. But Mimi dies in the last act, Maestro."

"Of *tuber colosi,* not plane crash, *cara mia.* You are safe with me!"

While the old man attempted to reassure Barbara, I went over to a wall phone and rang up Toots. He answered on the fifth ring, and sounded like a man curled into a fetal position.

"Napping on the job?"

"Resting," he told me. "I never sleep at my desk. What's up? Any more excitement?"

"Nothing but." I filled Toots in on the morning's mayhem at the Starlight Motor Hotel and then told him of my impending flight.

"You're going to land at Idlewild with the real Toscanini while Sarnoff is waiting for the ringer?" Toots sounded both incredulous and petulant.

"Exactly."

"So what's my exclusive, Jack? Every fucking paper in town's gonna be there."

"But you're going to be the only one who's gonna have any idea what's really going on."

"Jack, if Lansky and Lucky are involved, you don't think they're gonna have their muscle at the airport? What's to stop them from grabbing your old man again and hustling him into a car? Saying that *he's* the fraud."

"Nothing, except that I'm not going to let it happen. I've schlepped him this far; no way I let him get nabbed in my own backyard. Don't worry about it. By tonight, you're gonna be waltzing your way to a Pulitzer Prize."

"If I survive. This puts me out in the open, too."

"I wouldn't sweat it. One thing about Meyer and Lucky, they don't go after newspapermen. It's bad for business. Shooting private dicks—everybody loves that."

"What time you say you're getting in?"

"Around four o'clock. General Aviation at Idlewild."

"Don't try to be a hero."

"I am a hero, Toots; it just comes naturally."

I sat back down with Barbara and Toscanini and thumbed blindly through a six-month-old issue of *Collier's,* not registering anything except a photo of Lana Turner nibbling on an ear of corn. My palms were slick and I realized that I was a lot edgier than I had admitted to Toots. Barbara produced a deck of cards from her handbag and started to deal solitaire on a small metal coffee table. Maestro beamed, happy just to be near her, and began offering muttered advice in Italian. Barbara furrowed her ivory brow and studied her cards. When she looked up, she caught me watching her and smiled demurely, then reached over and squeezed my arm. I fell ever deeper for her, like a guy spinning down a well in a fairy tale. It's the little things that count, the small exquisite gestures—the straightening of a wayward collar, the instinctive squeeze of flesh. If she was not reading my thoughts, then she was certainly intuiting my fears—of crashing to earth in a flaming Piper, or getting my skull bashed in at Idlewild by some of the world's most accomplished thugs.

I had been thinking while pretending to read *Collier's,* and the more I thought, the more I agreed with Toots—the logical play for Lansky and Lucky was to snatch the Maestro again. As for Barbara, she probably knew way too much to be allowed to live; it would pain Lansky for at least a week and a half, but he would ultimately allow her to be rubbed out.

As for me, I was not only expendable, I was radioactive. If everything didn't go perfectly, I knew I'd be dead by tonight.

Fifteen minutes later, Vern walked through the door from the hangar and waved at us to join him. Barbara gathered up her cards and put them in her bag. I went over to Toscanini and helped him get up. He was positively buoyant.

"We are like Lindbergh, Boston Blackie."

"You like to fly?" I asked him.

He shrugged. "*Mezzo-mezzo.* But to go home, to orchestra . . . has been long time." His eyes got moist. "Makes me strong." He clutched my arm hard. "*Avanti!*"

The three of us walked behind the counter and out into the hangar. There were a half dozen people working there and they stopped whatever they were doing the instant we appeared. At first I figured it was Barbara, and God knows the men watched her with awestruck attention, but then they began to applaud, and I knew it was for Maestro. It was the goddamnedest thing—a bunch of Hoosier grease monkeys paying tribute to the great man. Toscanini turned and touched his tweed cap in acknowledgment, then headed for the abbreviated stairway to the plane.

"*Piccolo,*" he exclaimed, looking at the Pacer. "So small!"

"Well, maximum weight allowed is eighteen hundred pounds," Vern said. "So I guess we're all right with this group."

"Have been on diet, *signore,*" Toscanini told him, and the men all laughed some more, then Vern assisted him up the three steps and into the PA-20. It was a plucky-looking little plane, about twenty feet in length, with a single engine and wings that appeared to be shorter than the others in the hangar. After Barbara boarded the plane, I turned to Vern and asked him if I was just imagining that the wings were smaller.

"No, the wingspan is about six feet less than the other Pipers."

"Tell me that's a good thing."

"It's a very good thing, Mr. LeVine. Means it climbs a little slower, about two-thirds slower than the cub, as a matter of fact, but it also allows the plane to go twenty miles an hour faster." He clapped me on the back. "No need to worry, sir. It's gonna be a hell of a ride."

I took a deep breath and boarded the plane.

"Boarded" might be too grand a term to describe entering the Pacer. "Slinked" or "crouched" might fit the bill a little better. The plane looked to be ideal for transporting small dogs or circus midgets; if you were over four feet tall, standing erect was out of the question. Four cloth-covered seats were set in two rows and you got to the second row by climbing over the first, which Barbara had already done. She was seated with her hands folded, as pale as a denizen of Death Row. Maestro was already buckled into his seat in the first row.

Vern got on board carrying a large and fragrant paper bag.

"Coffee and doughnuts and sandwiches," he announced.

"Bravo, capitano!" Toscanini cried out.

"You want something now, before we take off?"

"Sì, sì, capitano. Doughnut, *caffe."*

I realized I was starving. Vern distributed the coffee and doughnuts to us all, and then started busying himself in the tiny cockpit. "There's water for later, and let's save the sandwiches for when we stop in Pittsburgh," he said. "We should have pretty smooth air by then. Just might be a little choppy till we're near Columbus."

"How far is that?"

" 'Bout a hundred and seventy-five miles. You all belted in, folks?"

We were indeed belted in, contemplatively sipping coffee and munching our doughnuts, which were still warm and tasted like something fashioned by God's own hands, if God were a plump housewife from Indianapolis. Toscanini looked as if he had never eaten a doughnut in his life, studying the circle of fried dough like someone who had just swum onto a deserted island and picked it from a tree.

"Delizioso," he said, and then Vern started up the engine and it suddenly got very noisy in the cabin.

"I advise you folks to finish your coffee," Vern shouted back over his shoulder.

We did so. Vern started maneuvering the small plane across the tarmac. It was a quiet morning at the Indianapolis airport. A pair of American Airlines planes were being washed down by a crew; to the east an old military transport, its Air Force markings faded but still visible, was slowly rolling down the runway. Everything seemed to be happening at half speed. Barbara leaned over and kissed me lightly on the lips. She smelled of coffee and warm doughnut and the promise of my lost youth.

"Good luck to us all," she said.

SEVENTEEN

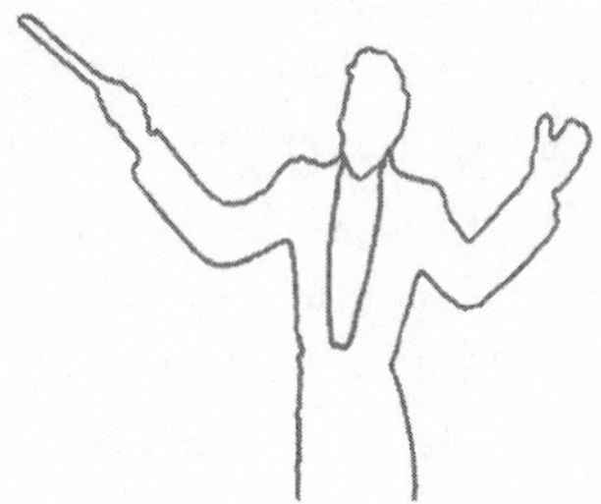

Vern was correct. The first part of the flight was not smooth. Not even close. We bumped and ducked and rolled. The old man stared placidly out the window and admired the agrarian world below, despite the continuous whoops and swoops of the air currents. As for me, I felt like I had gotten on the Coney Island Cyclone after a spaghetti dinner. I closed my eyes and attempted to conjure up clean and unnauseating images—hansom cabs at dusk, Rizzuto throwing a runner out from deep shortstop—but it was not entirely successful. My stomach was clenched like a small damp fist. Barbara wasn't doing much better and after an hour or so, my shoulder began to ache from the number of times she had dug her nails into me.

"This chop is going to end real soon, folks," Vern shouted out from the front of the plane. "Just hang in there! And if you can't, just use the bags. We discourage barfing out the window." He chuckled as if he had said something funny. "Never know who might be walking around down there!"

My head was slick with sweat; when I turned and looked at Barbara, she was milk-white.

"Soon," I whispered.

"Maybe crashing would be better," she said.

"Don't think about it, don't talk about it."

"You're not sick?"

"I keep trying to think of Phil Rizzuto throwing to first base."

She smiled very grimly. "That does nothing for me."

Vern looked back over his shoulder. "How are you doing, Mr. Toscanini?"

"Bene. Bella scenaria!" The old man pointed out the window, then turned to me. "Boston Blackie, no like the ride?"

"Don't you have a stomach, Maestro?"

Toscanini patted his middle. "Very strong. Always."

"You're very fortunate."

"Maybe am just happy because soon I have clean underwears!" He laughed hoarsely.

"Okay, guys," Vern announced. "Gonna climb to some smoother air! We want everybody to be happy."

The little plane rose another couple of hundred feet, fighting through some dark clouds, and suddenly—miraculously—the turbulence ceased. The currents turned smooth, then smoother. My stomach was immediately becalmed, as if I had ingested a wonder drug.

"Should be basically okay from here on," Vern announced. "Can't guarantee it, of course."

Toscanini looked at me and smiled. "You were almost to vomit, Boston Blackie."

"Me?" I said incredulously. "No way. I just like to turn colors as a party trick."

The old man nodded happily. "You still have stomach of a young man. And you, *cara mia* . . ." He gazed at Barbara.

"I'm not a great flyer, Maestro."

"You are great everything," he said, and blew her a kiss. You had to hand it to him: At eighty-three, he still had all the moves.

At ten minutes of twelve, we landed at Pittsburgh to refuel. Maestro elected to remain inside the plane and enthusiastically began to wolf down a bologna sandwich, but Barbara and I were eager to disembark. It was an enormous relief to feel solid ground beneath my

Florsheims, to let the westerly breeze dry my sweat-soaked suit and shirt. The skies over Pittsburgh were gray and unpromising; a procession of planes ascended regularly into that ashy sky and I watched them with a strange mixture of agitation and relief. Barbara and I walked a prudent distance from the fuel pumps and lit up our Luckies. I had no appetite whatsoever, but the cigarette tasted shockingly good.

"Nervous, honey?" Barbara asked me.

"I'm past that."

"Meaning what?"

"Meaning you reach a point where you think you have all the information you're ever going to get and you hope that's going to be enough to get you through whatever happens."

"And what do you think's going to happen with you and me?"

She asked the question very simply; it was just a fastball over the outside of the plate and I could take it or swing at it, but it was probably a strike either way.

"I don't know," I lied.

"Sure you do," she said evenly. "You think it's over. You think you're too old for me, you think I'm too dangerous, you think I could never stick with one man for very long."

"That's what I think?"

She took a drag from her Lucky. "Mmm-hmm. That's what you think."

"You're right. That's what I think."

She tossed her cigarette to the tarmac and ground it out.

"Don't be afraid of me," she said without looking up. "That's all I'm asking. Give me a chance."

I couldn't think of an apt reply. Over her shoulder, I saw Vern waving at me to return to the plane.

"Pit stop's over, sweetheart," I told Barbara. She hooked her arm through mine and kept her head tucked into my shoulder all the way back to the plane.

* * *

The flight from Pittsburgh to New York was smooth enough to allow for generous and prolonged slumber. Toscanini partook of the opportunity, beginning his rhythmic snoring somewhere west of Harrisburg. I was dog-tired, but there was as much chance of my falling asleep as there was of my doing a Mexican hat dance out on the plane's wing. With each mile approaching Idlewild, my innards tightened a little more. Barbara occasionally reached over and clutched my hand; her palm was as moist as mine.

"I see water, Jack," she said suddenly. "What's that?"

There was indeed a large body of water looming in the distance.

"Vern, what's that lake?" I shouted to the pilot.

"Delaware Water Gap," he hollered back. "We have about an hour and a half, hour forty-five to go. The tailwinds aren't much to speak of today, otherwise I could get you there a little quicker."

I checked my watch. It was twenty past two. This was going down to the wire.

I wasn't asleep, but I was clearly lost in my thoughts, staring out the window and noticing that we were flying over fewer farms and more clumps of squat suburban houses, when I felt a tapping on my shoe. When I looked up, Vern was speaking to me in a sort of stage whisper.

" 'Bout a half hour, Mr. LeVine. Maybe you want to start rousing the troops here."

"Yeah," I mumbled, and rubbed my mouth.

This was it.

I was able to make them out at about three hundred feet. As we made our final descent, I could see the lights, the stalks of microphones, and the crowd of reporters and photographers standing on the tarmac beside the General Aviation Terminal. It looked to be a hell of a turnout, maybe a hundred in all.

"Jack," Barbara said in neutral but charged tones.

"The press, baby. Out in force."

Maestro was strangely impassive, running a comb through his hair as the plane approached the runway.

"Welcome home, folks," Vern announced, touching the Pacer down at precisely seven minutes past four. As we taxied toward the terminal, I saw another private plane, larger and fancier than ours, spinning to its final stop like a housefly dying on a windowsill.

"That's a Piper Clipper PA-16," Vern announced. "Little bigger than this one, and a bunch slower."

Two flunkies in windbreakers were industriously rolling a red carpet across the tarmac. We kept going.

"Where do we stop?" I asked Vern.

"They want me to tuck it next to the terminal, about a hundred yards from this Clipper."

"Can we get any closer, like fifty feet?"

"We can try." Vern radioed the tower while I looked out the window. As we taxied toward the terminal, I could see that I had underestimated the press turnout. Stuffed behind a rope barricade, their numbers looked to be closer to a hundred and fifty, including newsreel cameramen.

I heard Vern listening to some rapid-fire static from his radio and then he said, "Roger," which I didn't know that grown-ups actually said. He turned to me and shook his head. "We can't be closer than a hundred yards from the Clipper," Vern called out. "They say this is a special event of some sort, and that's the best slot they can give me."

We were now passing the Clipper. The plane had come to a final stop and had shut off its engine, but its door remained shut. And now I saw why—a limousine the approximate length of the *Queen Mary* was cruising slowly across the tarmac, headed toward the cluster of microphones. The limo bore a flag on each fender: one bearing the ever-popular Stars and Stripes, the other bearing the less-sacred colors of the Radio Corporation of America.

I had no doubt that David Sarnoff, the head of RCA, was inside that limo.

"What's our plan?" Barbara asked me.

"We get out and walk toward the microphones."

"You're serious."

"Totally."

The Pacer PA-20 kept rolling, a little bumpily, across the tarmac, until we finally reached our designated slot. Vern shut off the engine and the plane fell shockingly silent. I stood up as straight as I could, which still only allowed me the posture of Quasimodo, and handed Vern the rest of his dough. He thanked me and put the money in his shirt pocket without even glancing at it.

"Got to file some papers inside, then maybe I'll come out and see what all the excitement's about."

"Hope it's not too exciting," I told him. "In any case, thanks for everything. You just helped save Western civilization, at least for the next couple of weeks."

"It was my privilege." He got out of his seat and pushed the door open, then helped get Maestro out of his seat.

"Va bene," the Maestro told him. "You are better pilot than Smiling Jack from funny papers!"

"Thank you, sir. Was an honor to fly you, and if you wouldn't mind . . ." Vern thrust a sheet of paper in front of the old man, which Maestro happily signed. Barbara crawled over the front seat and watched. Vern reverently folded the sheet of paper, put it inside a leather case he kept in the cockpit, then turned and opened the door.

"You folks just give me a second." The pilot lifted a cover and pulled out a three-step metal staircase, which he lowered out through the doorway.

He disembarked.

"Okay, guys!" Vern called out, and then the three of us, hunched over like question marks, made our way out of the plane and down the staircase and onto the tarmac. The pilot shook each of our hands in military fashion.

"Good luck," he said.

"Good luck to you," I told him. Vern turned and headed toward the General Aviation Terminal.

And there we were.

I extended my arms.

"Show time, ladies and gentleman." Barbara took me under one arm, and the Maestro grasped the other, and we began jauntily crossing the tarmac, like we were off to see the wizard, the wonderful Wizard of Oz.

EIGHTEEN

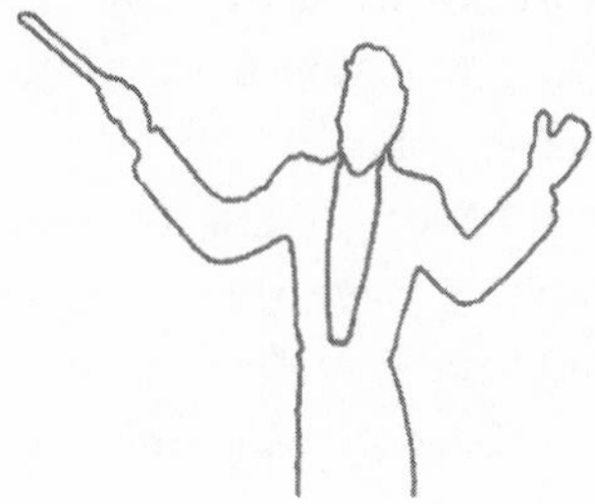

The limo had come to a stop and the man who liked to call himself "General Sarnoff," in deference to his unbloodied but heartfelt service to the nation in the recent war, emerged from the vehicle's depths and strode toward the microphones. He was a compact man with the build of a college wrestler; his broad and muscled arms could barely be contained by his dark blue pin-striped suit. Sarnoff's story was the stuff of corporate legend: the young Jewish telegraph operator—on duty the night the *Titanic* went down—who had battled his way to the top ranks of American corporate titans. He had cultivated a reputation for both pugnacity and excellence, for financial acumen and cultural overreaching. All of the above had led him to this bizarre moment of the double Toscaninis. Sarnoff slipped behind the microphones, pulled an index card from his jacket pocket, studied it, and then folded it in his hand.

"Stop here," I said to Barbara and Maestro. We were now about fifty yards from Sarnoff. "I don't want to make a move until the double comes out." The three of us slipped behind a gasoline truck and listened as Sarnoff's amplified voice boomed out across the airport.

"Ladies and gentlemen, this is a great day for lovers of good music and a great day for the National Broadcasting Company and the Radio Corporation of America," he announced. The doors of the Clipper were still shut; it was obvious that this had all been carefully programmed. "Our beloved Maestro has returned to us in good health, ready to assume the reins of the great orchestra which he built and which has been such an enormous source of pride to all of us at RCA. Now, before he steps out, I have been asked to inform you that Maestro is unfortunately suffering from a severe bout of laryngitis. . . ."

"Nice," I said to Toscanini and Barbara. "The ringer comes out, mutely waves his arms for the newsreels, and then they hustle him into the limo."

Sarnoff was still going. "So please join me in welcoming this great man. . . ."

"Let's do it." I said. The three of us stepped out from behind the gasoline truck and started marching toward the stand of microphones.

It was thirty yards away.

Sarnoff had turned to the airplane. "Welcome, Maestro!" The door to the Clipper swung open and out stepped the ersatz Toscanini, happily waving both of his hands. Standing just behind him was Giuseppe LaMarca, blinking nearsightedly into the predictable but nonetheless blinding explosion of flashbulbs.

We were fifteen yards away.

The faux-Toscanini stood and waved very convincingly at the cameras, pointing to his throat in mock dismay. I turned and looked at the genuine article standing to my right. He had never laid eyes on his double before and was genuinely astonished; he squeezed my arm tightly, and then his face turned so red it was nearly purple. He let go of my arm and began to shout at the top of his fine Italian lungs.

"Infamia! Vergogna!"

What happened next perhaps took ten seconds, but time had slowed to surreal and outsized units. All the clocks seemed to stop.

"*Vergogna,* David!" he screamed again. "Shame!"

As Toscanini bellowed in rage, the members of the press began to turn around. Sarnoff lifted his head, searching for the origin of the shouts, but his face was draining of all color: He knew that voice.

"Infamia! Disgrazia!"

And now more and more reporters and photographers were whirling about, as agitated as wolves on the hunt. They snapped, they whirred, they shouted incoherent questions, startled by the presence of this second Maestro.

"For shame, David!" the old man screamed once more.

When he finally locked eyes with Toscanini, Sarnoff turned whiter than a Siberian Christmas. He stared blankly for two numbing seconds, trying to process what must have been an almost unimaginable piece of information—that his company and reputation were dangling on the very precipice of ruin.

Then David Sarnoff did something quite brilliant.

He began to shake with rage, and then turned his powerful body toward the Clipper. He pointed to the utterly confused ersatz Maestro and screamed, "Who is that man?"

The double didn't move, but Giuseppe LaMarca, a.k.a. Joey Blinks, took immediate and imprudent action. He drew a small revolver from his jacket and, astonishingly enough, aimed it at Sarnoff. It was panic, pure and simple. A couple of terrified reporters shouted, "Gun!" which distracted LaMarca for a split second, and during that brief unit of time a city cop whipped out his pistol and shot the gangster just above the elbow. LaMarca dropped his pistol, clutched his arm, and stumbled onto the tarmac, where two bulky and raincoated members of RCA's security force fell on him like bullies in a schoolyard. The faux-Toscanini just stood there, and then ran into the plane, but a couple more members of the RCA Gestapo went hustling up the stairs and into the Clipper.

"Ladies and gentlemen," Sarnoff declared, his voice trembling, "I can assure you we will get to the bottom of this situation. Maestro"—and here he extended his hand to Toscanini—"I don't know what happened here, but I extend you a heartfelt welcome, and may I only say how happy I am to see you back to New York."

By now the press had turned a hundred and eighty degrees and was shooting photos and newsreel footage of the old man and Barbara and me. I caught sight of Toots Fellman at the edge of the herd and gestured to him. When he stepped forward, so did a mob of other reporters, but I held up my hand.

"Sorry, fellas, he has the exclusive."

I was then assaulted by an outraged cacophony of press abuse, much of it in deeply intemperate language, the gist of which was who the fuck was Toots to get an exclusive, who the fuck was I to make such a decision, and who the fuck was I anyhow? But the choleric reporters had to make way for Sarnoff, who was pushing his way through their massed legions to get at Toscanini. He reached Maestro and threw his arms around him with Academy Award–winning fervor as a thousand flashbulbs detonated. You might have seen the pictures—they were famous at the time: Sarnoff is smiling apprehensively and Toscanini is staring at him with a fearsome countenance.

While Sarnoff was hugging Toscanini, he looked over the old man's shoulders and up at me, his eyes broadcasting both contempt and sheer terror. Reporters were screaming wall-to-wall questions.

"Who was the second Toscanini?"

"Was that an attempt on your life, General Sarnoff?"

"Maestro, did you have a heart attack or not?"

"Let's get out of here," I told the general. "We've got a lot to talk about it."

"Yes," he mumbled, and then gestured for his RCA minions to clear a path through the reporters, which they did with totalitarian efficiency. The old man, Barbara, and I strode unimpeded through the mob, with a very happy Toots bringing up the rear. Photographers had a field day with Barbara, shooting acres of film and screaming for her name.

"Barbara Stern," was all she said, like they should know who she was.

We got into Sarnoff's limo—the three of us, plus Toots, plus an NBC security man who sat up front with the driver. It was a deluxe and heady vehicle, speaking volumes about life at the apex of corporate life: The seats were the finest cowhide, and all the appointments—door handles, ashtrays, window cranks—were finished in mahogany. And plenty roomy—you could have played ping-pong in the back of this car. A very nice means of transportation for a man who, at this moment, was terribly frightened. Sarnoff sat in the rear seat, all the way to the left; Toscanini was beside him; and Barbara sat on the right. Toots and I were perched across from them on a facing, and identically upholstered, seat. The car started speeding along the tarmac toward a chain-linked gate. Photographers raced alongside, furiously flashing away.

"Who are you?" Sarnoff barked at Toots. I wasn't sure that he knew who Barbara and I were, but I suspected he did.

"My name is Toots Fellman," he replied, totally unruffled, "and I write for the *Daily News*."

"You'll have to get out of the car," Sarnoff said.

I shook my head in the negative.

"He gets out, we all get out. That's the deal. Wasn't for Toots, you don't get your Maestro back. And isn't that the way we're going to play this? That you wanted him back?"

The general's eyes almost bulged out of his head. "Of course I wanted him back! What are you talking about?" Sarnoff pushed a button on a roof panel and a steel divider rose silently, walling us off from the driver and the security man.

"Pretty neat trick," I said cheerily. "Maybe I should get one of these babies."

Sarnoff ignored me, in full panic. "You cannot report on any of this," he said to Toots. "It could be extremely dangerous."

"Dangerous to who?" I asked. "Besides yourself."

Toscanini just stared straight ahead. He looked angry, but also tired.

"To the business climate in general, and to certain highly sensitive negotiations my company is involved in." Sarnoff turned to the Maestro. "When we heard you'd been kidnapped, I have to admit we all panicked."

"That's a load of crap," I told him.

Sarnoff folded his arms and glared at me.

"In fact, everything you've said so far has been a load of crap," I said, then stared out the window. "Where the hell are we going?"

"I think we should drop Maestro off at Villa Pauline," Sarnoff said.

"Is he going to be safe?"

"Of course he's going to be safe. He gestured toward the closed divider. "Roger Atkins is my personal security man; he was a marine captain, five citations for bravery. He's going to stay with Maestro." Sarnoff patted Toscanini's arm. "You're home now, Maestro. You'll be well protected."

Toots looked at me and rolled his eyes.

"And after we drop him off?" I asked.

"Then we can talk," Sarnoff said.

Toscanini finally spoke. "I am old man—"

Sarnoff went right up his ass. "No, Maestro, the youthful spirit—"

"Basta!" Toscanini said with some force "I am old and there has been much in my life." He paused and his eyes got bright with tears. "But this man"—he nodded at me—"this Boston Blackie, he is special person, David. Very important to me. Nothing can happen to this person ever."

I was speechless. Me, Mr. Snappy Comeback himself. It was all I could do to keep from bawling.

Sarnoff took it all in, and then turned to Barbara.

"And, Miss . . ."

"Stern. Barbara Stern."

"Of course," Sarnoff said solicitously. "Fritz's daughter. Can we drop you somewhere? I'll phone for extra security if you'd like."

Barbara just shook her head and stared at me.

"No," she said. "I'm with him."

A little less than an hour later, the limousine pulled into the long circular driveway of the Villa Pauline and we all got out. The sun was casting its last rays across the lawn, shining from the Palisades right across the Hudson and onto the house. A diminutive woman stood by the door, shielding her eyes from the glare, and in back of her hovered a pale, bespectacled man whom I took to be the Maestro's son Walter. When the old man got out of the car, Mrs. Toscanini shrieked with joy, then covered her mouth with both her hands. Toscanini turned and looked at me, and did not immediately start for his wife. He grasped my hands in his.

"I am safe now?" he asked.

"Yes you are," I told him.

"Bene." He nodded, and looked happy and exhausted and a little lost. *"Bene."* He hugged Barbara. *"Cara,"* he muttered, and kissed her on both cheeks and then on her lips, as his wife waited patiently; she knew her husband all too well. Finally, Toscanini turned to his family and went to them, and was encircled by their arms. Seconds later, they all disappeared into the house.

He never looked back.

Barbara watched him go and burst into tears. Sarnoff stood with his hands behind his back, then nodded to Roger, his security man. Roger walked to the front of the Villa Pauline and took a position with his arms folded across his chest. Just like he was taught.

"Thank God Maestro is safe," Sarnoff told me. "What a harrowing couple of weeks for all of us."

"General, let's can the philosophizing and go someplace cozy."

Sarnoff nodded. It was obvious that he wasn't used to being addressed in so blunt a manner, but it was also obvious that he knew he was in no position to get huffy.

"Fine," he said. "Let's do just that."

It was a very quiet ride into Manhattan, down the West Side Highway, then cutting across town. Toots and I sat in our seats like a pair of mute twins, while Barbara was still brushing away tears.

"Quite a man, isn't he?" Sarnoff said to her. "Has such an incredible impact on everyone he meets.

Barbara just nodded her head.

"I have to tell you, Miss Stern," Sarnoff said unctuously, "that it was such a tragedy, what happened to your father, such a terrible waste." He looked at me. "I'm sure you have your theories, Mr. . . . *LeVine,* is that correct?"

"The 'LeVine' is correct, and also the first part of your statement. But what I think happened isn't a theory." I gestured toward the closed divider. "You sure you want to talk about it in here? This thing is totally soundproof?"

Sarnoff took out a monogrammed handkerchief and patted down his brow. "Let's wait." He looked toward Toots. "And I must tell you again, Mr. . . .

"Fellman comma Toots," Toots told him.

". . . Mr. Fellman, that whatever we say between us this evening is totally off the record."

Toots nodded gravely. "I write for the *Daily News,* Mr. Sarnoff. You can trust me with your life."

The limo pulled into the basement garage of 30 Rockefeller Plaza and stopped at a red carpet that led to an elevator marked PRIVATE. The elevator door was already open and a uniformed operator was hustling over to open the door to the limo.

"Evening, General," said the elevator jockey, a gray-haired Negro who looked at the rest of us with undisguised suspicion.

"Evening, Buster."

We all got into the elevator and were rocketed up to the forty-sixth floor. Nobody said a word. Buster didn't hum or even tap his feet. When the doors opened at the forty-sixth floor, our party was met by a tall and severe-looking woman who wore her gray hair braided intricately on the top of her head. She greeted us with the warmth usually accorded escapees from a chain gang.

"General?" she asked in some astonishment.

"The little office, Helen," Sarnoff said to her.

The obedient Helen turned on her heel and marched away from the elevator bank. Sarnoff indicated that we should follow. We walked down a long corridor marked by very few doorways. This was the eagle's nest, the land of offices the size of ballrooms. At the end of the hallway was a set of double glass doors. Helen pushed them open and gestured for us to enter—this was Sarnoff's executive suite. In the reception area, two women sat behind facing blond-wood desks, their fingers flying over matching typewriters. They didn't so much as stir when we entered, not even looking up when Sarnoff strode imperiously past their desks.

The steely Helen opened an unmarked office to her left. We entered. The "small" office was about twenty-five hundred square feet and furnished like a sitting room in a London hotel, with clubby leather couches and chairs. The walls were covered by dozens of plaques, presumably awarded to Sarnoff, as well as a few second-rate oil paintings of hunting dogs. I don't think Sarnoff had ever hunted for anything besides Treasury Bills, but it helped give the room a cozy and Protestant feeling. The general entered the room and slammed the door so hard that one of the plaques fell off. I picked it up and studied it. It was a Brotherhood award from the Catholic Charities.

"I always liked the Catholic Charities," I told Sarnoff. "Glad to see you feel the same way." The general just grunted in reply and I hung the plaque back on the wall. Sarnoff sat himself in a leather chair and indicated that we should do likewise. Toots and Barbara made themselves comfy on the couch. I leaned against a mahogany buffet.

"Think I'll remain standing, sir, if you don't mind," I told him. "Been on my butt all day."

"Whatever you wish," the RCA chairman muttered in reply.

"Been a very long day," I continued. "Started with a shoot-out in Indiana, and that came after a terrible murder in Salt Lake City, which you may have heard about."

Sarnoff's face was as blank as a slice of turkey.

"A wonderful young woman named Kim West was shot down in cold blood at the Salt Lake airport. All she had done was to drive Barbara and Maestro and me up from Vegas. I'm wanted for her murder, by the way, and I'd appreciate it if you could assist in my defense. The whole thing is a trumped-up—"

"Charges were dropped," I thought I heard him say.

"Excuse me?" I asked.

Barbara crossed her trousered legs, but even a glimpse of her ankles was enough to embarrass me. "He said that the charges were dropped, Jack," she said, taking a cigarette out of her bag. Toots leaned over to light it.

"Certain people we both know had the charges dismissed." Sarnoff sat back in his chair and loosened his tie. "Mr. LeVine, I'm not going to play any games with you. Our great company got enmeshed in an unfortunate situation with some very dangerous people, and you have enabled us to extricate ourselves. That's why poor Sid Aaron went to you in the first place."

"Wrong," I told him. "Aaron went to me because he didn't want me nosing around on my own." I pointed to Barbara. "It was her father that started the ball rolling."

"And got killed for it, as did Sid," Sarnoff said.

"But there's a big difference. Fritz Stern just wanted to know the truth about the old man; Aaron got himself splattered because his eyes got big when he went out to Vegas."

"That's totally incorrect," Sarnoff said very firmly. "He was killed because he had hired you in the first place."

"Come on. . . ."

"You can believe me or not, but it's a fact. Sid's problem was that he thought he could play it either way: If you failed to track down Toscanini, he figured he would have ingratiated himself sufficiently with Lansky to work something out, and maybe get a little taste for himself. I don't deny that. But if you succeeded, he'd have Maestro back, which is what he really wanted in the first place. I'm not saying he was perfect, God knows, but Sid was very much dedicated to the continuation of the NBC Symphony."

"Are you?" I asked.

Sarnoff made a little steeple of his fingers. "An appropriate question, which I will answer by saying that I deeply love and honor Maestro, but the orchestra has become a terribly expensive proposition.

That said, I had nothing to do with the kidnapping and was willing to pay any amount for Maestro's safe return."

Toots cleared his throat. "So what was this charade with the heart attack and waiting for the double at the airport?"

"I had no choice; I was afraid that Maestro was going to be killed if I didn't play my part in what you quite accurately call a charade."

"Lansky didn't offer you an interest in the hotel he was building?" I asked.

Sarnoff nodded. "He did, but I declined. Wasn't worth the exposure, wasn't worth the risk." He nodded toward Toots. "Wasn't worth smart guys like you finding out. I didn't want to be in the hotel business. What is certainly true is that at some future point, it will be necessary for RCA to get out of the orchestra business. But not yet. Nature will run its course; Toscanini is eighty-three years old." He arose from his chair. "I am aware that Sidney offered you twelve thousand dollars if you brought Maestro back, which you have done, and magnificently."

"He already paid me half."

Sarnoff smiled. "The incorruptible LeVine. If I gave you forty thousand dollars, you wouldn't accept it?"

"It would depend on what you wanted in return."

"You coming to work for me."

"Doing what, running a quiz show?"

"Being my eyes and ears in this company."

"You mean a corporate spook?"

"Forty thousand a year, Mr. LeVine." Sarnoff raised his eyebrows. "Surely you don't earn that as a private detective."

"Surely I don't, but the corporate life doesn't appeal to me. I'm an old-fashioned boy; I'll take the six grand you owe me and call it a night."

Sarnoff nodded. "Fine. Helen will give you an envelope when you leave."

"And that's it?" I asked.

"I offered you a job, Mr. LeVine, and you declined." Sarnoff smiled. "It was a pleasure to meet you."

Barbara rose, as did Toots.

"I want my father's murder avenged," she said quietly but forcefully.

Sarnoff looked at her for a long moment, then looked at Toots. "Off the record, Mr. Fellman."

"Absolutely," said Toots.

Sarnoff pursed his lips, then locked eyes with Barbara.

"Miss Stern, my guess is that your father's death has already been avenged."

She stared at the General, not understanding.

"He means LaMarca was offed, sweetheart," I said. "Case closed."

"That's what you mean?" Barbara asked him.

"I really have nothing I can add to what I already said. Good night, Mr. LeVine, Mr. Fellman, and especially you, Miss Stern. I only knew your father slightly, but I never would have guessed his daughter would be the most beautiful woman in New York."

Barbara nodded. She heard it all the time.

"That's very flattering, but it doesn't bring my dad back."

Sarnoff didn't have a ready answer to that, so he simply shook her hand, then Toots's, then mine.

"If you ever wish to reconsider my offer, just call Helen," he said to me, then turned and walked out of the office.

Five minutes later, the three of us were standing on Fifth Avenue. The streets were packed with people leaving work, fighting each other for cabs, streaming toward the subways. Oh, the humanity, like the man once said on the radio. I felt like a stowaway who had just stepped out of a steamer trunk after a month at sea.

Barbara read my thoughts.

"Your head spinning, too?" she asked.

"I'm not sure it actually is my head."

Toots lit up his pipe. "I'm going back to the office, you cute kids.

That's some story, but I think it's for my memoirs. Too dangerous, too off-the-record. My editors would think I was smoking hop if I brought this to them."

"I agree." I put my hand on his shoulder. "Thanks for everything, Tootsel. I owe you a major dinner. Your choice."

"Let's go to Brooklyn, then, get some steaks at Luger's." He smiled at Barbara, tipped his hat. "Might you join us?"

"I might," she said.

"Good. Jack and I tend to run out of conversation pretty fast." He buttoned the top of his coat. "Gonna walk back. Newsmen can't afford these swell cabs," he said, and started down the street.

Barbara took my hand and gave it a squeeze. "I better go home."

I nodded. "Yes, you should." Suddenly I felt as shy and disoriented as a teenager. "Can I give you a call later?"

Barbara didn't answer. She put her arms around me and kissed me for a long, hungry time. When she stopped kissing me, she buried her head in my neck and I could feel her tears. I didn't say a word, just held her, there on Fifth Avenue, in front of Atlas holding up his sculpted world. When the crying ended, she looked up at me and said, "Yes, please call me later," and then went out onto Fifth Avenue and hailed a cab.

I grabbed the next one and twenty-five minutes later I was walking into my lobby in Sunnyside. Mr. Winkler from apartment 4C was exiting the elevator, being dragged by his ever-frantic wire-haired terrier.

"Jack, where the hell you been?"

"Out of town," I told him. The terrier's nails were madly scratching the lobby floor.

"Son of a bitch bastard," Mr. Winkler said for the thousandth time, and disappeared out the door, his arm nearly pulled from its socket.

It felt very good to be home.

I let myself into my apartment with a great feeling of relief. I expected it to smell dank and closed-in, but it didn't.

It wasn't even dark in the apartment.

In point of fact, the windows had been thrown open and the lights turned on and Meyer Lansky and Lucky Luciano were seated in the living room drinking my scotch.

The two of them were seated side by side on my sofa, like guests at a party that hadn't begun. Lansky was at ease and comfortable; Luciano, wearing dark slacks, a blue shirt, and a cardigan, looked like a homicidal accountant.

"Welcome home, Jack," said Lansky. "How was the trip?"

"I would have to say there were very few dull moments," I replied, taking off my hat. "How's my scotch?"

"I've had a lot worse. I've had a lot better, too," Lansky said, and flashed that sour smile. Luciano stared at me like I was something in a store window. His brown eyes seemed strangely outsized behind his steel-rimmed glasses, and he appeared both mousy and irritated.

"You ever meet Charles Luciano?" Lansky asked.

"I haven't had the pleasure."

Luciano finally opened his mouth. "You're very smart," he said hoarsely. His voice had a lot of Italy in it; raspy yet melodic. "I give you a lot of credit. We fucked this up good, but still, you're very smart."

"Where's Barbara?" Lansky asked.

"Went back to her mother. Mind if I wash my hands?"

Lansky held out both his small hands. "Be our guest."

I took my jacket off and went to the bathroom, lathering up my shapely paws. Maybe I was just punchy, but it was strangely unsurprising to see those two mobsters in my home; I knew they weren't here to kill me, because it wasn't the kind of work they did personally. But God only knew why they had shown up.

I returned to the living room and headed for the open breakfront that I use as a bar.

"Is it stupid of me to ask how you got in?"

Lansky nodded. "Very stupid."

I grabbed a tumbler and dropped in some ice cubes that Lansky and Lucky had thoughtfully put into a bucket.

"Rumor is that LaMarca is no longer among the living," I said, pouring out three fat fingers of bourbon.

"I wouldn't know about that," Lansky said, sipping at his scotch.

"It didn't seem very bright of him to pull a gun on Sarnoff, did it?"

Luciano grunted. "He was always a crazy dumb fuck. Too impulsive." He looked over at Lansky. "Is that the right word?"

Lansky nodded. "Good enough."

I took a long pull on my bourbon, let it wash around my mouth for a soothing moment, and then took a heartfelt swallow. It felt like a week's vacation.

"I know that LaMarca killed Fritz Stern." I said it as a matter of fact.

Lansky glanced over at Lucky with an expression that said, *What's to lose?* then looked up at me. "Like Charles said, he was always a hothead. But he won't be in the future, okay? Enough said; you don't need a map." Lansky got up and poured himself another scotch. "Now all that stuff I told you on the plane," he continued, "looks like it's moot, as the lawyers like to say."

"You're not going to build that hotel?"

Lansky shook his head. "Not immediately. Eventually, for sure, but we need an attraction like Toscanini. This move might have been premature, Jack. Too complicated, too many elements. RCA was a royal pain in the ass; I found Sarnoff very difficult to deal with. A very treacherous man."

"Sarnoff told me he didn't want to be a part of this," I said.

Luciano let out something like a laugh and spoke up. "If that's what he said, then that's what he said. He's a captain of fucking industry, isn't he? Those guys never lie, right?" Lucky stared at me with a chilling mixture of curiosity and indifference. It was a stare that said I could be killed like a raccoon on the highway; left for dead and no one would ever care.

"You're very resourceful, aren't you?" Luciano said, his tone turning dark. "Lost a bunch of good fellas in this deal because of you. Mikey Blond was a good fella. . . ."

"The guy who got hit by the bus? He's a bad pedestrian, that's all. Wasn't my fault."

"Freddy Brancati in Salt Lake was a good fella. . . ."

"My mother always said to carry a loaded gun out West."

"You have a big mouth," Lucky said.

The hell with it. I didn't need to listen to this self-important crap. Screw Lansky. Screw Luciano. "Yes I do, and I'm tired and beaten up and I can feel myself getting a little bourbon-headed, and if you're dumb enough to come out to Queens and shoot me yourselves, go ahead and do it."

Lansky waved his arms. "Jack, for crissakes, who do you think we are?"

"All I'm saying is that as far as I'm concerned, this matter is closed. I was hired to bring the old man back and to find out who killed Fritz. It's done."

"That's why we're here, Jack," Lansky said. "Just to close the books."

I finished off my bourbon and poured another.

"I'm glad to hear that," I told him. "But if any of your more impulsive associates ever has the idea that they could improve their standing by knocking me off, let me just tell you the following—there are a number of people who know the story of what really went on here—"

"That asshole from the *News*?" Lansky said.

I ignored him and continued my spiel. "And there are letters to be opened in case of my death, sitting in various safe-deposit boxes"—this part was total bullshit, but I thought it had an authentic and lawyerly ring to it—"so if anything happens to me or to Toots, it's not only front page in the *News,* with all names named, but in a half dozen other papers as well."

Luciano's face flushed to a sort of pinkish red. Lansky just sipped merrily at his scotch.

"Very prudent of you, Jack," he said. "I'm sure Charles agrees. We want no harm to come to anyone. We just want to do business. Charles isn't supposed to be in this country in the first place."

"I'm going back to Italy tomorrow," Luciano said, transforming himself into lovable Uncle Charlie. "Can't take New York anymore. Too many goddamn nervous people. Too much fucking traffic."

Lansky smiled. "Charles just wants to grow his tomatoes. Me, I go back to Havana." He finished his second scotch. "You want to come down, bring Barbara, be my guest. I'll be there most of the winter. Just call the Nacional."

Lansky put his glass down and Lucky pulled himself up off the couch. They looked much less imposing standing up.

"Matter's closed, right?" Lansky said. "You'll tell Barbara that I said so. That it was taken care of, that her father's death was avenged. I want her to know that."

"That you put the contract on LaMarca."

Lansky smiled. " 'Contract.' You talk like a fucking star reporter. I don't know from contracts. I know from taking care of your friends and loved ones and doing business. Period."

"I'll tell her."

We all shook hands and then the two gangsters brought their glasses into my kitchen and put them in the sink, just like their mothers had taught them.

Then they walked out the door and out of my life.

NINETEEN

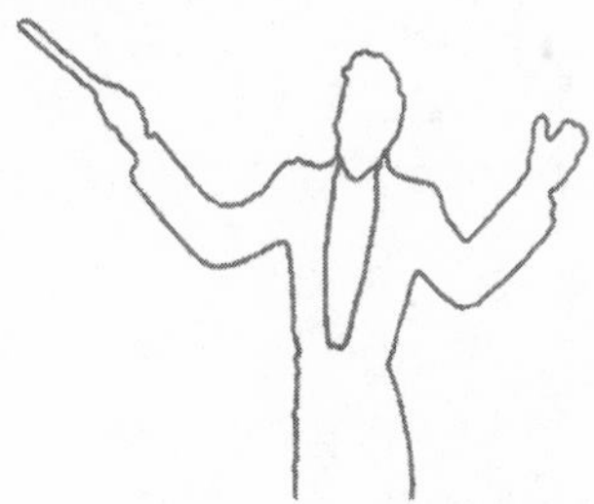

The next night was a Friday and I traveled up to Washington Heights to have dinner with Barbara and her mother and her sister Linda. The kid seemed to have perked up in the past couple of weeks, but Hilde was still living in the cemetery. The circles under her eyes were dark and deep, and she sighed frequently, but she dutifully observed the Sabbath and tried to play the host. She brought out a pot roast that weighed as much as a jukebox and served it with noodles and mixed vegetables and it all smelled like Central Europe on a platter. Then she went back into the kitchen and returned with a shiny *challah* in a silver bread basket and asked me if I would say the blessing. I dug into my memory bank and managed to remember it.

Barbara took my hand and recited it along with me.

I heard a clattering against the windows. It had begun to rain. I felt safe and sound and very contented.

Call me a softy. Go ahead, I can take it.